'This tender and evocative story of the power of love, grief and memories will resonate with so many readers thanks to the power of Vanessa McCausland's storytelling and her understanding of human nature.'

Sophie Green, author of *The Inaugural Meeting of the Fairvale Ladies Book Club*

'Tense, evocative and eerie, a story that will stay with you for days. Like the slow-moving river that flows through the story, this compelling mystery will creep up on you and pull you in.'

Josephine Moon, author of *The Tea Chest*

'This book is pure reading pleasure! Evocatively written and with beautifully realised characters whose loves and losses play out against a lush and mysterious backdrop, I kept turning the pages, desperate to know what would happen, but also wishing it would never end.'

Cassie Hamer, author of *After the Party*

'A tender look at love, grief and sisterly secrets. A gently flowing tale of heartbreak and hope.'

Belinda Alexandra, author of *Tuscan Rose*

# By Vanessa McCausland

*The Lost Summers of Driftwood*

*The Valley of Lost Stories*

# VANESSA MCCAUSLAND

**HarperCollins**Publishers

**HarperCollins*Publishers***

Australia • Brazil • Canada • France • Germany • Holland • Hungary
India • Italy • Japan • Mexico • New Zealand • Poland • Spain • Sweden
Switzerland • United Kingdom • United States of America

First published in Australia in 2020
This edition published in 2021
by HarperCollins*Publishers* Australia Pty Limited
ABN 36 009 913 517
harpercollins.com.au

A catalogue record for this book is available from
the National Library of Australia

ISBN 978 1 4607 6031 4 (paperback)
ISBN 978 1 4607 1133 0 (ebook)
ISBN 978 1 4607 9442 5 (audio book)

Cover design by Amy Daoud, HarperCollins Design Studio
Cover images: Roses by Marija Savic/stocksy/669699; wooden panels by
Ashkan Forouzani on Unsplash
Typeset in Bembo Std by Kelli Lonergan
Author photograph by Sally Flegg Photography
Printed and bound in Australia by McPherson's Printing Group
The papers used by HarperCollins in the manufacture of this book are a
natural, recyclable product made from wood grown in sustainable plantation
forests. The fibre source and manufacturing processes meet recognised
international environmental standards, and carry certification.

*In loving memory of Noël Cooney*

PART ONE

# *Ripples*

# THEN

The sun is hot and syrupy on their young bodies. Their eyes glint with mischief and the freedom of days spent in and out of the water. The river teems with the sounds of summer: cicadas, frogs, jumping fish.

Camilla is outstretched on the warm wood of the jetty, her small face trained skyward. She is only eight but already she understands the way she must arrange her body on her towel to look good. Her swimming costume is hot pink. She has matching sunglasses.

Jez splashes through the water, hooting with delight. He dives deep and feels the cool water run through his hair as he emerges toothy and smiling. Phoebe perches on the jetty watching him, her hair a tangle of salt and knots from the long, hot January days. Her eyes squint tight against the river's glare. She considers whether to join Jez's game, to feel the jolt of joy that comes from being near him.

Tommy is out deeper than the others, past the place where the eels are and way past the end of the jetty. There have been tales of sharks in these parts, near the bend in the river where they breed. But Tommy is twelve and isn't afraid. He can feel them all watching the perfect arc of his arms as he slices through the green water.

Karin is out not so far, but far enough that she can't touch the bottom. She doesn't like the feeling of the mossy rocks beneath her toes, but she is brave, almost as brave as Tommy because of being the second eldest and the tallest of them all. Even so, she is getting tired. She tries to float but her arms are growing heavy. She dips her long legs down and nothing is there to meet them. She gasps and the water goes into her open mouth. She coughs.

'Jellyfish. Lots of them!' Camilla shouts. She is standing, pointing wildly, a bright pink beacon on the jetty. All the children cry out and there's the thrash of limbs. *Please don't let me get stung*, Karin thinks. She imagines she can see them, luminous, pulsating, like tiny white hearts. It feels like they are tangling through her legs, their tendrils in her hair. She tries to lift her head but she can't. She wants to cry out but she can't. They are all on the jetty now—her sisters and the Driftwood boys.

Her body is as heavy as the old fish bucket on the jetty when it's full of water. If only someone would pull the rope to heave it out. *Pull the rope*. She is screaming but only bubbles come out. There is nothing to push off. Everything is turning green, as green and murky as those mossy rocks.

Karin feels Phoebe's arms around her before she sees her. Warm skin pressing against hers, the familiar brown of her hair against her cheek. Karin is being pulled through the water on her back. A lone bird soars overhead against the blue sky and she feels as fast and free as if she were flying.

Tommy's face flashes past, white with fear. He's yelling but Karin can't make out the words. She hears crying and wonders if it's coming from her but nothing happens when she tries to speak. Camilla's cheeks are wet with tears and she's down on the sand gasping as though she can't breathe either.

Warm breath on her cheek. Karin looks up into Phoebe's eyes, which are not scared but fierce. She presses against Karin's chest once, twice, and then it feels like the whole river is coming out of her mouth.

'Phoebe,' Karin says as her sister turns her onto her side on the sand and smooths the hair from her face, 'you saved me.'

# CHAPTER 1

Phoebe traced the straight line of the horizon with her finger, the sun sinking over its lip. She could almost smell the salt from the deep blue sea. She cropped the image tight and added hashtags: #champagnemoments #islandholiday. The couple in the photo were in sharp silhouette, his broad shoulders offset by the elegant slope of her hat, a bottle of champagne between them.

She was the gatekeeper of perfection. The champagne house Joet et Halo was aspiration in a bottle. It was her job to make sure the brand's social media accounts reflected the joie de vivre of the wine. Polo parties filled with young people laughing, picnics in fields of purple lavender, girls in tilted hats with balloons. And always, a glass in hand and the promise that there was a beautiful life out there somewhere.

*This will be me soon*, she thought, and pressed upload. Her last post to Instagram for the day. She glanced at her watch. Nearly 4.30 pm. Half an hour until Nathaniel was due to arrive. Phoebe's heart swooped in expectation. They would take a cab straight to the airport, maybe have a quick drink at that nice new bar with the mirrors before boarding, then they would be on their way to Hawaii. Joy fizzed inside her—how long had it been since she'd felt like this? There had been so many dark days, and darker nights. But now, things would be better. Things would be perfect.

Kate, her boss, twisted the gold bow at the neck of a champagne bottle she placed on Phoebe's desk.

'Well, here's your holiday gift. I saved one of the vintage limited editions for you. Don't forget to take a stunning pic and upload it.' She lowered her voice. 'Maybe just after Nathaniel ... you know what ...'

'Thanks Kate.' Phoebe's face grew warm and she smoothed her dress over her knees.

Kate cocked her head. 'Oh, you're so excited.' Her expression shifted. 'You deserve it, Phoebe, after everything you've been through.'

Sometimes it felt like this fantasy world they peddled was all that was keeping the sadness away. She clung to its flimsy beauty even when it didn't feel real.

'Lucky you, he's early,' said Kate, straightening abruptly and holding out the bottle of champagne towards Nathaniel.

He was wearing the new clothes they'd bought for the trip. Phoebe smiled seeing the crisp white of his shirt—he was usually in sweaty active wear. She tried to catch his eye, to exchange a little glimmer of anticipation, but his eyes only skimmed hers as he took the bottle from Kate, nodding with approval. 'Thanks Kate. Very nice. Very nice indeed.'

Phoebe got up from her desk and moved towards him.

'I'm glad you're early.' She squeezed his shoulder.

'I know how you get about missing planes,' he said. 'Everything has to be running like clockwork for my Phoebe.'

She rolled her eyes and ignored the tone in his comment and tried to focus on the fact that he was smiling and pulling her towards him as he said it. He planted a quick kiss on her lips.

'You ready to relax? We'll be lying on a beach soon with not a care in the world,' he said.

'I so need this. I can't believe it's finally happening.'

'Well, we've planned it down to the wire, so it better be happening.' He shook his head and laughed, his eyes soft with affection. 'Come on, let's get out of here.'

Phoebe busied herself at her desk, closing down her computer. Her eyes caught on the tiny photo stuck to the side of her monitor. It had been taken on her sister Karin's Instax Mini camera the moment she'd opened it for her birthday. Their two faces were squished together in a pale blur, their eyes squinting with laughter. It seemed like yesterday. Phoebe gently peeled away the photo and held it in the palm of her hand. Karin would never know about this holiday. She would never be maid of honour at Phoebe's wedding. Phoebe slipped the photo into her bag and brushed away a tear. She knew her sister would want her to be happy, to keep living her life, but sometimes it felt impossible. She shook her head and took a deep breath. No, this holiday was going to be happy. She was going to try to let go.

It had been a stressful few months. Nate had started a new personal training job at a gym in the city and they hadn't seen much of each other. Phoebe owed it to him to try to find the joy in life again. She needed this holiday. He, more than anyone, knew that. They just had to get on that plane and then everything would play out just as they'd planned.

She slung her bag over her shoulder, strode forward and gripped his hand. 'Well, paradise is waiting,' she said, a smile planted firmly on her face.

*  *  *

Dusk was falling, soft with sea mist. The sound of gulls, the beach breathing and the low beat of the bars reached her. *Tonight*, Phoebe thought, stepping onto their balcony. *Tonight is the night.* The bottle of vintage champagne sat in an ice bucket, sweating into the humid air. Her mood moved between jittery and strangely calm.

The breeze coming off the water was cool. Their hotel room looked directly over the North Pacific Ocean and the smell of the hotel barbecue mixed with the leftover scents of the day—salt, sunscreen and sweet coconuts.

Phoebe arranged the neckline of her dress and felt a droplet of sweat run down her chest. She had saved her best dress for last. Nate would propose tonight. It had been the most incredible day.

'Do you think we'll be doing this when we're old?' His question had drifted over to her while they lay under the full white sails on the charter yacht earlier.

She laughed. 'Why not? Doesn't everyone say things get better with age? Like a fine wine. I should know … And I have that vintage bottle ready to open at any moment by the way.' She nudged him playfully.

Nate nudged her back and shook his head, saltwater from his hair pinging her hot skin. She cried out.

'Your parents might just have to buy the yacht for us,' he said.

'Money doesn't matter if we've got each other, right?' She slid closer to him and planted a kiss on the burning skin of his shoulder.

'Yeah, you're right.' He smiled and wrapped his arms around her. 'You happy?'

'So happy. I haven't felt this happy since Karin ...'

He nodded, 'I know.' His gaze was far away, towards the horizon.

'Are you coming in one more time?' She stood, readying herself to jump off the side of the boat.

He lay down, stretching his body out on the deck.

'Come on, one more swim, they're about to pull anchor,' she said, her toes finding the edge.

'No, I've had enough,' he said, but she was already jumping off.

Nate stepped out onto the balcony now, dressed in a black shirt and pants, despite the heat. Phoebe looked down and saw his feet were bare too. *I will always remember this detail*, she thought. *We both had bare feet when he asked me to be his wife.*

Their eyes met and his gaze was more solemn than she'd expected. He reached into his pocket and Phoebe realised she was holding her breath.

# CHAPTER 2

Phoebe opened her car door but didn't get out. The night was thick with the smell of high summer. Her sister's home was lit with fairy lights, strung from the white-painted eaves and woven through the fragrant frangipani trees. From the elegant Federation architecture to the white Audi in the drive and the handsome investment banker husband, Camilla had it all. Phoebe shoved her heels onto her feet and located her handbag in the nest of empty water bottles on the passenger seat. She examined her face in the visor mirror, reapplied her lipstick, and stepped out of the car.

She pressed the doorbell and felt her stomach tighten. The music that had been playing inside stopped abruptly and Phoebe felt the hairs on the back of her neck rise. Something was off. She wasn't sure what, but something didn't seem quite right. For a start, her niece and nephew were usually the first to the door, tumbling down the hall towards her, breathless and sweet.

'Phee Phee,' Camilla swung open the door. She was wearing the equivalent of a white ball gown but had somehow managed to make this look completely fine for a family dinner. Phoebe ran her damp palms down the flimsy fabric of her dress and kissed her sister's perfumed cheek.

'Where's that handsome fiancé got to? Run off already?' Camilla laughed and Phoebe fought against the lump in her throat to speak. It was now or never.

She squared her shoulders. 'Camilla, it's off.'

'What is?'

'Nathaniel and me. It's over.'

She grasped Phoebe's arm. 'What? No!' She lowered her voice. 'No.'

'I know. I'm reeling.' Phoebe rubbed her temples. 'I mean, it was all so sudden and I thought of calling you but I just thought it would be better … in person. I don't know.'

'What? I mean, how?'

'He just didn't …'

'Propose?'

'Yeah. Said he just couldn't.'

'Where is he now?'

'I have no idea. We went our separate ways at the airport the night before last. I think I'm still in shock.' She gave a hollow-sounding laugh.

Camilla's face seemed to take on a crimson brighter than her lips. 'Oh, I'm so sorry, hon. You see …' She leaned in close and Phoebe caught a hint of vanilla and coconut. Her sister always smelled like a Caribbean holiday. 'I've kind of … organised something.'

Phoebe's hand shot to her mouth. 'No! You haven't.'

Camilla's lips lifted into a hopeful smile.

'A surprise thing? For our … engagement. Oh my God. The whole family? Everyone?'

Camilla nodded, and Phoebe felt sick. She eyed the front door and thought about running. 'Oh my God. I can't.'

Camilla patted her arm and lowered her voice to a whisper. 'They're all waiting right there in the dark, ready to shout "surprise".'

'What do we do?' Phoebe was shaking.

'Can we maybe … say Nathaniel's sick? Everyone will be heartbroken.' There was a patter of little feet as Sophia, Camilla's eldest, started down the hall towards them.

Camilla put her finger to her lips, indicating for her daughter to be quiet. Oscar stuck his head around the door frame. 'Do we have a choice?' Camilla wiped under Phoebe's eyes with her thumbs. 'Let's just go in there and we'll figure it out, okay?'

Phoebe felt her heart collapse and shrink, like a piece of paper folded too many times.

Her arms and legs felt numb as Camilla guided her down the hallway.

'Here, drink this. It'll help.' Camilla handed her a glass of champagne.

Phoebe saw a second glass on the side table, the one meant for Nathaniel, and it filled her with despair. She thought back to the bottle of vintage Joet et Halo on their hotel room balcony, untouched. Unphotographed.

'Don't worry, I'll do the talking,' Camilla said, too loud in her ear.

Someone flicked a switch and a chorus of happy, eager people yelled 'surprise'. The kitchen was festooned with balloons and lights and paper flags. It looked like something out of *Home Beautiful*. And among the beauty and the colour she saw the glowing faces of everyone she loved. Her heart ached.

'Where's that lazy bugger got to?' Uncle Jack yelled and everyone laughed.

Camilla stepped forward in front of Phoebe, her voice full of emotion. 'Nathaniel's sick.'

Phoebe stiffened, her hands curling into balls. She tried to catch Camilla's eye.

There was a joint 'Oh' of disappointment from the crowd. And then there was a moment of complete silence while everyone waited for an explanation. What was Nathaniel sick with? Was he okay? How was the holiday? How did he pop the question? A deep pool of answers, lies, began to form in Phoebe's mind. She would humiliate herself completely when everyone found out next week that Nathaniel never did ask her to marry him. But she didn't have the strength to fight this.

'Stomach bug,' she said, making a face and exchanging a panicked glance with Camilla. She hated herself for lying.

She saw her father at the back. He was standing next to the only picture of Karin that Camilla kept in the house. It lived in a beautiful silver frame above the fireplace and Phoebe found herself looking at it often. Wondering how Karin, with her long dark hair and pale skin, would have looked now with a year more living on her face.

Her dad glanced at the photo and picked it up. He used his shirt front to gently brush away the dust from the glass and placed it back on the shelf. The tenderness in this tiny gesture brought tears to Phoebe's eyes.

Her aunty made an alarmed 'Oh no!' sound at the sight of the tears. Phoebe felt fleshy arms encircle her.

She was sick of pretending that everything was perfect in this family. Camilla and her mother wanted life to be all fairy lights and frangipanis, but you know what? Sometimes it was just shadows and bare branches. Maybe if their family hadn't been in a place where pain could be soothed by material beauty and denial, Karin would still be here. Phoebe's chest ached with the familiar pang of grief.

Phoebe turned to face the expectant crowd. She would tell them the truth. Come clean. Camilla linked arms with her and whispered. 'I have no idea what we're doing. Just smile. I'm so sorry you have to go through this, honey. I wanted this to be perfect for you.'

Phoebe stood, immobilised before everyone. The words 'we broke up' were trying to form on her tongue but they wouldn't come. She couldn't ruin everyone's night, Camilla's party.

Her voice was false, upbeat. 'It was plane food everyone. He'll be fine. Please, eat, drink, be merry.'

Phoebe spotted the elegant turban of her mother's silk-wrapped hair. *Please no, I can't deal with this right now*, she thought.

Her mother moved deliberately through the crowd towards her, the bodies parting in her wake. She placed a kiss on both of Phoebe's cheeks. Her face was pale with the expensive powder she kept in a gold compact and touched up regularly, as though she were a 1930s film star.

'Oh darling, we've been waiting for this proposal for a while, haven't we? I'm truly happy for you.' Her glance flicked to Camilla. There was pity in both their eyes and the sight of it made Phoebe's heart sink. Her mother's pity was that it had taken her so long to get her life on track. Little did she know that she was now adrift and lying to everyone she loved. This was why she hadn't called Camilla or her mother as soon as

Nathaniel had told her the proposal wasn't going to happen. She couldn't stand their judgement.

Her mother made a tut-tutting sound. 'And what's this about Nathaniel being ill?' She shook her head. 'Silly boy.' Her mother had no time or sympathy for illness, as though it was some moral failing.

A thick dread moved through Phoebe's limbs. How was she ever going to tell her mother the truth when even the lie had sparked disapproval?

'Your sister has put so much thought into this celebration for you,' she said, tucking a strand of hair behind Phoebe's ear. 'It's such a shame Nathaniel can't be here.'

Phoebe felt her jaw clench and pasted a weak smile onto her lips. She wrestled herself out of her mother's grasp, wishing she was anywhere but in the middle of this room.

Her mother's breath was in her ear. 'Please thank everyone for coming out for you.'

Phoebe looked around hopelessly.

'I think now would be a good time,' her mother urged, manoeuvring her so she was once again facing the room.

Phoebe forced down the hot ball of hurt in her gut, squared her shoulders and raised her chin. 'Thank you so much for coming tonight, everyone. It means so much to …' His name felt thick in her mouth. She swallowed. 'Nathaniel and me.'

There was a burst of clapping and hooting and someone turned up the music. Phoebe's throat ached with the emotion she couldn't let out. She had to get out of here. She couldn't go home; it was suffocating there, too. She'd come back to all the tiny reminders of their life together, like skeletons scattered through the house. Innocent, awful reminders of how her life had been perfectly on track only ten days ago.

There was really only one place left for her to go. A shiver ran through her. She hadn't been there since Karin's death. Camilla and their father had cleaned out Karin's things. Phoebe had wanted to help but she just couldn't do it. Maybe part of her didn't want to spoil the memories. She thought of that slow-moving river, the kookaburras at dawn and the smell of eucalyptus and river salt. It was the magical place of childhood holidays and the source of their family's greatest pain. A place they'd all abandoned for the shame of it.

It was close to a year now. How could a whole year go by without her sister in it? All that was left was memories, overshadowed now by what Karin had done. Perhaps that was what had made Phoebe so keen to marry Nathaniel, to lock down life, forge some meaning, some permanence. She was nearing the age her elder sister had been when she took her own life. Karin must have felt like a failure at thirty-eight. No husband, no child, alone in the middle of nowhere. Nothing compared to their younger sister. The suicide sat unspoken and heavy over all the family gatherings. But just how dark and hard things could get, Phoebe had never understood. Not really. Until now.

She slid out a side door off the lounge room and escaped out the back door. She knew she was a coward for leaving but it wasn't hard to go without anyone noticing. It was Camilla's party, after all. And Phoebe had a five-hour drive south through the night towards memories of the very person she was afraid she had become.

# CHAPTER 3

The road snaked before her, long and black and empty. Phoebe had never felt more alone, and now she was heading towards the loneliest of places. Her stomach twisted at the thought of reaching the cottage in the early hours of the morning. She hadn't thought that far ahead, only that she needed to escape, to be alone to grieve the end of her domestic dream. The end of Nathaniel.

He hadn't been cruel. Every night he'd tried to find the courage to tell her that he couldn't marry her and every night he'd failed. He'd been afraid of hurting her, he'd said. And then on that last night he had looked so sad on that balcony and when she looked into his eyes, even before he spoke, she knew.

'I'm sorry,' he said.

She shook her head, not wanting to hear what was coming next.

'I can't.'

Her voice was tiny. 'Why?'

'It feels like we've been planning this instead of actually living, you know? It feels like some kind of military operation instead of something … I don't know, something natural.'

She took a step away from him and he reached out for her but she pushed his arm away.

'I'm so sorry Phoebe. I know how much this means to you.'

'How much this means to me? This is my life. This is our life.' She could hardly get the words out.

'I know, I'm sorry. I just … I need something … more. Different. It sounds horrible, I know, but I have to be honest. I've been wrestling with this for days. Weeks.' He sighed deeply and shook his head.

'Oh my God. Why did you make me go through all this? Buying the ring together? Planning the trip. Telling people?' Her face was wet with tears.

He put his head in his hands and was quiet. For a few hopeful seconds she thought he was reconsidering.

'I'm so sorry,' he said softly. 'Maybe I just went along. I knew how much you needed it. After Karin and everything that happened. I wanted you to be happy.'

'But you don't love me.'

He shook his head. 'It's not that simple.'

She laughed now, at how naïve she'd been. Of course it was simple. Nathaniel's unhappiness had probably been there all along and she'd just refused to see it. She'd been running too hard from the pain of Karin's death. And now look at her. She was driving through the darkness, running from everything and everyone. The headlights of her car fell on the trunks of tree after tree, white and still, like ghosts.

Phoebe thought about Karin making this trip, alone in her little vintage VW. It had felt like an abandonment when her sister left Sydney to move to the Bay but Karin was excited. There had been a florist business for sale in town, and the rent and lifestyle was so much more affordable than Sydney's lower north shore, where they'd all grown up. Karin had moved into the cottage, always intending to get her own place when the business was more established, but she was a lover of old things. The house had belonged to their grandparents, and where Camilla and Phoebe saw old people's stuff and dust, Karin saw treasures. She loved the lace curtains, and the faded orange lamps. They all knew the lure of the move had been the house just as much as the business. Karin had seemed so happy.

Phoebe wound down the window. The night air was still warm on her face. She could hear the earth breathing, the insects humming with the leftover heat of the day. She remembered this part of the trip, her sisters on either side in the back. The sunlight flickering through the trees was like looking through a kaleidoscope. She could still taste the hard-boiled butterscotch they were given as a treat on the drive. A wave of sadness rose through her body. How could that be so long ago? How could so much have gone wrong?

When someone you loved took their own life, all you were left with were questions. Questions about Karin's mental health, even though she had their father's emotional stoicism. Questions about how she had died. Phoebe had been so sodden with grief at the time that the details had seemed almost irrelevant. It was Camilla who had viewed the body and talked with police and the coroner. Her practical, together sister had pulled them all through it. The coroner had concluded that Karin had taken her own life in the river. But something deep inside Phoebe had said 'no', very clearly, very loudly, right at that moment of being told. Karin was afraid of the water, no one knew that better than Phoebe. But it was the coroner's verdict, the narrative that had wound itself about her family, whispered in hushed tones, a filmy, sticky web, almost invisible to the eye but felt on the skin.

The gravel crunched as Phoebe pulled into a petrol station, fluoro-bright on the side of the road. She filled her tank and smiled at the lanky teenage boy behind the counter as he looked up from his phone. She realised she hadn't eaten properly in days. She remembered all the elaborate meals her and Nathaniel had shared overlooking sun-bleached beaches. She'd been so expectant, waiting so naïvely for her perfect life to begin. When she closed her eyes she could still see the glow of Nathaniel's burned, bare shoulders at dusk. She bought a loaf of bread, a litre of milk, a jar of Vegemite, some cornflakes and a four pack of toilet paper. She grabbed a chocolate bar and watched the coffee machine dispense black liquid into a paper cup.

Back in the car, Phoebe switched on the engine to get the aircon going and bit into the sweet chocolate, hard and cool. She'd treated her body like a temple for weeks leading up to the holiday and with the prospect of a wedding on the horizon — she'd hardly touched sugar or caffeine. Now it didn't matter. There was a kind of relief in the simplicity of the sweetness, the buzz that ran through her as she tipped the coffee cup back to get the dregs.

It occurred to Phoebe that she hadn't brought spare clothes or make-up, or her pill—not that she needed to take it anymore. There were no lists of things to remember. No plan. This was so unlike her. She hadn't even brought her phone charger. Her phone sat on the seat beside her, uncharacteristically silent; she had switched it off after Camilla's first text. There was no mobile reception at the cottage anyway.

She knew these roads in the way she knew the bumps and grooves of her own skin. She didn't have to think, she just drove. She tried not to let Nathaniel into her mind. She tried not to think about Camilla. How would she be feeling after her wasted party? She knew her sister. She'd be mortified that Phoebe had snuck out but she would have made up some socially acceptable excuse. Anyway, she was beyond caring now. All she could think about was Karin.

You never knew the last time you saw someone was going to be the last time ever. Why hadn't she listened more carefully when Karin had told her about her business idea of mixing her florist with a tea salon and a vintage book and furniture store? They were all her passions and it was a great idea, but Phoebe had despaired that while it might have worked beautifully in Sydney's hip eastern suburbs, the residents of the Bay might not be so sophisticated. Karin had defended them. There was a lot of wealth coming in on weekends and holidays out of Canberra, she had said. There were a lot of holiday rentals to furnish. And the people here were simpler, it was true, but a cup of tea, a paperback and a bunch of flowers were simple too, in their way. Phoebe had thought back on her last conversations with Karin so many times, looking for clues, but she couldn't see any. Not even a glimmer of what might have made her sister walk into the river only a few days later.

The smooth traction of the road changed as the tyres moved onto the unsealed road. Fatigue was heavy on her shoulders and it made her eyes feel gritty and dry. There were no streetlights and Phoebe reduced her speed to a crawl. She rounded the corner and the river glinted like a dark mirror through the trees. She felt a rub of excitement run through her, the leftovers of childhood, like remnants of a pleasant dream. But as the metal gate came into view, the feeling changed. It was chained shut and panic tightened over her chest. Would she even be able to get in? The front door key had always been hidden under a stone frog in the yard but she hadn't thought about whether it would still be there. Was the electricity even connected? She had no mobile reception and she was in the middle of nowhere, in the middle of the night. Phoebe didn't believe in ghosts but her skin suddenly felt clammy with cold at the thought of the dark, empty, abandoned house. Why hadn't she just called Hellie and bunkered down with her for a few days? No. Hellie had a new baby, and the spare room was now the nursery. She hadn't even had the courage to tell her closest friend that the proposal hadn't happened.

She opened the car door and the smell of eucalyptus surrounded her, tart and familiar. Her breath hitched in her throat. Karin was in the smell, the sound of the river moving behind the house. It was Karin as a child, playing on the jetty, and Karin gone but still here, moored in the bark of the trees, the lonely shut-up house.

Phoebe wiped her eyes and got out of the car. The gravel was loose under her feet and she made her way carefully in the path of the headlights. Relief made her gasp as the chain fell away easily and the gate swung open. The house came into view, windows darkened, paint peeling like flaky skin. She remembered it bigger, newer. Memory always played that trick.

The air had cooled in the early hours and it nipped at her bare arms and legs. In the headlights she found the stone frog next to the tank where it had always been. Underneath was a rusty key, caked with dirt and time. Her heart was beating loudly in her ears as she wiped the key off and eased the metal into the lock. Part of her felt like an intruder, part of her felt like a refugee. She was scared about what she would find inside, but she pushed the door open and went in.

# CHAPTER 4

Phoebe opened her eyes to see dust particles dancing in the morning light. It took her a second to locate herself. To remember why she was here. The feeling settled like a stone in her gut and she shivered in the morning cool. The mohair blanket smelled slightly of mildew but she pulled it up to her chin anyway. She had flicked on the lights, collapsed onto the sofa and slept a long, dreamless sleep. In the daylight she could see how little the place had changed.

Her grandfather had built the house in the 1960s but evidence of Karin was everywhere. Under the fine layer of dust was a carefully curated melange of vintage artefacts. Karin had ripped up the decaying carpet to reveal polished wooden floors. She had stripped the wallpaper and painted the walls white. The furniture was mostly different from how Phoebe remembered it. The sofa she'd slept on was a newer type that had been covered in a beautiful stitched and beaded throw. The coffee table was made of raw wood and topped with her grandmother's cut-glass vases. There was a basket of shells, collected over a lifetime, held up to the ears of children to hear the sea.

Phoebe picked up one and ran her fingers over its rivulets. She went over to the cracked leather armchair and smelled it. Tobacco. She could still see her grandfather smoking his pipe here after dinner. She smoothed the spines of the *National Geographic* magazines dating back from the 1980s and the old leather-bound books, which still sat in the bookcase like dignified old men.

There was a picture of the whole family at the Mogo Zoo, the three of them standing in front of their parents. Phoebe was shocked at how young her parents looked. Her mother had yet to enter her turban-wearing phase, but even then she'd been partial to hats. She looked elegant in a wide-brimmed black hat, angled just so, and what looked like a silk jumpsuit. Camilla had inherited this ability to effortlessly shine, even somewhere like a zoo, but Karin had been the truly beautiful one. Phoebe had been called beautiful in her life, but sometimes looks were relative to who was standing next to you. In the photo, she was sandwiched between her two sisters—Camilla, honey skin and hair, with eyes the colour of the sky in high summer; Karin, her photographic negative: winter's version, with black hair, grey eyes and pale skin. Phoebe was in the middle in every sense. Her skin and hair were neither dark nor light, and her eyes were hazel as though they couldn't decide between green and brown.

Camilla wore a pink dress with sparkly ballet flats, and Phoebe and Karin were in shorts, T-shirts and thongs. Karin was laughing at Phoebe poking her tongue out. Karin had been the happiest, the simplest. She was the peacemaker and the fun-maker. She was like their dad. She was not the kind of person who walked out into the river and decided to die.

A breeze brushed her back and Phoebe turned, feeling fright jump in her chest like a startled bird. And then she saw that it had come from the window she'd opened when she'd arrived. She looked at the picture of her smiling sister. She didn't want to feel afraid. She wanted to remember Karin fondly, but the gap in understanding what she had done was a dark gulf that Phoebe couldn't seem to cross.

She wandered into the kitchen. Where some would have seen narrow benches and an impractical old electric stove, Karin had seen history. She'd kept it all except the florid carpet. Carpet in the kitchen was too retro, even for Karin, and she'd replaced the overhead fluoro light, too. Phoebe sat down at the dining table overlooking the river. It was covered in the same lace tablecloth that had always been there. It had been on this tablecloth that Karin had left her suicide note.

Phoebe stood up, abruptly, the image of dead and rotten flowers crowding her mind. She needed air. She had to pull hard to open the glass sliding door. It gave with a crack, and she stepped out onto the deck her father had built over one summer.

Through the white gums that lined the bank she could see the green of the river, still in shadow. A motor boat scooted past, a loud wound in the morning air. She smelled motor oil and eucalyptus. She realised she was hungry. Back in the kitchen the kettle looked new. Camilla probably bought it when they were down here to clean up Karin's affairs. Phoebe remembered that the water was from the tank and needed to be boiled before drinking. She filled the kettle and flicked the switch. She found the toaster, also new, and went about the comforting ritual of making Vegemite toast. She couldn't think of the last time she'd had toast. She carried her breakfast outside to the wooden table. The timber was brittle and cobweb-covered and she used a stick to scuttle away the wisps.

Her feet were bare and her hair was tangled and she was eating toast. It had been a long time since she'd been like this. Allowed herself to be like this. She was still wearing the dress from Camilla's party. Usually at this hour of the morning her hair had been tonged into loose waves, her face made up, and she was at her desk drinking a super smoothie blended in the office bullet with chia, blueberries and almond milk. She was almost certainly wearing a new-season dress that was worth nearly as much as she was paid weekly. Sometimes this meant counting every cent at the supermarket and ordering only an entrée at restaurants, but it was a trade-off she had somehow felt necessary. Now it seemed absurd.

For a long time Phoebe had convinced herself that the glossy surface of things was enough. There was a certain kudos working in the marketing department of a luxury champagne house. Everyone knew Joet et Halo. Everyone loved the bottles she gifted them. Nathaniel would boast that they had bottles of champagne coming out their ears, that once he'd found a few stashed in the bathroom cupboard. But for all the gloss, all the fabulous Instagram posts and the parties, the job itself was actually menial. When your favourite person in the world died, it was hard to find meaning in pretty pictures. Her dissatisfaction made its presence felt like an insect bite, waking her in the middle of the night. But even before Karin's death, Phoebe had known that one day maybe she would need more. She'd earned distinctions at university even if it was only an arts degree. She wasn't quite sure how she'd ended up cutting and pasting pretty pictures all day and pretending she had the best job in the world.

She brushed the toast crumbs off her fingers and pressed the palms of her hands into her eyes. She felt tired. This was not the way she'd imagined spending the last week of her holidays.

She looked up to see that the sun had just hit the river, making the deep green water sparkle. She found an old pair of thongs by the door and slipped them on. They felt good, rough and cracked, like dry earth beneath her feet. She picked up her mug and the long grass tickled her legs as she made her way towards the jetty. She'd been dreading going there. It was where Karin had died, but it was also tied to such happy times—fishing off the end, swimming in the cool water, picking pipis and oysters off the rocks. It was the first place they'd run to as children on arrival and the last place they'd go to say goodbye.

The timber was sun-bleached and the tin bucket they'd used to collect oysters was still there, like an ode to the passage of time, its salt-sodden rope rotting and barnacle-laced. Phoebe could almost smell the pungent fish guts, see the sparkle of scales as her father cleaned his catch with a rusty knife. She took off the thongs to feel the sun-warmed wood. Had Karin clambered down the side onto the sand and waded out to her waist, let the tide pull her under? Or had she gone down the ladder at the end into deeper water? That same ache that had been there for nearly a year swelled fresh in Phoebe's chest. What had Karin been going through to push her that far? Why hadn't Phoebe visited her in the two years she'd lived here? It had always seemed too far to drive. Work was always so busy. Why hadn't she ever brought Nathaniel here before? He and Karin had got on well, though the rest of the family had taken a while to warm to him.

It had been early December. Phoebe had invited him to her aunty's wedding in the gardens of a grand old home on the outskirts of Sydney. It was to be the first time the family would meet Nate, even though he and Phoebe had been dating for months.

The garden hummed with humidity and the hushed chatter of guests as they waited for the bridal party. It was already hot even though it was barely 11 am.

Karin had done the flowers for the event and wore tea roses in her hair. She'd found her dress—an old-fashioned lilac silk slip—in an op shop and had sewn silver beading into the fabric. She had looked so beautiful.

Nathaniel had been running late and Phoebe scanned the crowd nervously.

She saw Karin's face—quizzical and amused—before she saw Nathaniel.

'Babe, what the hell?' she'd said, grabbing his arm and pulling him close, as though this would somehow hide him. His breath had the sharp smell of stale alcohol and his hair was a matted mess, as if he'd just come out of the surf. His eyes were red-rimmed and bloodshot and his suit looked like he'd been rolling in the grass.

'What?' he replied, but looked sheepish. 'It was the work Christmas party last night,' he added, rubbing his eyes.

'Tell me you haven't come straight from there.' Phoebe looked around wildly for her mother. It wasn't too late to sneak Nate into the bushes and pretend this had never happened.

'No, the boys dropped by my place so I could get dressed,' he said, smoothing the crumples in his pants. 'I didn't want to be late.'

Her heart softened a little. She must really like this guy, but it didn't ease the panic stretched across her chest. 'Oh God, you know how judgemental my mum is.'

'Hi Nathaniel, lovely to meet you,' said Karin, moving over to them and planting a warm kiss on his cheek. 'Phoebe's told me so much about you.'

'This is my sister Karin,' said Phoebe, thankful for her calming presence. 'Nathaniel has come straight from his Christmas party. And I mean, straight.'

'Oh, I just thought you were some kind of rock star,' said Karin.

Nathaniel scratched his head, looking both puzzled and pleased. 'Sorry. Maybe I should go. I think I'm still a bit drunk.'

Phoebe rolled her eyes. 'You think?'

Karin laughed. 'Don't worry, everyone here will be drunk in an hour. I know, I just arranged flowers on the champagne table.'

Phoebe shot Karin a helpless look. There was no way she wanted her mother, or Camilla for that matter, to meet Nathaniel looking like this.

'You know what?' added Karin. 'I have some things in my car. Hairbrush, deodorant, Panadol, bottle of water. I've been tasked with keeping Aunty Claire and the wedding party looking decent.'

Nathaniel stared, his eyes glassy with exhaustion, and Phoebe had to give him a shove towards the car park. Karin put her hand protectively on his back, as though he was an old man rather than a hungover young one.

Phoebe was breathing a sigh of relief when Camilla emerged out of the crowd like a spectre. She had managed to flout the garden party dress code by wearing a black dress, but looked incredible nonetheless. Phoebe felt a new rush of adrenalin.

'Was that—'

Phoebe put up her hand. 'Don't even. I can't, Camilla.'

She widened her eyes dramatically. 'Oh my God. That's Nathaniel? I mean, honest to God, I thought it was a homeless person who had wandered off the street. Maybe one of Karin's lost causes.'

Phoebe shook her head. 'Can you please not say anything to Mum? Karin's looking after things.'

Of course, Camilla told their mother, and Nathaniel had been labelled 'the hobo' for a long time, even though Karin had transformed him into something presentable and, as predicted, everyone had been tipsy within an hour.

Nathaniel had always liked Karin best too after that day. Why hadn't Phoebe brought him down here? Why hadn't they all spent time together here on the jetty where there was nothing but the water meeting the sky?

Phoebe walked the few metres to the end of the jetty and looked across to the rich green bush on the other side. There was still only one house there. The stories she and Karin used to tell each other sitting in this spot. An old crone, a zookeeper, a giant. She heard a voice on the wind. Looking downriver she saw a man sitting at the end of the next jetty on a stool, rod perched in the air. There was something about the curve of the back, the way he held his head. Her heart lurched.

He looked up as she stared at him. Even from the distance she saw his face break into a smile. He stood and waved.

Her whole body flooded with a familiar feeling, like sunlight on cold skin.

'Phoebe,' he called, and it echoed across the water.

'Jez?' Her voice was constricted with shock.

They both stood there with their hands shading their eyes. Phoebe was sure she'd heard they'd sold their property at the end of the road and that he lived in Canberra now.

Jez pointed to a rowboat and mimed his intention. It only took him a matter of minutes to reach her, rowing upstream. She watched his shoulders move the oars against the current. They were the same shoulders. It was the same boat. She could have been seventeen again. There was a shine on his brow by the time he grabbed the ladder and looped the rope through it. She thought he was going to climb up but instead he looked up at her from the tethered boat. She sat down on the end of the jetty, letting her feet dangle off the end as she'd done a million times before.

'Long time no see,' he said, grinning. There was an openness to his face that time had snatched from her memory. A curl of happiness moved inside her.

She shook her head. 'It's been so long. Ten, no, fifteen years?'

'At least. More than fifteen by my count.'

The way he said it made it sound like he *had been* counting. After all this time and even in the midst of the pain of the last few days, it made her smile.

'What are you doing here?' She looked downriver. 'I thought you sold Driftwood.'

'Nah. Couldn't do it. Too many memories. We're living back here full time now. Only moved six months ago. Got sick of Canberra. There's plenty of work for me here. The good thing about being a tradie.'

'What are you doing?'

'Electrician,' he said.

'I don't blame you, I'd forgotten how beautiful it is here. I haven't been here since ... for years.' She picked at a piece of lichen, bleached white on the jetty.

'I'm sorry. About what happened to Karin.'

It was awkward when people talked about suicide. They never knew how to put it, how to attribute blame. But Jez had always been good with words.

Phoebe pulled her knees to her chest. 'Thanks. It's strange being back here.'

'Are you alone?'

She laughed more cynically than she meant to. 'I guess you could say that.'

He narrowed his eyes, trying to read her meaning.

'It's a long story.' She wanted nothing more than to sit here and tell him what had happened in the past fifteen years, find out about him, when she saw a woman out of the corner of her eye. She had long blonde hair that melted into the white of her dress. She wore a battered straw hat and was holding two mugs.

Jez followed Phoebe's line of sight. 'That's Asha.'

She'd heard the name before. His wife.

Phoebe watched as Asha put down the mugs, straightened and squinted into the sun.

'Over here,' Jez called and waved from the boat. 'Just saying hi to the neighbour.'

Phoebe's chest contracted. That's what she was now—the neighbour. She chastised herself. She was being sentimental, that was all. Just because she didn't get her happily ever after didn't mean others couldn't. She bit her lip until the sadness retreated a little. What did she expect? It was she who had wanted to move to Sydney, travel, pursue a career. Jez had always wanted to stay here, have a family. He must have kids now, too.

She forced a false note of brightness into her voice. 'Well, it was great to see you, Jez.'

He hesitated and made a sweeping gesture with his arm. 'You know, come to dinner.'

'Oh, no, I couldn't.'

'No, we've always got a full table. We've got a bit of a gathering of drifters going on at the house. Too big for just me and Asha. The Texan's cooking tonight.'

'The Texan?'

'It's a long story,' he said and she smiled. 'We've got two boarders. The Texan, also known as Tex, his partner Wendy, who lives just up the road, and our other boarder, Flick. And Tommy and his family come most weekends. I think Mum would have liked to think that her house was always full of people.'

'Tommy. How is he?' Phoebe would always remember Tommy as the tall, lean boy of their childhood. Always the boss of every game. Always the one to win an argument. It was not at all surprising that he was high up in the Australian Federal Police now.

Jez nodded, picking at a piece of peeling paint on the boat's hull. 'Yeah, he's pretty good. You'll see him this weekend.'

The promise of time with Jez. Phoebe couldn't help how good that felt. She changed the subject. 'Your mum was ...'

She thought of Pauline, always wearing bright lipstick, working the vegie patch, cooking up big vats of jam, in her studio with clay-thick hands. 'You're like her, you know.'

He looked out onto the water and she recognised the expression on his face. It held the echo of someone who wasn't here anymore. Then his features softened. 'You mean in my old age.'

She shook her head. 'We're not old yet, are we?'

'No,' he said with a smile. 'Thanks for saying that. About Mum.'

'It's true. I couldn't see it back then but I can see it now.'

'Jez.' Asha's voice rang out, bell-like across the water.

'I just invited Phoebe for dinner. She's an old friend,' he called back, his voice loud on the wind.

It was hard to make out Asha's face, shaded by her hand, but she didn't reply.

'Are you sure it's okay?' Phoebe wrinkled her nose. She didn't want to make anyone feel uncomfortable. But then again, she didn't really have any food in the house and the thought of a table full of people she didn't know was more comforting than she could have imagined.

'Yeah, yeah, yeah, of course. Come round at six. We eat early here in the country.'

'Well, I have to meet the Texan, clearly.' She shot him a wry smile.

'Clearly.' He hesitated as though he was going to say something else but then he shook his head and looked downriver. 'Great, see you then.'

He untied the rope with the deftness of someone who was born on the water. The boat floated, as light as a leaf, swept by the current. When he climbed the ladder and stepped onto his jetty, Asha picked up the mugs and handed one to him. She was almost as tall as him and encircled his shoulders with one of her arms as they walked up towards the house. They looked happy. He raised his arm to wave, and Phoebe waved back.

The last time she'd seen him she'd broken his heart. Now here she was floating adrift in her own life after Nathaniel had broken hers. Her vulnerability felt like a nerve exposed to the air. Jez was another life; it wasn't hers anymore.

Phoebe took a deep breath, drank the dregs of her tea and stretched her arms. She would go into the Bay to get some supplies, and go to dinner tonight, but then she would come back here and keep to herself.

# CHAPTER 5

The heat of the day had ebbed and the late afternoon sun cast a long shadow on the road. The kookaburras were noisy in the branches high above her. Phoebe had walked this road between their homes so many times. Their lives had been a constant to and fro between the cool of the dam and the salty jump off the end of the jetty. The dam came into view first now. It was still lush, surrounded by ferns and ringed with high reeds, a small timber weir the only access point among the foliage. Her heartbeat stuttered. That dam had been the first place where she and Jez had explored each other's bodies, their own pleasure oasis.

The birdsong intensified as the metal gate to the property squeaked open. *Driftwood*. The word had been smoothed by the elements. She ran her fingers along the woodgrain, feeling the passing of time. This sign had not changed in twenty-five years. Was there some essential nugget of herself she could still find, now that all the things she thought had mattered were gone?

Phoebe knew the easy connection she and Jez shared was a tempting panacea for the pain. She just needed to keep her head screwed on tonight. She had gone into the Bay to buy some clothes even though it was unlikely anyone cared what she was wearing. She'd bought make-up from the chemist and found the lipstick she wore for work. She'd dressed in a cream silk blouse, tan leather sandals and denim shorts. She felt strange, as though she was living another person's life.

The house was still beautiful, like good bone structure under age-weathered skin. It was set against the line of gums that flanked the river, and had a generous bull-nosed wrap-around veranda. There was new paving leading up to the French doors of the entranceway. Frangipani trees flowered to the right like gorgeous intruders in the native scrub. As Phoebe walked the path, the wonder she felt at being back here was tempered by a wave of nerves and doubt. It was impossible to be here without feeling those stirrings of affection. Every part of this place contained a little piece of her history with Jez, like breadcrumbs of emotion to be picked up and crumbled between her fingers. It was right on these front steps that they'd had the talk that ended their relationship. The house was like a lush incubator of their youth, of that nubile sapling growth that only happened once.

She climbed the steps now and reached the front door. A waft of tobacco smoke mixed with the aroma of roasting meat and onions.

'Hi.'

Phoebe jumped at the voice and swivelled around. Asha stood barefooted, wearing the same white dress, a hand-rolled cigarette between her fingers. She proffered her other hand, the nails bitten to the quick. 'I'm Asha. You must be Phoebe, the neighbour.'

She felt a jolt. 'The neighbour'. But it was true; she was a stranger here now.

She smiled as warmly as she could as she shook Asha's hand. 'Oh, yeah, my parents own the property just up the road.'

'Jez said your family and theirs knew each other.' Asha's voice didn't seem to match her delicate looks. She had a deep, strong intonation with an accent that spoke of growing up in the country. She took a long drag on the cigarette, her eyes flinching against the smoke. 'Anyway, come in. I think dinner's nearly ready and the mozzies are getting fierce.' She crouched to stub the cigarette out in a metal tray on the ground, and then led Phoebe in through the French doors.

It was strange that this woman was Jez's wife. Phoebe wasn't sure why, but there was a softness in him that she couldn't detect in Asha. She shook the thought away. She was here as the neighbour for dinner, that was all. What right did she have to analyse their relationship?

The interior was largely as she remembered it—an open-plan living room that looked out of more French doors to the trees and the river beyond. Further along there was a window seat that stretched almost the width of the room. She and Jez had passed whole afternoons lying foot to foot reading, playing cards, napping. The adjoining kitchen was flanked by a long, floating bar. The sofas looked newer, their white cotton brighter, and there was more of a hippy vibe than Phoebe remembered. She guessed the Moroccan cushions, throws and rugs were probably Asha's influence, but the pieces of driftwood still sat over the stone fireplace, namesakes that had been there forever. Candles burned on the coffee table and in the heavy iron candelabra above the dining table, filling the air with a vanilla scent.

'You must be Phoebe. Come grab a glass of wine.' A tall man with a wild head of grey hair gestured with a wooden spoon from the kitchen.

She smiled. 'You must be the Texan.'

'I am indeed. Call me Tex. Straight out of the American south and into the New South Wales south coast.'

'I see you haven't lost your accent though.'

'And that gorgeous woman outside is my Wendy.'

The way he said it made Phoebe's heart ache, reminding her of what she had recently lost. She turned to see a woman with a grey bob and glasses talking animatedly with Jez on the veranda.

'Those two are always talking, talking, talking, making me jealous,' he said, shaking his head with mock exasperation and spooning a morsel of whatever he was cooking into his mouth.

Asha took a seat on one of the high stools along the kitchen bench. 'Well, she can't have him,' she said, banging an arm full of silver bracelets on the bench.

Phoebe winced and smiled awkwardly. 'Do you and Wendy live here?' she asked.

'I do. But Wendy lives up the road. You're probably only a few doors away from her. She's on the river side.'

'They have the perfect relationship,' Asha chimed in. 'They see each other every second or third day.'

'We don't overcrowd each other. She has her space, I have mine,' the Texan said.

'So you live in the studio out the back?' asked Phoebe.

'No, I'm in one of the rooms at the back, Flick's in the studio, lucky duck. We all came through Airbnb and then got comfortable and refused to leave.'

'Do you still even pay us rent?' Asha asked, smiling. She had dimples in her cheeks when she smiled.

The Texan took a swig of wine. 'I've been told I'm a half decent cook so I get ... what do you call it here? Mates rates, because I slave over this stove every night.'

'You love it,' said Asha, reaching for the bottle of white Phoebe had brought. The bracelets adorning her wrists jangled as she moved.

'I love your jewellery,' Phoebe said. 'Do you make it?' Asha had the air of a bohemian artist about her. Camilla and their mother would probably adore her.

Asha laughed. It was deep and rich, a smoker's laugh. 'No. My market stall's right next to a local jewellery maker and I pretty much keep her in business.'

Phoebe smiled. 'You seem like you're a creative person, too?'

She waited for Asha to elaborate but instead she got up and went into the kitchen and pulled a glass from the cupboard. She snapped the top, poured the wine, looked Phoebe right in the eyes and took a sip. *Who opens a guest's wine in front of them without offering them any?* Phoebe thought.

Asha leaned against the bench. 'What's cooking tonight, Tex?'

Phoebe felt a pull in her stomach. She wasn't imagining it, Asha was sending her a clear message. She pressed her lips together. Maybe it was just an 'every man for themselves' kind of house. Maybe Asha hadn't heard her. Maybe she didn't want to talk about what she did at the market. She told herself to stop overthinking things and relax. Isn't this what she'd done with Nathaniel? Overthought everything, taken the spontaneity out of their holiday, out of the proposal? He'd implied she had stifled him. If she'd just let things happen she wouldn't be standing here expecting things from strangers.

'Lamb roast with freshly picked rosemary and lemons, and a vegetable medley straight from the vegie patch,' said the Texan.

'Cheers to that,' Asha held her glass up and clinked it with his.

'Grab yourself a glass, Phoebe; my food is to be consumed with wine. That's the only rule in this house.'

Phoebe felt the muscles of her jaw relax. She had been reading too much into things. It was a free-for-all kind of household.

Jez and Wendy came in through the French doors. The cool air off the river came with them, laced with the smell of wood fire.

'Phoebe, hi.' Jez dusted his hands on the front of his shorts and reached for her shoulder, pecking her softly on the cheek. 'You've met everyone? Wendy, this is Phoebe Price. Her family has a holiday place up near you.'

Wendy was a thin woman with warm eyes behind her glasses and a sprightly manner that made her seem younger than she probably was. 'Lovely to meet you, Phoebe. Are you on the river side of the street?'

Phoebe nodded. 'Where are you?'

'I'm about halfway up the road. I'm surprised I haven't crossed paths with your family on holiday before.'

There was something kind about Wendy's face that made Phoebe want to tell her the truth. She snuck a look at Jez. His forehead was crinkled, his thumb resting against his closed lips. It was so hard to talk about death. It was a puddle to be avoided on the side of the road, a place no one wanted to see their own reflection.

Jez shot her a look loaded with meaning. 'You guys don't come down much anymore, do you?' He was giving her an out.

'No.' Phoebe glanced at him gratefully.

'It's a glorious part of the world,' Wendy said, sighing. 'I used to live in Canberra and one day I just woke up and thought, no, I want to die somewhere more beautiful than suburbia.'

Jez shot her another look, this time openly apologetic. Phoebe smiled at Wendy and tried to look sympathetic.

'And then she met me and realised she had another twenty years of bliss left in her life,' said the Texan.

'I take it you've met my lover,' Wendy said. 'He insists on being referred to as that. Doesn't want husband, or boyfriend, it has to be lover.'

'What can I say, I'm a sensualist,' the Texan said, coming out of the kitchen to hand Wendy his wineglass.

'Can I have my own, please?' she asked, flicking him away with playful disdain.

'That's what she said when I wanted to move in with her.' He stuck out his lip in feigned hurt.

'Best of both worlds,' Wendy said, winking and taking a sip.

Phoebe couldn't have imagined a set-up like this with Nathaniel. Wasn't that the whole point of living together? To have a cocoon for two, shored against the outside world? They had been cocooned. One of their favourite things had been to make coffee in their Italian coffee pot and sit in the sun on their tiny balcony. Phoebe would read the paper and Nathaniel would close his eyes and tilt his face towards the sun. Now she wondered if he'd been dreaming of another life.

How had she been so blind? They lived close to the beach—one of his greatest loves—and he got to surf every weekend, he ran on the beach, they ordered Thai takeout and watched movies. Wasn't that what contented couples did? He had seemed happy enough. Phoebe searched for a moment where she might have caught a flicker of doubt in his eyes. Sure, they'd had times when work stress or domestic frustrations made them short with one another, but she'd always been relieved that they didn't have big arguments. She thought that had meant they worked. But maybe that had been the problem—too much was left unsaid.

The Texan's booming laugh broke through her thoughts. She could actually see why Jez was content to live this way. There was a warmth here that Phoebe could feel herself drawn into already. Jez would never admit it, but Wendy and the Texan were clearly parent substitutes. He'd grown up with an absent father and Pauline had died in his early twenties. Phoebe supposed the board from the Texan and Flick also helped with the running of the house. She wondered how Tommy felt about these parent figures. Even when they were seventeen, before Pauline had become sick, Tommy had been fiercely protective of his younger brother.

'Sit, everyone. Feast,' said the Texan, gesturing to the food-laden table.

Phoebe was used to incredible food—it was a perk of working for a luxury goods company. But this was simplicity in its most luxurious form. There were no fancy tablecloths or starched napkins and expensive chinaware. The plates were piled in the middle of the table, the cutlery sat in a wooden box, and it was clear this food had been grown and cooked with love.

'I'll call Flick,' said Asha, leaving the room.

Jez handed Phoebe the glass of wine she'd been craving. 'Felicity's got chronic fatigue,' he said. 'Well, recovering from it. She's a lot better since she got here.'

'Must be my food,' said the Texan, passing Phoebe a bowl of steaming whole baby potatoes flecked with basil.

'Oh, not everything's about you,' chided Wendy. 'There are still days where it's hard for her to make it to the dinner table.'

'Does she need a lot of looking after?' asked Phoebe, spooning potatoes onto her plate.

'She's pretty self-sufficient unless she has a bad day,' said Jez. 'She's only had one really bad episode, right when she first got here. She and Asha have become pretty close.'

'That's nice,' said Phoebe, her estimation of Asha shifting slightly.

Flick was nothing like Phoebe had imagined. There was no hint of illness about her. She was tall and tanned with a wide, friendly face.

'Hello, family,' she said as she took up a place at the head of the table. The only clue that she was unwell was the slowness with which she eased herself into the chair. She gave Phoebe a wave. 'Hi, I'm Flick. Otherwise known as The Invalid.'

The Texan carried a platter of lamb to the table. 'So, Phoebe as you can see, we've got The Invalid, The Marrieds, The Lover, and Wendy the Ruthless Independent. You're going to need a name to sit at this table.'

Phoebe was about to suggest 'The Neighbour'.

'The First Love?' said Asha, reaching for a plate.

Phoebe felt her face go hot and her heart begin to pound. Jez's hand stilled while pouring a glass of wine, the muscles in his jaw working hard. Their eyes met and there was a seriousness in his look that did nothing to calm her.

Phoebe glanced at Asha but her eyes conveyed no emotion at all. The tension hung thick in the air, making her sweat.

The Texan cocked his head and his mouth scrunched to one side. 'First Love, hey. You only get one of those.'

Wendy elbowed him in the ribs and he yelped.

Phoebe swallowed a piece of potato with difficulty, wondering, with horror, if she was going to have to elaborate.

Jez squared his shoulders and took a sip of wine. He looked from Phoebe to Asha and back again. 'Yeah, it was a long time ago. We were kids, really.'

'Yeah, totally. We ...' Phoebe shrugged, trying to look casual, indifferent.

'Kinda grew up together,' Jez finished her sentence.

She looked at Asha, bracing herself, but she was passing the vegetables to Flick, a nonchalant look on her smooth, even features.

'It must have been a really lovely place to grow up,' said Wendy, steering the conversation into safer territory. 'The dam, the river, all that grass beneath your feet.'

'It was,' Phoebe said, taking a large sip of her wine.

'So, you've got a place just up the road? What brings you back here?' Flick asked. She sounded curious rather than accusatory, which was a relief.

*The collapse of my life*, Phoebe thought. 'Ah, just ...' She searched for the socially appropriate words. 'I needed some time out from all the business of stuff ... life,' she said, her voice breaking very slightly, mortifying her further.

She took a deep breath. She was not going to lose it here,

not now. She looked around the table. Everyone belonged here. A guy from the southern states of America, a girl with a chronic illness. They fitted. Phoebe tried to think of the last place she'd felt she belonged. It wasn't with her family. Sometimes her mother and Camilla felt like people you read about in high-end magazines, sailing through life effortlessly, stylish and distant. They had never felt completely real to her, as though they were shiny Instagram images she could upload and marvel at. She had wanted to belong with Nathaniel, make a life together, but that hadn't worked out either. She was an intruder at work, too. All the girls seemed to love their job, and Phoebe had made a good pretence of loving hers, too.

'Sounds like you've had a bit of a tough time of it,' said Flick.

'We've all been through some tough times,' Wendy said, passing Phoebe the salad. 'That's life. It goes up and it goes down.'

'Sure does,' said the Texan. 'That's why we have wine.'

Phoebe took a grateful sip of the red in front of her. She glanced up to see Asha widen her eyes at Jez. They seemed to have the perfect life here, surrounded by friends, eating food they grew themselves. Phoebe was a ring-in. Her life was second-floor apartment living, with twelve-hour days and checking emails on her phone at night. She still felt slightly sick to be out in the world without her phone. The only place with reception was in the Bay. She'd bought an iPhone charger on her shopping expedition but still hadn't been able to check her messages.

'You guys don't have reception here, do you?' she asked.

'Not a bar,' said Wendy triumphantly. 'Well, maybe one. But that's the way we like it.'

'Walk to the top of the hill just before the highway and you can get it,' said Jez. 'Or borrow Tommy's reception stick.'

Phoebe looked at him quizzically.

'He was getting all crazy not being able to check messages, so he worked out that the end of the jetty has the best reception. And if you tape your phone onto this wooden pole he made and stick it out further, your messages come in.'

'Which defeats the purpose of being here,' said Asha, rolling her eyes.

'You know Tommy though,' said Jez.

'How's his little boy?' Phoebe asked.

'Yeah, Harry's doing okay,' Jez said brightly. 'I mean, it's hard for them. Autism, you know.'

Phoebe nodded. She'd heard somewhere along the way that they had an autistic child. It was the sort of information that got passed on in a similar way to suicide, with hushed voices and sympathetic brows. It was the sort of thing that only happened to Other People.

'He's five now. He's improved heaps since he's been in a special program. You'll meet him this weekend.'

Phoebe glanced at Asha. 'Oh, I'm not sure I'll be around that long,' she said casually.

'Well, if you're still around, I know Tommy would love to see you,' said Jez, his silver wedding ring catching in the candlelight.

'And you must come and pick the new-season white nectarines,' said Wendy.

Phoebe remembered the sweetness of the flesh, the honeyed scent, the sticky hands after they had gorged themselves. The way they had laid on the grass looking up through the branches holding their full, aching stomachs. The warmth of Jez's hand on her bare thigh. This place was so infused with the past, with the rawness and simplicity of something that she couldn't quite articulate but that she recognised was now lost.

She wanted to stay more than anything. She couldn't face the thought of going back to the city, to the apartment filled with reminders of Nathaniel, to a job selling happiness and celebrating milestones that would not come for her. She would be thirty-eight soon. Camilla ran a business, had married and had two children and she was only thirty-five. All Phoebe had done was catch up to Karin. Karin, who at thirty-eight supposedly walked into the river. But she would rather be here with Karin's ghosts than back home with her own.

She looked up to see Asha's eyes on her, burning into her flesh, willing her to leave.

# CHAPTER 6

Phoebe woke with a throbbing head. She'd slept on the sofa again, and she sat up and looked out the window. The clouds moved fast across a low sky. A good day for driving. She pressed her forehead into her palms to stem the throb and wished she hadn't had so much wine the night before. Her whole body felt heavy as she shuffled into the kitchen. The jar of instant coffee was out of date but she didn't care. She switched on the kettle and poured herself a glass of water from the fridge. She took her coffee onto the deck and felt the hairs on her arms respond to the cool air. The weather had turned.

It was too soon to be leaving. She still had another week of holidays and the last thing she wanted was to spend it cleaning out the apartment and finding another place to live. She didn't want to face her family; she hadn't even told them where she was and there was a self-indulgent freedom in that, which she was enjoying. But the truth was, after last night she didn't trust herself here. The more wine she'd had the more her body had loosened. She'd found herself staring at Jez, remembering small things about him. It was like a snare, like a rip, the pull of him. The way his fingers flexed when he talked, the rub of his hands beneath his chin when he was listening. But then Asha would speak, or the familiar ache of Nathaniel would press on her, and the spell would be broken. She was clearly in a very strange place, needy and alone. The easy familiarity of Jez, the warmth of nostalgia and the wine had combined to intoxicate her. Her life was already in ruins, the last thing she wanted was to cause more wreckage.

She finished her coffee and took a shower. Under the warm water she studied the almost empty bottle of cheap supermarket shower gel. Had Karin used this? Had it lived on past her sister? She squeezed some into her hand but felt sick at the strong apple scent. Had Karin used this the morning she died? Had she known that day would be her last? That she'd die smelling like fake apples? Phoebe washed it off her hands and turned off the water. She stood shivering under her towel. She didn't know the part of her sister that had decided to walk into the river, did that mean she had never really known Karin?

Phoebe had found a forum on the internet for people who were trying to come to grips with the suicide of a loved one. She never contributed but she read all the posts. Many people felt the same as her. They had questions that sat inside them, leaking unease into their bones.

The forum had been important for Phoebe because the suicide had seemed to be so easy for everyone else to understand. Karin was a woman in her late thirties, living alone on a property in a bush setting. Phoebe remembered the words of one of the officers who had come to Camilla's house in those early days. 'It gets very dark in that part of the world at night. It's a lonely place.'

But Karin was always going to local business meetings for her florist shop. She might not have had a best friend, but that wasn't the sort of person Karin was. She was self-sufficient and independent. She spent her weekends on treasure hunts at local markets and vintage stores, or keeping the property under control. And she'd had Phoebe. They spoke every week without fail, on a Sunday.

Phoebe thought back to the last time the family had all been together. The restaurant overlooked the harbour, with white sails hovering above a polished deck area. Karin had driven up the coast to Sydney that morning with her own flowers and decorations for the long table.

'Happy birthday, Dad,' Karin said, squeezing their father into a tight hug. 'You don't look a day over sixty.'

He laughed awkwardly, brushing his grey hair to one side and straightening his navy slacks. He never liked being the centre of attention.

'No, it's true,' said Phoebe, pulling him into an embrace. 'You look a decade younger than you are.'

He shook his head, his face reddening. 'What you've done with the table looks great,' he said. They all turned to admire Karin's wooden planter boxes filled with paper lanterns and fresh flowers and herbs.

'You can plant the herbs in the garden afterwards. I know you don't like waste. Oh, and I got you this.' Karin passed him a gift wrapped in brown paper and tied with twine. 'You don't have to open it now. It's every Beatles record on vinyl. Well, every one I could find. You've got to be the only seventy-year-old to have recently discovered the Beatles and own a record player. That's what twenty-year-olds are doing.'

He was silent for a beat. 'That must have taken you forever.' His voice was soft with emotion.

'There are a lot of vintage shops around the Bay.' Karin shrugged. 'It's my hobby anyway, digging up old stuff and finding it a new home.'

Camilla interrupted with a peck on their dad's cheek. 'Happy birthday, Dad. I'm so glad you ended up doing something. Turning seventy deserves to be celebrated. And Karin, those planter boxes are very quaint.'

'Thanks, Cammie, they're my bestselling item right now.'

'And you're looking very swish all in black.'

Karin squeezed Camilla's arm warmly but Phoebe thought about punching it. Camilla was so transparent but Karin never saw it, or chose not to. The truth was, Karin had always been the most effortlessly chic of them all. Her long limbs and perfect posture meant she could wear anything and look gorgeous. For their dad's birthday lunch she wore a knitted dress with knee-high flat leather boots, which were so much more elegant than Camilla's unseasonable heeled sandals and floral pantsuit.

'I've actually got an idea to expand the business a little. I'm going to do some second-hand furniture.'

'What's this about your business?' Their mother was wearing oversized black sunglasses and a silk scarf at her neck. 'Darlings, we should probably sit down so we get the best seats, people are arriving.'

Karin pulled out their dad's seat at the head of the table. 'I was just saying I'm expanding the shop a little bit to do tea and sell some second-hand furniture and maybe vintage books.'

Phoebe saw Camilla and their mother exchange a look.

'That sounds beautiful, being surrounded by flowers and books and sipping tea,' said Phoebe, accepting a glass of white wine from a passing waiter.

'You don't want it to become too knick-knacky though,' said their mother. 'I thought you'd just got the fit-out of the shop polished. And as I've always said, it's better to err on the side of simplicity.'

'I don't think that applies to the Bay, Mum,' Camilla said over the rim of her wineglass.

'Shouldn't you be thinking about finding eligible men down there rather than tea and old books?' Their mother made a dismissive gesture with her hand.

'I'm too busy with the shop and the house to think about that,' said Karin.

'I think late thirties is a bit too late down there anyway. Don't they all have four kids by twenty-three?' added Camilla, a look of false innocence on her face.

Phoebe opened her mouth then shut it, momentarily stunned by Camilla's comment.

'We're not all superwomen like you, Cammie, who can have kids and a business,' said Karin, completely without sarcasm or reproach.

The truth was that Karin was just as much of a high achiever as Camilla but she did it with the same humility and grace as their father. Camilla and her mother's interior design business might have been the family focus, but their father was the one who quietly and diligently paid the mortgage through his work as an actuary.

Phoebe wasn't sure how Karin's dignity had been lost. How somewhere along the way it was assumed, in whispered tones at family gatherings, that Karin's suicide was linked to her lack of a husband and child, her loneliness. Never mind that she was passionate about her business, and looked after a house and property all by herself. Phoebe knew as much as anyone the pressure of social mores, but Karin wasn't held to account by such things, not in the same way Camilla was. Not, she realised, in the same way she herself was. Being back here among Karin's things confirmed what Phoebe already knew deep down. Her sister had not been someone deeply unhappy and isolated in her life. She had been someone who watched the quiet slipstream of the river from the deck and absorbed its peace.

Phoebe dressed in the same clothes she'd worn the day before and threw on Karin's khaki cotton jacket from the coat rack at the front door. It was stiff with lack of wear. That was the feeling: *abandonment*. Phoebe felt like leaving now was in some way letting her sister down, though she couldn't explain exactly why. She smoothed the rough cotton against her skin, remembering Karin wearing this jacket. The colour had suited her cool colouring and made her grey eyes look green. Phoebe closed the door behind her and stood in the grass. The lawn needed mowing. She checked her phone was in her pocket. She would walk to the top of the street to get her messages and stretch her legs.

She was only a few metres up the road before she needed to shrug the jacket off. The sun fell in long lines through the tall trees and she enjoyed its warmth on her bare arms and legs. The houses were as she remembered them, many small and weathered with faded awnings and the whiff of fibro decay, but with prime river frontage. A few were two-level brick monstrosities, complete with jet ski and motorbike in the yard— most likely the holiday homes of politicians from Canberra. But other than those, the street was the same, unpaved and hopelessly encroached upon by nature. She thought of all the changes, all the technology that now ruled her life, and yet this place had remained nearly untouched.

She reached the top of the hill, overlooking the abandoned motel whose pool was still mysteriously appealing despite the crumbling 1960s architecture. Her phone began to buzz as messages and missed calls filled the screen: Camilla, her mother.

Every time Phoebe saw or spoke to Camilla it was as though all the imperfect aspects of her life were magnified. She knew it wasn't her sister's fault, but that didn't make it any easier. Camilla was just one of those people who was completely at ease in the world. It wasn't just that she always wore the perfect outfit or that her life was a merry-go-round of weekends away, parties for her children or dinner parties with friends, she had something about her that made others want to be around her. It was as though people could sense her ease and confidence and were drawn to that. Camilla posted paintings she'd done with her children on social media, while simultaneously popping up a gorgeous house interior she'd styled. Phoebe had understood from an early age that their mother was made of exactly the same shiny, effortless fabric. It wasn't surprising to anyone when Camilla joined their mother's successful interior styling business at age nineteen. Everyone said she had a natural 'eye', and that wasn't something that could be learned or taught. It was assumed that neither Karin nor Phoebe were blessed with it.

It had always been Camilla and their mother, and Phoebe and Karin, with their dad playing the role of Switzerland, hovering good-naturedly on the outskirts. In fact, the only concession their mother had ever paid their father was allowing him to keep the cottage after his parents died and take them all on holidays there at Easter and Christmas. Her voice always took on an exasperated tone wherever the cottage was concerned, but Phoebe's memories of her down here were of her stretched out on a plastic sunbed on the deck, a book in hand and a glass of wine beside her. Phoebe suspected for all the complaining, her mother needed the time away from her glamorous, frenetic life. She had never seen her wear a pair of thongs but there was a pair of leather slides that she used to occasionally slip on to visit the jetty when the sunset was particularly stunning.

Their mother had always been like that, a distant but authoritative figure to whom beauty was paramount. It was a brilliant irony that she had married a man who couldn't care less about the way things looked. Her father was the kind of man who, had he been born in a different time, may have defeated the wall of male stoicism that surrounded him, but it was ingrained in his upbringing. Phoebe knew he was a softie at heart but he had no way of translating feeling into action. The result was a kind of emotional stagnation that had only intensified since Karin's death.

That awful day was etched into her being. She'd been in a café with Hellie deliberating over the menu when Camilla had called. Phoebe had probably looked at the caller ID and rolled her eyes.

'Phoebe, Karin's dead,' Camilla had said. Just like that. The words had been so simple—no preamble. There was none with death. No, *Everything's okay, but …* or *Don't panic, but …* It was done, and all that was left was to survive the crushing of her heart, and the dark, dark nights as the knowing began: that the person was gone and never coming back.

Phoebe had wanted to go to her mother and sister and put her arms around them and cry. But that wasn't their way. There were no lingering hugs or raw emotion over cups of tea. Only her dad had cried with her in a way she didn't know men could—bent over and silent except for the shaking of his body. When she saw this terrible trembling, she sensed, through the white haze of shock, that it was all real.

Her dad and Camilla drove down to view the body the next day. They kept talking about 'the body' as if it was a news report about another person, a stranger, not her sister. That was why Phoebe couldn't go. She couldn't cope with the thought of seeing Karin stretched out and lifeless, that same blue-grey on her lips that she had witnessed when her sister was drowning, all those years ago. This time she hadn't been there to save her.

Phoebe's phone kept buzzing in her hand as texts filled her screen.

Hellie had texted, asking for a photo of the ring, her message peppered with happy smiles and love emoticons. Phoebe's heart dipped. There had been a time when she would have called her closest friend from the oceanfront balcony where her world had come crashing down. But that time had passed. Hellie had a newborn child, and every molecule of her body was trained on her baby. The gulf that had opened between them was completely understandable, but that didn't stop it from being painful.

Hellie—with her doting husband, new baby, and lovely settled life—was part of the pain now. It was an awful thing to be jealous of a friend's good fortune, but right now Phoebe couldn't face her.

A message from Nathaniel came in. Seeing his name sent a sharp pang through her and she placed a hand on her stomach, hesitating. He probably just wanted to know when he could pick up his stuff from the flat. But there was a small sliver inside of her that glinted with the light of possibility that maybe, just maybe, he'd changed his mind. She opened the message, holding her breath.

*Hi Phoebe, I'm really sorry about how it all happened and how disappointed you must be. I hope that with time you'll see it was the right decision. Let me know when it's okay for me to come and start cleaning out the flat. I guess we'll have to talk about what to do with it. N*

His mixture of apology and perfunctory details made the still fresh wound in her heart hurt. She still didn't fully understand why he'd ended it. He kept saying he needed something 'more' and there was a lot of talk of 'finding himself'. At what point did a relationship die? Was it a slow death over weeks and months? How had she missed the signs?

Phoebe had believed Nate when he said there was no one else, but now she wondered. Wasn't it a cliché to fall in love with your gym instructor? Maybe he'd found someone who he had something 'more' with, whatever that meant. Her cheeks prickled with heat and anger sparked inside her. Had he been feeling doubts while they planned the holiday, picked out the ring together, and never mentioned them? They'd owned the flat together for more than a year, been together for nearly five years. It wasn't like this was the first step down the road of commitment. But a large chunk of the deposit for their tiny sunlit apartment had come from her parents, and Phoebe's income essentially paid the mortgage. Nathaniel had worked in computer sales, freelance marketing, and had just started personal training. They'd never been able to rely on his income. Had her being the main breadwinner taken a toll on his ego? And yet the security of her parents' money had been something he'd openly acknowledged and been grateful for. Maybe it had made him stay when he wasn't happy. She shook her head and rammed the phone hard against her thigh, swearing under her breath.

She stood there, immobilised by indecision. There was too much information to process. She should reply to everyone, walk down the hill, shut up the house and drive home. But instead Phoebe ignored the messages, slipped the phone into her pocket and took the road that led down to the river. She just needed to walk for a while. It was mid-morning now, and the low drone of motor boats was punctuated by the high note of an occasional jet ski. Some men were fishing from a small wharf. Phoebe could think of nothing better than buying some bait and throwing out a line at the end of the jetty, watching the sun move across the sky and feeling its languid heat on her skin.

She reached the bridge over the river and crossed it, hoping she might see Jez or the Texan as she glanced inside the little coffee and bait shop. She wandered slowly back to the cottage, trying to ignore the thick churn of her feelings. It was so quiet, save for the whips of bellbirds in the trees above. A few doors away from the cottage she saw Wendy's bobbed head leaning over her letterbox.

'Hi,' she called out, feeling a rush of warmth as Wendy lifted her head and waved.

'I'm mending my letterbox. Tex has been promising to do it for weeks and today I just thought, bugger it, why am I waiting for a man to do this job?'

Phoebe smiled. 'Good on you.'

'So, we're almost neighbours. How lovely. You look like you've had a nice walk over to the village. Have you tried Ross's burnt coffee?'

'I didn't take money with me.'

'Come in for some morning tea. I've made pumpkin scones. I'm nearly done here.'

Phoebe pressed her lips together and glanced over her shoulder. 'Oh, I really shouldn't. I should probably head back to Sydney today.'

Wendy's kind eyes searched her own. 'So soon? You just got here.'

'I know. I don't want to. It's just …' Phoebe felt her voice breaking and cleared her throat.

Wendy touched her shoulder lightly. 'Hey, just come in and have a quick drink and I'll give you one of my newly made jams to take home.'

Phoebe nodded and followed her through a garden spilling with native plants. It looked wild but well loved. They walked down the side of the fibro house and onto a covered veranda overlooking the river. A breeze had picked up and the leaves rustled overhead.

'They're predicting rain and I think it's going to storm,' said Wendy. 'Are you sure you should be driving in bad weather? Sit, sit, I'll bring us some tea.' The screen door banged as Wendy went inside.

Phoebe took a seat at a little wooden table covered in faded floral plastic. It reminded her of being a child in the 1980s when her family had similar table coverings.

'Are you okay down here by yourself?' Wendy called through the open kitchen window. 'I've got Tex just down the road, but even so, sometimes I get the heebie-jeebies. It's so quiet at night. I heard a young girl committed suicide not long back. Just walked into the river, apparently.'

Phoebe felt a chill run down the back of her neck, as though someone had thrown a bucket of iced water over her. Karin had become an urban legend to be gossiped about over morning tea.

Wendy came out carrying a plate of scones. 'It was just so sad. A few of the people in the street knew her. Such a happy, lovely person, by all accounts. Everyone was so shocked. I moved in just after it all but everyone was still talking about it. You would have missed all that being up in Sydney.'

Phoebe pressed her hand over her mouth. She didn't know how to tell Wendy that it was her sister, and she didn't have the strength to lie. A sob began to build at the back of her throat.

Wendy's face flickered with emotion—confusion first, then wide-eyed understanding, then horror.

'Oh, oh, Phoebe, I'm so sorry. You knew her.' Wendy took her glasses off and pinched the top of her nose as tears sprang to her eyes. She reached out to touch Phoebe's arm. 'Oh, I should have thought. I'm so sorry.'

Phoebe couldn't help it. She hadn't let herself cry properly since being here, or since what had happened with Nathaniel. She'd been in shock, on emotional autopilot, just hoping that with careful steering she might not crash to earth. Her chest was heaving but the sound coming out of her seemed to belong to someone else.

Wendy left and reappeared with a box of tissues, her brows drawn together.

Phoebe took some and wiped her eyes. 'Sorry.' She shook her head, appalled at her outburst to a near stranger.

'No, no.' Wendy touched her arm again. 'It's me who should be sorry. Was she a friend?'

Phoebe balled the tissues in her hands. 'Sister. My sister. Her name was Karin.'

Wendy's face fell and her hand went to her mouth. She was silent for a beat and when she spoke her voice was a whisper. 'Oh, no. Your poor family. It must be so hard.'

'We just … our family isn't good at talking about these kinds of things.'

'I should have put two and two together, given you and Jez being childhood …' She paused. 'Friends. He just never mentioned.'

'It's not an easy thing to talk about.'

'No. No, it's still a bit of a taboo, isn't it? Very hard to understand, I imagine.' She rubbed her chin. 'Oh, I'm so sorry.'

Phoebe took a deep, rattly breath. 'That's exactly how it is. Impossible to understand.'

'Well, no one could believe it. Like I said, people in the street knew and loved her, from what I could gather.'

Phoebe smiled. She felt happy that Karin had had some friends down here. She had never been the kind of person who needed lots of friends, she was too independent. She liked people but didn't feel the need to possess them. She'd rarely talked about her neighbours but Phoebe knew it was the kind of small community that looked out for each other. They would have been shocked by her death.

'She owned a florist shop, in the Bay,' said Phoebe. 'So people went to her for everything—births, deaths, parties, funerals. I remember she told this story of accidentally getting flowers for a baby shower party mixed up with the flowers for an old man's funeral. But nobody seemed to notice. She thought that was very poignant.'

Wendy smiled. 'She sounds wonderful.'

'She was.' Phoebe looked out at the river. The water had taken on the quality of mercury, shifting and oily, reflecting a leaden sky. 'I don't really want to leave,' she said, surprised at the force of her own emotion.

'Of course you don't.'

'It's more than Karin. I've just broken up with my fiancé. Well, he was meant to be my fiancé. We didn't get that far.' She laughed, as though her life were a joke.

'I hope you don't mind me saying this, but it sounds like maybe you might need a little more time before you head back to Sydney.'

Phoebe hugged her arms; the breeze had picked up, whisking the clouds into a frenzy. A storm was coming. She wasn't sure how much she should confide in Wendy but she said it anyway. 'It's just, after last night, I feel like maybe I shouldn't stay here.'

Wendy took her glasses off and cleaned them with a tissue before putting them back on and fixing her with a knowing gaze. 'You mean Jez. And Asha.'

Phoebe nodded, feeling terrible, but relieved to talk about it.

Wendy sighed. 'They've got their own story. I'm not sure it's my place to tell you but …' Wendy looked towards the river as though deciding whether to go on. 'Jez confides in me a lot and … you know, they've had it pretty tough. Years of trying for a baby and losing some pregnancies. They were doing IVF in Canberra. It's all Asha has ever wanted, but it just isn't happening for them. The difficulty they're having is because …' She paused. 'Let's just say their inability to have children has created a lot of tension in their relationship. Their struggle seems to have forced them apart rather than bringing them together sadly. And now, I'm not sure a baby is going to be the thing to patch things up, even though they seem to believe it will. I'd love for them to have another chance, though Asha is back to smoking cigarettes at the moment, so I don't know where that leaves them.'

Phoebe felt a mix of emotions: sadness for Jez, and relief that she wasn't the cause of the unhappiness she could sense in Asha.

Wendy took Phoebe's hand in hers and patted it. 'Such young hands. So lucky.' She smiled. 'So, what I'm saying is that it's much bigger than Jez's childhood sweetheart coming to town. I think you need some time here, by the river, surrounded by your sister's memories. Jez and Asha have been through a lot but that's their story, not yours. Right now, I think you've got to look after yourself.'

Deep down, Phoebe knew that a childhood sweetheart turning up when your marriage was rocky wasn't the best scenario. But as she rolled the cool jar of homemade jam in her palms and promised to try it on the freshly baked scones wrapped lovingly in foil, Wendy's logic seemed practical. Rain had rolled across the river by the time she waved Wendy goodbye, promising her she wouldn't drive home in the storm.

# CHAPTER 7

The days passed without clocks. Phoebe luxuriated in the quiet still indifference of the trees, the slow crawl of the river. A gentle routine emerged. She would walk to the village each morning for Ross's coffee, check her messages at the top of the hill, and then return to throw in a line off the end of the jetty. She caught and threw back small fish, watching the quicksilver flick of their tails as they disappeared into the reeds.

She felt completely alone, and loved it. The only sign of life was the passing boats and the occasional bark from the dog next door. Karin had told her that an old lady named Ginny lived there. The dog was a guide dog because Ginny was blind. Karin had visited her sometimes. Phoebe felt guilty for not going next door and introducing herself, but she couldn't seem to rouse herself from this self-imposed hibernation.

She had texted Camilla and her mother, telling them where she was and not to worry, and informed her boss she would be out of range for the rest of her holiday. Their answers were full of more questions but Phoebe ignored them and switched off her phone. She didn't reply to Nathaniel.

She slept deeply at night, ensconced on the sofa under an open window, the breeze caressing her skin, the sound of the night close. She woke now to a scratching on the tin roof. Her heart was beating fast as she sat up and tuned her senses in the dark. Crickets and the soft rush of the river, nothing more. It was probably a possum. She looked out at the river and thought she saw a rowboat through the dark trees, drifting downstream. She shivered. This was the feeling Wendy had talked about: the silence like a blanket, a kind of thick, quiet desolation. She wrapped a jumper around her shoulders and went to open the sliding door. There was a nip to the air and Phoebe smelled smoke on the wind. She eyed the potbelly stove in the corner of the deck, longing to feel that warmth on her skin and see the comforting dance of firelight. She remembered how they used to toast marshmallows over that stove and wrap sticky damper around big sticks, licking the honey that dripped and ran down to their elbows. She opened the little metal door to find kindling already set up.

She went inside and flicked on the light in the kitchen, blinking as her eyes adjusted, and searched for matches in the drawers and cupboards. She padded down the hall to the main bedroom—Karin's room. The moon cast a square of light through the bare window. Phoebe hadn't been in here yet. She wasn't sure why, but it felt disrespectful, like she was invading her sister's personal space. She switched on the light and hesitated at the door. It was a beautiful room, sparse and simple. The bed was covered with the same white and silver beaded throw as the sofa. Karin had painted the walls white and pulled up the carpet to reveal floorboards. An Art Deco lamp sat on an antique bedside table. Phoebe sat down on the bed. She felt like a voyeur as she opened the drawer but she was also curious. There were hairbands, two notepads and some receipts. She picked up a band; there was a single strand of black hair wrapped around it. Her heart squeezed and she pulled the hairband over her wrist. The notepads were pretty, the kind bought from a gift shop at an art gallery, but they were empty.

She opened the drawer fully, searching right at the back, and pulled out a plastic ziplock bag with two small neat joints and a tiny lighter inside. Phoebe sat back on her haunches, shocked. She shook the bag as though to make sure they were real. So, Karin had smoked marijuana. Phoebe supposed it wasn't that strange, but she just couldn't picture the lover of flowers and granny chic having a habit, a dealer. She shook her head. Just because Karin had two joints at the back of her drawer unsmoked didn't mean she had a habit.

When the fire had taken and her hands were warm, Phoebe sat at the table, and took a joint between her fingers, breathing in the faint, herby smell. She had no idea what the effects of stale drugs might be. She lit the tip and inhaled, coughing when the smoke hit her lungs. She tried again, coughing again. Phoebe considered herself, right at this moment. The girl smoking a joint in the middle of the bush with bare feet, mozzie bites and fingertips that smelled of fish, bore no resemblance to the person she thought she was. How funny it was that she presumed to know everything about her sister.

The crunch of gravel down the side of the house pinged through her body like an alarm. A stick snapped underfoot. Phoebe sat up, listening, all the hairs on her arms lifting. She picked up a gumboot by the doormat and held it over her shoulder, calculating how long it would take to run to Wendy's house or Driftwood.

'Hello?'

The voice came from behind and she swung around, letting the gumboot fly. It missed Jez's head by a matter of inches.

'Oh my God, you scared me.'

He held up his hands. 'Sorry. I was knocking on the front door but you didn't answer.'

'That may be because it's the middle of the night.' She laughed nervously.

'That doesn't seem to have stopped you from having a little party out here,' he said, glancing at the joint burning softly on the table.

'I'm sorry, but, why are you here?' She looked at him properly as he moved into the light. He was wearing spotty boxer shorts with a hoodie and a pair of beat-up Ugg boots. A wave of fond memories hit her. All those times they'd snuck into each other's bedrooms in the middle of the night.

Jez rubbed his head. 'Sorry, you're probably wondering why I'm knocking on your door at this hour.'

'Something like that.'

He gestured towards the river. 'Looks like someone's stolen our dinghy, and I think they've taken yours as well.'

'Really?' A chill ran down her spine despite the fire's warmth. 'That's weird. Something woke me up—it was a possum or something—and then I looked out at the river and thought I saw a dinghy floating past. I'm not sure.'

'Yep. Sounds like that was probably them. I just wanted to check in. It's a bit freaky to have people like that around. It's usually so safe round here. And I know you're on your own.'

Phoebe hugged her jumper closer around her shoulders. 'I wonder how many they stole. Does Wendy have a boat at her place?'

'Nah, don't think so.'

'Let me get my thongs, hang on.'

They walked down to the jetty, the light from Jez's torch criss-crossing the grass, to find the slip empty.

'Yep. Bastards,' he said, picking up the rope. 'Cut it. No one bothers to lock anything up because nothing like this has ever happened before. River's getting busier.'

'Wow. I mean, the boat wasn't worth much but it's just the idea that someone would do that. Can you imagine this ever happening when we were kids?'

'No way. Things were simpler back then.'

They stood on the jetty looking out at the dark river. She wondered what Asha had thought of Jez leaving to check on her during the night. 'It's so dark. It takes some getting used to, the complete blackness.'

'Yeah. You don't get it in the city. Not like this.' He paused. 'Are you sure you're going to be okay here?'

She shivered. What was she going to say? It's not like she could stay at Driftwood forever, although she wished she could. Some houses seemed to hold something special within their walls, something that didn't diminish, even with the passing of time. There was an energy about Driftwood that made people feel welcome. Perhaps it had come from Pauline. Phoebe would always remember Jez's mother as one of the warmest, most hospitable people, so she wasn't at all surprised that so many people lived there now. The house was made for it and it's what Pauline would have wanted.

'It's okay,' Phoebe said finally. 'I think that's why I lit a fire. There's something strangely comforting about real flames.'

There was a pause before Jez spoke. She watched his face, the straight nose, the strong cheekbones: a silhouette against the moonlight coming off the river.

'I was really surprised you came back here … on your own,' he said.

She laughed darkly. 'I didn't have much choice in that matter.' She crossed her arms in front of her. 'Big break-up. I needed to get away from Sydney for a bit. Let's just say it was a spur-of-the-moment decision.'

'Sorry … about the break-up.'

'Yeah, relationships, huh,' she said and they both chuckled knowingly. Phoebe had missed so much of his life. His loves, his hurts. Standing here it seemed impossible that they had been apart so long. He was different, she could see that—he'd filled out; there was a certain consideration to his speech and actions that had come with age—but there was also something that was the same. Something about the two of them, some energy that felt exactly as it always had.

His foot scuffed the wood on the jetty and he shifted his weight a little awkwardly, as though he could feel it, too. Phoebe turned back towards the house. The glow coming from the deck indicated the fire was still alight. She knew she should say goodnight but she didn't want him to go.

'Do you want a cup of tea?' The material around her shoulders felt flimsy now against the breeze off the water. 'We can't really do anything about the boats until morning, can we?'

'Not really,' he said. 'A cup of tea? I thought you were going to ask me if I wanted a joint.'

She laughed and led the way up towards the cottage, keenly aware of his body behind her in the dark. 'They're not mine. They're Karin's.' It felt strange to say her name out loud. 'I practically coughed up a lung when I inhaled.'

'I would never have picked Karin as a pot head.'

'Exactly what I thought.'

They both fell silent as they reached the deck and into that silence came the awful reminder of what Karin had done. She expected Jez to ask something, talk about it, but instead he picked up the joint and studied it. 'I'm not a pot smoker. Asha smokes cigarettes but it's a bit of a ... bone of contention.'

Phoebe busied herself with checking the fire, which had smouldered to a low burn. She didn't know how to reply. She knew the comment was weighted with implications that went way beyond a smoking habit.

She threw another log on the fire, the damp making it crackle and hiss. 'So, no joint for you.' She stood. 'Tea, then?'

Jez nodded and followed her into the house, chin lowered, eyes downcast. He leaned against the dining table while she filled the kettle. 'It's so strange seeing you after all this time. It's like everything has changed and nothing has. I can still remember this tablecloth.'

The tablecloth. She couldn't bring herself to move it but she couldn't look at it or eat on it, either. She assumed Camilla must have washed it when she'd been down, but all Phoebe could see was Karin's dying flowers. She shook the thought from her head before it took hold. 'It belonged to my grandparents. Karin kept all their lace. She was big on lace—tablecloths and curtains and doilies.'

Phoebe busied herself with making the tea to avoid the intensity of Jez's gaze behind her.

She carried the mugs onto the deck. The night had softened, the breeze easing. Jez crouched to check the fire, then sat down at the table with her. There was such an ease about the way he inhabited his body. She'd forgotten how attractive it was.

'You remembered how I like my tea,' he said, smiling. 'Very milky.'

'With two sugars. And still a flat white for takeaway coffee?'

He nodded. 'Impressive. And you are …' He scrunched his face up, trying to remember. 'A latte. You used to drink soy in your coffee. Do you still drink that shit?'

She laughed. 'Worse. Almond milk. Or black.'

'Oh God. You were always way too sophisticated for me.'

'Oh come on, you've forgotten all those times we went camping and fishing and rode dirt bikes.' She nudged his leg under the table playfully. 'I was a little tom boy.'

'We had some good times on this river Phoebs, didn't we?'

She hadn't heard him call her that in so many years. The softness in his voice transported her back. Their bodies always so close, their skin coated in river salt.

'Life felt so easy back then Jez, didn't it? Was it just childhood that made it simple or …' *Or was it us?* she thought.

'I wonder if our names are still carved under the jetty?'

'Did we do that?'

'Don't you remember?'

She shrugged. Of course she remembered. J loves P using a pocket knife stolen from Tommy.

'Do you still do that weird thing where you plait your hair when you're thinking?' Jez asked.

'What? I never did that.'

'You so did. Little strands of it when you were deep in thought, like reading or watching a movie or something. You probably didn't even realise.'

She shook her head and laughed. 'You must be thinking of another girlfriend.'

'There hasn't been many of those since you.'

Their eyes met and Phoebe felt her pulse quicken. Some unspoken thing flashed between them. Phoebe looked away first.

'So, Asha's okay with you being here?' she asked, her voice hovering just shy of accusatory.

Jez paused, his mug at his lips, and then put it down without taking a sip. 'We had a fight about it, actually.'

She leaned back in the seat, pulling her legs to her chest. 'Oh.'

'She ... like the other night ... she gets a bit funny sometimes.'

Phoebe stopped herself from saying something rude about his wife.

'She's always felt threatened by you. Well, the idea of you being the first ...'

Phoebe felt her chest tighten and expand at the same time. 'Well, I can't say I blame her for not being thrilled about you coming over here in the middle of the night.'

Jez looked awkward. It felt like they were dancing around something big and obvious. She decided to be frank. 'Wendy told me a bit about what you two have been through,' she said, watching carefully for his reaction.

He made a swiping motion above his head. 'Moth. Yeah, Wendy's great. Sometimes I think I talk to her more than my wife.' He laughed but his gaze remained trained on his tea, as though he was afraid to look at her. 'When someone wants something so bad and you can't give it to them, it feels impossible, you know?'

'So ... is that why Asha smokes? Because she's given up on having a baby?'

Jez looked up and their eyes met. Where she expected to see sadness she saw amusement. 'I'd forgotten how perceptive you are.'

'It's probably just because that's what most women do. We can be self-destructive creatures.'

'She knows I hate it when she smokes. I still think it's possible for us to conceive but she's given up. She blames me. I feel like every time she lights up it's a smack in the face. She's so angry with me all the time in this kind of passive–aggressive way. It's not just the smoking. I feel like I can never do anything right.'

'She's going to be even angrier that you're here talking to me about it.'

He sat back in the chair. 'You know what, Phoebe? I'm done caring. I'm done. I just wanted to make sure a friend was all right and I got in trouble. I keep trying to make her happy, trying for this baby she's so desperate for, and then she throws it back in my face. I'm always trying to read her moods ... she won't talk to me, not properly ... it's like walking on eggshells. I don't know what she wants anymore but I don't think it's me.'

Part of Phoebe wanted to say they could never be just friends, and tell him to go home. The other part wanted to put her arms around him, comfort him and breathe in the smell of him. She could still remember it.

'What about what you want, Jez?' He had always been such a people pleaser. Phoebe couldn't imagine he was the type to walk when things got hard, but if he bottled things up instead, he might risk becoming a victim of his own good heart. Phoebe saw the dark rings under his eyes, the bone-deep tiredness that came with life's battles. For a second she saw Nathaniel. He could have ended up like this, she thought, trapped and resentful. She could have been Asha.

'I don't know anymore, Phoebe, I just don't know.' He looked up at her with such a pleading in his eyes that she felt a lump form in her throat. She had to shut this down. She could feel him hovering on the edge of an emotional dam. He wanted her to break it open, to pour everything out, have her comfort him.

She sat up and put her feet on the ground. 'Jez, I'm so sorry but you know I can't do this.' She indicated between them with her hand. 'There's too much ... history. I know you can feel it too. I'm not the one to help you with Asha. I've just come out of ...' She looked towards the dark river and took a deep breath. 'I'm just too weak right now.'

'Of course. I shouldn't have ...' He stood and brushed the tops of his legs. 'I'm glad you're okay.'

'I'm fine.'

'I should ...' He indicated downriver and then shoved his hands in his pockets.

Phoebe could see he was rattled. She wanted to say something to appease him but knew it would only make things worse. She watched as he walked away, head hung, and felt bereft. That was the only word for it. She wanted to hug him to her, listen to his pain, share her own, but she knew it was wrong.

He turned back before he rounded the corner of the house. 'I know Tommy would love to see you. He'll be up from lunchtime tomorrow.'

Phoebe smiled. She would like to see Tommy. She had a feeling it'd be easier between them with his brother there. 'Okay, I guess I could just pop over in the afternoon to say hi.'

'Stay for dinner. Or not. It's up to you.' He said it defeatedly, as though he already knew her answer.

She felt awful. But there was a naiivety about Jez that she had always known. Even now, he couldn't see what they were hovering at the edge of.

PART TWO

*Kindling*

# THEN

Karin tickled the dog behind his ears and let him lick her face. When she looked into his black, shiny eyes she could see something there that needed loving. She couldn't really explain this feeling to anyone so she hugged his neck and nestled into the rough fur. The dog made a little whimper and she hugged him closer.

'Come on, stupid, it's just a dog. And it's gross. It stinks. We can't take it with us.' Camilla crossed her arms and kicked at the dirt road with her thong, creating a plume of yellow dust.

'Yeah, we can, Cammie. Look, he's lost. No collar even.' She couldn't tell if the dog was old or young but from the way his eyes looked when you stared right into them, maybe old.

'He's not lost. He just lives somewhere round here. We can't take him on the boat anyway. Tommy and Jez won't let us.' Camilla turned and started to walk up the road towards Driftwood.

Karin straightened to her full height. Sometimes Cammie was so bossy for someone so little. Usually she would just let her win, even though she was only eight, but not today.

'Come on, boy.' She clicked her fingers and the dog followed her down the road, his nose wet on her palm.

'Where did he come from?' asked Phoebe, breathless from running to catch up. She gave the dog a scratch behind his ears and slung an arm around Karin's shoulders.

'Not sure, he just started following us. I think he's a cattle, maybe with a bit of dingo,' Karin said.

'Can I name him?'

'Sure.'

'No, I want to name it,' said Camilla, striding ahead but still listening, the sparkles on her cap catching the sun. 'Stinky Bum,' she called out, without looking behind.

Karin and Phoebe laughed and exchanged a look.

'Fine,' said Phoebe. 'Stinky Bum it is.'

Camilla stopped, glared at them and rolled her eyes because she hadn't managed to start a fight.

Cicadas droned in the trees as they got closer to the end of the street. The doors at Driftwood were flung wide and the air smelled like sunshine and cut grass. When they left the night before just as the dark was creeping in, they were flung wide then, too. Karin wondered if anyone ever closed them, not that there was much point—there was always someone here.

Last night Pauline had made them all cheese toasties for dinner because they'd been so tired none of them was hungry for a proper meal. They'd just wanted to watch cartoons, their sunburnt arms and legs flung over each other's on the cool floor. They'd spent the day by the dam and then making a cubby in the bushes near the bowerbird nest. Or had that been the day before? She couldn't remember. All the days melded together, like warm honey.

The echo of voices came from the river bank—the boys were already on the jetty. A whip of anxiety ran through her. Tommy had told her that she'd be safe and that there was even a life vest up in the garage she could wear, but she still felt nervous. It was their first time out in the boat with the new motor, so they could go much, much further up the river than they could just rowing.

They picked their way down the familiar path to the water, where Tommy and Jez were in the boat, tethered to the jetty by a thick rope. The dog, as if sensing adventure, broke into a run, his paws clicking over the wooden planks of the jetty.

'Hey, who's this?' asked Jez, climbing up the ladder to greet the dog with a ruffle of his fur.

'Stinky Bum,' they all said in unison, which made Jez laugh.

'Is he coming with us?' Jez had already put his arms around the dog as if to lift him down to the boat.

They all looked towards Tommy, who glanced up from the motor, his face squinting against the bright morning light.

'I said you wouldn't let them have the dog in the boat,' Camilla said, her hands on her hips and her head held high. She was using her baby voice to try to manipulate Tommy.

Tommy scratched behind his neck. 'Is he going to make you feel a bit safer coming up the river?'

Karin nodded silently, her fingers finding the dog's fur.

Camilla made a huffing sound, flipped one of her thongs off her foot and they all watched as it sailed through the air and into the river. 'Great,' she said. 'Can someone get it?'

'You did it. You get it,' said Phoebe.

Tommy shook his head. They all knew what Cammie could be like. 'Yes, we'll scoop it out.'

Jez held out some life vests. 'Come on. Let's go. Mum packed us lunch and everything.'

Karin watched her sisters scamper down the ladder and into the boat. She wished she could do that without feeling scared. Phoebe put on a life vest and held out her hand, nodding in encouragement.

'I'm not wearing that,' Camilla said, flicking the life vest away from her and adjusting the brim of her hat.

'You're wearing it or you're not coming,' Tommy said, throttling the motor into life. The smell of petrol filled the air. 'Oh, and no standing in the boat. Not unless I say.'

'Come on,' said Phoebe. 'You'll be okay.'

Karin took a deep breath and climbed down the ladder and into the boat. It was rocky and she felt a bit sick. She sat next to Phoebe, who threaded her fingers through hers. Pinned between the panting dog's hot body and Phoebe, she felt okay, even as the boat lurched forward and roared upriver.

'My thong,' shouted Cammie into the air rushing past them, but no one could hear her.

Tommy cut the motor to a low roar as they reached the part of the river they told Pauline and their parents they'd go. It was just on the other side of the big bridge, where you could see smooth grey stones in the shallow water and there was a grassy picnic area. There were a few people fishing from a rock wall and some others eating fish and chips from greasy newspaper. The salty, oily smell carried on the breeze.

'Can we go up further around the bend?' asked Jez, craning his neck to where the river curved and the bush got thicker and greener.

Tommy lifted his head to the cloudless sky. 'No, we should do what we said. Let's get out and have something to eat here.'

They used the oars to row onto the shore, the smooth rocks clunking along the bottom of the boat. Jez hopped out first. The water was cool around Karin's ankles, so she didn't mind it too much. It was hot now, the sun almost directly above them. She wished she'd brought a hat like her dad had told her to.

'Hang on. I don't have a thong,' said Camilla, hopping on one leg through the water onto the sandy bank. 'This isn't going to work.'

'Maybe you should've thought about that before you kicked it off,' said Phoebe.

Camilla elbowed her in the ribs and she yelped. 'Well, it's not my fault nobody helped me get it back.'

'Be nice, you two,' said Karin. Her sisters stuck their tongues out at each other.

'There'll be bindies in the grass,' said Camilla, her voice high and whiny.

Phoebe stopped and took off one of her thongs and gave it to Camilla. 'Here. Will this shut you up?'

Camilla smiled and nodded, slipping the too-big thong onto her foot. 'Can I have the other one? So they match?' Phoebe rolled her eyes, and took off her other thong and handed it over.

Jez sifted rocks through his fingers and skimmed the choice ones across the water. They all joined in, hooting as Tommy's nearly reached the middle of the river. Tommy tried to teach Karin how to 'put her shoulder into it' but hers still didn't skip more than twice. She found one shaped like a heart and secreted it into her pocket.

'Look, a shark egg,' said Camilla, kicking at it with her foot.

'Don't,' said Jez, picking up the black, spiky egg. 'I knew there were sharks breeding up here.' He nodded upriver. 'You're not meant to swim up there.'

'But can't the sharks be anywhere in the river then?' Camilla asked, her little face scrunched up.

Jez ran his fingers over the rim of the soft shell. 'Sharks are more aggressive when they're breeding.'

Camilla cocked her head. 'What is breeding anyhow?'

Karin and Phoebe exchanged a look. 'Come on, let's see what Pauline packed for morning tea,' Karin held up the backpack Jez had brought.

They picked their way over the spiky grass to a big shady tree, its branches and roots fat and strong. The boys were climbing within minutes. Karin opened the backpack and found a picnic rug rolled tight and a packet of sandwiches wrapped in grease-proof paper. Phoebe helped her spread the rug down on the grass and they took out plastic cups and a bottle of orange cordial.

Karin spotted some men while they were eating their sandwiches. She couldn't explain how she knew they were not good men, but she just did. She felt glad to have the dog with them, even if he was laid out next to her like a panting baby.

The dog seemed to be watching the men too, one eye closed and the other alert. One of the men was tall and skinny, and had a pointy-looking face, which was clouded by smoke from the cigarette in his mouth. Karin could smell it from where they were sitting. The other was short and fat and wore a fisherman's hat one size too small. No one else seemed to have noticed them except her and the dog. There was something odd about the way the skinny one kept looking around with squinty eyes, as though he was waiting for someone, or something. She imagined they were prisoners who had escaped from jail and were running from the police. Or maybe they were robbers planning on breaking into someone's house.

She looked over at Tommy to see if he'd noticed them but he'd disappeared high up in the tree and was hidden among the leaves. There was a pecking order by age: Tommy, Karin, Jez, Phoebe, Camilla. As the two eldest, she and Tommy shared the responsibility for keeping the others safe. They'd never spoken about it, but sometimes they would give each other a look and Karin would know that he was taking charge. She didn't mind. He was a year older and wanted to be a policeman.

Camilla was stretched out on the rug, taking up most of it. She threaded daisy stems into a necklace, humming a song Karin recognised but couldn't put her finger on. Karin picked a handful too and ran her fingers over their tiny, delicate petals.

'Let's see who can make the longest chain,' she said.

'I will,' said Camilla.

Karin thought about pointing out the men to Phoebe but she was sitting on the lowest branch of the tree, swinging her legs, and looking up at Jez with a soft smile on her face.

# CHAPTER 8

Eucalyptus leaves crunched under foot as Phoebe made her way down the driveway. She heard her sister's name on the wind and turned to find where the voice was coming from. The street was deserted. It was early and threatening rain—not the sort of weather for a morning stroll, but Phoebe needed to get out of the house. After her strange late-night conversation with Jez and now hearing Karin's name, she felt as though she was losing it.

She was checking the letterbox when she felt something brush her legs. A dog.

'Hello!' She looked up to see an old woman standing behind the fence in front of the small fibro house next door.

'Steffi, come. Leave the poor girl alone. Sorry, did I startle you?'

The old lady's hair sat in soft white tufts, like cotton wool around a small, alert head. Her features were neat and even— the kind that suggested past beauty. Her eyes were a milky blue, staring into the middle distance.

'No, no, you didn't. Is this your dog? She's beautiful,' Phoebe said, running her fingers through the golden retriever's thick mane.

'Sorry, for a moment I ... forgot. I thought you were Karin. I'm sorry. Are you one of her sisters? I've heard someone at the house.'

'It's okay. Yes, I'm her sister Phoebe.'

'Oh Phoebe, Karin told me about you and your glamorous job in the city.'

She laughed. 'Really not as glamorous as it sounds.'

Phoebe moved towards the fence, looking at the house properly for the first time—the neatness of its lawn, the proud slope of its roof. Although the woman was blind, she clearly looked after her little home.

'You must be Ginny. Karin spoke about you. I'm sorry I haven't visited earlier. It's just I wasn't sure how long I'd be staying here.'

'That's quite all right. I understand how busy you young people are. Karin was always off on weekends away. I don't know how you find the energy. I suppose I had it once. Anyway, you're here now. Will you come in for a cup of tea?'

Phoebe stiffened. Karin had never mentioned going away for weekends, not regularly. She wondered what Ginny was talking about. 'Was Karin away a lot? Overnight?'

'Oh yes, I was always keeping an ear out for her place on the weekends she was gone. Not that a blind old lady could have done much.'

A cold prickle ran down Phoebe's spine. 'Tea would be great, thanks,' she said, joining Ginny on the pebbled drive.

She remembered the angry man they used to call Old Tom who had once lived here. They had taunted him by throwing gumnuts over the fence while he gardened, Camilla and Jez egging each other on while Karin tried to distract them with freshly picked mulberries. Perhaps Old Tom had been Ginny's husband.

The air had the sweet and sour smell of crushed ants and eucalypt, and Phoebe tried to imagine Karin walking through the front yard to visit Ginny. She would have warmed to Ginny for the simple reason of her being vulnerable in the world.

Phoebe followed Ginny through a screen door. There was a swift scatter of paws on tiles as Steffi barked once, loudly.

'Oh shush,' Ginny berated the dog.

The dog's ears were velvety and her eyes squinted in pleasure as Phoebe rubbed them. 'She's very friendly.'

'The cleverest dog to ever graduate from assistance dog school. But I'm biased.' Ginny chuckled warmly. The lounge off the hall was dark as they moved deeper into the house. 'Sorry, I usually pull the blinds up, especially when I'm expecting someone,' she said, 'but when I'm on my own sometimes I forget.'

'That's understandable,' Phoebe said, feeling a twinge of sympathy.

The back of the house was brighter—a picture window filled with the weak sunlight reflected off the river. It was a large family room with a sofa, TV and dining table. This was obviously where Ginny spent most of her time. It was funny how humans always moved towards the light, even when they couldn't see it.

'This is lovely. So bright.'

'Yes, so I'm told. I can't see it but I can feel it.'

'The warmth?'

'Yes, but also it feels bright in here. It's hard for me to describe how.'

'I expect you have very heightened senses in other ways.'

'Oh yes, I rely on hearing, of course, and touch.' She eased herself into a chair at the wooden table. 'Take a seat, Phoebe. Oh, I wonder if I could impose on you to make us a cup of tea. I'm quite able to do it myself but I'm feeling a little tired today.'

'Of course, I'd be happy to.'

'The teabags are in the tin next to the kettle, and there are some biscuits in the pantry—Scotch Finger, my son usually buys them for me.'

Steffi padded into the kitchen with Phoebe as she set about making tea. There were braille stickers on the kettle and the tea tin, and fresh daisies sat in a blue vase on the bench. The sight of them struck Phoebe as heartbreaking. But perhaps Ginny just enjoyed the scent, or the soft petals between her fingers. She set the mugs and the biscuits on a tray and returned to the living room. Ginny had picked up knitting needles and her hands moved deftly over them, feeding from a ball of red wool in her lap.

'Thank you, Phoebe. You're just as kind as your sister, I see.'

'Oh, I think Karin was much nicer than me. She and my dad are the good eggs in the family.'

'Do you mind talking about her? I wouldn't want to make you feel uncomfortable or upset.'

Phoebe smiled. 'No, I like talking about her. It's just … a little more painful sometimes because of what happened.'

Ginny nodded and her gnarly fingers closed around her mug of tea. 'I understand.' She paused. 'I don't know if this is at all helpful, but I had a dear friend who took her own life. Bonnie was her name. She was a sweet but troubled person.

Very vivacious. Got away with murder because of her looks. It was a long time ago and back then they didn't have the mental health knowledge that they do today. Looking back she probably had bipolar or some kind of depressive illness. Anyhow, her leaving the world in such a way was tragic but not unimaginable, but Karin ...' Ginny paused, as though deciding whether to go on. She smoothed the pelt of red wool in her hands.

Phoebe felt the movement of her own blood slow. 'You don't think Karin took her life either? Is that what you mean?'

Ginny dabbed her eyes with a handkerchief she pulled from her sleeve. She wasn't crying but seemed overwhelmed. 'Who am I to say such a thing? A blind old lady who used to chat with her a few times a week. But no, I must admit, it doesn't seem right that Karin would do that to herself.'

Phoebe swallowed and tried to gather her thoughts as they raced through her head. There were so many questions she wanted answered.

'Thank you for telling me that. I'm so sorry about your friend.' She wanted to reach out and touch the old lady's hand but was unsure about the etiquette with blind people. 'Karin was terrified of the water,' she went on. 'She nearly drowned in this river when she was eleven and didn't go back in the water again after that. I just can't accept that she would have done it like that, if she was going to ... you know.'

'And tell me, Phoebe, why did they conclude it was a suicide?' asked Ginny. 'I only know what my son Chester read out to me from the paper. I think they said it was not suspicious. Surely an accident would have been more likely if she was afraid of water and not a strong swimmer?'

Phoebe took a deep breath. 'There was a suicide note.'

Ginny shook her head. 'I didn't know that. The papers didn't report it.'

Phoebe looked out the window. Still, after all this time it hurt to say it out loud. 'It was written in flowers. It said, "I'm sorry".'

Ginny's mouth turned down. 'I didn't know that,' she said again.

Phoebe tried to talk but her voice had abandoned her. She cleared her throat. 'I think because she was a florist they thought that flowers were a reasonable way to write a goodbye ... even though anyone could have put those flowers there.'

'Can I ask what they were?'

'What type of flowers, you mean?'

The image was seared into her like a scar. The police had given them a photo. The flowers were laid out over the white lace of the tablecloth, still in the shape of her final words. Phoebe would never forget the sad bow of the rose's heads, the tangled brown stems of the snapdragons and the stiff and brittle peony petals. For months they were the only things she could see when she closed her eyes. She had never allowed herself to picture her sister dead, instead she saw the flowers.

'Wild roses, peonies and snapdragons. They were all dead by the time they found her. A fisherman called the body in.' Phoebe hadn't allowed herself to think about the gruesome details in a long time. 'And I guess they didn't see how it could be homicide. She was a friendly person in the community who didn't have any enemies. And there were no signs of struggle or trauma.'

Ginny's lips trembled. 'A note made of flowers seems like something lovely and thoughtful Karin would have done, not ...'

Her voice trailed off and she angled her face towards the light. 'The reason I asked what flowers they were, is because Karin knew what all the flowers meant.'

'What do you mean?' Phoebe felt a tingle run from the nape of her neck to her toes.

'She used to bring me flowers all the time—cuttings left over from the shop. I think she felt bad I couldn't see them, so she used to tell me the story of each one. When she put together her bouquets in the shop, she'd take into account the meaning of the flowers. She was so thoughtful like that. I still remember—pink roses and geraniums are for true friendship. She found a book about it on one of her antique hunts. She gave it to me as a gift. It's in the bookcase, in the lounge.'

'Here? Do you mind?' Phoebe got up, hands trembling and head light. She found the book next to an old leather-bound bible: *Flowers and Their Meanings; A Victorian Custom.*

The book was reed thin, and coming away from its spine. It smelled like tea leaves and dust, the pages flimsy with age. Phoebe stood there, transfixed in the dim light. She opened it carefully, skipping the introduction. The flowers were in alphabetical order, and accompanied by a finely drawn sketch. She found each one, methodically, her heart a mess in her chest. Red roses were love. Yellow roses meant friendship or jealousy. Snapdragons meant graciousness and strength, or in the negative, deception. Peonies were for compassion and shame but also a happy life and marriage.

The beat of her heart was the only sound in the room. What did it mean? Did Karin really leave a hidden message in her final words? Should Phoebe read the positive? Love, friendship, strength, compassion—everything that Karin was? Or the negative? Deception. Shame. Jealousy. What did Karin have to be jealous about?

Phoebe went back into the living room to find Ginny still facing towards the river. 'I found it.'

'Well, what do they mean? The flowers she left.'

Phoebe read out directly from the book, and Ginny let out a soft sigh.

'What do you think?' asked Phoebe, sitting down and smoothing the book shut.

'I don't know. I guess the police know what they're talking about.'

'Did they question you?'

Ginny blinked. 'A young policeman came to the door and asked if I'd noticed anything suspicious. When he realised I was blind he didn't ask many questions. He didn't tell me it was suicide, maybe they didn't know at first. He said that my neighbour had drowned in the river. He kept calling her "Your neighbour" instead of using her name. I couldn't stand it. I can't tell you how shocked and saddened I was. I had to call Chester to leave work. I couldn't be alone. Just the thought of Karin alone in the river ...'

Out the window the water was twinkling innocently, throwing light into their eyes.

'Did you know she was found with all her clothes on?' Phoebe said. 'That's why they think it was a suicide, as well. People who are going to kill themselves don't want to be found naked. I think about that all the time. How can someone not care about their own life and the pain they'll cause others but care about being found naked?'

Ginny smoothed her hair behind her ears. 'When they found Bonnie, she was in her best dress and shoes. It was a purple ball gown with gold trimming she'd worn for her twenty-first birthday. All the boys wanted to dance with her in that dress. And her hair was braided.'

Phoebe felt humbled by Ginny's story. Sometimes grief was so selfish, you forgot you weren't the only one suffering. 'Do you still think about her?'

Ginny smiled sadly. 'Oh yes. The pain eases with time but it never goes away.'

'I dream about Karin every night,' said Phoebe. 'I wake and see this woman out in the middle of the river in a boat. She has long dark hair, like Karin, and she's wearing white. It takes me a minute to realise it's her because sometimes she's Karin as a child. But then I know I have to save her, and I get up and run down the hill and dive off the end of the jetty. And I'm feeling around in the cold water, getting tangled in the white gown but I can never find her. I wake up holding my breath.'

Ginny reached out and squeezed her hand. 'You poor girl, what an awful dream.'

'I'm sorry. I'm just blubbering now.' Phoebe straightened and dabbed under her eyes with a napkin from a dispenser on the table. She had thought it might be awkward quizzing Ginny about Karin but the opposite was true. It was so nice to talk to someone who understood. She took a deep breath. 'I wanted to ask you about what you said before ... that you thought Karin went away on weekends. I used to talk to her every Sunday night without fail, it was our thing, and she rarely mentioned she'd been away. Do you know where she went? Why?'

Ginny reached down and as if on cue Steffi arrived to have her ears scratched. 'Good girl … I never felt it was my place to ask but I always assumed … there was someone, wasn't there.' It was more a statement than a question.

'I don't know, was there? None of us was aware she was seeing anyone.'

Ginny pressed a finger to her lips. 'Well, let me see. I must admit, I didn't take a lot of notice. Karin was intensely private about these things and it wasn't the kind of thing we talked about. We usually chatted about our gardens, the state of our tomatoes, or the abysmal state of the herbs—we had a resident possum. She told me about who she was doing flowers for in town, what had happened that week—births, deaths, marriages. Though she wasn't a gossipy person, just someone people spoke to during important milestones in their lives. I think she knew it made me feel like I was part of the community.'

'And she went away on these mystery weekends a lot?'

'Oh, probably one or two weekends a month. Yes, I think it was mostly weekends, but I don't pay a lot of attention to which day it is. No one seemed to visit her here. I rarely heard her with anyone next door.'

'And she didn't talk about anyone? Mention why she was going away?'

'No. Well, yes, I suppose she used to talk about going to the trade shows in Canberra sometimes.' Ginny paused. 'So you must wonder why I assumed she was seeing a man.' She took up her knitting and sat back in her chair. 'If I had to explain it, it was that when she returned after being away she was always more … wistful, a little sad. When you can't see people's expressions you pick up a lot from the tone and volume of their voice, the words they use.'

It was hard for Phoebe to ask, but she asked it anyway, 'Sad enough to commit suicide?'

'Well, no, it wasn't unhappiness as such. More a longing, a distraction. It came out in her voice. The way she trailed off from her sentences. And she'd visit me more, as though she didn't want to be alone.'

Phoebe thought of all the Sunday nights she'd talked to Karin on the phone. Had she spent some of those weekends away and not mentioned anything? Where did she go and why did she hide it?

Phoebe took a sip of her tea. She realised it had gone cold and put it down.

'You didn't drink your tea,' said Ginny, and Phoebe laughed. 'Can you tell?'

'And you have only taken a bite or two of your biscuit.'

Phoebe shook her head. 'That's amazing.'

'I'm sorry I can't tell you more about this mystery man. Or even if there was one. I'm afraid I've led you on a wild goose chase, haven't I? Your sister was a very kind, generous person but she didn't talk much about herself. She was very practical. It takes a lot of hard work to keep a property going on the river. I think we both shared that stubborn spirit. She was strong, your sister. I think that's what doesn't make sense to me. She wasn't like my Bonnie; Karin was too strong and grounded to take her own life.'

Phoebe reached out and put a hand on Ginny's. 'Thank you for saying that. Do you mind if I keep the flower book?'

'No, of course not.'

'Everything you've said I've been thinking. I can't stop thinking it. My mum and sister never question Karin's death. My dad might have, but he's so passive; he doesn't want to rock the boat or upset anyone any more than they already are.'

Ginny smoothed the perfect square of red wool flat on the table. 'Sometimes rocking the boat is the only way forward.' And for a second Phoebe could have sworn she had perfect vision.

# CHAPTER 9

Phoebe watched the river glistening through the gum trees. It was hot. A languid breeze murmured through the she-oaks, and on it was the smell of bushfires. The air had a toffee quality, as though it had been burnished over low heat. The things she'd spoken about with Ginny rolled over in her mind, and she didn't know what to do with these questions and thoughts. She had truly believed she'd known her sister so well. But she'd known nothing of these mystery trips away or that Karin arranged flowers according to their meanings. Why hadn't she known all this? A feeling of helplessness settled in her. What else had she missed about her sister?

She went inside and took a six-pack of Heineken out of the fridge then retrieved the straw hat she had bought in the Bay that morning. She didn't want to take more, didn't want to presume she'd be staying all that long.

The walk down the road was dusty and dry but the grass at Driftwood still looked lush. The area had once been swampland and Phoebe imagined the plant roots reaching into subterranean pools and sating their thirst. The sound of voices and splashing came from the dam. The water shimmered, reflecting the low sky, and Phoebe shielded her eyes against the glare and watched Jez take a run off the pontoon to bomb into the middle. Hoots of protest hailed with the spray of water. She laughed, remembering all the times he'd done that in their childhood. He was still that boy who had kissed her for the first time in the warm afternoon sun sitting on the edge of the dam, legs dangling in the deep. She shook her head. No, he was somebody else's husband and a man who would always feel special because of what they'd shared. But that was all it was.

As she watched the others swim she longed for the delicious coolness of water on her skin. It felt even hotter here than at the cottage, the air thick with humidity. She wished she'd thought to wear her swimming costume under her shorts. She made her way to the dam's entry—a timber weir with an old rubber tyre attached to its side.

Wendy spotted her first. 'Phoebe! Did you bring your costume? Come on in. It's wonderful.'

'Hotter than Texas in these parts,' the Texan chirped, waving from the shallow end and pouring a bucket of water triumphantly over his head.

Phoebe laughed. Tommy was waist deep, holding a little boy who bobbed around in yellow floaties. He turned and waved. 'Hi, Phoebe!'

'Hi, Tommy!'

He gently pushed the boy towards her on the pontoon. The boy became distressed, his high-pitched cries piercing the air. Tommy took a red train he must have had in his pocket and placed it in his tiny hand. He whispered in his son's ear and the boy immediately calmed. 'This is Aunty Phoebe. Phoebe, meet Harry.'

Phoebe crouched, passing a hand through the cool water and smiling. 'Pleased to meet you, Harry.' The boy was very fair, with wavy white-blond hair, nothing like his father's dark hair and eyes. 'You're a good swimmer, Harry,' she said, trying to meet his eyes. Despite his cherubic looks there was a distance, an absence. A wave of sadness passed over her and she forced a smile onto her mouth to hide it.

'He's gorgeous,' she said. 'Those curls. How old is he?'

Tommy looked up and she could see pride in his eyes. It moved her, and she thought of Jez, wanting to be a father. 'He's five. It's so great to see you, Phoebe.'

She felt a wave of affection for Tommy, a warm nostalgia that wasn't accompanied by the complications of romantic feeling.

'And your wife's here?'

'Jenna's on gin and tonic duty.' He nodded towards the house and then at Harry. 'I like to give her a bit of a break, you know.'

Phoebe nodded, 'Of course.'

'He loves swimming but doesn't like water going in his eyes so it's a bit of a challenge with Uncle Jez doing bombs, isn't it?' Tommy said.

She laughed, her eyes seeking out Jez. He was star-limbed on his back in the deep end with Asha and Flick. Asha's hair floated out from her head like pale mermaid tendrils. She was such a beautiful woman. Maybe that's what had made Jez stay so long. That and his loyalty. He was made of something solid, something simple. She couldn't blame him for not wanting to move to Sydney with her when they were young. She could see now that this was where he belonged.

Flick lifted her head out of the water and waved.

'Are you coming in?' asked Jez.

Relief flowed through her; he didn't hate her for sending him away. 'Didn't bring my cozzie.'

'Just jump in, in what you're wearing,' said Asha, her voice a challenge.

Phoebe had hoped that Asha might have cooled off, but the tension was still there, still raw.

'Go on,' said Flick, her voice more friendly. 'We won't care.'

Phoebe wiped a lick of water across the back of her neck. It felt so good. So cool. The afternoon was like a furnace and she longed to escape it. Something in her body released then. She wasn't going to let Asha spoil what might be her last time here. She kicked off her thongs and steadied herself on the edge of the pontoon. She remembered doing back-flips as a kid, the feeling vibrant and zinging in her chest and limbs.

'I think this is our cue to exit,' said Tommy, lifting Harry up onto the edge and pulling himself up to a seated position. She noticed that his body was hard and sinewy, probably not like many other dads nudging forty.

'We'll get the cheese platter out and make a start on this beer. Thanks, Phoebe,' said the Texan, helping Wendy out of the water and picking up the six-pack.

Phoebe knew the topography of this dam as well as she'd known Jez's body. Its dips and depth; where you could dive and touch the bottom, where you had to tread carefully for sticks. Where the eels lived. She did a shallow dive and the cool enveloped her head and body, cascading through her, making her whoop to the surface. She craned her head to the sky and floated, feeling the lip of the water caress her legs, her arms.

It was so easy to forget how weightless the body was in water; the simple pleasure of it. Karin came to her mind, as she so often did now around water. Karin had never been able to feel this easy enjoyment. For her, water was fear. Phoebe had been beside her in the river that day. There had been no kicking or screaming, just silence. Drowning was soundless. The blue-grey lips, the rolling back of Karin's eyes, had played so many times in her head that it was a memory tattoo. Phoebe had saved her big sister, everyone said afterwards, but it always felt as though she'd failed Karin in some essential way. If only she'd noticed earlier maybe Karin would not have developed the deep phobia that had defined so much of their childhood.

Phoebe kicked over to the other three, feeling the reticence of being so close to Asha coil in her belly. 'How nice is it in?' she commented, keeping her distance, finding the soft muddy bottom with her toes.

'They said it hit forty-three degrees in the Bay today. You can smell the fires,' Jez said.

'Where are they? Do you reckon they're close?' asked Phoebe.

'As long as we've been here there's never been a bushfire. That's what? Thirty-five years,' said Jez.

'Just because you always think it's going to be okay doesn't mean it will be,' said Asha, disappearing under the water and swimming to the other end of the dam, her legs slapping against the water's surface.

'She's in a particularly delightful mood today,' said Flick, picking a piece of reed out of her hair.

Jez snorted and wiped his hands down his face. They all watched as Asha pulled herself onto the platform, pale skin gleaming, picked up a packet of cigarettes, lit one and breathed deep. The air was so hazy that the smoke coming out of her lips was invisible. Phoebe glanced at Jez but he avoided her eyes.

'I think maybe we're all still recovering from the bad night's sleep because of the boat thieves,' said Phoebe, wanting, illogically, to excuse Asha. 'I haven't bothered calling the police, have you?'

'Yeah, I mean, no, but Tommy said he'd put in some paperwork on Monday. You should report yours,' said Jez.

'So how long have you two known each other?' asked Flick, her face trained skyward, her arms making small circles in the water to keep her afloat.

Phoebe looked over at Asha, who was now lying prone in the eerie orange light. It felt like a betrayal talking about the past. She met Jez's eye and a jolt of energy passed between them. She went under, opening her eyes to the deep green-brown. Her limbs looked translucent, a dirty white. She pushed off the soft ground and glided backwards away from him.

'How long?' asked Jez when she broke the surface.

'I don't know.' She was breathless from staying under too long.

'Well, we've know each other since we were eleven, but how old were you when we got together?' He sounded angry.

'I don't know, sixteen I suppose.' Her heart was hammering against her chest. She pushed a wet strand of hair out of her face. She didn't understand why he was being so aggressive suddenly.

'I was your first boyfriend and you don't know how old you were when we got together?'

*What's going on?* she thought, but she looked at Flick, who seemed unperturbed. Thankfully Asha was too far away to hear.

She felt trapped between Jez's emotional barrage and Asha's physical blocking of the dam's exit. 'I was sixteen. We got together in September of that year, okay? That makes it, I don't know … a long time.'

'Their family came here every school holidays after their grandparents died,' said Jez. 'It was a holiday romance.'

Phoebe felt the sting of his words. He knew it was far more than that. They wrote to each other during term time, spoke to each other every other night; he came up to Sydney for her birthday. For a long time they just assumed they'd get married, though the details were never fully fleshed out.

Was he punishing her for pushing him away? She felt a surge of anger. She turned to face Flick. 'Actually, he was the love of my life.'

Flick's eyes glazed with a faraway look and a wry little smile came onto her lips. Phoebe looked at Jez but he ducked under the water. Silence hovered over the dam, opaque as the smoky air.

'Hey guys, you better come in,' Tommy called from the veranda. 'The fires, they're getting close.'

'Oh my God, really?' replied Flick, swimming towards the pontoon.

Asha raised herself onto one elbow and squinted into the sun. 'I think the dam's the best place for us to be then,' she said.

Flick towelled herself quickly and then linked her arm through Asha's and they picked their way over the grass towards the house. Phoebe's stomach turned.

Why did she just say Jez was the love of her life in front of Flick? Would she tell Asha? It was like Jez had set a trap and she'd fallen straight into it. It was true, she had thought about him many, many times over the years. Was it just the seductive spell of nostalgia?

Phoebe watched Jez pull himself up onto the pontoon and shake water from his ears. She'd been stupid to let him get to her, to let her emotions out. She raised her nose to the air. She couldn't tell if the smoke was stronger or not. Things crept up on you while you thought you were safe, while you thought you had complete control. She realised she was alone in the dam with no towel and no dry clothes to change into. But the thought of going back to the cottage in this eerie half-light made her shiver. She swam towards the edge, got out, wrung her hair and walked dripping wet towards the house.

# CHAPTER 10

Phoebe tiptoed across the floor of the entranceway, feeling bad to be leaving a trail of water behind her, but she stopped short when she reached the lounge. Everyone was crowded around the television. Harry was on the floor pushing his train on a track. A woman, who must have been Jenna, sat beside him, cradling a glass of wine between crossed legs. No one looked up when Phoebe entered; their eyes were fixed on footage of several homes that had been razed by fire. The newsreader's voice was strangely emotionless as she listed the towns that had been affected, and then read out the names of several streets in the Bay that backed onto bushland and had already been evacuated. The fire was expected to worsen, with strong winds forecast overnight and tomorrow. Phoebe swallowed down the acidic taste of panic rising in her throat. She was okay here, with everyone. Tommy was in the Federal Police; he'd been in far more drastic situations than this and he no doubt stayed calm in emergencies—that was the best kind of person to be around, wasn't it? The newsreader explained that residents in high-risk areas were being sent text messages and had the tough decision of whether to stay and protect their homes or evacuate.

'Yeah, what about people who have no reception because they're in the middle of the bush?' asked Jez.

'I'll get some info from the fireys,' said Tommy. 'I'm sure we'll be fine here. Bloody media always beating things up.'

Jenna shook her head. 'I don't think this is a beat-up. You just have to look outside to see how close the fires must be.'

Tommy crouched in front of her, his face close to hers. 'Hey, look at me. Babe, do you trust me?'

Jenna's mouth scrunched and she looked him in the eyes.

Tommy gripped her shoulders. 'I won't let anything happen to him, okay?'

'Are you sure? It's just—'

Tommy stood abruptly and clapped his hands. 'Hey, people, can we turn off the TV now? It's not helpful watching this. If I've learned anything from my job, it's that anxiety makes everything worse.'

'Isn't it kind of vital information?' asked Asha, stretching her legs out.

'But we're just sitting here passively. We could be doing things to get the property fire-ready,' said Tommy.

The Texan held up a hand in protest as Tommy grabbed the remote from him. 'Who put this guy in charge?'

*He's always been the one in charge*, thought Phoebe.

Tommy disappeared down the hall and came back with a towel, holding it out to her.

'Oh, thank you. It's so hot I think I'm nearly dry,' she said.

'You should ring your family. They'll be worried when they see the news. And you should stay here tonight—you and Wendy—just to be on the cautious side.'

Phoebe didn't even think to question Tommy. An image came to her of him sitting high in a jacaranda tree brandishing a plastic sword and shouting orders to his 'crew'. 'Thanks. I might call them now if that's okay.'

She thought of her family and a terrible idea struck her. Maybe it would be easier for them all if the cottage burned in the fires. They could move on, rather than continue with the unspoken and unresolved pain of Karin's death. Phoebe felt a wave of fierce protection then. No, she would fight to save everything that the cottage stood for, as painful as it was. She knew Jez and Tommy would stay and fight for Driftwood. The house was more than just a building, it was the memory of their mother, full of all the small things that made up a life, but came to hold meaning after death. She wished her family thought of the cottage in the same way, instead of regarding it as a thing of shame and dead memories.

Tommy disappeared and returned with a cordless phone. Phoebe took it outside onto the front step. The air was choked with smoke now and the raucous dusk birdcall was absent, there was only the sound of the hot wind in the trees. The taste of it caught in the back of her throat and she coughed.

She knew Camilla's mobile number by heart. She took a deep breath. They hadn't spoken since the engagement party. Would she hold a grudge? She had too many other things going on in her life, surely.

Camilla picked up on the second ring.

'Hello, Camilla speaking.' Phoebe imagined her sister standing in the kitchen cooking, simultaneously orchestrating some kind of magnificent craft endeavour for the children.

'Hi, it's Phoebe. I'm calling from a landline.'

'I'm putting you on speaker phone.' She heard the clunk as Camilla put the phone down on the marble benchtop. There were the muted, indistinct voices of a television in the background. Oscar and Sophia watching cartoons probably. 'Are you back home yet?'

Camilla was all practicality. Phoebe didn't expect her to ask how she was coping post-Nathaniel. 'No, I'm still down south. Have you heard about the bushfires? I'm not sure if I'll be able to get back up the highway for work on Monday. Lots of homes have been lost already.'

'I didn't realise it was close to you.'

'We're okay now, but—'

'You're with someone?'

'Oh, I'm at Jez and Tommy's. They're all here. Jez lives here now, with his wife. And Tommy's here with his family. There are quite a few of us, so I think we'll be okay. They're not sure if the fires might come this way.'

'Oh my God, I haven't seen those boys since we were teenagers.' There was a surprising warmth in Camilla's voice. There hadn't always been so much tension between them. Once they had been close. Once they had all been friends, in that innocent, easy way of children. Phoebe felt a pang, of the past, of what it took and didn't give back. Of what it left behind to wonder about.

'I know. It's amazing. Tommy has a little boy now and Driftwood is still gorgeous.'

'I talked to Mum today. I think she's worried about you.'

This was the second-hand way Camilla and her mother communicated to her. Emotions were conveyed, not shown or expressed.

Usually Phoebe acquiesced and glossed over, reassured, made sure things didn't get too messy, but there was something raw and real and immediate about being here that gave her strength. 'What, is she worried I might end up like Karin?'

There was a long pause on the line. Phoebe didn't know why she'd said that. She knew Camilla didn't have the capacity to respond to it.

'Hang on. Sorry, Oscar is pulling Sophia's hair.' She heard Camilla admonish the children.

'Sorry, Phee Phee. It's all happening here.'

*Typical Camilla diversion*, Phoebe thought. 'You're probably in the middle of dinner. I just wanted to let you know I'm okay and I won't be back until the highway is open.' She paused. She had been going to say sorry for ruining the engagement party and disappearing. That would be the usual dynamic—apologising for something that Camilla had coaxed her into. But she stopped herself. Camilla seemed to have decided to ignore it had ever happened, so Phoebe would too. 'Tell Mum not to worry.'

After she'd hung up, Phoebe sat on the steps for a while. Her clothing was stiff against her skin. It was a blood orange dusk, beautiful, apocalyptic.

She heard footsteps behind her and turned.

'You must be Phoebe.' Jenna was slim and small, with wispy brown hair pulled into a thin ponytail. Under her eyes were the bruised smudges of parenthood.

Phoebe shifted over on the step. 'Hi, and you're Jenna.'

'Do you mind? I just need to get away from all the drama on the news.'

'No, sit.'

'It's a weird light, isn't it?' said Jenna, squinting into the haze.

'I was just thinking how it's beautiful and a bit scary.'

'It's good that you're here rather than up at your place, alone.'

'Do you think you'll try to make it back to Canberra tonight?'

Jenna looked down at her near-empty wineglass. 'I don't think Tommy would ever abandon Jez and he wouldn't want me and Harry driving back alone when there are fires around.'

'That makes sense. You're lucky to have this as a second home.'

Jenna shook her head. 'You have no idea. It's amazing. Harry's so happy here. It's as though the nature calms him. He's always loved it. That's why we come almost every weekend. We're so glad Jez and Asha moved back here.'

'It sounds like, if you don't mind me saying, he's quite high functioning ... on the spectrum.'

A small smile lit her lips and crinkled the papery skin around her eyes. 'Thank you for saying that.' She nodded. 'He's getting better. We've done a lot ... a lot of work to get to this stage.'

A silence fell between them but Phoebe felt no discomfort; they just stared out into the falling evening. It was funny how you could know someone for five minutes and feel comfortable around them and others you could interact with for years and still not know how to act or what to say to make it feel right.

'What about you, Phoebe? Married? Kids?'

'Ha.' She took a deep breath. 'I couldn't be further from either, really.'

Jenna shifted beside her. 'Sorry, I didn't mean to—'

'No, no, it's fine.' Perhaps it was because Jenna had opened up about her own struggles, it felt safe to admit what a mess her life had become. 'I was actually meant to be newly engaged at this point. She wiggled her empty ring finger. 'It's funny. I had it all so planned out. We'd get married and buy a house with a backyard and have kids, just like everyone does. But I didn't even stop to think if that's what I really wanted, it was just what needed to happen.'

Jenna smiled. 'Yeah, I was meant to be a mother of two—one boy, one girl, two years apart, neither with a disability, of course.'

'Life just doesn't work like that, does it?'

'No. But it goes on. And you learn to deal with what you've been given.' Jenna laughed suddenly. 'You know, I think it's this weird end-of-the-world light that's making us all so deep.'

'And the fact that we could all be trapped by bushfires overnight,' Phoebe said, laughing darkly.

'Do you think it's that bad? God, no wonder we're sharing our crushed hopes and dreams.'

Phoebe smiled. 'Everyone needs someone to have authentic conversations with. I guess my sister was that person for me.' She was mortified to discover her face was suddenly wet with tears. She flicked them away with impatient fingers. 'Sorry, being here just reminds me of her.'

She saw a shadow of recognition in Jenna's eyes.

'I'm sorry. Tommy told me what happened,' Jenna said, her face crumpled with sympathy.

Phoebe stared out into the smoky air. She didn't know why she'd raised the topic of Karin, or what to say now. *My sister was actually a really strong person. She was dreaming of expanding her business. I would have known if she'd been mentally ill or in such a bad place she was going to kill herself. She told me everything.* A small part of herself whispered, *except her weekends away twice a month.*

There was a patter of feet behind them. Harry was naked except for a nappy. He seemed too old to be wearing one and Phoebe's heart squeezed with the implication of what that meant.

'Oh, hello,' Jenna said. 'Daddy's given you a bath has he? Are you hungry for dinner?'

'Dinner. Dinner. Dinner.'

Tommy appeared behind Harry. 'He'll keep saying that until there's food in his mouth.' He tickled his son affectionately. 'That's one of the things with his condition. He has this incredible body clock. Dinner has to be at exactly the same time every night. We have no idea how he knows it's 5.30 pm, but he does. Ignore it at your peril.'

Harry repeated the word over and over and Jenna smiled and took his little hand in hers. She looked up at Tommy. 'Phoebe and I were just talking about Karin.' She turned to Phoebe. 'I actually met Karin at the coffee festival,' she said.

'Oh, you met her?' asked Phoebe, the promise of some extra snippet of information about Karin warmed her. As though an ordinary memory of an ordinary day could bring some part of her back. People didn't realise that when you lost someone, talking about them was the only thing you had left.

'She was selling tea and flowers,' said Jenna. She indicated towards Tommy. 'You hadn't seen her in, what? Years. It's so lovely that you all spent summers down here.'

'I remember that,' said Phoebe, shaking her head, as though to set the memory free. 'She had a stall with vintage tables and stools and served tea in second-hand china. It was in Canberra.' *Maybe that's all it was. Business. Maybe she was going to lots of markets and trade shows around the place on these mystery weekends away,* Phoebe thought. 'Karin was the only one selling tea at a coffee festival. So typical of her. She mentioned she ran into you.' Phoebe looked up at Tommy.

'Gosh, yeah, I'd forgotten that,' he said, scratching his head. 'Well, we'd better get this one fed,' he said to Jenna. 'Do you know where his medicine is?'

'I think it's in the car. I'll get it,' said Jenna, checking her watch.

For the briefest moment Karin's memory was alive. But it was over, blown away on the hot wind. Phoebe understood. To the living, the dead were just dead. It was only those who cherished them who still thought of them as alive.

The mood inside was sombre; the stifling heat of the day trapped inside the house despite the high ceilings. The wide lounge windows had been shut to limit the smell of burning bush and people were strewn over the lounge and on the floor. Everyone was drinking beer. The television was on again and droned like an insect in the background. Phoebe was unsure of where to sit and felt out of place in the face of Asha's obvious dislike and Jez's unpredictable behaviour, so she perched at the kitchen bench. At least Tommy and Jenna seemed like neutral territory.

'I can't be bothered cooking, it's too hot,' said the Texan, his drawl more pronounced than usual. He took a long pull of his beer. 'I was going to barbecue but that's not happening. What's Harry having? Maybe we should all have that.'

'Ah, a boiled egg and toast soldiers,' said Tommy, who was placing a pot of boiling water on the stove.

'Sounds perfect,' said the Texan.

'Come on, you've got an army here to feed. We need our sustenance,' said Wendy. 'What about I boil up a big pot of pasta and you can whip up that basil pesto you make from the garden?'

'Sounds great,' said Jez. 'We need something to line our stomachs. We've all been drinking since midday.'

'Did we even have lunch?' asked Asha. 'Oh yeah, I had an apple. In my alcoholic apple cider.'

'So, you're all wasted and we're possibly looking at having to deal with a bushfire either drunk tonight or hungover tomorrow,' said Tommy, placing two eggs into the saucepan. 'Great work, guys.'

Phoebe could tell by his tone that he was only half joking.

'See, you're failing in your role as chef,' said Wendy, elbowing the Texan in the ribs. He made a huffing sound and eased himself off the lounge. 'As long as the possums haven't attacked the basil, or the heat hasn't wilted everything.'

'It's not like we can prep the house now,' said Jez.

'Well, actually we could,' said Tommy. 'I'll hose as much as I can tonight, give everything a good soaking. Wendy and Phoebe, we could do that for your places tonight too. But I think everyone should stay here to sleep, just to be safe.'

Phoebe's eyes flew to Asha, who was stretched out on the lounge with the insouciance of a cat. She and Flick had changed the channel to a soapie, their legs intertwined despite the heat, as they fished strawberries out of a punnet on Asha's belly. There was no way Flick wasn't going to tell Asha what Phoebe had admitted about her husband. She glanced over at Jez who was gazing out towards the river, sipping the dregs of his beer. Everything felt so surreal.

The unrelenting heat of the day took its first casualties early in the evening. Jenna and Harry went to bed while they all ate the fragrant, herb-laced pasta the Texan had thrown together with lashings of garlic and good-humoured grumbling.

'He gets tetchy when he's drunk,' Wendy explained. 'But who can complain when he whips up meals like this?'

Phoebe had avoided eye contact with Jez all night, instead drinking more wine than she should have and chatting with Tommy and Wendy about having been through the terrible Canberra bushfires in 2003. Wendy looked at her watch; everyone else had gone to bed.

'Gosh, it's nearly eleven. We should get some sleep. You take the spare room, Phoebe; I'll sleep with grumble bum. He snores ... that's part of why it's best that we live apart.'

Phoebe laughed. 'If only more people were so honest, there'd probably be a lot more happy couples in the world.'

She thought of Nathaniel. Had they been honest? No, they hadn't, obviously. Had Nate just not had the courage to say it out loud? It was easy to think that she'd missed the signs but maybe she hadn't wanted to see them. The way she'd always seek out his hand to hold, but it was never reciprocated. Excuse: he's not as physically affectionate as me. The way she told him things sometimes but when she looked into his eyes they had a vacant expression, as though he wasn't really there. Excuse: he's tired. The way she'd interpreted his quietness and lack of excitement leading up to Hawaii as him having a lot on his plate with his new job, or maybe nervousness. There were so many ways to stay blind to the truth in relationships, so many ways to hold on.

'Snoring is the enemy of love. Take it from a woman who's had two husbands,' Wendy said.

'I don't doubt you. You're very wise.' Phoebe squeezed

Wendy's arm, feeling a rush of liquor-induced affection. 'I think you should take the spare room, I can just sleep on the sofa,' she said, in no hurry to be in the room next to Jez and Asha.

'You're a sweetheart. You sure?'

Phoebe nodded.

Wendy widened her eyes and nudged her, whispering. 'You're a lifesaver.'

For all the joking and ribbing, Wendy clearly adored the Texan. There was a difference between Wendy's playful teasing and Asha's snide teasing. She thought back to Wendy's comment that Jez and Asha's relationship was full of resentment. But maybe it wasn't even that. Maybe as soon as a couple stopped being kind to each other, it was over.

Phoebe moved to the longest sofa under the windows, set the cushions up to support her head and pulled a light throw from the other lounge. There were tea cups on the coffee table and the stub of a cigarette in an ashtray. No one else smoked. She thought about how odd it was that humans self-sabotaged. Why was she smoking when they were trying to conceive and why was Asha so angry at Jez? Why didn't she leave him if she was unhappy? Why punish him? Was it just habit? Financial security? And yet Asha seemed jealous and protective of Jez. Phoebe remembered her arm around him when they'd first met on the jetty. She'd thought they were happy. And yet the more she saw the less she believed they were. She wondered what went on behind closed doors between them; she just didn't want to find out tonight.

She must have fallen asleep mid-thought because she woke with a jolt. She raised her head. A sliver of artificial light came from the kitchen. It was just someone getting a drink from the fridge. She closed her eyes again and felt the soft pull back into sleep.

'Oh, sorry.' Jez was above her, holding a glass of milk.

Phoebe rubbed her eyes. 'What? What is it?'

'I didn't realise you were sleeping out here. Can you see that glow?'

Her limbs were slow and heavy as she sat up, as though she'd been asleep for hours. The tops of the trees on the opposite side of the river looked lit from behind. A spike of adrenalin needled through her, snapping her awake. 'They're not on fire, are they?'

He shook his head and rubbed the back of it, as he was prone to do when thinking. 'No, but I think it's the glow from fires burning across the river somewhere.'

She straightened, instantly on alert. 'Should we wake the others?'

He skolled the milk in his glass and put it down among the empty beer bottles. 'Maybe. Let's go down to the jetty and take a closer look.'

Phoebe slid on her thongs and followed Jez out the French doors. The air outside was thick and she resisted the urge to pull her top up to cover her mouth and nose. 'It smells worse.'

Jez picked up a torch at the door. 'Look at the air.'

In the bright torchlight tiny particles floated like ashen snowflakes. Phoebe felt a chill run along her bare arms despite the suffocating heat.

'I can't see the glow from here,' she said, pointing towards the treetops.

'Strange,' said Jez, starting down the narrow track towards the river.

Phoebe looked back at the dark house, her instinct telling her to wake Tommy and the others, but instead she followed Jez as he picked his way down to the water. The air on the river was fresher, cooler. They walked to the end of the jetty and Jez switched off the torch. The night rumbled around them, as though in protest at being set on fire.

'It feels … a little easier to breathe here,' she said, relishing the feeling of fresher air in her lungs.

Jez turned to her and she could see the whites of his eyes flash in the dark. 'You know having you here—'

'Jez, I'm so sorry.' The words rushed out of her. 'I know it's all just too weird. As soon as it's safe, I'll go.'

'No, that's not what I was going to say.' He sighed and looked up. 'No stars. Must be too smoky. Will you sit with me here for a bit?' He must have felt her hesitation. 'Please?'

She swallowed. What she wanted was to sit here with him and talk while the rest of the world burned—that was the problem. She sat anyway, feeling a wave of tiredness well up through her bones.

'I was going to say that having you here has made me realise just how unhappy I am. And ironically, I'm taking it out on you.'

Her heartbeat rose in her throat and she took a deep breath to calm herself. She licked her lips. They tasted like smoke. 'Jez,' she said softly. 'You've got a wife. You're trying to have a baby.'

'I need to know if what you said was true.'

Her chest was aching now. Phoebe turned away so Jez couldn't read her expression. She'd never admitted it to herself, she realised, until right now. She had loved Nathaniel, she was sure, but how to explain the difference between her love for Nathaniel and her love for Jez? The love she felt for Nathaniel was the practical sort. They had always liked the same things, had the same friends, and they'd talked of their future as though it was inevitable, sensible. It was the same way they'd done everything; even their love-making was a need to be met. It all just fitted. And she was not naïve. Such a thing was not easy to find or manufacture. Her life with Nathaniel had been full and good. But somehow they had manufactured it, the both of them. Nathaniel had felt the absence too—he'd just been braver in deciding that he wanted more. Phoebe wondered if she would ever have admitted this to herself if it hadn't been for Jez, turning up right when her wounds were so exposed.

With Jez, what they'd had when they were young had never been predicated on practicality. They saw each other infrequently, and yet every time they were near each other it was there. With Jez it was always a feeling, as simple as it was strong. Phoebe had once heard a woman talk about how when she looked at her husband after many years of marriage, she still felt moved that this handsome, amazing man had chosen her. Phoebe was with Nathaniel when she'd heard this, and she'd thought it slightly insipid and overly romantic. She suspected she'd had this kind of connection with Jez, but she could always dismiss it as the freshly plucked yearnings of first love.

But now, here they were, both injured from the ravages of half a lifetime. So much time had passed, and yet in the still quiet of the night, in the small gap between their bodies, they could have been teenagers again. A wave of emotion ran through her and she wrapped her arms around herself. Perhaps it was the chill lifting off the water, perhaps it was realising that it might be possible for a love like this to erase so much of her pain.

'It was true, what I said, Jez. You know it was true.'

'It was, or it is? I mean, have you thought about us over the years? You were about to get married. Were you happy?'

Phoebe sighed. She would never tell him that he crept into her dreams, and she'd wake with the sound of his voice in her mind. 'Yeah. Marriage was the plan. It was what I wanted.'

'But you weren't marrying the love of your life?'

She slipped her hands under her knees. 'I think we both know that it's a bit more complicated than that.'

'But why? Maybe it's not, actually. Feeling those fires so close, you start to think about what matters. What you'd leave behind. What you would save, no matter what. And it brings everything into focus. Why live life being so fucking unhappy? Trying and failing so hard. Maybe this thing … this meeting of minds, or hearts, whatever it is we have, maybe it's that simple.'

'But, Jez, it wasn't that simple, remember? We wanted different things.'

'That's changed. We've both grown up. I think we were both naïve, don't you? I've lived my life, and what we had …'

He trailed off but she knew what he meant. When you were young and deeply in love you thought there would be other loves, that they would be waiting, lined up to be tried on, discarded and replaced until you found exactly the right fit. But then you found that love wasn't a dazzling costume shop. You found that a love that had sparkle, that was pure and deep, was elusive. You realised that love could be a dull thump in your heart, or a need to be met, or a wound to soothe, or a monotony.

'What if what we both want has changed?' Jez asked, his voice low and steady.

Hers wasn't so calm. 'That's what dating is for … seeing if you're compatible with someone and I'm not going to date another woman's husband.'

The low growl of a boat motor from high up the river echoed around them.

'I'm going to leave her, Phoebe.'

Her heart felt like it slowed. 'Jez.'

'Will you promise me you won't go? Not yet.'

'Jez. I have work next week. I …' *I'm on the rebound, I'm lost, I'm weak and too needy, I'm still grieving*, she wanted to say.

'Use the fires as an excuse. They might not even be an excuse anyway. You're probably stuck here for a while.'

Phoebe could feel the heat coming off his body. The right thing to do would be to leave. The truth was she couldn't afford to jeopardise her job, especially now she was single. Even though it didn't fulfil her, she had to make a living and everyone would think she was crazy giving it up. The illusion she peddled was strong. Would she miss it? Why did she need fancy events and free wine? So she could boast on social media about how cool her life was? Phoebe cringed at the thought of her last status update—a pair of cocktails sweating lazily against the setting sun. A post that was meant to convey the dreamy perfection of their lives in a single image. The sound of Nathaniel's exasperation came back to her as she arranged the glasses just so for the picture. Of course, she hadn't read it as contempt. She hadn't read it for what it was: her arranging their lives, as though happiness would be inferred by the tilt of a straw.

How far away that moment seemed now. But this river. Jez. Karin. They felt more real to her than any small detail from that life.

'I think that's really courageous,' she said softly. 'If you're really unhappy and you've tried and tried to make your marriage work, then maybe leaving her is the right thing to do. But if you leave Asha, it can't be because of me,' she said, turning to face him.

There was a soft touch on her shoulder.

'Why not?' asked Jez, and for a moment she thought it was Jez's fingertips but then she felt it on her cheek, the tops of her thighs, her hair. Charred leaves were raining from the sky, still warm.

Phoebe's heart was beating fast as they ran towards Driftwood.

# CHAPTER 11

Warmth seeped through the window pane and Phoebe flattened her palm against the glass. The air outside was ashen, but it was the wind that was scary. She scanned the river for evidence of fire. It had felt so close the night before. There would be no going home, no doing anything but preparing for the worst. She lay on her back and listened. Voices came from deeper in the house. She heard the low crack of Jez's voice. She had replayed his words in her head until sleep had finally snuck in. Her dreams had been full of him—him and Asha, him and her, the world burning around them. She had no idea how she was going to approach this day—Jez with his secret exposed only to her, or Asha, with her scalding comments.

A deep thirst made her pull her body up from the sofa. She tiptoed down the hall to find the bathroom empty. She drank straight from the tap, scooping water into the cup of her hand. She'd never worn much make-up but she wished she had a few things to help with the tired face looking back at her. She needed to go home to get her toothbrush and a change of clothes but had no idea if it would be safe. She opened the top drawer of the bathroom vanity and found a make-up bag.

Asha's. She ran her fingers over the tinted moisturiser, concealer, mascara and blush, and was tempted to use just a little. There was something so intimate about seeing the tools a woman used to cover her flaws. Phoebe shut the drawer and looked at herself in the mirror again. Was she really the kind of person who could steal another woman's man?

She opened the drawer again and picked up the blush. She could really do with a little colour in her cheeks. Would it be bad if she just used a tiny bit? Phoebe was staring at her reflection when the door opened. She jumped when she saw Asha and shoved the blush into the drawer. Asha's face was hidden behind a tumble of blonde hair and her eyes were red-rimmed, as if she'd been crying.

'Sorry,' Phoebe said, startled, hoping to God Asha hadn't seen her. 'I'll be out in a sec.'

Asha shook her head. 'No, it's okay. I just need to pee.' She pushed past her to the toilet, pulled up her nightie and sat on the seat, hair still hanging over her face. Phoebe was so shocked she couldn't move for a second.

'Sorry,' she said again and quickly left, pulling the door shut behind her. She felt, again, like an intruder.

Jez and Tommy were at the dining table. Jenna had Harry on her hip in the kitchen. Jez looked up and something tentative passed between them. Tommy ate toast, sipping on coffee while he chewed. He rapped his thumb on the paper open in front of him when he saw Phoebe.

'Good timing, Phoebe. We're just working out the plan for the day. I went into the Bay early, got some supplies, the papers, and had a chat to some mates at the station. Road's still clear so we've just been deciding … You could drive to the

Bay and camp out there in a hotel and see this thing out, but you'd need to get going soon.' He glanced at his watch and then up at her. 'Like now.'

Phoebe felt Jez's eyes on her. She thought about how easy it would be to go stay somewhere that had internet access and was safe. She could return to her normal life, drive home as soon as the highway opened. But that dream from last night was still inside her, a promise and a curse. She couldn't help it—she didn't want to leave Jez yet. She didn't want to be on her own and go back to her shell of a life. And she thought of the cottage. All the beautiful antiques Karin had collected, her grandfather's ancient reading chair, the family photos, the place Karin had last been alive. She couldn't abandon it. She heard Ginny's voice in her head, *'But no, I must admit, it doesn't seem right that Karin would do that to herself.'* Something wasn't right, Phoebe was sure of it now. And the book of flower meanings that Karin gave to Ginny … was the note Karin left a hidden message? What about the weekends away? There were too many unanswered questions. It would feel like she was abandoning her sister if she left now.

'I'll stay and fight,' she said.

Tommy glanced up at her, surprise lighting his features. 'You know we mightn't have the manpower to …' She could tell he was going to say 'save' but changed his mind. 'Fireproof everyone's places.'

Phoebe nodded and chewed at her bottom lip. 'I know, Driftwood and Wendy's place are the priorities. My place being just a holiday house …' But as she said this she realised it wasn't just that anymore. It held so many memories, memories of her sister. She couldn't lose the cottage, too. Her family might not care, but she did.

Tommy and Jez exchanged a glance. Tommy stood, his body poised on his fingertips. 'We'll do our best to look after everyone's places.' He straightened and clapped his hands. 'Where is my team? Is everyone still asleep?'

Jenna called out from the kitchen. 'There's sourdough here for toast and OJ in the fridge. Make sure you eat. And Tommy's bought a whole heap of bottled water.'

'I'll see what Asha and Flick are up to,' said Jez, getting up from the table.

Phoebe went into the kitchen. 'Hello there,' she said to a Vegemite-smeared Harry.

He gazed back at her without expression and spun the wheels of his red train with a tiny thumb. Last night, Tommy and Jenna had described some of his tantrums but Phoebe couldn't imagine this placid boy in a state of agitation.

She poured herself a glass of juice and drank it quickly. Jenna passed her a slice of freshly buttered toast. 'What are you and Harry going to do?' Phoebe asked.

'We'll stay here, fill the baths and the sinks,' said Jenna, wiping Harry's hands and face with a washer.

Jez returned and began to rinse the breakfast plates. 'Thanks,' he mumbled, and their eyes met fleetingly. 'For staying to help out.'

Phoebe wanted to whisper in his ear about her dreams, exorcise the messed-up feelings in her body, but she just nodded. 'So, what's the plan, then?'

Tommy stepped into the kitchen and clapped his hands. 'Can we get a move along, people? Leave the goddamn dishes.

Get Harry dressed. This isn't a lazy Sunday brunch, there are people's homes at risk.'

'We need to eat,' said Jenna, her eyes flashing. She put Harry on the ground and Tommy picked him up.

'I'll get him ready,' he said.

'No, I'll do it,' said Jenna, prising Harry from his arms and leaving the room.

Tommy looked at his watch, agitated. He started putting the water bottles in a plastic bag. 'This is the plan. Jez will come with me to help out at Wendy's. Jenna, Asha and Phoebe will fill the baths and sinks, hose and rake around the property.' He sighed. 'Does anyone know where Flick is?'

'She's not up for helping,' said Jez, putting down the tea towel.

Tommy rolled his eyes and left the kitchen with the bags full of water bottles. His anxiety was like tinder catching.

A buzz of intense worry started in Phoebe's chest. She considered the prospect of being stuck here in this smoke cocoon with Asha. 'How long will you be at Wendy's?' she asked Jez.

'I'll just go up there for a few hours then come back before lunch. Wendy and Tex have decided they want to stay and fight if the fire gets close. I want to help them.'

Phoebe swallowed a mouthful of toast with difficulty. 'I need some long pants and sneakers from the cottage. Do you mind if I walk up with you? Then I'll drive back.' The thought of venturing into the opaque air alone was frightening.

She suddenly thought of Ginny. 'Jez, I think we need to check on Karin's neighbour, Ginny.'

She realised her mistake when she saw the surprise on Jez's face. 'I mean, *my* neighbour. She's very old and she's blind.'

Jez nodded. 'We'll check in on her. Come on, we'd better get going. I'll meet you at the front gate in five. Grab a wet towel from the bathroom to put over your mouth.'

It was only a few hundred metres up the road but in the haze it seemed much further. Sunlight fell in smoky streaks in front of them. The crickets and birds that usually dominated this stretch of bush were quiet. They walked in silence, towels over their mouths, like actors in a post-apocalyptic film. Phoebe's eyes stung, and the inside of her nose burned as though all the tiny hairs inside had been singed. When they reached the cottage she gave Jez a wave at the drive.

'Grab what you need. I'll wait here,' he said, his voice muffled against the towel. 'You're not going back on your own.'

'I'm okay,' she said, even though she didn't feel it. 'I'll just drive back.'

'Go on, I'll wait.'

She went inside, heart hammering, and grabbed Karin's jacket from the coat hook. She hesitated in front of Karin's wardrobe. It had felt disrespectful to help herself to her sister's clothes, but now a sense of urgency overruled. She found a pair of Karin's joggers, one size too big, and jeans that looked roughly the right size. She shoved her pyjamas, toothbrush and cosmetics bag into a supermarket tote. On the way out she grabbed her mobile phone, charger and the car keys.

'Ready,' she yelled to Jez, who she could just make out at the end of the drive.

He jogged towards the car and got in. She could feel him studying her from the passenger seat. 'I thought I would have scared you off.'

She glanced at him. His hair was a greasy mess, his T-shirt had a hole where the collar band was coming away and his skin was pink-tinged with sunburn. She had a strong urge to kiss him. She manoeuvred the car carefully down the drive. She didn't trust herself to answer him.

He faced her, one hand on the dash. 'Can we talk?'

Phoebe jammed her foot on the brake, the blinker sounding as loud as her heart. She wasn't used to talking about feelings like this. Nathaniel had always been uncomfortable dissecting their relationship. 'Let's get through today, okay?' The words rushed out of her and she was surprised at how breathless she was. 'We're in the middle of a bushfire. I'm going to need to call work and tell them I'm not coming in next week. I'm feeling …' She stopped. 'Ginny. Next door. We need to check on her.'

Jez took a moment to register her words, his eyes trained on her intently. 'I'll go.'

He got out of the car and loped down the drive. Phoebe hoped someone had come for Ginny. She knew she had family locally.

Jez was breathless and coughing when he returned. 'No one's home.'

Phoebe's shoulders slumped in relief. 'Oh good, someone must have come and got her.' She could feel Jez watching her again.

'Thank you. Thank you for just staying here and not leaving yet,' he said.

She didn't know how to reply. Was she giving him false hope? Could she really let him back into her life, her heart? Could she do that to Asha? Her mind felt as choked as the air and she squeezed her eyes shut. When she opened them he wasn't looking at her anymore.

They drove the short way to the end of the street in silence and Phoebe stood and watched while he drove back up the hazy road, the sound of her heart in tune with the muted thrum of cicadas.

The work was hot and the air stubborn, refusing to refresh their lungs. They had been clearing for what felt like hours, raking leaves from the grass and picking up sticks to pile at the end of the garden as far from the house as possible. Now the sun was high, and the heat rising from the ground made Phoebe feel as though she was trapped inside a glass jar. She leaned on her rake, watching as Asha sat down on the front step and wiped her arm across her forehead. She had hiked her white dress up to her thighs, tucking it into the band of her underwear.

'I feel like maybe I need to apologise,' Asha said, kicking off her gumboots and shaking them.

Phoebe looked behind her but there was no one there but them. 'What for?' She tried to keep her voice light.

'Being a bit of a bitch.' Asha took a deep breath and scraped her hair off her face. She leaned back on her arms. 'I've been known to exhibit hostile behaviour. I was the same with Flick when she first came. Now we're besties.'

Phoebe fought to look natural as she batted a fly away with her hand. A tight knot of guilt pulled in her stomach. 'Oh, you know, I get it. It's always a bit weird with ex-girlfriends.'

Asha shot her a small smile and pulled a cigarette out of the pocket of her dress, rolled it between her fingers and then put it down on the deck beside her. 'You know what? I actually don't feel like smoking when I can't breathe. Weird, huh?'

Phoebe laughed cautiously. 'Yeah. Or no.'

'It's a dirty habit, anyhow. Want a beer?'

'Definitely.'

Asha went inside and Phoebe sat on the shaded part of the step and brushed the burned leaves away with her hands. They crumbled at her touch. So now Asha was going to give up the smokes? Just when Jez had decided to leave her. Phoebe rubbed her burning eyes and sighed deeply. Life could be so ironic.

Asha returned and handed her a sweating VB, and Phoebe rolled it behind her neck, feeling the coolness ease the woozy exhaustion. Her hands came away blackened but she had nowhere to wipe them.

'Probably not the swanky Sydney beer you're used to but it does the trick,' said Asha, sitting beside her on the step.

'Don't worry, I've drunk my share of VB,' she said, trying not to sound as snobby as Asha obviously thought she was. 'It's an Aussie teenager's rite of passage.'

Phoebe chinked bottles with Asha and they both drank. 'What was Jez like as a teenager, anyway?'

The prospect of talking about that was only slightly more appealing than the thought of getting up and continuing work in the unforgiving heat. At least Asha was trying.

'Um, okay, that's hard. It was so long ago.' Phoebe paused to let that sink in. 'I guess he wasn't unlike he is now, but there was just an innocence that isn't there as much anymore. Maybe he's more cynical now.' She shook her head. 'It's hard to tell, really. Everyone probably gets more cynical as they age.'

'That's funny, I don't see any cynicism in him. I think he's still blind to how life really is. He's always seeing the good in people, but in my experience, that's just not realistic.'

Phoebe thought about everything that Asha must have been through with the miscarriages and felt for her. 'Maybe that's why you're a good match—he needs someone with their head screwed on.'

Asha pulled her hair into a low bun against the nape of her neck. 'Do you really think we're a good match?'

She looked up and their eyes met. Where Phoebe expected to see defiance, she saw instead vulnerability. She saw, suddenly, the thick armour that Asha cloaked herself in, beetle-like. But underneath Phoebe could see all the fragile little legs kicking. Part of her wanted to warn Asha just how unhappy Jez was.

Phoebe shook her head. 'I don't know you well enough to judge. I mean, Wendy told me that you'd both been through a lot trying to have a baby. That can't have been easy.'

Asha laughed her deep, throaty laugh. 'So, that's a no, then.'

'No, I mean, how can we judge anyone's relationship? You're asking me, who just had her partner tell her he couldn't marry her with the ring sitting there right in his pocket. The ring I chose.'

'Really?' Asha's eyes widened and she put down her beer. 'So you knew he was going to propose but he didn't do it?'

'Yeah. We were in Hawaii to get engaged. It was the whole purpose of the holiday. I mean we were both busy with work. We'd planned it, but we'd had to fit it around work and stuff. We'd been living together for a while; I wasn't expecting some surprise engagement, like out of a Hollywood movie. We'd chosen the ring together, and I knew that one of the nights he was going to propose. I guess you could call it practical, but …'

'Were you the one driving it? The getting married thing?' Asha shook her head. 'I mean, sometimes I wonder, is it just me who really wants a baby? Is his heart in it, or is he just going along with it?'

Phoebe felt tiny pricks of tears behind her eyes at Asha's admission. They were both loved by a man who was not *in* love with them. She thought back to the recent wedding ceremony of a friend. The minister had said that love should be more than romantic love, that a lifetime of marriage required loving someone more than merely being *in love*. She'd felt conflicted hearing that. Part of her wanted the minister to be wrong, part of her knew he was probably right. And she still felt unsure. Was it too much to ask to still feel a spark, even after many years? Or could you feel it at first, only to have it snuffed out by the drone of so many days together? And did it matter if the spark dimmed to an ember?

'I don't know,' said Phoebe, taking a long pull of her beer. 'I mean, we were both ... how do I put it? Maybe we were more in love with the idea of marriage than what it meant to spend the rest of our lives together. I'm not sure that I wanted *him* as much as I wanted a husband and a child and everything that goes with that. I felt ready for it.'

Asha nodded and ran her thumb over the condensation on the beer bottle. 'And then at some point you realise that nothing is actually perfect. So the question is, should both of you have persisted with getting married to someone who was a pretty good match, even though you weren't madly in love— whatever that is—or is it best that he decided to walk away?'

Asha could have been asking the same thing of her own relationship. Maybe she was. Phoebe looked at her with her pretty hair, bottle of VB resting on the white flesh of her thigh. She had underestimated her. She could see the woman Jez had fallen in love with. But now, perhaps through the small injuries they had dealt each other over time, he could no longer see Asha for who she was, and she couldn't show him either.

It struck Phoebe that Asha might be considering leaving Jez. She could tell Asha what Jez was planning to do, free her from the same awful bind of being loved but not *loved*. But it wasn't Phoebe's place and she would never betray Jez.

'I truly don't know the answer to that.' She took another sip of her beer. It was warm now and it mixed with the thick smoke in the air to make her feel ill. 'Is it just me, or is it getting even more toxic out here?'

Asha stood and walked down the steps of the veranda, shielding her eyes against the glare. 'Maybe we should go inside. I feel like it's a hopeless fight at this stage. If the fire comes, it comes.'

Phoebe wondered if Asha was only talking about the bushfire. But when she searched her face, she realised that Asha had no idea what had already been lit.

# CHAPTER 12

They fell asleep that night draped in damp towels, their skin still smeared with ash. The electricity had failed, so they lit candles and then blew them out. The naked flame felt dangerous. No one wanted to be alone in the hot, close night so they all slept in the lounge room. Phoebe was dirty and hungry, but a physical peace eased along her limbs as she lay in the makeshift bed of cushions beside the coffee table. All the tension felt like it had been flushed out by the intensity of the day. The fire had roared right to the riverbank on the opposite side, but the sparks had not crossed the water. And then, like sorcery, the wind had changed. Sometimes simply surviving made everything make sense. Even Jez and Asha had fallen asleep turned in towards each other on the sofa. After their chat, Phoebe had felt the tension between her and Asha slacken, loosen and fall around their feet. She let sleep come now, content in the knowledge that they were all safe and maybe, just maybe, they were friends.

The morning dawned like a gift—blue clouds and the smell of rain on the horizon. It gave them all an energy that the orange heat had sapped. When the first rain sounded on the tin roof of the veranda they ran outside to lift their faces to the sky. Steam rose up from the soil and the clean smell filled their nostrils.

There was work to be done as the earth cooled. Phoebe swept burnt leaves and ash from the hardwood floors until her arms ached. Asha cleaned the smoke film from the grimy windows. Jez saw to getting the power back. Tommy and Jenna drove into the Bay and brought back two kilos of freshly cooked prawns, which they all ate with their fingers, ripping fresh bread off uncut loaves. It was after the third bottle of white wine had clinked its way to emptiness and the clouds had peeled back to reveal a tentative afternoon sun that the Texan suggested a swim in the river.

Had she not been so hot and exhausted, Phoebe might have hesitated, toes curled over the edge of the jetty. She'd have thought she could never swim in this river again, let alone right here, so close to where Karin had nearly drowned as a child and then supposedly walked into the water as an adult. But Phoebe thirsted for the water, as though it was a tonic for her body. As she pushed off into the cool green she realised that for the first time in ages she felt okay. Good, even. Cleansed. The charred trees on the opposite bank were like burnt matchsticks poked into the ground. The smoke had seeped into everything; it was in their hair and on their skin, but with it had come something Phoebe had not expected. She thought back to her life in Sydney. All its deadlines, its small, needling stressors. The feeling of inadequacy that one social media post could incite. But here none of that mattered. It didn't even exist. All that existed were the people in front of her, the daily necessities—safety, food and rest. Time idled along on its own, and Phoebe had given up reaching for her absent mobile phone to check and control it.

Feeling the coolness envelop her body she finally understood what made Karin come back here and make a life for herself. Their mother and Camilla had judged her so harshly for it. What would she do? How would she meet someone decent? Wouldn't she be lonely? And all the time, it was her sister who had it right. She was the one closer to the heart of what actually made a person happy. It was her sister, with her meaningful job and much-loved house, who had the better life.

It struck Phoebe deeply, this knowledge. She felt it as the river ran over her, through her. She felt her smallness against the pull of the current and it made her heart swell with gratitude at living. Karin wasn't an unhappy childless spinster, just as she had never been an unhappy child or wayward teenager. She was an easygoing, warm person who loved nature, treasured old things, and was a member of a small community.

Their very last conversation drifted into Phoebe's mind.

'I think I'm going to get a dog Phoebs.' Karin's voice was warm with excitement.

'It'd make me feel better,' said Phoebe, clucking her tongue. 'I've wanted you to get a dog ever since you moved there.'

Karin made a sound that even though they were on the phone, Phoebe knew meant she was rolling her eyes. 'It's perfectly safe down here. Which you'd know if you ever visited.'

'I'm sorry, I'm so slack. Work has been so busy. So many events at night at the moment. I'm buggered. I promise when I can take my next lot of holidays I will come.'

'We can buy prawns and eat them on the jetty, and drink all the free champagne you're going to bring me out of Grandma's gorgeous vintage glasses. I'm saving them for a special occasion. I just found a set of six of them wrapped in newspaper on top of the fridge. I have no idea why they were stashed there. They're absolutely exquisite, Phoebs. Worth an absolute fortune.'

'Random. I think Grandma was pretty eccentric. Dad said she was exactly like Camilla, but nicer.'

Karin laughed. 'Poor Cammie.'

'It's strange how we never thought Grandma was weird when we were kids. We just thought all grandmas sunbaked topless.'

'While drinking from her Waterford crystal champagne glasses, in the middle of the bush. Anyway, I'm saving them for a special occasion so you'd better get your arse down here.'

Phoebe changed the subject so she wouldn't feel so bad about not visiting. 'I don't think you should get a puppy, more of a mature dog. You're too busy with the shop to raise a puppy.'

'No, I've talked to the shelter and they're keeping an eye out for a lovely dog for me that needs a home.'

Phoebe sighed. 'Knowing you, it'll be missing its front paws or something and end up needing twenty-four-hour care.'

'Funny you should say that. There was one special-needs dog called Jack that they think—'

'No!' Phoebe laughed. 'I'm not letting you get a special-needs dog, Karin. It needs to look after you.'

'Why? I'm perfectly fine.'

*I'm perfectly fine.* Those words would never leave Phoebe now. The innocent ring of them. She had no text messages left to pore over—Karin rarely used her mobile. So the sound of her sister's sweet voice tolled in her head like a bell. *I'm perfectly fine. I'm perfectly fine. And two days later you were perfectly dead.*

The sound of a dog barking from across the river pulled Phoebe back to the present. She was getting cold. She swam back to the jetty and pulled herself up the ladder. Jez was standing with Harry in the shallows as Tommy and Jenna watched on from the jetty. They were talking, their brows furrowed as if discussing something stressful. It had been a hard twenty-four hours and Tommy had taken the brunt of the responsibility for saving their homes. He must be mentally exhausted. Phoebe could just make out their voices, loud and urgent whispers on the warm breeze. She froze on the ladder, not wanting to poke her head up and interrupt what was obviously a strained conversation.

'Just for a few more days. Maybe the week. Look, Harry is so happy,' said Jenna.

'I can't. Work's too busy.'

'But he and I could stay. There are plenty of extra hands to help out. You can come back on the weekend.'

'No, I told you. You're not staying here without me.'

'But why? It's so much easier for us to be here with the others. You're hardly home. Your hours are not family friendly. It's—'

Tommy thumped the wood. 'We're not going over this again. I said no and I meant it.' He got up and Phoebe could see him shielding his eyes, surveying the river, as though the jetty was a boat moving through the water that demanded his attention.

'We'll leave after dinner,' he said and started down the jetty, the sound of his boots loud. Tommy never wore bare feet. Even as a kid, Phoebe remembered he was always shod, as though ready for anything at any moment, as though not willing to feel the sand between his toes.

She felt bad for Jenna and wondered why Tommy was being so insistent. Maybe he was extra protective of Harry, or he was worried there would be more fires. She supposed all couples had their sticking points. She and Nathaniel had certainly had theirs.

Phoebe snuck up onto the jetty when she was sure Tommy had gone. She sat down a little bit away from Jenna and returned what she thought was a sad smile. She could tell Jenna didn't feel like chatting and they sat in companionable silence, letting the afternoon smooth out around them.

'Are you okay with him for a bit longer?' Jenna called to Jez, who was now picking shells off the sand with Harry. 'I'm just going up to the house for a moment,' she said.

Jez gave her the thumbs up.

If there was more tension between Jenna and Tommy, the tension between Asha and Jez seemed to have shifted, as if the proximity of destruction had created a certain peace. Phoebe felt relaxed and welcome. It was as if the defending of Driftwood had conferred a place for her in it. She stretched her legs and noticed how brown they had become. Her skin hadn't been that colour since she was a child, playing on this same jetty.

'Gosh, you're brown as a berry,' said Flick. She sat down and swung her legs over the side.

'You know, I was just thinking that. I totally forgot about sunscreen. It seemed a low priority these past few days.'

Flick cocked her head. 'It's interesting, despite what we've just been through, you seem much more relaxed than when you first arrived.'

'Do I?' Phoebe felt a flush creep up her face. 'It took me a while to leave the city behind. And not having my mobile beeping at me, and, I don't know, things being ... simpler.'

Flick nodded. 'Back in Sydney I used to pay my psychologist nearly one hundred dollars an hour to get the same benefits that I get from sitting right in this spot. Just look at Harry. Jenna says he's a different child when he comes here.' She squinted into the sun overhead. 'It's to do with being closer to trees, grass, his little feet running on the earth, you know? The more I think back to my old life, the more I think I can never go back. I feel like this place is healing my chronic fatigue. I mean, I still have crashes when I can't get out of bed, but it's rare now.'

'That doesn't surprise me, that you're getting better here.'

'I was so much lonelier in the city. Here we have a little community. You should come to the markets in the churchyard one weekend. You'll feel it for yourself. And you said it before— it's about simpler things. I have a fulfilling life contributing to the garden, writing bad crime fiction. Though my lawyer self sometimes balks at how slow my life has become.'

Phoebe thought about what it would be like to leave her job and set up a life here, even if just for a while. Could she actually be brave enough to do it? She imagined the judgement from their mother and Camilla. Saying goodbye to the security and the kudos of working for Joet et Halo. But looking at Flick, her face still trained towards the sun, she thought maybe she could.

'You're a writer? And a lawyer?' Phoebe had imagined Flick as a professional sportsperson, with her athletic physique.

'Worked in child protection for many years. The kind of job that can burn you out.'

Phoebe felt an intense shame mixed, strangely, with envy. Her own job was so vacuous, so pointless compared to what

Flick had dedicated her life to. Phoebe had got the marks to study law, and had contemplated it seriously, but the women of her family were all so creative. She'd spent her whole working life attempting to be like them, without a thought to what was actually important to her. 'Why did you leave? Was it the chronic fatigue?'

'That, and disillusionment. It was rewarding but heartbreaking too, because you don't always get justice. Things aren't always fair. It's hard to handle, especially when kids are involved.'

Phoebe shook her head. 'I can imagine. Can I ask you something weird?'

'Sure, I've seen some weirdness in my life, I can tell you.'

'You must have been pretty good at reading people?'

Flick shrugged. 'Well, you could see the creeps a mile off. And believe me, there were a lot of those.'

She shuddered, and Phoebe wondered what horrors Flick must have witnessed. It was no surprise her body had given up on her.

'No, but I mean ... did you ever read someone, read a situation wrong? Did you ever doubt your own judgement?' asked Phoebe.

Flick stretched her legs out and looked thoughtful. 'I know what you mean. Like was there someone who I thought was guilty who was actually innocent, or vice versa?'

Phoebe nodded.

'Mainly, I think I was right. I've always had ... my mum used to call it my "Flick-o-meter". I've always been able to judge people pretty well.'

Phoebe thought of Flick and Asha's friendship. Maybe she had grossly misjudged Asha at the start.

Flick turned to Phoebe and smiled warmly. 'Take you, for example. You probably don't see how amazing you are. You're beautiful and smart, and always look incredibly put together, even if you're wearing thongs. It's infuriating.' She laughed.

Phoebe laughed too, flushed and confused. 'Really?' She shook her head. 'You should see my sisters and my mum. I've always been the dag of the family.'

'Wow, your sisters must be knock-outs.'

Phoebe paused with the realisation she was still referring to her sisters in the plural. She felt vulnerability catch around her shoulders and she drew them inwards.

Flick must have noticed because she hesitated. 'Or, you don't like talking about it?'

Phoebe shook her head. 'It's not that. I just … I still say sisters, when now I have only one.'

Flick remained quiet, allowing Phoebe to go on.

'You know my sister committed suicide?' Phoebe was shocked at how easily it slipped out of her mouth.

Flick's eyes flashed with sympathy, and she twitched her lips in the way Phoebe had noticed many people did when suicide was mentioned. It was almost like a suppressed grimace.

'I did hear that,' said Flick. 'It's so sad. I'm sorry.'

'It was right here. Well, just up at the cottage's jetty. It's so weird saying that out loud.'

'This place will always be special then, won't it? In a sad way.'

Phoebe nodded.

'It must be so hard, knowing in retrospect that someone you were so close to was suffering, likely had a mental illness and you couldn't help,' said Flick.

Phoebe bit her lip in frustration. 'That's the thing. I don't think she did have a mental illness. I know the stats. I've read them for myself. Ninety per cent of suicide victims are mentally ill, but with Karin … I just … you know, I knew her. She was my best friend.'

Saying it out loud made the spear of constant sadness twist a little harder in her chest and her voice wobbled. 'I feel like no one else knew her quite like I did. We didn't speak every day but that was because of proximity, and life, you know? But I still knew her. We still called each other every weekend. I knew what her week looked like. I knew what she was eating for dinner.'

'That's why you asked me if my instinct about someone was ever wrong. You have an instinct about your sister.'

Phoebe felt her eyes prick with tears. 'She was wise, you know, in that way some people are? They seem to get what the essence of life is and they're more content because of that.'

'Mmm. Maybe she was actually a really sensitive human being. I consider myself an HSP. Highly Sensitive Person. A lot of chronic fatigue sufferers and deep thinkers are.'

'Yeah, I know what you mean, and she was sensitive, but Karin also had this practical side to her. It kept her from dwelling on things too much, unlike me. It kept things simple. Well, I thought they were simple until what happened … happened.'

'So, you're left feeling like you never really knew her?'

Phoebe shook her head and gazed out to the river. It was that still time, where the afternoon hovered on the cusp of dusk. 'I don't know. I spoke to Ginny, our neighbour, and she said some things about Karin that I didn't know about and that really threw me. But Ginny didn't think Karin was the type of person to take her own life, and deep down I don't either. She cared so much about people, I just know she would never have wanted to put us all through this.'

Wendy came up behind her and crouched, putting a warm hand on her bare shoulder. 'Thinking about your sister?' she asked softly.

Phoebe smiled a sad but grateful smile. 'I'm always thinking about my sister.'

Flick squeezed her forearm.

The Texan clapped behind them. 'Righto. That's what all you Aussies say, isn't it? The barbecue is fired up. Who wants steak, who wants chicken? Is everyone having ...' He affected a bad Aussie accent. 'Snags?' and the sound of their laughter echoed across the water.

Phoebe felt a pulse of uncertainty. At what point was she going to overstay her welcome? A few short days ago she couldn't have imagined feeling so comfortable. But her place was just up the road. There was no reason to stay another night, or even for dinner. But she wanted to, desperately.

'I should probably head back to my place,' she said.

Flick and Wendy both hooked their arms through hers.

'We can walk back up together after dinner,' said Wendy. 'You're part of our little community now,' she said.

'You are,' said Flick, nudging shoulders.

Phoebe felt a lump rising in her throat and she swallowed it down. 'As long as it's not too much trouble.'

'Don't be silly,' said Wendy.

They ate together at the big table on the veranda overlooking the river, slapping at their ankles as the mozzies came in. The sausages were burned and the salad from the garden was a little limp after the heat, but no one cared. They relived the fears of the past two days and drank too much wine as the night folded softly around them. The Texan admitted he'd been drunk on 'that awful VB stuff' the whole time because he was so scared.

Then Asha said, 'Well, we had sex for the first time in forever. I know, you do crazy things when you think you're going to die.'

The table went quiet and Phoebe felt her face grow hot. The sound of the mozzie zapper punctuated the silence. She could feel Jez's eyes on her. Had she really taken Jez's declaration to leave Asha to mean abstinence? How naïve. Why wouldn't they have sex? They were married. It wasn't impossible that the fire, the physical brutality of that day, had made Jez seek out the physical comfort of his wife's body. An image arrived in her mind—the morning sun falling in slants across Nathaniel's bare back. The easy way they would roll in towards each other. Sex could be a balm, a refuge, Phoebe knew. She missed that, and the loss was a deep ache inside her. It had been real. For a while, it had been enough.

'I wish it had that effect on Wendy,' said the Texan, scuttling the tension and making everyone laugh, except Phoebe.

Wendy slapped him playfully. 'You just admitted you were drunk the whole time the fires were going.'

The evening cooled and Phoebe felt a nub of dread settle in her stomach. She hated how she watched every interaction between Jez and Asha. She felt like a spy, and yet she couldn't leave. After dinner was cleaned up and they'd waved goodbye to Tommy, Jenna and Harry, they all walked down to the fire pit—a clearing near the dam with a large cast-iron bowl.

Jez and Wendy lit kindling and Phoebe wandered away from the group to find sticks for toasting marshmallows.

'You remember doing this as kids?' Jez came up behind and handed her a choice stick. It was long, tapering to a thin point. It looked like a weapon.

'Yeah. Wow, that's a goodie.' She fought to mask the hurt in her voice. The fire illuminated half of Jez's face. He was beautiful in a way that Nathaniel had never been. It seemed awful to compare the two but there was something about physical beauty that was so raw, so subconscious. It drew you in, it hooked you, without you even realising.

'Jez, it's good that you and Asha seem …'

He looked at the ground, his hands finding his pockets, his boots kicking the dust. 'I just … I realised I was being a dickhead.'

'No—'

'It wasn't fair on her, or you, to go on the way I did.'

Phoebe felt herself slide, as though she had slipped down a steep precipice, gaining speed, picking up burrs and grazed by gravel on the way. She couldn't speak.

'I'm in love with you, Phoebe,' said Jez. 'I was then and I am now. I can't be near you without feeling it.' He shook his head, a small smile playing on his lips. 'Just having you around makes me happy in a way I can't even describe. But everything you said is true. I have a commitment to Asha. I can't just abandon her when things get tough.'

Phoebe swallowed hard and snapped off the top of the stick, pleasantly sharp against her palm. It was what needed to happen. He was right. But still, the hurt yawned inside her, dampening down the anger. 'Should I stay away? I should stay away.' She whispered the words.

'No.' He grabbed her hands and then quickly dropped them, as though suddenly aware they weren't alone. 'Please. And it's not just me who'd miss you—everyone loves you.'

She managed a smile. She wanted more than anything to stay a part of this odd little group, she just didn't think she could watch Jez and Asha play happy families, especially after everything Jez had told her. 'Are you sure?'

He nodded. 'It's been good for you down here, hasn't it?'

Phoebe felt the warmth of the fire as it flared to life. The sound of laughter mixed with the pop of the damp wood burning. 'I'm taking another week. I don't know that I even care if I lose my job anymore, not after what we've just been through with the fires. It's put everything in perspective a little bit.'

'Don't you have, like, some shit-hot job selling wine, or something?'

She shrugged. 'Yeah, you know what? I've never really admitted this to anyone.' It was true, not even Nathaniel knew the true extent of how far the reality of her job veered from the illusion. 'It's actually not that amazing a job, it just sounds good. I just put up pretty pictures to make everyone think that life is perfect, when it's not. Story of my life, faking it,' she muttered and shook her head. She felt a small, satisfying rush admitting this.

'Kind of the opposite to mine. Being an electrician sounds pretty lame-arse but I like it, you know?'

'At least it's actually helping people instead of selling them a false dream. That kind of sums up the difference between us, don't you think?'

He shot her a quizzical look. 'Well, we'll feed you if you do lose your job. Could be the best thing that ever happened to you. Maybe I could …' He shook his head and cleared his throat. 'Maybe Wendy could even help you plant your own vegie garden.'

*That's the thing*, she thought. *If you plant that vegetable garden with me something will happen. You know it and I know it and yet you're telling me to stay. But I'm here for my sister,* she thought. *I need to understand what happened to her and find some kind of peace before I can leave this place.*

# CHAPTER 13

Driftwood was in afternoon shadow as Phoebe knocked on the door and called out a 'hello'. She kicked off her sandals, peeled off her hat and listened. Silence. She had stayed away for a while after her painful conversation with Jez but the pull to come back here was too strong. She opened the door and peeked in.

Flick looked up from her laptop, which sat in the middle of the dining table surrounded by empty mugs. 'Oh hi,' she said. 'Sorry I'm off with the fairies.'

'You reckon it's gin o'clock yet?' Phoebe held out the lime offering from her front yard and smiled.

'I don't care if it isn't, I need a break. It's too hot to write.' She stretched and fanned herself with her hands. 'I've had too much coffee. I need a downer.'

'Have you had a productive morning? Killed off any characters?'

Flick laughed. 'I'm never going to be a good thriller writer. I can never kill anyone.'

'Occupational hazard. Maybe you need to try a different genre,' Phoebe said, moving into the kitchen and beginning to slice the limes. The scent of the citrus filled the air.

'What's this? Gin and tonic time and no one called me.' The Texan peeled off his straw hat and rubbed his hands together. 'Come and look what our garden grew.'

Phoebe and Flick examined his basket filled with fresh basil, mint, tomatoes, lettuce and zucchini.

'No one would ever know you used to be a big-shot banker,' said Phoebe. 'You've got gardener's hands now.'

'It's in my blood. My family ran a cattle ranch. I was so sure I wasn't going to work on the land and now here I am, up to my elbows in dirt. By choice.'

She smiled. 'Sometimes life seems predestined or circular or something, doesn't it?'

He shook his head. 'Sometimes I wonder what my life would have been like if Jenny hadn't got sick.'

Phoebe shot him a sympathetic look. He sometimes talked about his wife dying of cancer. It was clear Jenny had been the big love of his life and still influenced him a lot. It made Phoebe feel closer to him somehow. They all shared this sense of loss. Tommy and Jez had lost Pauline, their mother, the same slow, painful way. Even Asha, with her pregnancies that never came to be.

'How's your little vegie patch going, Phoebe? Jez said you were plotting one,' the Texan asked, his positivity kicking back in, as it inevitably did.

Phoebe cringed. 'I'm not a natural gardener, I'm afraid. But I do have lots of limes.'

The Texan nodded. 'Very handy. Have you seen the price of those buggers at the supermarket? With the amount of gin we all drink, we'd be broke if it wasn't for your abundant citrus tree.'

Phoebe laughed. She measured the gin into tall glasses and topped it with tonic water, ice and lime wedges. She handed the drinks around and settled herself at the picture window with her own. The sun was low over the trees and the river was as still as a millpond in the hazy afternoon heat. The Texan began washing and cutting his produce and the smell of basil and garlic infused the air.

Wendy gave Phoebe a wave as she came inside, then washed the dirt from her hands at the sink and poured herself a white wine.

Asha came into the kitchen barefoot, wearing what looked like her nightie with her hair tied into a knot on top of her head. 'Yes, I've been napping. I worked all morning in the studio but it's just too hot in there this afternoon.'

'Oh, a nap sounds good,' said Wendy.

'So what's happening?' Asha slid her hand along the kitchen bench.

'I'm cooking, everyone else is doing nothing,' the Texan said, taking a sip of his gin and giving the frying onions a stir.

Phoebe and Wendy shared an amused glance.

'Hmm, I see,' Asha said absently.

She seemed happier since the fires, her face more open. Phoebe hoped this might translate into her not being as prone to cutting remarks.

'I need some feedback. Anyone got a sec?' Asha asked, rearranging the bun on top of her head.

'Feedback on what?' Phoebe replied.

'There's this painting I've been working on. I never paint but a friend gave me a canvas and, I don't know, I just need to know if it's done, or if it's complete crap, in which case I won't take it to the market.'

Phoebe hadn't seen inside Asha's studio yet. She was curious, but it felt like entering dangerous territory. Their relationship seemed less fraught since their talk during the fires but there was still a frisson there, something unspoken. She wondered if Asha really wanted her feedback, but before she could ask, Asha grabbed Phoebe's gin and tonic.

'Come on, alcohol is allowed.'

The studio was little more than a shed with a tin roof, attached to the back of the house. Phoebe remembered it filled with clay pots and figures, the smell earthy and rich. It had once been Jez's mum's pottery studio. Now the last of the afternoon sun streamed through its grubby windows, illuminating the drying fabrics strung like washing from the roof. It smelled strongly of turpentine and chemicals.

'They say if you want the truth, ask your greatest enemy, not your best friend,' said Asha, handing Phoebe her drink.

Phoebe felt the jab of Asha's words hit her. 'Thanks,' she said sarcastically. Asha's brutality came on so fast, like a swift uppercut to the jaw. Phoebe was constantly side-stepping, gauging her mood.

'Well, you know what I mean. We're never going to be besties, are we?'

Phoebe made a non-committal noise, trying to shrug off her increasing discomfort.

'There'd be no point asking Flick. She'd just tell me what I want to hear.'

Asha ducked under some of the drying prints and Phoebe followed. She should be used to bluntness—she'd grown up with Camilla. The painting was a simple still life—a bowl of fruit, candles and a jar of flowers. The colours were luminous and it had the same ethereal quality as its creator.

'It's beautiful,' said Phoebe.

'Really? You sound like you're telling the truth.'

'I am.'

Asha picked up her paintbrush and dabbed at the canvas a little, chewing her lip. 'I haven't done this like, ever, but a friend is thinking of opening a gallery in the Bay and asked me to do some paintings, so I thought I'd give it a go.'

'You call that giving it a go? It's amazing.'

'I've never liked painting,' Asha said, flinging the paintbrush into a jar. 'My mum was a painter. Everything was about Mum being a bloody painter. I swore I'd never do that to my children.' She paused and Phoebe felt the weight of her words hang, heavy as the damp fabrics surrounding them.

'Your mum, was she good?'

'When she wasn't smoking weed or hungover, yeah, she was great. She taught, and won a big prize once. She pretty much acted like she was rich and famous from that day on, even though we never had any money.'

'The life of an artist always sounds a bit too romantic,' said Phoebe.

'Yeah, if your idea of romance is asking the neighbours for food because your mum has gone off with her new boyfriend and there's nothing to eat in the house.'

'She didn't feed you?'

'Oh, you know, when she remembered she had kids.'

Suddenly Phoebe saw Asha's longing for a child in full relief. She wanted someone to nurture as she had never been. And she understood why Driftwood was so precious to her—a place of plenty and safety.

'What about your dad?' Phoebe asked.

'He was a bloody artist as well. He went off to find himself, of course.' Asha picked up another brush and let out a long groan. 'And Mum let him, because, you know, free love and all.' She tucked a strand of hair behind her ear with the end of her brush, like she'd been doing it forever.

'But he never came back. He went and remarried some Italian woman and lived on the Amalfi Coast. He used to send us pictures of them on the beach. Mum pretended to be all cool about it, but she'd go into a drug stupor for days after those letters and it was me who had to make sure me and my brother got to school and ate.'

Phoebe was about to say how hard that would have been, when Asha continued. 'So, you think it's really okay? My painting? Honestly?'

'It's incredible, Asha, you've obviously got your mum's talent.' Phoebe could feel herself softening. 'Where is your mum now?'

'Living with a boyfriend—Len. Deadbeat,' Asha said under her breath. 'They're not that far ... maybe forty minutes from here. He's been around for the longest of them all. I don't visit them, it's too depressing. My brother does. He's a better person than me.'

'You're not a bad person.' The force of Phoebe's response surprised her. 'I don't really have a relationship with my mother either.'

Asha looked up, surprise brightening her face. 'What sort of number did your mum do on you?'

The studio felt suddenly airless. But Phoebe wanted to share this congruence in their lives. 'Think of the most stylish woman you can imagine. That's my mother. She's an interior stylist, very successful, but there's nothing else. The way things look is everything to her. I don't even think she knows who I am. If she saw me now the first thing she'd comment on would be my outfit, and it'd be a criticism.'

Asha was silent and their eyes met for a second. A flash of something passed between them, but then Asha looked away, busying herself with putting lids on paints. 'Sounds like our mums would get on,' she said. 'That must've been shit too, just with more food to eat.'

Phoebe laughed. 'Yeah, I guess I shouldn't complain too much.'

'Oh, hi Phoebe.'

She swung around to see Jez standing inches away from her, his head ducked awkwardly under some of the fabrics. She felt her cheeks grow hot.

'Hey, babe,' Asha seemed nonplussed about them all being in such close proximity. 'I was just showing Phoebe my painting. You like?'

Jez took a moment to reply. He looked between Phoebe and Asha and scratched his head. 'But you don't paint.'

Asha rolled her eyes. 'Yeah, get with the program.'

Phoebe was stuck between the two of them. The air was thick with turpentine and she felt light-headed with the smell.

'I'm with the program, babe. I just thought you hated painting 'cause of your mum,' he said, moving a piece of fabric out of the way carefully.

'Jose is opening a gallery in the Bay.'

'Oh, yeah?' He moved closer to inspect the painting. 'Yeah, it's good, babe.'

Phoebe couldn't remember or imagine Jez ever calling her 'babe'. They seemed to use it almost like an insult. She wished she could melt through the dusty, paint-splattered floor.

'Good? Just good?' prompted Asha.

'Well, I can hardly see it.'

'Here, let me move,' Phoebe said, grateful for an excuse to get out.

'Oh, dinner's nearly ready,' said Jez as their shoulders brushed.

'Oh, okay.' Phoebe was breathless by the time she reached the door.

# CHAPTER 14

Homegrown citrus winked in the sun and golden apples lolled in wooden barrels, their leaves still attached. There were slabs of sticky honeycomb and rolls of snowy goat's cheese under muslin. The churchyard was filled with meandering market-goers and the air was thick with the smell of barbecue and sweet incense. A sense of warmth ran through Phoebe and it wasn't just from the sunshine on her bare skin. She had always loved farmers' markets for the sense of community and the freshness of the produce. A fresh breeze shifted along the small hairs of her arms, making her shiver pleasantly. She knew what this feeling was. It was freedom.

Phoebe had resigned. She'd had a decision to make when her extra week of leave was nearly up. She'd finally charged her phone and driven into the Bay. The café was a chain of the kind she usually would have avoided in Sydney. It sold coffee in various sugary incarnations and muffins sat bloated behind the sweating glass counter. There was nothing gluten-free or with activated nuts, but none of that seemed to matter to her anymore.

Out of habit she ordered a short black and then reassessed. Why couldn't she have dairy? That's how she actually preferred her coffee. She changed her order to a latte, remembering how easily Jez had recalled her favoured drink. She found a corner booth and sat down, heart beating fast as she opened her email. Her job was the last thing tethering her to her old life. Could she really let that go? It had always been as though working for Joet et Halo somehow conferred the champagne brand's wealth and effervescence onto her person. She thought of her boss, Kate, who famously drank one glass of champagne every night without fail to remind her of how special and rare life was. For a long time Phoebe had loved that idea and aspired to be like Kate, with her smooth hair and her pared-back, monochrome designer clothing.

But life could not be appeased by a bubbly drink. The pain could not be eased with the smoothness of hair cuticles or the satisfaction of owning three charcoal cashmere tops. Phoebe thought about what Flick had said about nature, about how it was healing her. Is that what was happening to Phoebe, too? Was the river, with its endless ebb—muscular and frightening one minute, sparkling and mischievous the next—teaching her something? Her life had never felt smaller, less important, but she had never felt more free.

Her coffee arrived and she took a sip, enjoying its rich creaminess. Her fingers stumbled over the opening words of the email but she pressed on.

*Hi Kate,*

*Thank you for being so understanding of my taking extra time off on account of the bushfires.*

*I'm afraid that I'm making contact to resign from my position. I've been through a bit of a difficult time lately. The engagement to Nathaniel fell through and it has forced me to reassess my priorities.*

This was where she paused. She was about to write something banal about taking time out from office work but instead her fingers started moving more swiftly over her phone.

*To be honest, I was never entirely happy in my role. I'm not sure how I ended up spending all my days peddling a glamorous life that had become so far from my reality. Part of me loved the beautiful pictures, the parties, the veneer. But it's not me. It never made me happy and now I think I finally understand why.*

*Thank you, Kate, I always respected and looked up to you.*

*Best wishes,*

*Phoebe*

She pressed send before she lost her courage. Her hands were shaking as she wrapped her fingers around her coffee cup, but her insides were singing so loudly she felt dizzy. She would never drink a short black again.

She thought about how she would have acted if she'd gone back there. She knew she would have framed the breakup with Nathaniel differently, as a mutual decision that they were both happy about. She would have delivered the news with a strong, fake smile and then opened her computer and felt herself getting smaller and smaller, like Alice in Wonderland, tricked into thinking that if you imagined something, it became real.

Phoebe knew her resignation and breakup would now become the gossip of the mostly female office. She cringed, imagining the mixture of pity and false sympathy flashing from screen to screen, eye to eye. But she had nothing to lose. She wasn't going back. She would wake tomorrow with the sun to the sound of kookaburras echoing across the river.

The gentle bustle of people moving past her at the market brought her back to the present. She picked up a lychee and rolled its rough skin between her palms, inhaled its sweet scent. Maybe she'd make lychee and mint martinis at Driftwood tonight. She stood still and watched the Saturday morning crowd. Mothers pushing children in prams, older people wearing sensible sun hats, families and a few young people out enjoying the sun. She saw things, absorbed things into her body now in a way she couldn't ever remember doing before. To take her mind off her resignation, Wendy had helped her plant tomatoes, lettuce, carrots and potato in the back garden, and for the past week she had spent the cool of the morning working there. She enjoyed the soft grit of the soil, its new-rain smell. The work was simple, mindless, nothing like the exhaustive detail of the menial tasks she'd performed in her job. Her skin had browned and her hair had honeyed from the hours spent outside. She laughed when she told Flick and Asha how much she usually spent on self-tan and hairdresser appointments to get the same effect. She thought about all the handbags she'd lusted after and saved for, the designer dresses she'd felt special and powerful in, the make-up, the shoes. They had been important. They'd made her happy, in some fleeting, heady way, but it had never lasted. And then she'd needed something new.

Here she had been rotating the same few items of clothing, handwashing to conserve tank water and hanging clothes out to line-dry in the fierce midday sun. It reminded her of backpacking through Europe. It was astonishing how little you really needed when your sense of satisfaction was coming from somewhere else. She knew it was coming from Driftwood.

Phoebe spotted Asha's stall at the far end of the market, overlooking the sparkling bend in the river below. Asha saw her and waved. It felt like something had shifted between them since their chat about their mothers in the studio, despite the awkwardness of Jez turning up. Asha had already sold her painting—Wendy had adored it and begged Asha for it until she'd relented.

Phoebe had promised to come and see Asha's market stall. What she hadn't realised until this moment was that Asha made baby clothing from the screen-printed fabrics drying in the studio. Her heart ached as she walked towards the trestle table, strung with brightly coloured fabric flags and piled with tiny bibs, singlets and a few cushions. Asha was putting a singlet into a paper bag for a woman carrying a baby in a sling. Phoebe brushed her hand over the soft cotton with a pink and purple elephant pattern.

'Do you like them?'

'They're very cute,' Phoebe said.

Another woman with an older baby, chubby legs kicking in a front pack, approached and cooed over the bibs. Asha smiled, but Phoebe could see vulnerability in her eyes. The woman paid for a pack of three and left.

'So, mums are a big customer base?'

Asha rolled her eyes.

'That must be hard,' Phoebe said, hoping for honest Asha, not brutal Asha, to respond.

Asha straightened, as though bracing herself against the question, but then her shoulders collapsed in defeat. 'Out of anything I've ever made, the bibs sell the best. I manage to get rid of the soft toys, but without the bibs and singlets I wouldn't have a livelihood. It's just life's way of being ironic, I guess.'

Phoebe shot her a reassuring look. 'You know, my best friend has just had a baby. I'll take a three-pack as well,' she said, reaching for the elephant print. 'As long as you don't mind.'

Asha laughed and waved a hand. 'It's okay. I've accepted that I'm going to be the crazy old lady who makes beautiful bibs for other people's children.'

Phoebe pressed her mouth into a sympathetic line.

An older woman approached the stall and bought a pack of the bibs for her granddaughter's baby.

'Like hotcakes around here,' said Phoebe.

Asha raised her eyebrows. 'I'm not even joking. Jez doesn't know. He tells everyone I sell cushions.'

'When was the last cushion you sold?'

Asha laughed dryly. 'Oh, probably a few months ago.'

The moment was broken with the approach of a heavy-set man with a serious expression, wiping a handkerchief across his forehead.

'Hankies. What about hankies with purple elephants on them?' suggested Asha, pressing her hand to her mouth as she tried to suppress a laugh. 'Bibs and hankies, something for the very young or very old. Pretty much sums up the people round here.'

That set off a wave of giggles in Phoebe but the man stopped next to her and she straightened.

'Sorry, you don't know me.' He cleared his throat. 'My mother lives next door to you. Phoebe, isn't it? I've seen you in your yard.' He stuck out a sweaty hand. 'Chester Hill.' He had a friendly demeanour and the same sun-worn face that so many men had here.

'I just wanted to introduce myself. Ginny is quite fond of you already. I know she's happy to have a new neighbour after …' His voice trailed off. 'After what happened.'

Phoebe shook his hand awkwardly and shielded her eyes from the glare to get a better look at him. 'Your mother is quite remarkable. I can't believe she's blind and lives on the river by herself. Well, with Steffi.'

Chester shook his head. 'She's as stubborn as a person with 20/20 vision. I've been trying to get her into a nice retirement village for years but she insists on staying on the river. She's never listened to anyone. From what I've heard, your sister was just as headstrong and independent. They were a match, those two.' He smiled. 'Sorry, I hope you don't mind me talking about it. It was just such a shock when … Mum took it very badly.'

Phoebe's eyes pricked with tears. 'No, it's okay.'

Chester rubbed his chin. 'Sorry, I just wanted to come and say hello, and if you ever need anything, I'm sure anyone in the street would do anything for you. I've got a full tool box if you ever need any handyman help.'

Phoebe smiled weakly, overcome by the emotion this man had just expressed. 'Thanks, Chester, that's really kind of you.'

'Mum's just over by the church in the sun. She asked me if she could have a word with you when I said you were here.'

'Oh, she's here? Sure, I'll come over.' Phoebe looked at Asha who was quietly sorting singlets, but she could tell she'd been listening.

'See you later?'

Asha nodded and flashed a small smile, and for a second Phoebe thought she saw sympathy on her face.

Ginny sat at a table in the make-shift café next to the old stone church. Steffi was by her side.

The dog greeted Phoebe with a small bark and several licks and Ginny smiled up at her. 'Oh Phoebe, is that you?'

'Hi Ginny, you look like you've got a lovely place in the sun here.'

'I'm so pleased you're here, I've been meaning to talk to you about something for days.'

'And I've been meaning to bring you some limes and one of my lemon and yoghurt cakes and tell you about my vegie patch.'

'Come, sit,' Ginny patted the chair beside her.

'How have you been?' Phoebe asked, moving the chair closer.

'It's just that I remembered something. My memory is terrible. Not what it used to be. But anyway, I was napping the other afternoon and I woke up from a dream about Karin. And for some reason the dream made me remember a conversation I had with her.' Ginny's hand fluttered at her throat. 'She'd gone away one weekend but I was quite poorly and Chester was in Sydney, so Karin had said she'd have her mobile phone on the whole time in case I needed to ring someone.'

Phoebe helped Ginny take a sip of water, feeling her pulse quicken at Ginny's mood. 'Sorry Phoebe, I'm just feeling a little emotional today.'

'That's okay,' Phoebe said, reaching out and patting her hand.

'Anyway, I did need to call Karin and I called her very late at night. Silly, really, I should have just called an ambulance but

I just wanted to hear a friendly voice, I suppose and to know I wasn't overreacting. And ...'

'What happened?' Phoebe's throat constricted.

'Karin answered ... I woke her up. And I was very feverish at the time and she helped me because she rang the ambulance for me, sweet girl. And I'm not sure I even properly registered it at the time because I was so unwell, but there was a man's voice in the background.'

'In the background as in he was beside her? And you said you woke her? She was sleeping?' Phoebe's mind was spinning.

'I think so, yes. As you know I'm more attuned to sound than most and it was definitely a man close to the phone and not background noise like a TV.'

'What did he say?'

'I can't really remember, it's all a bit of a blur, just that he was talking to Karin.'

Phoebe's hand trembled as she squeezed Ginny's hand. 'And that's why you subconsciously thought she was seeing someone on those weekend trips.'

Ginny squeezed back. 'Yes, I know I'm a doddery old lady but that's why I thought she was involved with a man.'

Back at the house, Phoebe found herself standing in front of Karin's open wardrobe. She still avoided this room, still slept on the sofa, even though there were two other bedrooms. She took down the shoeboxes stacked on the high shelf above the clothes. She wasn't sure what she was expecting to find. Old letters? A diary? Some evidence of this man Ginny had heard her with? No, it was all too introspective for Karin. Theirs wasn't the kind of family to go combing through private things.

As far as she knew, no one had gone through Karin's phone or email. Had the police even looked? She had no idea. If only she had been stronger, she could have, should have, but she just hadn't had the strength to face it.

A phone conversation with her dad came back to her, shrouded in a haze of emotion so thick her throat made a strangled sound. It had been a day after they'd been told Karin had died.

'Honey, the police are asking some questions.' Her dad's voice sounded different, and yet so familiar. He was talking to her as though she were a child again, as though he were trying to protect her from the world. 'We're not really sure how to answer them, but you were closest to her.'

'What? What have they found?' She was keenly aware of the desperation in her voice, and then she realised it didn't matter what they'd found because Karin was gone.

'They're asking about a Jack. There was a piece of paper with the name "Jack" written on it next to her landline, and a time—2 pm. Do you know who that could have been?'

She hadn't known. Her mind had been unable to focus on anything but the pain. Thoughts were scattered, awful things. All she could do was surrender to her feelings.

'No,' she had said. 'No, she didn't know anyone called "Jack".'

But now, kneeling before her sister's closet, smelling the faint note of flowers mingled with dust, she remembered. Maybe it had been talking to Ginny. Maybe it was walking into Karin's room and staring at her things. Jack had been the name of the special-needs dog Karin had fallen in love with at the kennel. The one Phoebe had forbidden her to get.

She laughed out loud. Karin had made a time to go and see him, despite Phoebe's discouragement over the phone. That was so completely Karin.

*You were about to pick up a dog with special needs. You did not kill yourself. Who were you with that night Ginny called and how did you end up in that river?*

She sat on Karin's bed, running her hand over the quilted cover as though her fingertips could find the answers she needed, here where Karin had slept. Phoebe didn't know where to put this new information. She felt like screaming it out loud. Making it real. Was it real? Or was being back here just sending her slowly mad? She looked at the old analogue clock, still steadfastly keeping the time on Karin's bedside table. There was still an hour until gin and tonic time at Driftwood but she needed to be around other people.

'Where is everyone?' Phoebe asked, finding Jez making a sandwich in the kitchen.

He looked up and smiled. 'Want some? I can make runny honey bread for you.'

She laughed. It had been so long since she'd heard someone call it that. She'd hated sandwiches as a kid and the only thing she'd ever had on bread was honey. She hadn't even wanted it to be called a sandwich. Nostalgia swept through her, sweet and aching. Jez knew her.

'You okay?' Jez put down the knife and studied her. 'You look a bit ... I don't want to say "off" but ...'

'Um ...' She squeezed her eyes shut and grimaced. 'I don't know. I just needed some company, I think.'

'What's happened?'

He knew her better than she knew herself. He always had. Nathaniel had never had a particular interest in seeing into her, and gradually Phoebe had stopped expecting him to notice how she was feeling. Somehow, she'd convinced herself along the way that it was a man thing—that men couldn't read emotions. And yet here was Jez, opening her stuck-together pages. She sat down at the kitchen bench and took two limes out of her pocket. She rolled one and sniffed it. 'You're not usually around for gin and tonic time.'

'Would it go with a ham and cheese sandwich?'

'Gin and tonic goes with everything.'

Phoebe fixed the drinks as he ate with the same big, hungry bites as when he was a kid, leaving the crusts and wiping his mouth with the back of his hand. They sat at the table, and he told her about his morning visiting a mate and his wife's newborn at the hospital, awe and sadness in his voice.

He brushed crumbs from his fingers. 'Asha can never come to these things. Too painful for her. Then there'll be the christening and the first birthday and it will just keep going.'

'It might still happen for you guys.' Phoebe said with false cheer. She felt torn. She wanted to reassure him, make him feel okay but doing so held its own awkwardness.

Jez pushed his plate away and took a gulp of his drink as though it were soft drink rather than hard spirits. 'I can tell something's up with you. I've told you about my crap day. You were never good at hiding your feelings.'

She ran her hands down her face and took a large sip of her drink. 'Just before the fires, I met my neighbour, Ginny. The one whose house you checked on. She's blind and ...' Phoebe paused, slightly unsure of whether to open this whole thing up to Jez. 'She knew Karin, but she said a few odd things. Anyway, I haven't been able to let them go. And today we had another chat at the markets. But it just ... I don't know. Apparently Karin used to make bunches of flowers for Ginny based on their meanings, because she's blind and can't see them. She'd given Ginny a book about it and ... you know Karin's suicide note was written in flowers? And Ginny mentioned Karin went away every few weekends. I wasn't aware ...'

It was possibly the effect of the alcohol, but tears crept into her eyes. 'And the worst thing is that maybe Karin was closer to her blind neighbour than to me. Maybe I didn't know my sister at all. I thought she told me everything but she didn't.' Phoebe sniffed and wiped under her eyes with her fingers. 'Sorry, I don't know why this has suddenly affected me so much.'

Jez stood and moved behind her. He gently folded his arms around her shoulders. She was seventeen again and caught in the intensely personal smell of him. With this smell came the feeling of the first time he kissed her, water from the dam cool on his lips, lily pads at her shoulders. She remembered the watery buzz of a dragonfly hovering, his lips on the back of her neck. The longing made her unable to stop crying.

'That's not true,' said Jez. 'You did know her, of course you did. But people are complex. You can't know everything about someone.'

Phoebe turned and looked at him. Close up, the creep of time had made lines, like paper softly folded, around his eyes, but the blue-grey of his irises had not faded. 'Small things, yes. But someone taking their own life? Someone doing things that no one but a blind old lady knew about?'

Jez shook his head and then looked at her. 'This isn't just about meeting Ginny, is it? You don't believe Karin killed herself, do you?'

Phoebe swallowed. 'No,' she said with a force that she hadn't anticipated. 'No, I don't. But there were things about my sister that I'm just finding out. Maybe I didn't know her as well as I thought I did.'

'You did know her, Phoebe. And if you don't think Karin walked into that river by choice then I believe you.'

Phoebe took Jez's hand. 'Thank you,' she said.

Jez, squeezed her shoulders and then moved towards the French doors. 'Have you told your family any of this? What do they think?'

She hung her head and sighed. 'Mum and Camilla think she was depressed about not being married with kids at her age. Or lonely, or something, because she was here, where they thought was the middle of nowhere.'

'But not you. You didn't think that.'

'I spoke to her every week. She was good. She was as happy as any of us. Her life wasn't perfect—sometimes the shop stressed her if it was too quiet, but she was coping fine. She had a new idea to expand the florist business, and she had made an appointment to adopt a dog.' Saying this out loud made Phoebe cry more. She looked at Jez but he was nodding, his eyes soft with emotion.

'She didn't have depression or anxiety. I would have noticed if she'd suddenly changed.' *It was up to me to notice.* 'But I don't know, Camilla and Mum didn't really question her suicide. Maybe they didn't know her like I did.'

\* \* \*

A memory returned to her, faintly, a whisper.

'I want them to be sunflowers.' Phoebe's voice was small. The sadness, days of crying, had made her voice so small.

'Darling, that would be entirely inappropriate.' Her mother shook her head and caressed the froth of cream roses in front of them. Her mother seemed to only ever use words of affection when softening a blow.

'But she loved sunflowers,' said Phoebe, wishing she could muster more strength, more fight.

'They smell terrible,' said Camilla, scrunching up her nose. 'So big.'

They were on their way to the funeral home to plan Karin's service. Her dad was getting everyone coffees and there was a florist next to the café.

Her mother pursed her lips. 'It's just not suitable.'

'I don't think we could really say Karin had a favourite flower,' said Camilla. 'She was a florist, she appreciated all flowers. Oh, these are gorgeous.' She picked up a bunch of poppies, their little faces manic and bright. 'Too red though.'

'Why? Karin would have wanted bright flowers. She was bright. She loved colour,' said Phoebe.

Her mother fixed her with a look—the look she'd learned as a child that cautioned her not to go any further. 'You can't put bright flowers, let alone sunflowers, on the coffin of someone who has taken their own life.'

Phoebe had felt a rage form within her and she wanted to grab the cream roses and shred them with her fingers, throw them in her mother's face. 'She didn't kill herself.'

Her mother made a huffing sound.

Phoebe looked to Camilla. 'Is that what you think, too? That she really did that to herself?'

Camilla picked up a bunch of tulips, hiding her face behind their elegant foliage. 'It's not us who think that, it's the police. They said her death was not suspicious.'

Phoebe pressed her palms into her eye sockets. 'But this is Karin we're talking about. Our Karin.' Phoebe felt her dad's presence behind her and was grateful for it. She turned to him, hoping for support. 'Dad?'

His eyes met hers but dropped to his feet. And then the moment was lost, and Camilla was reaching for her macchiato, saying how tired she was. They had gone to the funeral home and there had been no colourful flowers on Karin's coffin. They had never spoken about the way Karin had died again.

The warmth of Jez's hand on her arm roused her from the memory.

'You did know her best, Phoebe,' he said.

'I didn't even put her favourite flowers on her coffin.'

The sun flashed as it caught a movement in the water. 'Sometimes I feel like if I stare into the river I'll see her face. Sometimes I feel like she's still there, just below the surface. Like she's in the river now.'

Jez opened the French doors to the sound of the breeze in the she-oaks. He faced away from her, towards the river, transfixed as it transformed into a sheet of light. 'I couldn't believe it when I heard. I mean, Karin and I kind of missed each other as adults but ...' He paused. 'I remember once— we must only have been about thirteen—we were playing hide and seek and you had the most awesome hiding spot under the jetty, and we were all looking for you for ages. I mean, it felt like the whole day in that kid way of when days just went on and on.'

Phoebe smiled. 'I loved those days.'

'And Cammie was the first to give up, because she was hot and tired and needed a drink.'

'Typical.'

'Tommy was annoyed that you'd outsmarted even him, and me and Karin were trying to figure out where the hell you were. It was getting to the point of calling the parents, but Karin was like, "No, she's all right." And I asked how she knew, and she said that you'd saved her life in the river, and ever since that day it was her mission to look after you. It was like a superpower—she could always feel if you were okay.'

Phoebe felt his words smart in her chest. 'She said that?'

Jez pursed his lips together. 'You know, when I heard she died, I thought back to that exact moment. She kept looking and looking when we'd all given up.'

'And she was the one who found me, freezing, standing in the water up to my waist.' Phoebe smiled even though her cheeks were wet. 'She wasn't even angry with me. It was so strange. I remember how sometimes she felt older than me and other times I felt older than her.'

'Maybe it was because you were both looking after each other.'

Phoebe shook her head and tried to breathe. 'Except I couldn't in the end, could I? Since she died I feel like I've been running and running because I've felt so guilty. Instead I looked to Camilla. She has the husband and the kids and the big happy house. She seems to have it together, you know? You have no idea how many hours I spent researching my wedding, Jez. I think that's when Nathaniel and I grew apart—I was plotting my perfect life with him, while under the surface it was disintegrating around me and I couldn't even tell. I don't know when the point came that he decided he didn't want me, that he wouldn't do it. And I don't remember knowing that it was him I wanted, really him. Maybe it was just the idea of him? Maybe it was just the thing you do? It was all my idea to get married. I remember the exact way his face looked when I said we should get married. It was noncommittal. But I couldn't accept it. I tried to make him propose to me even though he didn't want to.'

Jez shook his head. 'Give yourself a break, Phoebs. You were grieving. You'd lost your sister and best friend. So what? You wanted love and stability.' He looked at her with such tenderness that she wanted to reach out and touch him. But then he turned back to the river and laughed under his breath. 'The perfect life. What is that? It's having two children.'

She made a sad, clicking sound with her tongue. 'Oh Jez, who's to say that's perfection?'

'Asha.'

'If she wants it so badly, why doesn't she leave you?'

His laugh was joyless. 'It's as though we both chose the worst person to try to make babies with. She had problems initially, but then she had an operation for endometriosis that they think pretty much fixed it. But we still couldn't conceive. Then they realised that it was me. It's got lots of technical names but long and short of it, I can't make her pregnant. I've changed my diet, exercise, taken vitamins and supplements. Everything.'

He'd given up so much for her, it must have been like a slap in the face that she kept smoking.

'We could use a donor but I don't want to. She blames my pride. She blames me for it all. She suggested Tommy, but I know him. He won't because of the autism risk—it's why they won't have another child … and it would all just be too weird. I wouldn't even ask him and she hates me for that.'

'It sounds like it's been hard.'

He shrugged and walked out onto the veranda, and Phoebe followed. The sun slanted low and warm into their eyes. She leaned her elbows on the railing.

'Do you ever think back to how simple our love was?' he asked, eyes half closed against the glare. 'Playing each other mix tapes in my room and lying on the jetty for hours? We were so …'

She thought he was going to say 'naïve' but instead he said 'hopeful'.

'Everything was before us and we thought we'd do it all together. It felt like everything would be lit with this … I don't know how to describe it—light. If we were just together.'

Phoebe's heart raced and her stomach churned. She knew exactly the feeling he was talking about. The way her whole body illuminated in his presence. Every nerve cell reaching for his touch. She felt exactly the same way now standing right here. None of it had diminished, not a single bit. 'Did we talk about living in Sydney together? I can't remember,' she said.

'I think it was the only thing we didn't talk about. You were going to go travelling and then come back here. I don't think we ever really went into the details past that point. I knew you wanted to go to university and have a life in Sydney and I guess I thought I was capable of it. But when you came back from Europe you'd changed somehow. You were, I don't know, more worldly or something. There was this distance between us that made it impossible to ... you know what happened. I just knew I couldn't leave here, I suppose.'

'It's funny, I always thought I abandoned you,' she said.

'No, it was me who abandoned you.'

'And then your mum got sick.'

'Asha came along at that time and she and Mum got on so well. I suppose part of what's kept us together all this time is that Mum absolutely loved her. They shared that creative spirit, I think. I feel like I'd be somehow letting Mum down ...'

'I knew your mum, too. I think she'd just want you to be happy, Jez.' Phoebe didn't feel bad about saying it because it was the simple truth.

He turned to her. 'Do you think we could be happy? In that way we once were? Or was it just because we were so young and we'd had no pain yet? We hadn't lost people ... We hadn't looked into someone's eyes and seen resentment where we'd expected love. We hadn't felt like failures.'

She started to cry, but silently, bracing her body against the railing. She pressed her forehead against the cool wood and cried for his pain and for how hard he was trying. For the love he had for his dead mother. For Asha who just wanted to have a family with him. She cried for Tommy not having another child because of autism and she cried for herself and the deep hurt of rejection and being let down when so much was riding on being buoyed up. She cried for Karin, who she didn't protect after all.

When all her tears had been spent, she felt Jez's warm hand curl around hers. His eyes were wet.

'I don't want to hurt anyone,' she said.

He kissed the back of her hand. 'That's why I love you.'

# CHAPTER 15

The rain fell in sheets across the river and Phoebe picked over a bowl of dry cereal. It stuck to the roof of her mouth and she could barely swallow.

Phoebe had never thought herself capable of being the other woman. It was something that women with more cleavage and less empathy did. But this was Jez. They had done nothing but hold hands as the sun slid towards the water, but a line had been crossed, she knew that. It wasn't a physical line as much as an emotional one. Phoebe didn't know if she believed in soulmates, but sitting there overlooking the river, she felt as though she had never been closer to someone. And she realised that maybe this was what Nathaniel had been talking about when he told her something was missing. Maybe it was simply being vulnerable to someone and feeling seen and held and safe. It was glimpsing someone's hurts and pains and still loving what you saw. She didn't know why she couldn't do this with Nathaniel. She just couldn't.

She thought back to the beginning with Nathaniel. Had there been an opening up about their feelings? An emotional connection? No, not like she had with Jez. If she was completely honest, Nathaniel had always had a slightly distracted quality, as though there was something going on somewhere else that he was missing out on. She'd never taken it personally, but perhaps she should have. The irony was that it had initially been him who had pursued her, even though her heart hadn't at first been in it. If only she'd listened to her own feelings—perhaps they'd been telling her that she needed something more. Their relationship had been a sphere that turned on the axis of dinner dates with friends and who would do the vacuuming on the weekend. Of course, she'd never lived with Jez and shared those practicalities, but somehow she knew the deeper thread of their communication would make things different. It was strange now to think that the more superficial relationship she'd had with Nate had been enough. It was strange how little you could know yourself and hide your own feelings.

And Jez. He wasn't one to hide from anything. He would never have gone looking for a bit on the side, Phoebe knew that. But unhappiness and circumstance had woven a particular kind of net, steeped in the honeyed nostalgia of their past. They had known each other in that difficult time of late childhood, so their becoming, their movement into the world, had been shared. It was as though something formative had fossilised in their brains and their bodies.

Phoebe had wanted to still time on that veranda yesterday, his hand in hers. The first sounds of others in the house and they had parted, Jez to shower and Phoebe to help Wendy and the Texan with dinner, guilty and elated and pouring too much gin into the cocktails. She avoided eye contact with Jez for the rest of the evening but she could feel the pull of him on her body like a rope, tethering a boat to the shore just beneath the waterline.

She got up now and put her cereal bowl in the sink. The rain thrummed louder and lashed against the windows. The river was pewter and pock-marked with it. There would be no gardening today and how could she go to Driftwood and face everyone after what had happened? She and Jez hadn't had time to discuss the mechanics of how to inflict as little pain as possible. There was no temptation afforded by surreptitious text messages, or any kind of electronic communication, because there was none here. For that she was grateful. She was adamant that she wouldn't allow anything to happen until Jez left Asha. But how would Jez leave Asha? And what would the shape and texture of something new look and feel like? The fallout would be huge. Surely Flick would leave with Asha, and what about Wendy and the Texan? Wendy knew Jez and Asha had problems but even if the break was clean, it wouldn't be really. Everyone would wonder when it had begun between the two of them. And when had something begun? She remembered back to the night of the missing boat. The things Jez had said.

She found her mobile phone abandoned on the windowsill above the kitchen sink and scrolled through the unread messages from the last time she'd been in range. She stopped at Hellie's. It had been too long since Phoebe had texted, let alone spoken to her closest friend. She couldn't believe she'd been here for several weeks. It had been too hard at the time to admit even to Hellie that things with Nathaniel were over. Hellie was the one person she couldn't hide from. Hellie knew that the decision not to get engaged wasn't mutual. She knew how all-consumed Phoebe had been with wedding plans. Speaking to her would be like having to stare into a mirror and not look away.

It was 10.15 am; Hellie would probably be at home for Ava's morning nap.

She picked up after the first ring.

'Hi Hellie, it's Phoebe.' It was strange addressing her friend so formally. They had long ago lost the need for naming each other in greeting but she was calling from a landline.

'Oh my God.' There was relief in Hellie's voice and it made Phoebe feel bad about not calling sooner. 'I was just saying to Mum that I felt like putting out a missing person's alert.'

'I'm sorry. I'm sort of a self-imposed missing person.'

Hellie paused. 'Oh Phoebs, it's so shit. It's really over then with Nathaniel. Over, over?'

'Yep.'

'And you just wanted to escape from everything?'

'Yep.'

'Isn't it hard being at the cottage though?'

This was what she loved about her friend, she was so intuitive. Phoebe's voice was husky with withheld emotion. 'Yes. But don't feel too sorry for me. I've quit my job to grow vegetables.'

'No. What? How? When?' Hellie's voice had the bright tinge of hysteria. 'How will I survive without my freebie bottles of champagne? My plus one invites? I would have done your job.'

'You've got a baby.'

'What baby?'

Phoebe laughed, imagining Hellie's straight face. She had never admitted her real feelings about her job, even to Hellie. She enjoyed taking her to the parties and lavishing free wine on her. It had been enough for a while.

'Hellie, I know I haven't gone into the whole Nathaniel thing with you. I don't know if I have the energy.'

'I don't even have the energy and I haven't lived it.' She paused and there was a rushing sound as she moved the phone. 'Just picking up Ava. She's hungry. I'm a mobile cow right now.'

'How's it going? Is she beautiful? Are you getting more sleep since we last spoke?'

Hellie sighed deeply. 'You have no idea. No one tells you how hard this is going to be. Why don't they? I may not have reproduced if I'd known.'

'I guess that's the point. It's a biological imperative to ensure the survival of the species.' Phoebe thought of Asha, desperate for a baby, Jenna's shattered dream of a normal child. She felt like telling both these women's stories to Hellie but her friend had her own journey, and it was hard as well. 'So, still no sleep?'

'Not enough. Broken sleep is just torture, really. But here am I whingeing and you've just been through ...' Ava's cry ricocheted down the phone line.

'You need to feed her, it's okay. Go, go.'

'You're not off the hook that quickly. Hang on, I'll put you on speaker phone.' There was a little yelp from Ava and then she settled. Hellie's voice was more distant now. 'She's on the boob. Aren't you lonely down there? Does it feel strange?'

'No, strangely, it feels right. It's where I need to be right now.'

Phoebe considered how much to tell Hellie. She knew Jez was her first love. Hellie had a first love too—Marc with a 'c' who had been a very sophisticated struggling poet, in the way only twenty-one-year-olds could be. Phoebe wanted to know whether what she and Jez felt was merely a circumstance of their past. Would Hellie feel unmoored by seeing Marc?

'Hells, I need to ask …' If she opened this particular door, Hellie would launch into a barrage of questions Phoebe didn't yet know the answers to.

'I still can't believe it. You and Nathaniel were good together.'

Phoebe paused. 'Were we?'

'Yeah. It made sense, you know?'

'No, but now that you know it's over, tell me—did we have chemistry? Were we right? He doesn't think we did, that we were, obviously.'

Hellie was quiet and baby sounds filled the receiver. 'In my experience, if you have to ask someone else if you have chemistry then you probably don't. But you looked great together.'

'So, no.'

'Yeah, but we both know that chemistry isn't the be all and end all. Look at you and Jez, and me and Marc. Sometimes it's just nice, better to have chemistry as a pubescent memory.'

'Hells … Jez is here. I wasn't going to tell you but—'

'What, living there? I thought he was married and living in Canberra.'

'He was, until recently. They moved back into Driftwood and run it as a guest house of sorts.'

She clicked her tongue. 'Why am I sensing there's more to this particular story?'

Phoebe went quiet. She didn't know what to say, where to start.

'Oh my God. There's something going on.'

Phoebe sighed. 'Yes. Something, but I don't know exactly what, or why, or … but I just—'

'You're feeling bad. He's married.'

'Not happily though.'

'Is any cheating man happily married? Sorry ... I'm just worried that you're on the rebound and all those first love feelings are just stirring up—'

'I know, I've been so aware of the rebound thing and keeping my distance, but I can't explain it, we just seem to always end up alone talking—just talking, but there's this thing between us.'

'Chemistry.'

'Maybe. Yes. I don't know. And then there's all these feelings I've been having about Karin.'

'Of course you have. Everything of hers is down there. The anniversary is coming up.'

'It's more than that though.'

A knock on the front door interrupted her. 'Hang on, sorry, there's someone at the door and this phone isn't cordless. Give me a sec.' She placed the handset on the bench.

Her heart thumped thickly against her chest when she opened the screen door to find a police officer on the step. He was short and muscular with a neck and shoulders that looked too big for his body; the human version of a bulldog. He wore dark glasses, which he slid up to sit on top of his closely shaved head. 'Sorry to disturb. Are you Phoebe Price?'

'Yes.'

'You reported a missing dinghy.' He studied his notepad. 'A rowboat, a few weeks ago?'

'Yes.' A rush of relief took her adrenalin down a notch. 'It's not worth much but I just thought I should let the police know there are people taking things from the river.'

'We've located it.' He flipped through the notepad with deft fingers. 'Down at Burra Lakes. A whole heap of stolen goods, motorbikes, boats, jet skis. Trying to sell them at a garage sale, if you can believe that.'

'Really?'

'We have one of the suspects in custody. A pretty violent individual to be roaming this area, so it's good you brought the theft to our attention.'

'Oh?' Phoebe replied, feeling a shiver run through her.

'Yeah, but there's nothing to worry about, forensics will release the boat shortly if you'd like to pick it up.'

She felt like mentioning her feelings about her sister's death to this policeman but she'd seen enough crime shows to know that he would look at her kindly, as though she were a bit simple, and repeat the facts at hand.

'Oh, I'm not that keen to have it back, to be honest. What about the other boats that were stolen on the same night?'

The policeman's shoulders lifted. 'Yours was the only one found at this stage. We think it was probably the same people, but they may have already gotten rid of the others.'

'And who was the man you arrested and what did he do?' She crossed her arms and hugged them to her.

'The man we have in custody is on domestic violence and manslaughter charges.'

Phoebe felt her stomach drop but she smiled and thanked the man. Was she really now imagining that Karin could have been hurt by some random violent thief? But Ginny's words came back to her. She'd been sleeping next to a random man that Phoebe never knew about.

She watched the policeman walk down the drive then remembered Hellie and rushed back.

'Sorry, a policeman was at the door. Can we continue our conversation another time Hellie? And yes, I promise I won't sleep with Jez.'

PART THREE

*Undercurrents*

# THEN

'Can we go up a bit further?' asked Jez, one hand on the dog's back, the other skimming the water as he and Tommy pulled the boat off the sand into the deep.

Tommy bit his lip and stuck his finger up, as if testing the air for something. Karin wondered what it was. He looked down the river towards Driftwood and then upriver. 'We could just motor up to the bend, I guess,' he said, checking the face of his watch. 'It's still early.'

'Are you sure we should do that? We told your mum we'd just go to the picnic area,' said Phoebe, hopping into the boat, her eyes meeting Karin's and asking silently if she was okay with it.

As second in line, if she said no, they wouldn't go. Karin shrugged off the uneasy feeling those strange men on the bank had given her. They were still near the rocks but they looked like they were packing their fishing stuff into the back of their big truck anyway. She actually did want to see what was beyond the bend of the river. She'd never been that far and it was where the sharks breed, and it would be kind of cool to see one.

She nodded her agreement and squeezed Phoebe's hand to let her know it was all okay. Tommy revved the motor, the boat once again cutting through the glassy water like a knife. It was hot with the life vest snug around her body and Karin wanted to lean out to dip her hand in the cool water but she wasn't game this far out. It was so deep with nothing but green underneath them.

Ever since that day she'd nearly drowned, she'd avoided going in the water. It was hard to explain to her friends back in Sydney, but everyone in this boat had been there. In a strange way, that actually made her feel safer.

The river was a darker green at the place where it bent and narrowed. The sun didn't reach this part, and it was as though an entirely new shadow-world existed beyond the bend, one that was quieter and cooler and more remote. There were no houses on the banks here, just trees.

'Hey, what's that?' Jez's voice was small under the sound of the motor.

Tommy cut the engine and there was suddenly silence. They glided through the green. A sheer rock wall reached up to their right. A cockie screeched.

Karin was expecting to see a shark and she felt her heart beat faster, but Jez was pointing to something up in the trees on the left bank. She squinted but she couldn't make out what he was pointing at.

'Can you see anything?' she asked Phoebe.

'Nup,' said Phoebe, letting go of her hand so she could strain forward.

'It's like, I don't know, there's like something in the trees.'

'What, an animal?' asked Camilla, standing up.

'Sit down,' called Tommy.

'No, no it's wooden. Like a treehouse,' said Jez.

To their left was a narrow mouth where the river snaked off, dense bush crowding the banks.

'Get the oars out,' said Jez 'It's shallow here. Let's go up this little stream here so we can check it out.'

The clunk of the wooden oars as they sliced through the water was calming. Jez and Tommy rowed, their shoulders working hard. The air smelled damp and mossy here, like mosquitos and water lilies. They were all craning their necks to see what was in the trees.

'I can see it! Yeah, it looks like a treehouse,' said Camilla. For once she sounded excited instead of bored.

'Look, there's a sandbank. Let's pull up there,' said Phoebe.

The dog began to bark.

'Shhh, boy, it's okay.' Karin hugged his neck. 'I don't know, it seems a bit far away from everything,' she said, the hairs on her arms lifting. She hugged the dog closer and he made a little whimper.

'What if someone lives there?' asked Phoebe, also wrapping her arms around the dog.

'I don't think it's anyone's house. It's just a rundown treehouse in the woods,' said Tommy, steering the boat towards the shore. The certainty in his voice was reassuring. She and Phoebe exchanged a look.

The boat hit the shore and they all piled out, the dog last. Crabs scuttled into tiny holes in the sand and a kookaburra's cry cut through the trees above.

'Look, there's a path,' said Tommy, making his way past a bank of dense green mangroves.

They followed the narrow path cut through the bush. 'Snake,' shouted Jez, and then laughed.

'You shouldn't joke about that,' said Tommy. 'There might be snakes.'

Jez laughed again. 'This is so cool; the path leads right up to the tree. It's as though it's been made to lead there.'

From the ground, the treehouse seemed high up. Planks of wood had been nailed into the gum's trunk, leading up to the small house, camouflaged from where they stood by leaves.

'Cooee, anyone there?' shouted Tommy, his head back, hands cupped around his mouth.

They all stood still, listening, but they could only hear the wind in the leaves and the tide pulling out.

'Who's first?' asked Jez, looking to Tommy.

'We'll go. You girls stay here and keep watch,' said Tommy, already on the first rung, testing it for strength.

'Why do you get to go first?' asked Camilla, hands on her hips, bottom lip stuck out.

'Because we're older than you,' said Tommy. 'We'll just make sure it's safe first.'

They waited, the dog's whines piercing the strange, quiet atmosphere.

'It's a bit spooky here,' said Phoebe, linking her arm through Karin's.

'I know, it is a bit,' said Karin, thinking of the men at the picnic area. She knelt, playing with the dog's ears. 'It's okay, boy,' she said. 'They'll be back. It's only a treehouse.'

But even Camilla was hugging the dog close to her body.

Jez came down from the treehouse first. He landed on the spongy ground with a thud. His face looked flushed. 'It's just an old treehouse. Tommy says it's a bit rickety and dangerous for you girls to come up.'

'It doesn't look rickety from here,' said Karin, craning her neck skyward. She set her mouth into a line and shared an annoyed look with Phoebe. They weren't going to let the boys leave them out of this adventure just 'cause they were girls. 'It actually looks like someone's made it really carefully. It even has a window and a kind of balcony thing.'

The treehouse had been made with long planks of light wood and it even had a sloped roof and small window overlooking the river.

'I want to see what's up there,' said Camilla, her hands on the lowest rung of the ladder.

'Me too,' said Phoebe, slapping at a mosquito at her ankle.

Jez looked up and scratched his head. He looked torn. 'Tommy said you shouldn't though.'

Karin stood to her full height. 'Well, I'm the second oldest and we want to see it, too.'

Jez shrugged and kicked at a tree root.

Karin gave the dog a quick hug. 'You stay here, boy, okay?' As if understanding, he settled his body against the tree trunk.

'They're coming up,' Jez yelled into the sky.

Tommy's head appeared out of the small window. 'I told you not to let them.'

'You're just saying that because we're girls,' shouted Karin, hoisting herself up onto the first rung. She might be afraid of water but she wasn't afraid of heights. She wanted to see what the river looked like from the tops of the trees.

'Go on,' said Phoebe, letting Camilla go ahead of her. Karin knew it was because Phoebe was bigger and wanted to be behind Cammie in case she slipped, but she would never let on.

Her arms and legs were aching a bit by the time she reached the top. There was a rope to make it easier to get off the ladder and onto the wooden platform. She helped her sisters.

They could see all the way down the river and she got a rush of exhilaration that went from her toes to her fingertips at being so high. The river looked like a long, green snake. The wind in the leaves filled her ears.

'Hold on tight,' she told the others. 'It's a bit windy up here.'

Jez and the dog looked tiny on the ground. The dog barked twice, two yips, as if in greeting.

Karin carefully inched over the wooden planks to the little cabin fitted snugly into the 'V' of the huge old branches, as though it had always been part of the tree. It wasn't very big. Inside Tommy was bent over. Even his twelve-year-old frame was too tall to stand straight. She was eleven but a few centimetres taller. It was a bit of a competition, their heights etched in pencil on the corner of the kitchen wall at Driftwood.

She entered the cabin and it smelled like rain and damp ground and something else sharper, maybe urine. There was a makeshift bed in one corner; some old blankets and a faded blue cushion. Tommy was kneeling now at the other end, in front of the window. There was a funny expression on his face that Karin hadn't seen before. His eyes flicked to Phoebe and Camilla who had just squeezed in behind her.

'Are you okay?' asked Karin, inching closer, her head skimming the roof even though she was bending her knees.

He had his hands behind him. She could see a pile of magazines in the corner next to him. The rude pictures on the cover made her stop short.

He'd seen her see them. 'I told you, you shouldn't have come up,' he said, his hands fumbling behind his back.

'What's wrong?' she asked again, because she could sense that he was nervous, an emotion she'd never really seen in all-confident Tommy.

'It's just …' He hesitated and bit his bottom lip.

'Ewww,' said Camilla. 'This is so gross. It smells in here. It's a homeless person's treehouse.' She pinched her nose and pretended to vomit, but then she saw the window and stuck her head out. 'Nice view though.'

Phoebe snorted. 'Don't touch anything,' she said, pulling Cammie away from the window.

'As if I would. It's gross. Don't pull me,' Cammie said, smoothing down her T-shirt.

Tommy nodded for Karin to come closer. 'Look behind me,' he whispered, his neck rigid.

She gasped as she spotted a black gun lying on a blue plastic milk crate.

'It can't be real,' she said, her hand over her mouth so the others wouldn't hear, but he nodded and widened his eyes.

'It's heavy. Toy guns are never that heavy,' he said.

'You haven't touched it, have you?' She felt breathless.

Tommy's mouth scrunched at the corner, which meant he had. Everyone knew that Tommy wanted to be a policeman so Karin was pretty sure he knew what he was talking about even if he was only a kid.

'What are we going to do?' Her eyes searched Tommy's and she felt cold suddenly and shivered. She thought of the men she saw at the picnic area and her stomach ached.

'Oh my gosh,' said Phoebe, seeing the magazines. 'Don't look, Camilla.'

But their little sister was looking. For once she was speechless, her eyes wide like saucers.

# CHAPTER 16

The white tablecloth glowed in the early autumn light. It was April now and Phoebe had been here for months, but time had stretched and yawned and the days ran together like summer holidays, like when you were young. They had assembled a long table under the old willow tree and the sound of the wind in the leaves accompanied the clang of cutlery being laid. Phoebe stood on a ladder, stringing white lanterns through the leaves. She was relishing the cooler turn of the shortening days, and the sun was losing its sting. She didn't remember feeling the seasons as much in Sydney, but here her days were spent outside, tending the vegetables in her garden, raking leaves into small piles, fishing from the jetty and stoking the fire on the deck at dusk.

Tommy's birthday party would be the last of their alfresco celebrations. She had been at Driftwood since 8 am, mixing punch, assembling paper lanterns and chopping vegetables for salads. The Texan had joined her to knead loaves of sourdough for the oven. Someone was always in the Driftwood kitchen, no matter the time of day. And it wasn't like the share houses of her youth where people hoarded their own food—it was the opposite. If Wendy had lettuces from her garden she'd bring them. If milk was on special at the supermarket Phoebe would buy bulk and leave a few litres in the fridge. The Texan was always whipping up rhubarb to have on yoghurt or baking muffins, which he insisted were eaten straightaway, fresh from the oven.

The Texan had taught her some of his recipes and she found herself behind the kitchen counter helping him, more often than not. She learned to make a fragrant chicken curry with fresh coriander and ginger from the garden, and tasty dhal with lentils that had been soaked overnight. She baked bread and cultured yoghurt from scratch. These were all things she had consumed in her former life from packets, never imagining she would have the time or inclination to create them herself.

Flick brought out a tray of wineglasses and Phoebe climbed down the ladder and helped her arrange them along the table.

'Do you think Tommy's freaking out? Forty's a big milestone,' said Flick, brushing leaves off the tablecloth.

Phoebe laughed. 'Somehow, I don't think Tommy does "freaked out". Mildly concerned perhaps ...'

Flick nodded. 'True. And it's not like he doesn't have everything you're meant to by this age. Bastard.'

Phoebe felt her neck muscles tense. She knew what Flick meant but resented how the passage of time needed to be accompanied by socially acceptable milestones, even in a joking fashion.

'You know what?' She hated how defiant her voice sounded but went on. 'In society's eyes I'm in the worst position of my entire life right now. I've gone from having a glamorous job and owning a nice apartment with a guy, to single, unemployed, living in the country, but I'm the happiest I can remember since I was a kid.'

Flick smiled indulgently and narrowed her eyes. 'Really?'

She nodded forcefully. 'Really.'

Flick raised her eyebrows and shrugged in surrender. 'Okay. I mean, don't get me wrong, we've got a great little thing here, but God, what I wouldn't give for a gorgeous guy to come and sweep me off my feet.'

As if on cue, Jez appeared, carrying a bag of ice on his shoulder.

'Speaking of gorgeous guys,' Flick said loudly.

Phoebe reddened and bent down on the pretence of steadying a rickety table leg. Jez had been sending her letters. She found the first folded into a tight square inside a small envelope in the letterbox.

*Today you looked sad. Just checking you're okay. I'm here if you need me to fix anything.*

She knew he meant more than a broken light. She wrote back, telling him how the melancholy thread of her sister sometimes wound itself around her until she couldn't breathe. He told her he was lonely, that he couldn't reach Asha. That he was trying, but he couldn't sleep at night with the confusion he was feeling.

But mostly the letters were short and simple and written in his loose, tradie scrawl, torn out of pages of a notebook. He told her about his days. The view across the rough waters of the Bay where he'd eaten his Vegemite sandwich and drank from a thermos of coffee on Tuesday. Various amusing dramas involving wildlife encounters in people's roofs. Sometimes he imagined their future together. The simple things they'd do:

come home to each other, sleep in the same bed, watch TV together. And he told her about his dreams. She was in them. The unborn child he couldn't have was in them.

Phoebe could see that he was wrestling with the same guilt as she was. He delivered the letters daily as he drove past on his way home each afternoon. By that time she was already at Driftwood. Just as her love for Jez had grown, so had her attachment to his home and its inhabitants.

His arrival after four each day was heralded with the thump of his heavy boots being kicked off in the hall. The Texan, Wendy, Asha and Flick were usually in the kitchen by that time, snacking on the Texan's hummus, almonds, baby tomatoes, or whatever other thing had been plucked from the garden that day. Phoebe couldn't help but watch Jez's interactions with Asha closely. The way he kissed the top of her head in greeting, the way he'd pour her a glass of wine. Knowing all the while that a letter was there, waiting for her. She hated this. Jealousy and guilt had become two sides of the same coin. She hated herself for their emotional deception but she couldn't stop herself. Their every interaction was cast with tiny, shining lines, caught beneath the surface like fishing wire. She held tight to the knowledge that they had not been physical with one another. You could call what they had a deep friendship, but really, in the darkness of the night, when she woke breathless and panicked at 2 am, she knew this was not an excuse.

She would read his letters, curled on the lounge, right before sleep. Most days she wrote back at breakfast time and left her letter in the box for him to pick up. Sometimes if she was early enough, he'd collect it on his way to work. She told him what she had planned for the day—a little gardening, going to Driftwood to make chicken soup for Flick whose chronic fatigue symptoms had flared unexpectedly. Picking up some medication for Ginny in the Bay and dropping in a batch of her lemon and almond muffins.

But there had been no letter from Jez for three days. Phoebe had tried to calm herself—he was busy with Tommy's birthday surprise, maybe he didn't have a lunch break this week—but she couldn't help thinking something had shifted. Something was wrong.

Jez was behind her suddenly. 'The table wobbly?' He put down the bag of ice and crouched beside her. She was acutely aware of his body so close. 'Here, let me fix it.'

She looked around. Flick had gone inside. She felt his hand enclose around her wrist and he pulled her under the table. No part of her resisted. It smelled like cut grass and autumn leaves. She could feel the moisture coming up from the earth through the grass, the warmth of his body and then his lips. She couldn't tell who kissed who but everything else disappeared. The taste of him had not changed. It was the same as it had always been. It took her back like a long forgotten song, clear and remembered. Her body trembled in the places his hand touched. Her arm, her shoulder, her cheek. She wanted to stay here with the tablecloth billowing around them, in this cocoon of light. But they were both listening out for the sounds of others and the guilt was like stones in her stomach, worn smooth from shifting and moving.

People talked about the excitement of affairs and Phoebe couldn't deny the feeling that coiled in her belly every time she saw him. But there was sadness too, and stress. Why were they in this situation? This emotional pull with no clear direction? Had she become what so many women before her had? The woman a man will never leave his wife for? Everything had changed so slowly, like the summer leaves crisping to autumn. Now he controlled the way the world looked when she woke. She hated and loved him for this in equal measure. She pushed him away gently and her voice was a whisper. 'It's so hard, Jez, doing this.'

She waited for his response but he drew her into him again, pressing his face into her neck.

'It's not fair to Asha.' She hated herself for pushing him away.

His face went pale or maybe it was just the bleached light reflecting off the tablecloth. She searched his eyes for some clue but the sound of Asha's voice floated over the lawn.

'Jez, we need you to tell us how much beer we need.'

He stiffened. 'Coming,' he yelled, trying to mask any urgency. He placed his hand over Phoebe's. 'We need to talk. Tonight. After the party.'

She wanted to feel relieved, to smile, to kiss him again, but her gut was churning in the way it always did when she was picking up cues she didn't understand. She was torn between pushing him for more and escaping, and then the sound of a car on the dirt road roused them both.

'Tommy's here,' he said, and was gone.

\* \* \*

Harry squirmed with what may or may not have been delight as Asha snuck a tickle under his arms. He was moving trains around his track with the same fierce intensity that rarely left his little face. They sat on the picnic rug in the shade of the liquidambar, Harry dressed as Superman and Asha cross-legged and also in uniform: one of her long white cotton dresses. Phoebe had been surprised when Asha had volunteered to babysit to give Tommy and Jenna time to enjoy their lunch. She usually approached Harry with caution, clearly unable to invest in something she was denied.

Phoebe thought, not for the first time, that Asha looked like a haunted character out of *Picnic at Hanging Rock*. What would happen to the dresses as the cooler weather set in? At first Phoebe hadn't been able to marry this sweet, innocent image with Asha's caustic remarks but as their relationship thawed, she saw that this whimsy suited Asha. She was a maternal hippy, really. She wanted a life of barefoot children and making things with her hands, but she also wanted the stability Jez afforded—so different from her own upbringing with her neglectful mother. Phoebe could see she was single-minded about this. Asha would not be poor and struggling again and Jez was the key to this. It didn't matter that their relationship was dysfunctional. Phoebe couldn't help but feel Asha was using Jez, and her power lay in her looks. Phoebe suspected that Jez had become accustomed to having something that other men desired. Perhaps they had ensnared each other equally.

Phoebe felt her heart ache. She had walked into such a mess. And now Jez had kissed her. She should just walk away right now but she had been preparing for this party for days. She felt a measure of pride at how much Tommy and Jenna had been moved by the surprise lunch. The long table was piled with plates of roast and cold meats, salads and breads. Phoebe was seated at the sunny end of the table between Jenna and one of Tommy's work colleagues. The guy wore his confidence like a loose tie about his tanned neck. He was a new Federal

Police recruit. She could see it in his eager eyes, the arrogant way he tipped his beer back. As soon as she sat down she knew there was some kind of unspoken set-up going on, probably instigated by Tommy. She wondered if he had any clue about what was going on between her and Jez. The two were close but affairs were not things to be easily shared, even with the people who you trusted most.

'It's nice to see Asha playing with Harry,' said Jenna, interrupting her thoughts and leaning over to fill her wineglass.

'Thanks,' said Phoebe, taking a sip, happy not to have to hear any more about the fitness routine of the guy whose name she'd already forgotten.

'Sometimes I feel like it's too painful for her to interact with him, but Harry really likes her. He won't sit and be entertained by just anyone. He's very picky. She'd make a great mother, don't you think?'

Phoebe nodded mutely, her skin crawling with what felt like tiny biting insects. She tried to remain still, to ignore the erratic beat of her heart. She tried to press the thoughts out of her head. Surely Jez had been careful, given everything that had been happening between them. *But she's still his wife. They still have sex.* The thought lodged in her like the piece of ill-chewed meat in her throat.

'This means so much to Tommy. Thanks for making it all so beautiful. He comes across as very sure of himself but really … this means a lot.'

Phoebe shook her head, willing herself to focus. Jenna's eyes had become misty and Phoebe was glad of all the effort everyone had gone to in making the day special. 'It was all Jez's doing. He's been planning it for ages.'

They both watched Tommy, reclining in his seat, wineglass balanced precariously in his hand. He was holding court, his defences loosened by alcohol and adoration. It was rare that he told a work-related story.

'And this guy, we bring him in and he's all tough guy, tatts, steroid abuse, a string of priors, the whole bit, and he's, you know, he's been on our watch list for a while.'

Jez began shaking his head, a knowing smile on his lips. He'd obviously heard this one before.

'And we've got his laptop, and our guy has checked it and there's nothing incriminating, but the guy's got this weird obsession.' Tommy paused, the whole table quiet, hanging on his words. 'Nothing criminal, mind you, but ...' Jez squeezed his eyes shut trying to control his amusement.

'They're called Bronies—men who are into My Little Ponies. We're talking every episode, chat rooms, Ebay searches for figurines. It's a thing.' Tommy shook his head and finished his wine in one gulp. 'More disturbing than most of the stuff I've seen, Jesus.'

His mates slapped their thighs, doubled over in mirth.

Jenna cocked her head and narrowed her eyes. 'I'm pretty sure he told me that was classified.' Phoebe laughed and Jenna rolled her eyes. 'Maybe I just need to get him drunk more often, so he'll tell me more about work.'

'And what about the dude who had the Smurf sex fetish? He had to be painted blue,' said Jez, elbowing Tommy in the ribs.

'Looks like Jez gets all the juicy stories,' said Phoebe.

'It's lovely how close they are,' said Jenna. 'What, with their mum gone.' She took a sip of her rosé. 'Were you like that with your sister? Before ...' She trailed off.

Perhaps it was the wine or the lingering anxiety over what was going on with Jez, but Phoebe said what was in her heart. 'Yes, we were best friends, just like Jez and Tommy. It's the anniversary of her death next week and I just can't stop thinking about her. She would have turned forty next year.'

Jenna's delicate features darkened and her large eyes searched Phoebe's. 'Oh, Phoebe, how awful for you. And here we are all celebrating.'

Phoebe's throat constricted but she managed to shake her head. 'No. It's okay, life goes on. People are still allowed to have birthdays.' She gave Jenna a comforting smile. But if she was honest, sometimes it didn't feel like it was okay. Sometimes it felt like every celebration, every new birth, everything that showed that life went on and was good, was a kick in the face to Karin's memory. A lot of grief's journey was working through these feelings and trying to come to a place of acceptance.

Jenna looked into her lap, wringing her serviette, clearly trying to find the right words. 'I'm just so sorry. I had no idea the anniversary of her death was next week.'

Phoebe took another sip of wine. She was becoming pleasantly numb. It was the only way she could cope with the uncertainty over what was going on with Jez. She looked at Jenna, head hung, and over at Asha, smiling on the rug. Both of them lived with uncertainty. How their child would survive in the world, and whether a child would ever come. Solid ground was a myth; it had just taken Phoebe this long to realise it.

She felt a tap on her shoulder and swivelled in her seat to see a bottle of white wine held aloft and a raised, questioning eyebrow. She was surprised to find that her wineglass was empty. She was drinking too much but she allowed Tommy's mate to refill it.

'You ladies were looking a bit serious. I thought I'd cheer you up.'

She forced a smile onto her face and their glasses clinked in cheers. Jenna left to join Asha and Harry on the picnic rug and Phoebe felt relieved and a little drunk. Maybe Mr New Recruit was okay. Maybe she just needed a bit of fun in her life. Everything was too intense, too serious. What did they say about just having fun for a while after a big break-up? She'd certainly skipped that step. She shot Charlie, that was his name, a more genuine smile. He actually wasn't bad looking. He leaned in and she could smell his cologne.

'So tell me about yourself, Phoebe.'

It was easy to edit her life to sound good. She mentioned working for Joet et Halo, being in charge of their social media and how that meant going to lots of amazing events and travelling, all the promotional parties she went to, the freebie champagne stashed in every room in the house. He didn't need to know she'd quit. The apartment she owned—he didn't need to know it was now being rented out to cover the mortage, while she and Nate got their act together to sell. She mentioned her successful family, omitting the small detail of the suicide. He nodded and made a whistling sound when she told him where her parents lived. She remembered this feeling, how addictive it was. It was like trying on her old self, her old life.

She thought about how her social media accounts looked right now. They were suspended, frozen in the same filtered version of her life that she'd just told this stranger. The last photo she'd posted was of her and Nathaniel drinking cocktails on the beach at sunset. There were no lonely tears in the dark, faces staring up at her from the river depths, affairs. Even now, she knew she could manipulate things to make them appear perfect. Her Instagramable organic vegie patch, the little community at Driftwood—like a second family. Even her affair with Jez could be made glossy. They were childhood sweethearts, destined to be together after all this time.

She put her hand over her glass as her companion went to top it up again. But she fumbled and it fell, spilling wine over her dress and the table. His laugh was a boom and his hand was suddenly patting down her lap with a napkin. She began to giggle. When she looked up she saw Jez standing beside her. His face was serious. More serious than a spilled glass of wine warranted. Was he jealous? She stood and the world tilted. She steadied herself on the back of her chair and suppressed another giggle. She muttered something about needing to use the ladies and focused on staying upright while she found her equilibrium. She thought Jez was going to take her arm, but of course he didn't. He couldn't. Everyone was here. Everyone would see. He began mopping up the spill with serviettes. She steadied herself again on the back of the chair.

'I'll be back,' she said, her voice sounding slow in her ears. She made it to the bathroom and sat on the cool toilet seat with her head in her hands. When she stood against the bathroom vanity the world was still spinning. She tried to find herself in the face staring back in the mirror.

'What are you doing?' she asked the girl with the tanned skin and the eyes, hooded with wine. But there was no answer.

# CHAPTER 17

The party went on into the night. The fire pit was lit and people sat on logs in the clearing, warming their hands against the cool river air. Frogs chirped and the laughter became louder as the fire crackled in the darkness. Tommy and his mates passed a bottle of Scotch between them, taking swigs, their knees spread, necks tipped back in bravado. The spirits made them sentimental, arms hooked around each other, voices husky with emotion.

Phoebe sat nearby, painfully sober by now. She was grateful for the warmth of the fire on her face and the hot chocolate in her hands. A headache throbbed from the base of her neck, up into her skull. The beginnings of a hangover. She would have gone home but she needed to talk to Jez. The whole day his warm mouth, the look in his eyes at the table, jealous and yet restrained, had haunted her. The knot of anxiety in her stomach would not unfurl, even after all that wine. Some of the others had gone to bed. Jenna and Harry and Flick all retreated as the sun slid behind the trees. She watched the Texan and Wendy frying the last of the sausages on the barbecue, near the house. She envied their easy way with each other. Wendy snapped at him playfully with the tongs. They seemed able to give each other freedom as well as security. The power was spread evenly, not tipped to the extreme as it felt with her and Jez. She had been so powerful at first. Jez's underbelly had been exposed; his immediate attraction and his neediness for emotional connection was stronger than hers. She wasn't sure why or when or how, but somehow it had tipped. Now it felt as though she was at his mercy. She hadn't realised how starved she'd been of emotional connection. It was his letters, so simple, in some ways, so innocent, that had hooked her.

She thought of her own parents. Did they have a good marriage? It was so hard to see them objectively. She knew in the deep, unexplained way children do, that her father had given up much of his freedom in marrying her mother. This place was his only concession—one she had grudgingly given him over the years. Phoebe knew her mother had suggested they sell after Karin died, but he refused. She wondered if he missed it down here. He must. *I could invite him*, she thought. He could drive down for a weekend. The feeling of warmth took her by surprise. Of course, he'd come. It was the anniversary of Karin's death. Phoebe had always loved her dad but they weren't close. He struggled to express his emotions in the same way so many Australian men did. Instead they were conveyed in the fixing of broken things. A toaster here, a car engine there. She had long ago understood that it was his way of showing love. She realised sitting here, as the night cooled around her, that he was the only one she could bear seeing. She warmed her hands against the bright flames. She would call him tomorrow.

There were loud hoots over by the barbecue as drunk, starving men picked sausages off the hot plate with their fingers.

Tommy and Jez threw a sausage back and forth between them until it landed on the ground and everyone bent over, defeated by laughter. Phoebe felt a stab of longing. She and Karin had had that closeness. They had laughed together until tears squeezed out of their eyes. She hadn't thought about that in a long time. She tried to remember back to the last time they'd laughed like that. It had been on the phone. She'd been telling Karin about Nathaniel's weird tan mark. Their niece, Sophia, had put a sticker in the middle of his forehead and he'd gone sailing without realising. A pale love heart had been etched into his forehead for a week. It had been funny at the time but telling her sister had made it deliciously so. She realised that she still hoarded anecdotes from her life to tell Karin, waiting for them to go from the banal to the sublime by sharing them with her. There was still some part of her that expected her sister to come, ready to sit down with a cup of chamomile tea with honey, to be filled in on everything that had happened since she went away.

She remembered the first person she wanted to call about Karin's death had been Karin. She had dialled the landline and let it ring and ring and ring, sure her sister's sing-song greeting would eventuate on the line.

Phoebe felt her heart vibrate and she brushed away tears. She watched the men eat the sausages with their fingers and wipe their greasy hands on their shorts. They were back to drinking VB. Maybe Jez was too drunk to talk tonight. Phoebe was tired and the thought of sleep nestled in her mind. She was shaking her numb legs in readiness to stand when Charlie, the flirtatious guy, sat beside her. He held a sausage in one hand and a joint in the other.

'Care to join me?' he asked, holding out the sausage suggestively.

She shook her head, exasperated, as though he was an annoying older brother. 'I'd prefer the joint actually. But hang on, can't you arrest me? Is this an undercover sting?'

He arched an eyebrow. 'You don't even want to know what these boys get up to.'

She sat forward, resting her arms on her knees. She was sweating now in front of the fire. She pressed her palms against her burning cheeks. 'But … call me naïve but you're cops. You can't just go around giving drugs to people. Can you?'

'Haven't you watched TV?'

'Really?'

He nodded and produced a lighter, lit the joint and inhaled with more drama than was necessary. Phoebe's muscles stiffened as the smoke curled around her. She knew Jez's aversion, and the thought of Tommy even smelling it made her heart race. Charlie offered it to her and she shook her head.

He scoffed and kicked his boot in the dirt. 'You think these guys care about a bit of marijuana?'

Phoebe felt him watching her and it made her squirm. She shrugged and pulled her knees to her chest.

'You worried about Tommy?' He shook his head and laughed.

She locked eyes on him, searching them. She found only heavy-lidded redness. 'As I said, watch some cop shows on TV. Least of our worries,' he said, his eyes narrowing against the plume of smoke coming out of his mouth. 'Let me tell you something. I haven't been a cop for long but the biggest thing I've learned in my training when dealing with anyone—

housewives, murderers, kids, whoever—never assume you know someone.'

A shiver slid down Phoebe's back, as though someone had traced her spine with a shard of glass.

'Not that I'm going to reveal all the Feds' secrets to you. No matter how pretty you are.'

Phoebe grimaced. She didn't like this guy. He was drunk and obviously talking shit to try to impress her.

Asha and Wendy appeared as though sensing her discomfort.

'Come in, we're making more cocoa,' said Wendy, holding out a hand to help her up. 'It's getting cold.'

Charlie made a face. 'Party pooper.'

Phoebe shot the girls a grateful look.

Inside was warm and Wendy had laid out some shortbread biscuits and was pouring cocoa from a large thermos. The Texan had started on the piles of washing up in the sink. Phoebe grabbed a garbage bag and cleared beer bottles from the table.

'You're like the mother we never had,' she said to Wendy, sipping her cup of hot chocolate. 'Thanks for rescuing me from that guy.'

'What about me?' asked the Texan.

'Oh, yeah, you too, Dad,' said Asha, pulling up a seat next to Phoebe. She smelled of wood smoke but not cigarettes.

'I'm sure your own mothers would never let you drink so much.' Wendy shot Phoebe a knowing look.

Phoebe held up her hands in defeat. 'I may have had too much white wine earlier.' She took a sip of the warm, sweet milk.

'My mum's worse than me,' said Asha. 'Don't forget, I'm a bogan at heart.'

'Well, I think you were the only one who stayed sober.' Wendy nudged her. 'And why exactly was that?'

Asha's face flushed crimson and she shook her head and picked up the thermos. 'Is this ready to pour?'

Phoebe felt a rush of blood in her ears. Her heart hammered so loudly she was sure Asha could hear it. Panic burned the back of her throat and she could taste white wine and sausages. Her stomach turned. This was it. This is what Jez was going to tell her. This was the dread that had sat in her belly like a dead weight all day.

Wendy's eyes flashed and a look of mischief came into them. 'Are you avoiding my question, Asha?'

She looked uncharacteristically flustered. 'I ...' Her face broke into a smile. 'I can't hide anything from anyone in this house, can I? Jez will kill me if he finds out I told you.'

Wendy clapped her hands under her chin. 'I knew it. As soon as I saw you playing with Harry. And you've stopped smoking. Good girl. How many weeks?'

It felt like the world fell out from underneath Phoebe and she was falling. Everything was spinning and she knew she was going to be sick. Everything was mashing together, guilt, anger, confusion, jealousy. How could Jez have let this happen? He knew how much Asha wanted a baby. He knew he didn't want one with her now. He'd said so in the letters. What was the word he'd used? Relieved. Now that he could see clearly, he was relieved not to bring a baby into such a toxic relationship. But he'd known Asha was pregnant when he'd kissed her, under the table today. He should have told her, not kissed her. Her fingers made fists and she clamped her jaw to stop the tears. How long had he known?

The front door slammed and Phoebe jumped. Jez and Tommy came into the room, laughing, drunk.

'Why are you all drinking tea already?' asked Tommy, swaying slightly. His hair was wild, which made Phoebe flash back to when he was young. 'It's my party and I command that you all drink more beer. Or wine. Or something else.' He produced a fat joint and a cigar from his pocket. 'Someone bring me a lighter,' he said, putting both in his mouth and extending his arms dramatically.

Jez lunged at Tommy and grabbed them from his mouth. 'Dirty,' he said, flinging them away.

'Hey,' said Tommy, wrenching Jez's arm behind his back so hard he cried out. The two of them wrestled and ended up on the kitchen floor laughing. Phoebe wondered if he'd got the drugs from the dodgy new recruit. It was obvious Tommy was smashed.

'This man is turning the big four O and you're drinking tea at, what is it? Nine o'clock?' said Jez from the kitchen floor, slapping his brother on the back. 'You're all lightweights. Lightweights!'

'You listen to my little brother,' said Tommy, getting Jez in a neck lock and ruffling his hair.

Wendy cocked her head. 'It's ten actually, and someone has to look after your wife, now, don't they?' She paused for effect. 'And you better start get used to going to bed early, Jez.' She winked.

Jez's face froze mid tackle. All the colour drained from it. He looked at Asha and she beamed at him, at them all. 'Sorry, they got it out of me. I would have been telling them soon anyway.'

He was drunk and Phoebe could tell he couldn't mask his emotions. Their eyes locked and his face passed through shock, into anger. And then she could see before she looked away, sorrow. She didn't pause to wonder if anyone else had seen this strange reaction from a father-to-be who had hoped for a child for so long. Phoebe put down her mug and rose unsteadily. Her chest felt tight, as though her heart was an oyster that had been prised open, the contents stolen. How soft, how ripe she had felt these past weeks. Now everything inside her felt like rubber. How stupid she'd been. He was never going to leave Asha. She was simply a diversion in the bump of their marriage.

She heard Jez admonish Asha, something about her not being far enough along and it being too soon to tell. But he was drowned out by everyone's joy. She watched it all play out in a strange slow motion, as though it wasn't real. Tommy was slapping him on the back, eyes glistening. Wendy was hugging Asha, the pair of them jumping up and down until the Texan suggested that it may not be good for the baby.

Phoebe realised she needed to contribute to the generally jovial atmosphere or it would look odd. She swallowed back the bile in her throat, hugged Asha and said, 'Congratulations, you must be thrilled,' as warmly as she could. She felt like a traitor, a fraud, and hoped Asha wouldn't feel the cold clammy sweat on her skin. She tried to find a place within her that was happy for this woman who had finally gotten what she'd longed for. But it was too soon. All she could see was the sadness in Jez's face. She knew he would stay with Asha now. And he should, but he didn't love or respect his wife anymore. He had admitted to that. He hadn't written for days because he was trying to figure out what to do, even though he knew what he must do. His torment, his loyalty, made Phoebe want him even more.

Jenna appeared in her pyjamas, shielding her sleep-addled eyes against the light. It didn't take her long to realise the reason for all the noise. She and Tommy shared a weighted glance. She slapped him playfully on the chest, telling everyone she'd strongly suspected Asha was pregnant but Tommy hadn't believed her. She hugged Asha, patting down her hair and placing a hand on her flat belly. The pair whispered the secrets of mothers, as though Asha now spoke that soft and knowing language, too. And for the first time Phoebe felt the full hollowness of being outside—outside of that special realm of motherhood and outside now, of the group. How could she remain? It would be too painful for her and for Jez.

Tommy and Jez sobered up quickly and dismissed the last of the revellers. Jenna pulled up a seat at the table and they drank the hot chocolate while Asha told them all about it. She'd had blood tests and her hormones were strong. She was feeling nauseous constantly and the doctor said it was a very good sign. So Jez had known for weeks that she'd been pregnant? Surely Asha wouldn't have kept it to herself. Phoebe longed to talk to Jez, to hear his side of things. But to what end? It would only be more painful for them both.

Everyone was tired and the excitement of the last hour had smoothed a silence over the gathering at the table. The Texan clapped his hands and reminded everyone it was bed time and that they'd been drinking since midday. Normally Phoebe might have crashed on the lounge, or someone would have walked with her up the road, but tonight was different. No one noticed as she slipped into the night without saying goodbye.

A letter was there the next morning, flimsier than usual, folded into a tiny square. Phoebe's heart leaped as her fingers found it but her brain admonished her heart. What was the point in hoping?

*I'm so sorry. Please meet me at my usual lunch place at midday so we can talk. J*

He usually signed off with a kiss but today there was nothing.

The wind whipped against the sea wall with a violence that caught her hair and stung her cheeks. Sails flapped and rigs rattled as the boats on the water braced themselves. Someone upwind was eating fish and chips. The oily, salty smell was the only comfort as she waited for Jez in her car, the window down. How many times had he sat here writing to her when he knew Asha was having a baby? She tried to push the thought out of her mind but it clung on. A cheap motel sat like a squat and ugly temptation across the road. The flashing red vacancy sign hypnotised her.

She got out of her car and pulled her hair back into a ponytail to stop it flying around her head. His ute pulled in beside her. He cut the engine. Her stomach did the same thing it always did whenever she saw him. But this time it was laced with pain rather than excitement. He wound down the window.

'Do you want to hop in?'

'No,' she said, her voice lost in the wind. She couldn't bear the smell of him in the close cabin.

He had work boots on even though it was Sunday. Maybe he had an emergency job to go to after this, or maybe he'd pretended he was working to get out of the house. She was angry at herself for even caring. She braced her arms against her stomach as he approached. His eyes were red-rimmed, as though he hadn't slept much either.

'Is your hangover as bad as mine?' he asked, rubbing the back of his head. He was awkward. There was a distance now.

'I think my hangover happened last night, about the same time as Asha's announcement.'

His face fell. 'Phoebe, I'm sorry. It wasn't meant to happen like that.'

A sour taste piqued the back of her throat. 'Like what, Jez?' The anger in her own voice shocked her but she went on. 'Letting me fall in love with you while all that time your wife was pregnant?'

'I didn't know, I swear it.'

She couldn't look at him. 'When? When did you know?'

He rubbed the stubble on his chin and he squeezed his eyes shut and then opened them wide as though trying to wake himself up. 'It's going to sound bad, but there's a reason.'

She waited, the wind roaring in her ears.

'I've known since about five or six weeks but—'

Her laugh was a bark. 'So basically all the time you've been writing the letters.'

'We've had miscarriages very early on, Phoebe. Neither of us thought it would get past six weeks.'

'But then it did, and you never told me.'

'I know, I should have. But I wanted you. I could feel you falling in love with me. I was selfish, but none of this changes the way I feel. I don't want to be with Asha. I don't want to bring a child into this marriage. I want to be with you.'

Tears stung behind Phoebe's eyes but her voice was hard. 'None of that matters now. How you feel is irrelevant. You made a choice and this is the result. I know you. You can't leave her and I won't let you.' She wiped her cheeks. 'I'm so torn. I'm just so sad.'

She stilled herself, holding her breath, willing the tears to stop. She could tell he wanted to reach out for her but her whole body was steeled against him, against the wind. She wanted to scream at him, *This was it. This was our chance at a big love. Not everyone gets that but we had it.*

Instead she shook her head and took a step away from him. 'I feel so sorry for Asha … sorry for us. The whole thing just keeps going round and round in my head, as though there's a solution if I just think hard enough. But there's not.'

A gull floated overhead, suspended in the headwind. Flying hard but staying still. She watched the bird and felt her own fast-beating heart.

'You can still visit. Stay for dinner most nights …' His voice trailed off.

Phoebe shook her head and looked out past the choppy sea to the jagged rocks of the island in the middle of the bay. 'No. You know that's not possible.' She affected a light, spirited voice, filled with falsity. 'Yeah, let's just be friends.' She sounded like Asha. Her voice darkened. 'There are some people who can't just be friends, Jez.'

'I can't lose you from my life forever.' His eyes were shining. He was crying. He leaned back against the bonnet of his car and hid his face with his hands.

She weakened then. She wanted to reach out for him but instead she looked out towards the island, steeling herself. 'I feel like I'm dying. Not because I've lost some big plan for my life, like with Nathaniel. You weren't even meant to be in the plan. It was a crap plan, a terrible plan. A plan that hurt. I just …' Her voice faltered and she took an unsteady breath. 'It's like something has been ripped out of me. And it's never going to fill back up.' The fast-moving clouds bathed them in a moment of sunlight.

Jez looked up. His eyelashes were wet. 'I'd do anything to hold you right now.'

She closed her eyes and felt the warmth of the sun on her face. She thought of that motel only metres away, imagined the feeling of him, close. This was his moment of weakness. He would regret it tomorrow. They both would. She opened her eyes and the sun was gone. 'Jez, you need to go home to Asha and try to make it work.'

He wiped his arm across his eyes and nodded, swallowing until he could speak. 'That's what I came here to tell you. I have a child to think about now. You're a better person than me, Phoebe.'

'I know you still care about Asha.'

'Yep.' His voice was clipped. His hands found his pockets.

She turned towards her car. 'Please don't write me any more letters. It's too hard.'

'It'll look strange if you disappear completely.' He was starting to think rationally, about what other people would think. He was drifting away from her.

'My dad's coming down. That'll be a good excuse not to be around. It's the anniversary of Karin's death this week.'

'I'm so sorry, Phoebe.' He rubbed his temples and pressed his palms into the sockets of his eyes. She could see he was trying to suggest something, help in some way.

'Don't, Jez. It's okay.'

'Not really.'

She paused, steadying her voice. 'No. Not really.' Then she turned abruptly, got in her car and started the engine. He was still standing there as she drove away.

# CHAPTER 18

To get Jez out of her mind, Phoebe worked. She was glad of the distraction of her dad's arrival. She scrubbed the benchtops until her fingers pruned, vacuumed and swept until her lower back ached. She stripped the beds and washed the sheets, hanging them to dry in the warm morning sun. Finally, she'd conceded to moving off the lounge, taking the bedroom she'd once shared with Karin. The room still smelled the same, like sunshine and varnish. It faced north and had two single beds arranged neatly along each wall. The room had been stripped of their childhood: the soft toys, the band posters. She wondered if it had been Karin who had got rid of it all when she did up the cottage. It had assumed the beige blandness of a guest room. Sometimes Phoebe felt as though life was like that. Childhood was so saturated in colour and detail, so alive, but as she'd moved through life the colours had faded. She suspected it had something to do with freedom, though she couldn't say exactly what. She lay on her old bed now and the nights telling scary stories came back to her in a flash. She would get so scared she'd hop into Karin's bed and fall asleep balled into her sister's back.

Her dad wouldn't want to take the master bedroom, which had become Karin's, so Phoebe put him in Camilla's old room. She folded a fresh towel on the end of the bed. It hadn't seemed strange to them back then that Camilla got her own room, that was just how Camilla was.

Phoebe was washing some dirt off the tomatoes in the sink when she heard the crunch of a car in the drive. She'd been so focused on cleaning up for his arrival, on not thinking about Jez, that she hadn't considered what it would be like to have her dad stay here. What they'd talk about. What they'd do. It seemed strange suddenly that in all her thirty-seven years they had never spent any time together like this. Did she know who her dad actually was?

He gave her a slightly rough, slightly awkward hug, as though she was a small animal he didn't want to crush. He looked tired from the drive, and with the objectivity of a little time and distance, Phoebe could see the old man he had become. His brown eyes were more watery and there was a puffiness about his face now. Capillaries made tiny red rivers from the corners of his nose across his cheeks. She realised with a pang that she hadn't looked properly at her dad for many years.

'Place looks good,' he said, hands on his hips, squinting against the sun.

'There's quite a bit that needs doing but you'll be happy to know I haven't broken too many things.'

'I've been glad to have someone stay in it, truth be told.' He gave her a warm smile.

'How did Mum feel about you coming down?'

He chuckled. 'Oh, you know your mother. She wished we'd sold it ages ago. She calls it the money gobbler.' He shrugged. 'She's right, of course.'

'It has slightly more sentimental value than that,' Phoebe snapped.

A look of concern crossed his face. 'How've you been down here, by yourself, anyway?'

She smiled. She didn't want to explain the whole thing with Driftwood and all the time she'd spent there, it would only make him want to pop in to visit. Her dad had that easy way with neighbours. 'I've been okay,' she said, running a finger along the red dust on the car bonnet. 'I just needed some time away from everything, you know?' She dusted her hands together. 'I'll grab your bags,' she said.

'I've only got the one. And a new fishing rod.' He shooed her away when she tried to help.

'I wondered if you'd fish,' she said. 'The boat got stolen, you know.'

'Really? Someone wanted that old dinghy? I'm shocked it didn't sink as they took it away.'

'The police came round and everything.'

'Did they find it?'

'Yeah, some bikie types, apparently, but I said we didn't want it back.'

He rubbed his hands together and chuckled. 'Well, good, that's one thing less on my "to do" list.'

They went into the house and Phoebe put the kettle on and set out a plate of biscuits. She had gone into the Bay specially to buy his favourite Lipton Tea and ginger biscuits. She'd also got some steaks and beers for dinner. She'd take him to the club for lunch tomorrow and maybe they'd have fish and chips one evening. It felt good to focus on someone else's needs.

She placed Karin's gorgeous French-style tea tray on the table outside and sat down, feeling her lower back protest after all the sweeping. The afternoon sun streamed through the gum trees, arranging itself in warm patterns across the deck. Lorikeets squabbled in the bird bath near the lemon tree and a kookaburra sat in the branches nearby, a single eye trained on them.

Her dad picked up his mug, his hands trembling slightly. 'You don't realise how special this place is until you come back.'

He sat down on the wooden bench and Phoebe noticed he was wearing shorts despite the cool clip in the air. He always wore shorts, even in winter. She put it down to his English heritage. She felt protective suddenly of his skinny legs and watery eyes, of the slight tremor in his hands. How heartbreaking it was to see time slowly exact its tyrannies on the people you loved.

She was about to ask what he wanted to do tomorrow when she saw that his head was bowed, chin to chest. Her heart skipped a beat. 'Dad?'

He straightened and wiped his arm across his eyes. 'Sorry, love, it's just ... emotional being back after ... last time.'

Tears spiked Phoebe's eyes. There was little that could dissolve her quicker than her father crying. She reached out and put her hand over his, the skin rough and leathery. 'It must be hard.'

'Your sister and I kept it together. We had to ... viewing the body and getting everything sorted, throwing out all the food in the fridge. We didn't have time to think too much, there was too much to do. But now being back ...' He shook his head. 'Sorry. Your dad has become emotional in his old age.'

She squeezed his arm. 'It's okay. It's nice actually to see I'm not the only one still feeling sad. Sometimes I think I shouldn't be by now.'

He took a handkerchief from his pocket, wiped his eyes and blew his nose. 'It feels like last week to me. As you get older the years speed up. It feels like yesterday that you were all born. All those summer holidays here. You think your children will always be little. You think things will last, but they don't.'

She laughed bitterly. 'Yep, I think I've learned that lesson lately.'

He nodded. 'It's been a hard time for you, hey? We've been worried about you. Mum wants me to bring you back. I think it's probably doing you good being down here, and someone may as well look after the place.'

Phoebe took a sip of tea and smiled at him. 'Thanks, I knew you'd be on my side.'

He took a bite of his biscuit. 'Thrown a line in yet?'

'I did, when I first got here. Only nibbles, but you know me, not the most patient person.'

'You were always in the middle. Not as patient as Karin but more patient than Camilla.'

She laughed. Deep down, her dad was more emotionally intelligent than she'd given him credit for over the years, or perhaps it was only now that he was able to show it. She wanted to ask him more—if he missed Karin, what he did with the pain, which seemed to be intensifying as the anniversary drew near—but staying with the practicalities felt more natural.

'Why don't we go down to the jetty now? It's going to be a nice evening. We might even get a sunset.'

'There would have been some good ones with the fires back in January.' He put down his tea, a deep furrow appearing between his brows. 'You realise it was silly to stay when the fires got so close. We've always got the guest room made up, you know? You could have stayed with us if you didn't want to go back to your apartment.'

'I helped out a bit at Driftwood, so I wasn't alone.' She hadn't been going to mention it but it was only a matter of time really. Besides which, if they went fishing they were bound to see someone on the Driftwood jetty.

'They're still living there? The boys?'

'Yeah, Jez lives there with his wife and Tommy's here with his family every weekend. And they have a few house guests that live with them, as well.'

'How's that, seeing Jez after all these years? We all thought the two of you would get married.'

Phoebe felt a rush of blood to her face. 'Well, yeah, that ship sailed a long time ago. Jez and his wife are having a baby now, and Tommy has a little boy, Harry. He's a really sweet little guy but they've had some challenges as he's autistic.'

'Oh, that does sound challenging. Of course I'm remembering Tommy and Jez both as young boys, not fathers. It's making me feel old, coming back here.'

'You and me both, Dad. You and me both.'

He drained his mug. 'Thanks for the cuppa.' He paused and looked awkward all of a sudden, his fingers drumming the table. 'I know there's a lot of pressure these days to get everything done in a certain time frame, but, you know, life is very long.'

'I think that's the wisest thing you've ever said, Dad. I'd wish you'd tell Mum that.'

'You know your mother. She has ...' He sighed a deep sigh and Phoebe saw the tiredness in his eyes again. 'She has certain ways she thinks things should be done.'

'Perfectly.'

'She does love you all though.'

'You're always defending her, even though she's so hard on you, too.'

He shrugged and looked around. 'Well, she's not going to talk me out of coming down here anymore, that's for sure.'

'Good.' Phoebe paused. The sting of tears was back in her eyes. 'I'm really glad you're here, Dad. For this week.'

He smiled his lopsided smile and suddenly he was the same dad who had sat here twenty years ago, playing cards and teasing them. 'Well, we were Karin's favourites, weren't we?'

She laughed. It was the first time she had been able to, while thinking of her sister. 'Yeah, we totally were.'

The river was on fire, burning pink and red as it rippled below their feet, a perfect twin of the sky. Her father took a sip of his beer. 'I see you found Grandma's champagne glasses and one hasn't survived.'

'Champagne glasses? What?' Phoebe screwed up her nose.

He pointed between his knees into the water. 'There in the reeds, I've just worked out what it is. It's been glinting at me all afternoon. I can even picture her holding that glass when I was a kid. She always said a woman needed good nails and good champagne glasses.'

Phoebe's heart stilled, as she looked at the almost intact vintage glass lodged in the sand. 'It must have been Karin,' she said.

'Hey?'

'It must have been Karin. I didn't use them. Why is it in the water?' Her pulse quickened as her mind retraced itself back to her last conversation with her sister.

*We can buy prawns and eat them on the jetty and drink all the free champagne you're going to bring me out of Grandma's gorgeous vintage glasses. I just found a set of six of them wrapped in newspaper on top of the fridge … I'm saving them for a special occasion.*

Phoebe felt a hot surge of anger at herself. If only she'd gone to visit Karin right then, as soon as she'd hung up, taken all those useless free bottles of champagne and driven through the night, maybe she could have saved her. Instead had her sister been sitting here drinking champagne out of a fancy glass alone? Had she knocked the glass into the river? Karin had loved to sit on the jetty at the end of the day despite her fear of the water. She would have loved it here now, the sky darkening to a blood orange. She sometimes went right to the end to call on a Sunday evening as it was the only place on the property that had any hope of mobile reception.

'Karin found Grandma's glasses stashed on top of the fridge. She told me about them the last time we ever spoke, right before …'

She watched her dad's face closely as he stared into the water. It was filled with sorrow. Did he share her doubts? She didn't know. He had been silent the one time early on that she'd suggested to Camilla and her mother that Karin wouldn't have killed herself.

'I'm sure she said there were six. I'm going to see if the other glasses are still in the house.' Phoebe got up, her joints stiff from sitting still so long. She went inside, then slid back the door of the side cabinet in the lounge room. It was where all the good crockery and glassware were kept, as was the fashion in the 1970s. The smell reminded her of her grandparents, talcum powder mixed with the sharp nip of liquor. She saw the glasses straightaway. Heavy crystal in a vintage style with a wide mouth. They were the kind you'd expect at an extravagant 1920s soirée. It had always struck Phoebe as odd that her grandmother owned and loved such beautiful things and yet was happy to live quite simply in the country. Perhaps her father had once hoped their mother possessed such a dichotomy. It had skipped a generation and manifested in his eldest daughter.

There were only four glasses. Phoebe counted again. Two unaccounted for. One glass at the bottom of the river. Where was the other glass? That same unsettled feeling wormed into her bones. It had only been two days after that phone conversation that Karin had died. Had she poured herself one last drink and thrown the glass into the river before throwing herself in? It was so unlike her sister. She would never disrespect her grandmother, or a beautiful object, in this way. She would never disrespect herself in that way. Or had she accidently knocked the glass into the water and gone in to retrieve it and been swept away? But where was the other missing glass? Was she drinking with someone? None of it made sense.

Phoebe shook the chill from her shoulders and closed the cabinet. She washed some dust from her hands in the kitchen sink. She thought about the secrets people might discover if she died suddenly. Were there any, apart from Jez's letters, smoothed flat under a lounge cushion? Would that really be a surprise to anybody though? Even her dad thought they'd been destined to be together.

She returned to the jetty. Dusk hummed over the water, the birds wrestling in the trees, frogs singing their night tune.

'Nothing. Not even a bite,' her dad said.

Phoebe sat down, the wood cold now. She wished she'd put on a jumper up at the house. She realised she was nervous. 'Dad, there's some stuff I've been wanting to talk to you about. About Karin.'

She could just make out his eyes against the darkening sky as she talked. She told him about Ginny next door, who couldn't believe Karin had killed herself, the mystery trips away, the man Ginny had heard on the phone, the joints, so out of character, and reminded him about the time Karin had nearly drowned right here off the jetty. As she spoke, the words felt flimsy in her mouth, like a grim fairy tale. She faltered as she wondered aloud if maybe something else had been going on, if it hadn't been suicide, like they thought.

When she finished, the dark was velvety around them. There was no moon. Her dad was silent for a few seconds and Phoebe waited, her heart drumming like a water insect in her chest.

'I hear what you're saying, I do. Some of that does sound a bit odd. But it's also quite normal for all of this to be stirred up because of the anniversary. You're thinking about her a lot.' He sighed deeply, sadly. 'As to being surprised to find things out about her. We all have secrets. And Karin lived alone. She liked her independence.'

'So, you think I'm imagining it.' She said it without bitterness.

'Of course, I have my doubts too, but I don't think we should stir things up too much. It's hard enough for your mum. She might not have shown it, but it's been very hard for her.'

'You wouldn't know it.'

He reached out and patted her hand. 'We all have our way of dealing with things.'

Phoebe knew what he was implying. She knew the conversation was over.

# CHAPTER 19

Phoebe watched the slant of sunlight inch across her bed. She couldn't move. The anniversary of Karin's death was tomorrow. The one person who could have helped her through it was lost to her. How would she have coped if she was still with Nathaniel? He would have kissed her on the head and told her to get on with it, not to dwell. He'd often accused her of 'dwelling'. That was the difference. If she was with Jez right now he would have held her, told her it was okay to cry, be happy to talk about it. And that would have taken away the loneliness. How had it taken until now to realise she'd been so often lonely with Nate? She buried her head in her pillow and wondered what her dad would think if she stayed in bed all day. Jez felt like something she'd imagined. He and his life at Driftwood were like a dream. She wanted to go back to sleep.

She heard her dad in the kitchen and willed her feet onto the dusty floorboards. Raindrops spotted the window pane. She shrugged on the raincoat at the door, slipped on a pair of old rubber thongs and went out to the letterbox. She'd done this each day, morning and evening, even though she'd told

Jez not to write anymore. There was a soggy newspaper, some pamphlets, and a letter addressed to Karin.

Phoebe's heart jumped, even though it looked like a bill of some kind. She carefully prised open the damp paper.

> *Dear Ms Price,*
>
> *Further to our last correspondence, this is a reminder that your custom-made dining table is ready. Please contact us to arrange delivery or to pick up at our Merimbula workshop. Please find your invoice enclosed.*
>
> *Kind regards,*
> *Woodend Hill*

Yes, she remembered this. She remembered Karin telling her about meeting a furniture designer down the coast in Merimbula and how much she'd loved his work, hewn from local wood and made by hand in a workshop that smelled like sawdust and saplings. She said when she expanded her florist into a tea salon, she intended to have a beautiful table made for the centre of the shop. And here it was. Phoebe flicked to the invoice. It didn't make sense. Karin was well into her plans for expanding the business, had paid a hefty fee for this custom-made table, and she'd fallen in love with a dog. Why would she just abandon everything? Phoebe looked at the sender— Woodend Hill. It was so like her sister to support the local artisans, and in turn they would buy flowers from her.

She remembered the way Karin described her beloved shop—the natural wood of the front door, with 'Miss Botanical' in cursive white writing; the delicate Parisian bird cages hanging from the ceiling; the vintage mirror she'd found in a garage sale that ran the length of the shop, and the blackboard on which she'd inscribe the specials and thoughts of the day. She planned to eventually advertise tea on that blackboard—herbal blends served in heavy cast-iron teapots. And the flowers, arranged with Karin's love and artistry, wrapped in brown paper or hessian, with a tag bearing a positive affirmation. Phoebe had encouraged her to set up an Instagram account to showcase her business, but that had been a work in progress—Karin hadn't liked social media and they hadn't moved past a few pictures she'd sent to Phoebe.

The business had sold quickly after Karin's death. Camilla had handled it all. But perhaps the table had taken many months to make. Phoebe wondered if Camilla knew about it. She wished she could get in the car right now and drive down the coast to pick it up. She would suggest to her dad that they make the journey before he returned to Sydney.

It was raining harder now and Phoebe headed back into the house. She found her dad fixing a broken latch on a window. She told him about the table and they agreed they'd make the trip, even though they weren't sure where the table would go or what size it was.

The rain wasn't easing, so Phoebe suggested lunch at the club in the Bay. Something to get them out of the house.

The club was a concrete and reflective-glass monstrosity that sat opposite the ocean; the type of place that had once been astoundingly modern and now looked like a cheap pair of reflective shades. It had been their family tradition to lunch here at least once during each holiday. As children they'd always been fond of the all-you-can-eat buffet, where the ice cream squeezed out of a machine and the sprinkles were infinite. The place had kept with the times; the buffet had been replaced by a Thai restaurant.

The shrill buzz of the pokies engulfed them as they moved past the tacky entrance foyer. It smelled like stale cigarettes and spilled beer.

They made their way onto the deck overlooking the grey water of the Bay. The sun was cutting its warm fingers through the clouds, gulls wheeling in the breeze. Phoebe saw her straightaway—Asha sitting with her back to the sun, her hair a glowing halo around her head. A guy with dark greasy hair sat opposite her.

A dull thump began in Phoebe's chest. Asha was the last person she felt like seeing today.

Her dad indicated a spot in the sun and began wiping the slightly damp plastic chair with a napkin. Phoebe must have looked distracted because he stopped and looked at her.

'You all right?'

She shook her head and blinked. Asha hadn't seen her yet. 'Yeah, yeah, I've just seen a friend.'

'Oh, do you want to say hi? I'll grab some drinks. I suppose you've progressed beyond lemon squash.'

She laughed uneasily. 'The house white will do, thanks, Dad.' A wave of gratitude washed over her. She was so glad he was here.

Asha glanced her way and Phoebe waved and made her way over. She felt a lump forming in her throat. She hadn't seen her since Tommy's party, since the pregnancy announcement. She felt too fragile for this but she couldn't just ignore Asha.

She pressed a smile onto her lips. 'Hi,' she said, trying to sound cheery.

'Hi Phoebe.' Asha's tone was neither warm nor cool.

'You having a pub lunch?' Phoebe hated herself right now for sounding so obvious and awkward.

'Yep,' said Asha, swirling a glass of what looked like wine in front of her. She must have seen Phoebe glance at it because she said, 'Don't worry, it's watered down. Fifty-fifty.'

Phoebe nodded in an exaggerated way, trying to hide her discomfort. 'Oh, yeah, cool.' She looked at the guy. He seemed young, in his early twenties, and was wearing a pair of dark sunglasses with a cigarette tucked behind his ear.

'This is Aiden. He's a friend from school,' said Asha, her voice emotionless, steady.

Phoebe stuck out her hand awkwardly and they shook. His hand was sweaty.

Aiden pushed his hair behind his ears and stood, fishing in his back pocket for his wallet. 'I'll get another beer. Want anything?'

'Oh no, thanks,' said Phoebe, scanning for her dad. She watched Aiden pick his way through the plastic chairs.

'I'm not having an affair, if that's what you're wondering,' Asha said. 'But I'm absolutely dying for a cigarette.' She feigned smoking, breathing deeply. 'That's why the wine. Thought watered down wine was better than tobacco.'

Phoebe shifted from one leg to the other, willing her dad to return with their drinks. 'Oh, yeah, no, definitely,' she said.

'You seem uncomfortable. You want to sit?' asked Asha.

'Oh no, no. I'm having lunch with my dad.'

'Is that why we haven't seen you around?'

'Yeah, I've been showing him around a bit, you know.'

'Nice. Where have you taken him?' Asha asked, stretching back and putting her feet up on a chair.

Phoebe's words felt stuck in her throat. She hadn't taken him anywhere. She didn't know what to say. Just at that moment, he reached the table they had saved, carrying two glasses of wine. Phoebe felt her body melt with relief. 'Oh, there he is. I better go.' She turned to leave but felt a cool hand on her arm. She swivelled and Asha leaned in, pulling her close. Phoebe could smell alcohol mixed with something sweet.

'I know,' Asha said, her voice low.

Phoebe shot her a quizzical look, her heart ramming against her chest wall.

'You don't have to pretend. We all like the attention of boys. I get it.' Asha nodded towards the bar area, towards Aiden. She let go of Phoebe's arm and leaned back, continuing with her mock smoking routine. 'We both know how to manipulate men. But Phoebe, make no mistake.' She paused and her eyes flickered. 'Jez is mine. I'm not gonna make the same mistake my mum did. I'm not gonna let the best thing that ever happened to me go.' Asha pointed at her with her invisible cigarette. 'I see the way you look at him.'

Phoebe felt her whole body go cold. 'Oh, no Asha, I—'

Asha put up a hand. 'Save it. I can see the two of you had something but you're clearly on the rebound, hon. And he was stressing over making this baby.' She patted her stomach. 'But what's done is done. Don't you think he'll be a great dad?' She took a slow sip of her wine, watching Phoebe over the rim.

Phoebe's head was pounding, anger rising up in her. Her hand went to her throat. Asha was enjoying this. She'd played it so cool for months, but really, she'd been biding her time, waiting to be able to laud this over her.

Phoebe fought against the tears that threatened to spill down her face. 'I'm sorry, Asha. You're right. I'm sure Jez will make a great dad,' She backed away from the table, but then she felt a spike of emotion rush through her. Asha might have felt like she'd won, but there were no winners in this situation. Phoebe straightened and met her intense gaze. 'I really hope you can make him happy, Asha.'

Asha raised her eyebrows and an amused smile played on her lips. 'Maybe we'll see you around some time, Phoebe.'

Phoebe turned and walked away, knowing that Asha meant the exact opposite and that Driftwood was no longer her refuge.

# CHAPTER 20

The garden was misty and spider webs glistened as though strung with jewels. Phoebe walked across the dewy grass to find his letter. She knew it would be there. Today and only today—Karin's death a year ago—eclipsed everything else. Instead of the small square she was expecting, her fingers found a long roll of thin cardboard. She stood in the cover of the eucalypt by the letterbox and unravelled it with shaking hands. A constellation of stars. Her sister's name. He'd had a star named after Karin. There was no note—he'd kept his promise—just the gesture. Simple. Heartbreaking. Phoebe sunk to her knees on the wet ground.

The sound of tyres on the unsealed road roused her. Was it Jez? Her heart leaped. She got up and brushed wet leaves off her knees. She was still in her pyjamas. Her heart shrank as she saw the dusty hood of the white Audi as it pulled into the driveway. Camilla wound down the window and stuck her head out. She was wearing big black sunglasses and an energetic smile.

'Surprise.'

Why did everything in life have to be exciting, a surprise? Even the anniversary of someone's death? The wound of the failed engagement surprise party, Camilla's selfishness, yawned in her chest. Phoebe scrambled to fathom Camilla being here at eight o'clock in the morning.

'You look like a little bush princess. You've got leaves in your hair.' Her sister ran her fingers through her own, foliage-free hair.

Phoebe laughed dryly. How nice it had been to be without judgement for so long. She'd almost forgotten what it felt like. She made her voice neither friendly nor hostile. 'What are you doing here?'

Camilla cocked her head. 'Come on, Phee Phee. Even I'm not going to forget today.'

'But—'

'I left at 3 am. It's a pretty quick drive at that time. I woke at about two and couldn't sleep. Then I realised why. I went online, cancelled everything from my planner for the next three days, woke Rich, packed a bag and came.'

Phoebe blinked as though to wake herself from a particularly strange dream. It was all typical Camilla. The spontaneity, the intensity, the lack of thought for anyone but herself. 'I don't know what to say.'

Camilla's face softened and Phoebe saw she looked tired. She felt sad that she was stressed about her sister's arrival on such an important day. She should have been thrilled to have the extra support, but it didn't feel like support.

'How about a coffee?' Camilla grimaced. 'I thought about bringing my Nespresso. And I don't suppose you have the ingredients for a super smoothie for breakfast?' She must have read Phoebe's look of incredulity because she winced apologetically.

Phoebe laughed despite herself and shook her head. She wanted to blast Camilla for imposing all her petty judgements and stupid food expectations within a few minutes of arriving. Instead she took a deep breath. She didn't want to fight. Not today. 'No kale in these parts, I'm afraid, but we do have organic tomatoes.'

Camilla's eyebrows rose. She scanned the garden. 'Do you have chooks?'

'Sorry, no free-range eggs from the garden but I do have some courtesy of the wonderful Coles supermarket,' Phoebe said.

Camilla waved a hand and flashed one of her most charming smiles. 'Perfect then.'

Phoebe rustled up the best breakfast she could for her sister. Poached eggs with tomatoes and basil from the garden, toasted sourdough, and a cup of free-trade coffee in the good mugs. She made enough for them all—her dad was happy to have a second breakfast and she knew she should try to eat something. They sat on the deck in the soft morning sun.

'I'd forgotten how pretty it was down here,' said Camilla, gazing out onto the river, arm stretched elegantly along the bench seat. 'And how quiet.'

It was a Friday and the river was mostly free of craft. A waterbird's cry echoed across the way and there was the rising insect-hum of the day warming up.

'Well, this is a treat, to have my two girls here today.' Her dad's eyes crinkled at the corners and glinted in the sunlight.

Phoebe smiled. She knew he was feeling as emotional as she was.

'I thought you'd appreciate it, Dad,' Camilla said between mouthfuls of egg. 'Mum would have come but someone had to handle the business. There's so much going on right now.'

Phoebe was relieved their mother wasn't here. Her father seemed to soften some of Camilla's spikier edges, as though his humility rubbed off just a little on her.

'So, what's the plan?' Camilla fluffed up her hair and looked at Phoebe. There was no wondering how anyone was feeling or what she'd been doing for the past few months. She'd finished her breakfast and now she needed a new task. There was no stopping with Camilla. 'So, I was thinking ...' She threw Phoebe a sidelong glance.

*I'm not going to approve of this*, Phoebe thought.

'Something small. Very low key.' Camilla flattened her hands on the table, her Hermes bracelets jangling down her arm. 'Dad, you could fire up the barbecue and I'll make my famous punch. I'm assuming they have guava juice down here.'

Phoebe flinched as a quiver of frustration brushed along her arms. Camilla hadn't even mentioned Karin's name yet or what they were 'celebrating'. For her, each milestone in life could be contained to an event rather than let loose as a feeling.

'Just a little gathering. Neighbours,' she went on. 'I can go and tell them now. The boys from Driftwood. Phoebe, you said they were around on weekends. We could do it tonight, or tomorrow night, depending on ...' She checked the heavy watch on her slim wrist. 'Availability.'

Phoebe clenched her hands into fists under the table. This wasn't some business lunch for high-flying executives, it was a day to remember their sister. 'I don't understand why everything needs to be marked by a celebration. We're talking about Karin's suicide here, Camilla. Maybe it's just enough for the three of us to be here.'

Camilla looked confused. Phoebe ignored the feeling of guilt building in her stomach and went on. 'I appreciate you wanting to do something nice, I really do, but it's not really like that round here. Anyway, people will already have plans.'

Camilla's eyes widened in disbelief. 'What plans?'

Phoebe bit her lip to stop the words that were forming from coming out of her mouth. She waited a beat and changed them. 'Despite what you think, people do have lives here. They might not be rich but they still have plans for a Friday or Saturday night.'

Camilla's cheeks flushed. 'I'm just trying to do something nice for our sister, Phoebe. I may not be able to abandon my entire life and move down here, but I can do my bit.'

Phoebe was angry now. 'You think that's what I did? It was just a decision I made one day? To abandon my life? You think I should have just gone and harassed Nathaniel until he agreed to stick to the original plan? To make your perfect engagement party a success? Is that what this is about, Camilla? Are you still angry that I ruined your party?'

Camilla's head jutted backwards as though Phoebe had slapped her. 'What are you talking about? You think I'm that shallow?'

Phoebe laughed without humour. 'No. No, not shallow at all.'

Camilla turned to their father, that wide-eyed, disbelieving look in her eyes again.

He held up his hands. 'I don't want to get into this. Can't you girls just be nice to each other, today of all days?'

Phoebe stood and started stacking the plates, enjoying the violent clanging. 'We're not having a party.' It felt good to say it, to take control. Camilla's mouth was pursed, her arms crossed tightly against her body. 'And if you must know, yes, I abandoned my life because I was so sick of comparing it to yours, Camilla.'

Camilla made a loud scoffing sound that reminded Phoebe of their mother. 'You think I don't want to abandon my life?' She laughed maniacally. 'Every second of every day. I'm the one who's jealous, of your freedom. Do you realise how frantic I am all the time? If I slip up for an instant the whole thing will come crashing down—the business, the kids, my marriage.'

Phoebe paused. She'd never thought about Camilla wanting to abandon anything. She'd always seemed so capable, so strong. It seemed impossible that Camilla was jealous of her. Phoebe's voice was softer now. 'At least you have all those things.'

'Would you like some help with those?' Their dad flashed Phoebe a hopeful smile and reached for the plates.

'No, it's fine,' she snapped, then grimaced at her own tone. 'Sorry.' She put down the plates. 'Dad, you shouldn't let Mum push you around so much. I know you don't like conflict but—'

Camilla made a disbelieving sound. 'Geez, any more hurtful home truths you'd like to share with us today, Phoebe?'

It felt impossible to stop now. Now that she'd started telling the truth, it was as though a tight place in her chest had expanded. It felt good, powerful. 'Yes, actually, there is something else.' She glanced at her dad, wincing a little. 'I don't believe Karin killed herself. Dad just wants to leave it alone, as usual, but I can't, not if I'm being honest. I just can't. There are too many things.'

Camilla shook her head slowly, obviously struggling to absorb so much in one hit. She was about to speak when there was a loud voice around the side of the house. Phoebe recognised it immediately.

The Texan appeared holding a container full of leafy greens and a few of his prize potatoes. 'And here I was thinking Phoebe might be lonely.'

She felt her cheeks redden. She wondered how much he'd heard. But despite the awkward look on his face, Phoebe felt like hugging him; she'd missed his jovial good-natured presence in her life. 'This is Tex. This is my dad, Peter, and my sister Camilla.'

Camilla's face lit up and she arranged the bangles on her arm. She was clearly thrilled to have a distraction from all the emotional talk. 'You're from Texas then, I assume?'

'I'm told my accent will never let me forget it, so I figured why not just go with the flow, as you Aussies might say. Retired Texan banker and cattle farmer who now devotes himself to the garden.'

'And the kitchen. He's a wonderful cook,' said Phoebe.

'How interesting,' said Camilla, reaching for the box of vegetables.

'No, he doesn't grow kale,' Phoebe said dryly.

Camilla shot her a withering look but it had a nip of playfulness at its tail. It was the first time either of them had admitted their vulnerabilities to each other. Phoebe wondered if maybe their relationship might have the capacity to change or whether the same dynamic would just reappear, over and over, as it so often did with siblings.

'We're not using up all my produce with one less mouth to feed, and you know that breaks my heart,' said the Texan.

Phoebe wondered if he and Wendy had suspected anything since her sudden disappearance from their daily routine. She tried to sound light. 'I've had Dad here, and Camilla arrived today.'

'Well, you must all come over for dinner. We have lots of vegies to use up.'

Phoebe felt jittery at the thought. There was no way she could handle seeing Asha after their encounter the day before, the tension would be unbearable. Her temples began to throb in anticipation. Camilla shot her a sidelong look and Phoebe could see her sister's mind working. She knew what she wanted. As much as it hurt her to let Camilla win, it was a better outcome than having to go to Driftwood. It would be easier on her turf. In truth, it would be easier the more people were here. She rolled her eyes and gave a small shrug of defeat.

'I've got a better idea,' said Camilla. 'We were just planning a casual barbecue.' She looked at Phoebe for approval, choosing her words carefully. 'We were thinking tomorrow night?'

'It's the anniversary of my eldest daughter's death today,' their dad added.

The Texan lowered his head, picked up a potato and rubbed its dusty skin in his hands. 'Jez did mention that. Sorry to hear.' His mouth flattened into a line of sympathy. 'Well, I thought Phoebe might need cheering up, but a barbecue sounds great. I'll bring along some salads.'

'Will Jez and Tommy be around?' asked Camilla. 'I haven't seen them in forever. They were like brothers when we were young.'

The Texan chewed at the end of a twig of lemongrass. 'Yeah, I think Tommy and Jenna will be down this afternoon as usual, and Jez and Asha should be around.'

'That's settled then. Why doesn't everyone come, anytime from what, 5 or 6 pm?' Camilla hesitated for a moment. 'Or, what time do you think, Phoebe?'

She shot her sister a look. It was the first time in their lives Camilla had ever deferred to her, small as the gesture was. 'Six sounds great to me.'

When the Texan had left they went inside to wash up, but not before Camilla had located a pair of hitherto undiscovered rubber gloves to protect her manicure. Phoebe wasn't sure if her questioning of Karin's death had been forgotten in the avalanche of memories from their childhood or whether Camilla was avoiding it. Before Camilla could ask, Phoebe just said it. 'And in case you're wondering, yes, Camilla, you may as well invite the rest of the neighbours, too.'

There was no magnificent sunset. Didn't the earth know what today meant? What had the sky looked like that night, one year ago? Had it been scarlet-torn, as though the fabric of the earth had been ripped away to reveal a glimpse of heaven, or had it been dull and low and grey, like tonight? Phoebe couldn't bear thinking about Karin's final moments, the last glimpse of sky she'd seen. Birth and death were both shrouded in the same cloak. They happened to us all but there was no real language to express the physical brutality of either. They were left for those hazy unknown places where dreams and nightmares took us.

She heard footsteps on the jetty behind her and turned. Camilla was holding two glasses of wine. They'd eaten fish and chips from the Bay on the deck earlier, licking the salt and lemon from their fingers. She and Camilla had opened a bottle of white wine and their dad had drunk the rest of the beer. They'd toasted Karin and remembered small things. She'd loved fish and chips and prawns, but hated hamburgers and Chinese food. She loved wearing hats and had one for every occasion. She discovered eyeliner at the age of fifteen and with the realisation that it made her look exotic, had worn it, always. She hated avocados. She would pick up a spider in her hand but was creeped out by frogs. There were so many small things that made up a person. Talking about them made her seem almost alive again.

But now Phoebe felt the full heaviness of what today actually meant. Wine and company were exactly what she needed. A rush of affection for Camilla took her by surprise. They clinked their glasses together gently, a silent toast to their absent sister. Phoebe was about to apologise for fighting when Camilla spoke.

'I went up the road to check my texts. Mum sent one. It was a bit cryptic, and half of it was about one of our clients, but I think she was basically saying she felt sad not to be here.'

Phoebe let a puff of air escape her lips. 'Well, I guess that's a big deal coming from Mum.'

Camilla bumped her hip against Phoebe's. 'Listen, Dad and I have been talking. We're both worried about you.'

Phoebe felt the small hairs on her neck rise. It had always been Karin and Phoebe against the rest of the family, and it felt the same now. She stiffened. 'I know what you're going to say. That I've had too much time to think down here. Yes, that's probably true, but it's more than that.'

'Well, you've got to admit, you went from such a busy, exciting life to ...'

'To what? This boring old place?' Phoebe drew a few deep breaths. She wasn't going to get angry again. Sometimes it felt talking to Camilla was like talking to a small child, explaining things that perhaps they had never considered properly or had the emotional maturity to manage before.

'I've come to love it here. Karin loved it here. You'll see that when you meet people.' Phoebe looked at her sister in the darkening air. She was wrapped up in layers of cream cashmere, her hair tucked into a grey, loose-knit beanie. She looked like she should be in a magazine. Phoebe's own hoodie and jeans would have once made her feel inferior; now she realised she no longer cared. 'Things are simpler here, if you let them be,' she said.

She could feel Camilla's eyes on her. Strangely, she didn't feel judgement, but something gentler.

'Okay, Phee, I'm listening. You think, what? The police got it wrong? Karin died by accident instead of suicide? Or someone killed her?'

When it was said so harshly out loud it sounded ridiculous, like the daylight recounting of a dream that had seemed so real moments before in your head. But Phoebe said simply what she had always believed. 'Yes. Maybe ...'

'We both know how careful Karin was around water and besides, she left a suicide note. And if some misadventure befell her ... I mean, who would do something like that?'

'Karin was seeing someone. I'm sure of it.' Phoebe tried to calm her voice, her thoughts, so as not to overwhelm and scare Camilla off.

'Her note, the flowers they found up in the house. They said, "I'm sorry". But what if they didn't mean "I'm sorry for leaving you all and killing myself." What if they were for someone specific, an apology of some sort? And Karin had used Grandma's vintage champagne glasses right before she died. Dad found one at the bottom of the river, and the other is missing. Why was she using two glasses?'

'But how would we ever know? If the police couldn't know, how could we? And if she was seeing someone, surely there'd be some evidence. Phone calls, emails, something more than missing champagne glasses, or whatever. She would have told you, for a start.'

Phoebe waited a moment, steeling herself before going on. 'It's not only me. Ginny next door thought Karin was seeing someone. She rang Karin late one night when she was away for the weekend and woke her up. She heard a man talking next to her. Why would she be with a man late at night having just woken up? Why wouldn't she tell me about him? Why would there be no evidence anywhere of him? And why didn't she tell me she went away every few weekends? The only conclusion I can come to was that she was having an affair. It's the only reason she wouldn't have told me any of this.'

Camilla laughed, disbelievingly. 'Karin, having an affair? What, all secretive … with a married man or something? Yeah, right. How is that any more likely than her committing suicide?'

'Love.' Phoebe was glad the night had wrapped them close and Camilla couldn't read her expression.

'Oh, still … Karin was so not the type to get into something grubby.'

The word felt like a slap. It was hard to hear the truth, that this was how other people inevitably viewed an affair. They didn't care about the feelings involved, the complications, the subtleties. There were no subtleties, there were only lies and deception when you looked objectively. She too might have once thought it impossible that Karin had hidden a secret lover. Now she knew it wasn't. Perhaps everyone was capable of it, given the right—or wrong—circumstances. 'Maybe it didn't feel grubby, maybe it felt like she couldn't help it,' said Phoebe.

'Oh, people can always help it.' Camilla crossed her arms in front of her and her mouth drew tight. 'You have no idea how little things can set your mind spinning. I mean, I trust Rich, I do, but I'm just being practical. He's an attractive man. He earns good money, and you know what? I get scared sometimes. When you have kids, it's not just yourself you're looking out for. Sometimes the pressure feels huge to keep looking young, so he won't, I don't know, run off with his secretary.' She took off her beanie and ran her fingers through her hair.

Phoebe cocked her head. 'Really? You worry about Rich?' Phoebe thought these were the worries that happened to other less confident women than her sister.

'Of course. Why do you think that every nanny I've ever hired is either old or unattractive?'

Phoebe scoffed. 'The nanny. That's such a cliché.'

'It's a cliché for a reason, Phee Phee. Let me tell you, I have friends who are living out the cliché right now, while their former nanny lives the high life with the father of their children.' Camilla shivered and linked arms with Phoebe. It felt surprisingly nice to be this close to her sister.

'What about hot friends, are you wary of them, too?' asked Phoebe, enjoying seeing Camilla's more human side.

'Yes and no. You know I'm drawn to beautiful people, so that's most of my friends.'

They both laughed. 'And then of course there's your stunning sisters,' said Phoebe, before she realised she'd used the plural again.

Camilla squeezed her arm. Her voice was softer now. 'Karin was more beautiful than both of us put together, wasn't she? How many men fell in love with her and how many did she reject? I guess it's not impossible that someone got obsessed with her, or a married man fell in love with her and she was too ashamed to tell anyone, to tell you, but say in some distant universe what you're saying is true, what are we going to do? Rock up to the police station insisting they find her secret lover, who somehow knows something about her death? Just because she might have been having an affair doesn't mean that person had anything to do with her death. Can't we just let her rest in peace? Today of all days. Here of all places.'

Phoebe's heart was hammering as she looked out across the dark water. A lone cry echoed around them and Phoebe felt Camilla move closer. They watched a crane glide, white against the night sky, and settle silently on the surface.

'Okay, that's kind of spooky,' Camilla whispered.

Tears filled Phoebe's eyes and she smiled. 'And I haven't even told you about my dreams. Karin won't let me abandon her, Camilla. We're bound by this river and she's here but she didn't want to be. She didn't want to abandon us.'

PART FOUR

# King Tide

# THEN

When Camilla saw the gun she screamed. The dog started barking down below and somewhere a flock of cockatoos took flight, their screeches echoing through the trees.

Karin's heart was hammering. She grabbed her little sister gently by the shoulders and looked her in the eyes, which were filling with tears. 'It's okay, Cammie.' She glanced at Phoebe. 'Why don't you go outside onto the balcony and see if you can spot any animals?'

'I don't want to,' said Camilla, but she let Phoebe lead her outside the treehouse.

She knew Camilla would be too proud to let Phoebe take her back down to the ground, but Karin didn't want to leave Tommy here with the gun.

'We should just leave it here,' she said. 'It might not even have bullets in it. Just don't touch it. You shouldn't have touched it.'

Tommy shrugged and squirmed. 'Well, I had to see if it was heavy. If it was real.'

Karin resisted the urge to reach out and touch it herself. She had never seen a gun in real life before. It was as black as a beetle and looked exactly like in the movies, but bigger than she expected a real-life gun to be. Even though her heart was racing, there was also another feeling in her body—excitement. She felt like they were true adventurers, in the middle of nowhere, with a gun. The most they usually found on their treks into the bush were things like half-smoked cigarettes, and once they found a lighter and a bucket filled with used fireworks.

'Has Jez seen it?'

'Yeah, he wanted to try firing it.'

Karin rolled her eyes. Jez never took anything seriously.

'What was that scream?' asked Jez, his head sticking into the cabin. He was breathless from climbing the tree fast.

'Just Cammie,' said Phoebe, shooting Jez a look.

'Well, it's pretty freaky here,' Camilla said, sucking on her bottom lip. 'Mum and Dad wouldn't want us being here with guns and rude magazines.'

'Yeah, but it's kind of cool though,' said Jez, a cheeky smile on his face. 'Hey, I saw two guys walking through the bush as I was climbing.'

'What?' exclaimed Tommy, his jaw dropping and his face going pale. 'What—towards us? Did they see you? Are they coming this way?'

Jez shrugged. 'They were quite a long way away. It was hard to tell.'

Karin felt all the blood drain from her body now. The strange men. This was probably their hideout. It was probably their gun. Her heart was beating loud in her ears and the silly song Camilla had been humming on the picnic rug was going through her brain on a loop.

Tommy's eyes locked onto hers and he whispered to her. 'Can you make sure no one touches the gun? I'm going to have a look. This could be their place.'

She nodded and swallowed hard. She tried to ignore the fear spiking under her ribs. She wished they were still sitting on the grass at the picnic area making daisy chains. She wished she'd been more responsible for her younger sisters.

Tommy pushed his way out of the cabin and she could hear his footsteps pacing the wooden planks.

He stuck his head back in. He was breathless. 'Everyone down. Now. And be quiet.'

'Why do we have to be quiet?' asked Camilla, her face red and tear-stained.

'What's happening?' Phoebe asked, her eyes large with worry.

'There are some men coming and we need to get down from here. But it's going to be fine.'

Phoebe gasped. She grabbed her younger sister's hand. 'You're right, it's totally gross here, Cammie. I'm starving. I wonder if there's any more food? Let's go back to Driftwood and make a cake.'

'There's no more food. Jez ate it all,' said Camilla, but she followed Phoebe to the ladder.

Karin watched her sisters descend, followed by Jez. 'Do you think it's their gun?' She turned to Tommy, who was scanning the bush, on high alert

'That's what I'm worried about. We're going to have to hide and just watch where they go. Hopefully they won't go down to the bank and see our boat. He held out the rope to her. 'You next.'

Her feet didn't feel as steady on the way down. One of the pieces of wood on the ladder was wobbly, and she had to stop herself from crying out when her foot slipped. Her hands ached from holding on so tightly.

The ground was a welcome feeling beneath her feet. She gave the dog a cuddle and they waited for Tommy. As soon as his feet hit the ground he pointed to the bank of mangroves where they'd come from.

'Let's head back there. We'll hide in the mangroves,' he said.

'Are we hiding from baddies?' asked Camilla.

As if to answer her question they heard the low sound of the men's voices. They all instinctively crouched as though ducking for cover from swooping birds. The men laughed and there was a swish swish as they moved through the dense bush.

Karin could hear her own breath. *What if the dog barks and the men find them hiding and come after them with the gun?*

They ran back down the path to the mangroves and squatted at the muddy roots, their hands sticky with sweat, and waited. In the dark of the mangroves, Karin's eyes met Tommy's. He nodded in reassurance. She patted the dog's neck, willing him silently not to bark and give away their hiding place.

The men moved closer through the bush, their voices becoming louder and louder until she could see their hairy legs going through the mangroves only metres away. They were carrying something. Karin was holding her breath. Their boat was right there on the sand. What if the men stole it, trapping them all here? No one knew where they were. They were meant to still be at the picnic area.

One of the men yelled and there was a huge splash. Karin jumped, pressing her hand over her mouth. But it wasn't a body or a gun being thrown into the water, it was a kayak. She felt all the tension in her arms and legs melt away. They weren't criminals or hobos, they were kayakers. She shared a relieved smile with Tommy and let out a long breath.

She looked over to see Camilla nestled into Phoebe. Jez and Phoebe were holding hands.

They watched as the men pushed off into the river with their gleaming silver oars. Even though the threat had passed, none of them moved. The heat of the day thrummed in the air as heavy as the cicada song in the trees, but it was cool and safe in their hiding place.

Tommy was the first to emerge. 'They're gone,' he said, stretching his hands above his head and letting out a big breath.

That's when Karin saw it. The shiny black of the gun tucked into the band of Tommy's board shorts, as though he'd done it a hundred times before, as though he was already a policeman.

'Tommy,' she said, shaking her head as she approached him. Her legs felt wobbly and her voice sounded wobbly. 'Why do you still have it?'

He swivelled towards her, his hands coming down and finding the gun, taking it quickly out of his waistband. He looked young. Younger than her in that moment. A rush of fear and anger surged through her and she scrunched up her face.

'Why would you bring it? I thought we said we wouldn't touch it?' She realised there was another feeling in her body. She felt betrayed. They had a pact, like kids in the adventure books they both liked, to protect the others.

'I just … I wanted to have it in case, you know, they were bad men. It's better for us to have it than them,' he said, his eyes flashing.

'But they weren't bad men,' she said, moving closer over the wet sand towards him. 'We're okay now. We should put it back.'

'We can't keep the gun,' said Jez, emerging from the mangroves with Camilla and Phoebe behind.

'Oh, I know,' Tommy said, but he didn't move.

Karin felt a jolt of protectiveness for her sisters, and she took a step forward. 'Maybe give it to me and I'll take it back up the tree.'

Tommy took a slow step backwards. 'I don't know, is that a good idea? For bad men to have a gun? Who knows who could find it up there in the treehouse? Anyone can see it from the river.'

'It's better than kids having a gun,' said Camilla in a small voice, hugging Phoebe's arm.

'Not really,' said Tommy. 'Maybe we should take it to our parents.' He was still holding the gun with both hands.

'You're scaring us,' said Jez in a tone Karin had never heard him use before.

Maybe it was Jez admitting he was scared, maybe it was the way Tommy was standing there as though he was going to run. Karin moved before she could stop herself. She was reaching forward, her hand touching the cold metal, and then there was a bang so loud her ears rang and for a moment everything slowed and went silent.

She saw the gun drop to the sand. Tommy fell forward onto his knees, and for an awful second she thought he'd been shot. But he was pressing his hand against the dog's back leg. The others all rushed forward, crowding around the animal. When Karin's ears stopped ringing she heard it. A shrieking, high-pitched and awful, coming from the dog. Then she saw it. Blood. Everywhere, blood. The dog was on his side, his eyes showing white. She dropped beside him, letting out a cry.

'He's badly hurt. The bullet's hit his leg,' Tommy said, his hands covered in blood.

'I'm so sorry. I'm so sorry.' The words fell out of Karin over and over and she felt her sisters crowd around her, hugging her shoulders. Her whole body was shaking.

Tommy didn't take his eyes off the dog but his voice was calm. 'It's not your fault. I don't know why the gun even went off. I thought the safety was on.'

He sounded so old, like a parent, and Karin realised it was she who had behaved like a child. She buried her face in her hands. She could barely look at the dog thrashing on the sand, his eyes rolling back. Part of her wanted to hold the dog's shaking body against hers, the other part wanted to run as far away as she could go. And then something solidified inside her. *We have to get him into the boat. To a vet.*

She tore off her T-shirt and wrapped it around the hurt leg. Tommy helped, knotting it tight, but there was so much blood. The white fabric was suddenly red.

Camilla was whimpering on the sand next to the dog's head, a smear of blood on her cheek. 'I'm sorry I called you Stinky Bum. Your real name is Bingo. You're a beautiful dog.'

'Someone help me get him up,' said Karin, hoisting the dog towards the boat by his shoulders. He was struggling and whining in pain, his back leg kicking madly.

But the others didn't move. 'Why are you all just standing there?' she cried. 'Help me. We have to save him. Get him to a vet.'

Jez, Phoebe and Camilla tried to drag the dog towards the boat but he was heavy and squirming and Karin could tell he didn't want to be touched. Tommy wasn't helping at all. She yelled at him but her voice didn't even sound like her own.

She saw Tommy shake his head, very slowly. 'He's not going to make it. He's in a lot of pain.'

He looked towards the gun, still lying on the sand. She shook her head and wrapped the dog up in her arms, smelling his wet, salty, bloody fur. She knew what Tommy meant. 'No. I won't let you. We'll fix this. We'll fix him. It's only his leg,' she said.

But Tommy had picked up the gun and was walking towards the dog. He pointed the gun at the dog's head and everyone went quiet and still. Even the river seemed to stop running. The dog calmed a bit.

'No!' Jez cried. But Tommy shook his head and stayed there. He had tears in his eyes.

'All of you go behind the mangroves. Now.'

'No, Tommy, you don't have to do this,' said Karin, pleading with him with her eyes, too frightened to get any closer. 'Please, I'm begging you, Tommy. We can save him. It's not far back down the river.'

'I have to do this. Get behind the trees. Now. Don't watch.' Tommy was standing over the dog, not touching him now. His eyes were glassy.

She looked to Jez and Phoebe, but their faces were pale, their eyes fixed on the dog who was howling softly now. Camilla had her hands over her ears, tears streaming down her face. Karin squeezed her eyes shut, then opened them and gave Tommy one last pleading look, but she could see that she couldn't reach him now. He had made up his mind.

She kissed the dog's head then grabbed her sisters and pulled them behind the mangroves. The silence was so loud she couldn't stand it. Waiting. Waiting for the shot to pierce the thick air. When it rang out they pressed into each other's bodies, trembling.

'It's done.' Tommy stood next to the mangroves and Karin couldn't see the gun anywhere. She didn't even care anymore what he did with it. The dog's body was limp, like a piece of seaweed on the sand.

She wanted to punch Tommy, hit him in his stupid chest and scream in his calm face, but she knew it wasn't his fault. Not really. She was the one who had made the gun go off.

'I want to see him. I want to see Bingo,' said Camilla through her tears.

'Okay,' said Karin, smoothing her little sister's hair. 'We'll say goodbye.' She had to be the grown-up now. She needed to look after her little sisters.

Jez knelt down next to them, still hidden in the mangroves. His eyes were large. 'Tommy and I will make a raft. We'll send Bingo out into the river on it. It'll be like a funeral.'

It took them a while to head out of the mangroves. It was as though something had changed for them all; the grown-up world had crashed into their little kid world. Karin knew Phoebe felt it, too. For Karin it was as if she was walking through thick water. Her arms and legs would not obey her. But finally she began to move and roused the others.

'We'll decorate the raft,' she said as she watched the boys begin to pick up sticks and crack them in half with stomps of their feet. 'I saw some flowers just a bit up on the bank. I think they were kangaroo paw and banksia. We can decorate the raft with them. Make it beautiful.'

Bingo's body looked like a deflated balloon. Karin had never seen a dead body. It was so strange and sad that it felt like a bad dream that she'd wake up from soon.

As they picked wildflowers from the banks of the river they talked about Bingo. They wondered whose dog he was really, and if he'd be missed. Was he a stray? Or did he just want to come on an adventure? The boys tied reeds from the river around thick branches they had broken with their bare hands and legs. Together they gently moved the dog's body onto the wobbly stick raft and placed bottlebrushes around his head like a crown, banksia over the wound on his leg and a big red waratah over his chest where his heart would be. The sun was sinking lower in the sky and they knew their parents would be worried. As the raft drifted out, they all held hands on the bank, watching until the river claimed Bingo, and he disappeared forever.

# CHAPTER 21

The tide was the highest Phoebe had seen it. The jetty met with
the lip of the water as though the river was going to consume it
whole. She thought about that abandoned champagne glass, of
all those old bones of fish and crabs and other dead things under
the water. She wished the river could whisper its secrets. Stories
of it flooding had been passed down from her grandparents, but
no one could remember actually having seen it.

Phoebe felt like she was caught in the tide. She had no
choice but to let it carry her, because everyone knew that
swimming against the tide didn't work. The water was too
strong, too deep.

The afternoon was unseasonably warm. They'd spent all day
preparing for the barbecue—thankfully, Camilla had stopped
calling it a party. Phoebe was glad of the distraction, and as
she watched her sister direct proceedings, she realised that this
was Camilla's way of showing her love for Karin. The deck
had been swept, the lawn mown, lights and lanterns strung up
and the smell of baking pastry wafted from the kitchen. There
were none of Camilla's usual flourishes. The food was going
to be basic—sausages and bread rolls, some mini quiches, bags

of crisps emptied into their grandmother's cut-glass bowls, and sandwiches cut into triangles. It had turned out, not as a showpiece for Camilla's entertaining, but her concession to something simpler. This was the sort of gathering Karin might have thrown herself.

Phoebe was putting beer and wine into an esky on the deck when she heard footsteps behind her. She turned and jolted upright. Jez was just standing there, as though he'd been standing there all along. He smiled at her. An easy smile. The kind that he used to have in the sun-honeyed warmth of the past. She blinked, confused. She looked around for Asha, senses acute.

'She's not here,' he said, reading her.

'You're early. We're not expecting anyone for an hour.'

She looked at his face, really looked. His eyes were soft and all she could see was hope.

'Can you come with me? Can we talk?' he asked, holding out his hand.

She could hear Camilla and her dad in the kitchen. 'Why are you here, Jez?'

'Everything's changed, Phoebe. Please, will you just come for a quick drive with me? Please.'

Phoebe ducked into the house. 'I'm just popping into the Bay,' she said. 'Need anything?' As she grabbed her car keys she couldn't help but feel her heart blooming with the same hope she'd seen on Jez's face.

\* \* \*

The beach was deserted. No one swam here because the sand was flecked with black mud from the estuary. The tide was high, the water having reclaimed the driftwood that usually lay in the shallows. Phoebe got out of her car just as Jez's ute crunched into the car park. Her whole body trembled as he waved.

He got out of his ute and now she could see that his emotions were mixed. There was heaviness in the way he closed the car door, as if it were taking all his energy. But that warm smile came easily to his lips as he approached.

'Let's walk,' she suggested.

He breathed deeply and nodded.

They took off their shoes and began towards the estuary, the late afternoon sun at their backs.

'I don't know where to start,' he said.

'Start at the beginning.'

'I'll start at the end,' he said, eyes fixed on the sand in front of him, voice steady. 'We lost the baby.'

Phoebe stopped and turned to him. 'Oh no, I'm so sorry Jez.'

'I've just come from the hospital.'

'How's Asha?' Her mind was spinning, like the seagulls wheeling above them.

He shook his head and took another deep breath. 'She's gone crazy with grief. Flick's with her now. She's not alone.'

'Of course. Good. That's good. But maybe you should—'

'She doesn't want me there. She's blaming me. Saying I didn't want this baby. But I did, Phoebe. I've wanted this baby for so long.' His face crumpled and he pressed his fists into his eye sockets.

'I know, I know you did.'

There were so many emotions running through her. Guilt, relief, love, pain. She felt the anguish as a burn in her chest.

'Jez.' She took a step towards him and gently pulled his hands away from his eyes. He was crying.

'I feel like such a bastard.'

She pulled him down so that they were sitting on the sand. She wrapped his wide back in her arms and he deflated. His head hung between his knees and his body shook silently.

'It's not your fault, Jez. You tried your best. You tried to be honourable, which is all anyone can do in life.'

He straightened and wiped his face with the hem of his T-shirt. His eyes were red-rimmed. 'The things she said.'

'She's grieving.'

'It feels like that baby was the only thing keeping us together. But I was trying. I was going to be a good dad.'

'And you would have been.'

'Then why do I feel so relieved, Phoebe? Why do I feel like I've escaped when the mother of my child is in so much pain? How can I be such a bastard?'

'You're not a bastard, Jez, you're human. You've been struggling with this for a long time. It's okay to feel two things at once. Emotions are not black and white.'

His whole body was shaking now and he turned to her, his eyes filled with tears. 'But that's the thing. It is black and white. I love you, Phoebe. I want to be with you. It's so clear and it's so awful. I just don't know what to do.'

'Hey, hey.' She spoke quietly, as though to a wild animal in distress. 'I'm not going anywhere.'

Swiftly then, she was in his arms and he was kissing her. It was hungry and slow and full of anguish and passion. Her mind was telling her to resist, that this was not the time or the place, but it felt like she was diving into him and there was no way out. She couldn't breathe but it didn't matter. Wet foam nipped at their feet and they rose, stumbling towards a fallen tree trunk at the mouth of the estuary.

Her body was alive as she lay on the powdery sand. He tasted like the ocean, his breath a shell held close to her ear. Her mind flatlined. All she could do was feel. Her bare back on sand, his skin rougher than she remembered. The sea surged around them as he entered her and it felt like the whole ocean engulfing her. She went under and opened her eyes. His eyes were open too, and she could see all the way into him. Her external senses closed down then, in the watery space between them and she wanted to stay in this secret place of theirs forever. And then she was gasping for air. They both were. And they clung together, their bodies shivering, but warm in their underwater knowledge.

They must have stayed like that for a long time. Phoebe felt honed by the forces of wind and water. They dressed slowly, the crash of the waves and the bird call intensifying as the evening put down its soft-footed paws.

He took her hands and guided her over the log that had shielded them from view. 'I don't have to tell you that I'll do anything to be with you.'

She smiled at him, a rush of gratitude filling her. 'I'm so in love with you.'

He kissed her hair. 'I don't think I ever stopped loving you.'

She looked into his eyes. The wash of sadness had retreated. 'Jez, I won't abandon you again, I promise.'

He hugged her to him as they walked back down the beach. 'I don't know what it's going to look like, I just know that I need you in my life. I don't care, I'll move to Sydney to be with you. Whatever it takes.'

She threaded her cold fingers through his warm ones. 'You know, I don't even think I want to be in Sydney anymore. I don't miss it at all. Thank you, though, for offering to shift your whole life for me, but I love it here, the river, the space. Living feels simpler.'

'Your seventeen-year-old self would be rolling her eyes.'

'I know, but what can I say? I've changed. I don't know what my plans are exactly, but I just can't seem to leave. I wonder why?' She looked into his eyes and he tucked a piece of hair behind her ear.

'Well, let's just take everything slowly,' he said. 'It's going to be hard, with Asha. I don't want to abandon her, but I don't want to give her false hope either. I've been lying to myself and to her for so long, and I can't do it anymore. I don't know if she can either. There's too much resentment. I think she knows we can't keep doing this.'

'You need to talk to her. Be honest, Jez. She deserves that, she's not stupid.' Phoebe squeezed his hand. 'I think you need to go back to the hospital when you've both calmed down and have a proper talk.'

'She's already told me she's never coming back to Driftwood. I feel terrible. It's her home.'

Phoebe shook her head. 'What a mess. She's lost so much.'

Jez looked out over the darkening ocean, his eyes sad. 'I know. I wish everything was different. I wish I'd had the courage to confront our issues instead of letting it get to this.'

'I think you both just wanted a baby so badly,' said Phoebe. 'And you wanted to make each other happy.'

Jez sighed. 'Maybe once upon a time we did, yeah.'

'What are Tommy and Jenna going to make of all this?'

Phoebe cringed. 'And how will they be, do you think, when they find out about us?'

'Well, they've had their own ...' He trailed off, eyes gazing seaward. 'He'd hate me talking about it.'

'What?' Phoebe's pulse quickened.

'There was something. Jenna never knew, but Tommy didn't cope very well with Harry's diagnosis. Not that he ever confided in me directly, but I think he might have been distracted momentarily by ... the possibility of something, or someone else.'

She stumbled in the sand, the looseness in her body tightening. His hand was under her arm. 'What makes you think that?' she choked out.

'You know Tommy, always got everything and everyone sorted. He never spoke in details. I just knew there was a bit of a struggle, and it wasn't just over Harry.'

Phoebe managed to hide the tremble in her voice. 'Another woman? An affair?'

Jez shot her a look and Phoebe felt its meaning ricochet through her.

'You've got cold hands,' Jez said, blowing onto her fingers.

'So Tommy had an affair?' she asked again. But Jez looked away, unwilling to elaborate. Of course he wouldn't—his allegiance would always be to Tommy. Phoebe swatted at the thoughts that buzzed in her ears, nipped at her mind. Had Tommy had an affair with Karin while he was running from his pain? A familiar face, a shared history full of nostalgia and happiness. A panacea. Phoebe knew how that felt. The man asleep beside Karin, had it been Tommy? Jenna's complaints about Tommy's job not being family friendly. He would have had plenty of time to slip in meeting up with someone else. But Tommy and Karin? It wasn't possible, surely. Karin was too old-fashioned for him; he was too controlling. Tommy liked women who were gentle and amenable like Jenna, not independent like her sister.

Maybe she was fumbling blindly for meaning where there was none. Had she projected her own guilt over her affair with Jez onto Karin? Perhaps imagining her sister was capable of an affair had eased her own shame. She thought about how fortune tellers so often gave a generic story, which people were willing to stretch to fit their own reality. If you looked hard enough sometimes you could find evidence for your own beliefs.

They reached the car park just as the wind began to howl, the shadows gathering around them. Phoebe looked at Jez, his hair full of sand, his tired eyes, and her heart squeezed. 'How do you feel?' she asked.

'Relief ... love ... hope ... sadness.'

She brushed his cheek with her thumb. 'Me too. You're a good man, Jez. I know you don't feel it right now but you are. Go and talk to Asha. Work things out with her.'

He kissed her tenderly. 'I don't feel it. But thank you for saying that. I know you have the party ... for Karin ... but ...'

'No, go, go.' She got into her car.

He waited, hands in his pockets, shuffling off the cold while Phoebe drove off. Her mind was full of everything that had just happened. She'd made love to Jez. He'd told her Tommy had had an affair. And every fibre of her body was telling her it had been with her sister.

# CHAPTER 22

Phoebe found Camilla in the kitchen taking quiches out of the oven.

'Oh my God, there you are,' Camilla said, adjusting the apron around her waist. 'There are so many people here already. Where have you been?'

'Sorry, I've ... too hard to explain,' Phoebe said, tugging Camilla's elbow. 'Can I have a quick word with you?'

'Hang on. I just want to get these quiches out to people while they're hot.'

'Camilla, please. It's important.'

Camilla huffed and put the plate down, grabbing her glass of wine.

Phoebe led her into Karin's old room. She sat on her sister's bed and Camilla sat next to her. 'I don't know where to start.'

'What? What's happened?'

Phoebe took a deep breath then grabbed Camilla's wine and took a big sip. 'I just had a conversation with Jez and I don't know how it came up but he confided that Tommy had an affair.'

'Tommy cheated on his wife?'

'When he was struggling with Harry's autism diagnosis, which I think would have been about eighteen months to two years ago ...' She gave Camilla a pointed look.

'What? You think it was with Karin?' Camilla took back the wineglass.

'The timing would make sense. It would make sense. The man Ginny heard on the phone, it could have been Tommy. They came into contact with each other—Jenna mentioned they saw Karin at a coffee festival in Canberra one time.'

Camilla pressed her fingers to her mouth. 'One time though ... Did you say anything about Karin to Jez?'

'No, of course not. He wouldn't even elaborate on it. You know how he and Tommy are.'

'I don't know, Phee. I mean, it's possible but ...' she screwed up her mouth. 'What are we going to do? Go out there and ask Tommy if he was sleeping with our sister?'

'No, I know we can't just ask him.'

'Well then, how are we ever going to know?'

Their dad stuck his head around the door then and they both jumped. 'Oh my God, you scared me, Dad,' said Phoebe.

'Come on you two, you're needed. I know it's a sad occasion but you tell that to these country folk. I haven't got nearly enough beer or sausages.'

Camilla squeezed Phoebe's arm and they followed their dad out onto the deck. The lights they'd strung up earlier glowed in the evening air and candles flickered on the table.

There were the familiar faces of people in the street. People who existed nameless on Phoebe's periphery, but whose consistency made them comforting. There was the man who was always hosing his garden no matter what time of day she passed. The old couple who sat on their veranda drinking tea from a yellow teapot and reading the papers. The lady who was always washing her car and Ginny and Chester. Some of them gave her hand a squeeze of recognition, others seemed there for the free feed and because Camilla was such a persuasive force. No one from Driftwood had arrived yet. Phoebe's stomach churned in anticipation.

Her dad brought an armchair out for Ginny, placing it near the potbelly stove on the deck. Steffi sat steadfastly by her side, ears pricked for movement, eyes alert. Phoebe felt like the dog. She offered Ginny punch in a plastic cup and apologised for not visiting her this week. She wished she could confide in her about Karin and Tommy but Ginny seemed quieter than usual, distracted. Perhaps she was overwhelmed by the noise of children racing in the yard, or the sausages and onion sizzling on the barbecue behind her. She seemed not the wise and thoughtful woman who had raised all those questions about Karin, but a slightly puzzled, old blind lady. Doubts started to niggle in Phoebe, like a forgotten item on a mental shopping list.

There were people who could go through life ignoring their inner niggles, and others who lived by them. Phoebe was neither. She never quite knew whether her instincts were true or mere anxieties. They felt like perched birds waiting for seed. If she made too much noise they would take flight and never return. So she approached them cautiously, neither feeding them nor sending them away.

Tommy appeared suddenly, little hands looped around his neck, carrying his son and an esky. Jenna walked a little in front of them, nursing a bowl of salad, her head bowed as though deep in thought. Phoebe had felt so strongly when Jez had hinted about Tommy's affair, but now seeing him before her with his family there was only doubt. How could Tommy really have cheated on Jenna, especially given what they'd been through with Harry? Or had a beautiful, dark-haired lover on a quiet river taken the pain away? Had their easy way with each other, a leftover from childhood, turned into something more? Had they smoked joints together on the deck? Drunk champagne together on the jetty? Gone away on weekends? Or was it all just a story, perched on the line of her mind, about to take flight?

Before being in love with a married man, Phoebe had held everyone up to her own chaste standards. Life had seemed more like a chess board: you landed in a black or a white square, and you had a choice about where you landed. It was a matter of good, or bad. Now she knew about the other pawns that were off to the side of the board. She knew about all those places on the board where the squares had rubbed off from daily wear. She found it harder to condemn Tommy knowing the places of the heart she knew now. But if he had been Karin's lover, if she was right about that, what did that mean for the way Karin had died? It felt like there was a whole new meaning, hidden just under the surface. And yet he was here, knowing this gathering was to remember Karin.

She hung back as Camilla greeted Tommy. He placed Harry on the ground with the careful grace of a good father. His face broke into a smile that crinkled his tanned cheeks as he touched Camilla's elbow, kissed her cheek. Jenna came alive too as Tommy and Camilla made hand gestures between them. It was clear they were explaining their history. Everyone laughed as Camilla made a joke.

Phoebe caught Camilla's eye as she knelt to be introduced to Harry, who was clinging to the fabric of Jenna's pants. Jenna carefully prised Harry from her leg, handing him into Tommy's care, and came over.

She offered a sad smile. 'It must be so lovely to have your sister here, today of all days.'

'It is.' Phoebe tried to arrange her face into a normal expression but the muscles around her mouth would not comply. She couldn't stand the feelings competing inside her right now—how lovely Jenna was, how helpless Harry was. The things she thought his father, her husband, capable of.

Tommy came over then, Harry on his hip, his face buried in his father's T-shirt. 'Say hello to Phoebe. You know Phoebe.'

Tommy leaned in and gave Phoebe a peck on the cheek. Her heartbeat was elevated, her senses on high alert. He smelled of soap and coffee. *He's a regular guy*, Phoebe thought. *What on earth am I thinking? Maybe Jez is mistaken about the affair.*

'Hi, mister,' she said to Harry, watching as Tommy adjusted the boy on his hip.

'You're getting too big for all this carrying,' he said.

'He's adorable. He reminds me of my little boy, who's quite shy,' said Camilla.

'Ha. You wouldn't say that if you'd seen him this morning.' Tommy shook his head slowly.

'We couldn't find his red train,' said Jenna, 'and God help us, we usually have about three of them stashed around the place. They're his security blanket.' She exchanged a look with Tommy. 'Well, more than that. He can't function without it. But do you think we could find even one at 5.30 am?' Jenna shook her head. She had purple smudges under her eyes.

'Tommy had to go into the Bay and buy one as soon as everything opened.' Jenna stiffened slightly. 'Babe, you did bring it, didn't you?'

'It's in my pocket.'

'Oh, thank Christ.' Jenna pressed a hand against her chest. 'I couldn't go through that again today.'

Phoebe watched Tommy as he held his son. His face looked tired but his laughter came easily. There was nothing in his person to suggest the kinds of things Phoebe was silently accusing him of. She tried to remember how he'd been as a kid. He'd been the boss, that was for sure, competitive with his brother, but that was normal. Had there been any suggestion of something between him and Karin? They were the eldest and that probably linked them in a way. She didn't remember them sharing any particular friendship over and above what they all shared, as a group. She tried to think about the last time they would have seen each other as kids. Their last ever family holiday.

An image came to her of the four of them—her, Karin and the two boys. They had covered themselves with a bottle of olive oil from the kitchen and were frying in the sun on the jetty. She remembered feeling self-conscious lying there, Jez's calf warm against hers. She must have been sixteen, Karin seventeen. It was the summer she and Jez had first made love. She could still remember the way his shoulders glistened in the sun. She had confided all her lovesick feelings to Karin. Surely if there had been something with Tommy, Karin would have confided in her? But Karin had always been the most self-possessed of the three of them. She was a listener rather than a talker. She had never been attracted to type-A personalities.

Tommy had managed to pass Harry into the care of the Texan and Wendy, who had just arrived. They sat with him on the step, making funny faces, which momentarily transfixed Harry. Jenna and Camilla had peeled off from the group near the punch bowl. Phoebe found herself standing next to Tommy. She didn't know what to do with her hands and her throat felt tight. She wished she had a drink, and was about to excuse herself to go help with the barbecue, when he spoke.

'I'm sorry, about today. You know, about Karin.'

He said her name softly, with more deference than Phoebe thought him capable. He had not mentioned her sister's death before now. They had never really had a proper conversation, one on one.

Phoebe had to clear her throat before she could speak. 'Oh, that's okay.' She cringed. *Why had she said that?* 'I mean, thanks. Thanks for coming.'

He opened his mouth as though to say something else, but then he must have thought better of it and shoved his hands into his pockets. 'Well, I'd better go find something for the little monster to eat.'

'Oh, sure, yeah. We've got plenty of sausages. I know how he likes his sausages.'

'Sure does.'

She watched Tommy move towards the barbecue and shake a neighbour's hand. He picked up a paper plate and a serviette. Phoebe's gut was churning; the birds in her mind were in riot.

Somewhere down near the river bank she heard the sound of someone yelling. Two of the older neighbourhood children arrived on the deck, red-faced and bright-eyed.

'The jetty's gone,' they said in unison. 'It's a king tide. The jetty's gone.'

Phoebe looked towards the voices and all she could see was the river giving up its secrets.

The music had been turned up and there were more people, not less as the night went on. The whole street had turned out. Phoebe smiled at the sight of a man with a massive beer belly swaying to the music with his eyes closed. Someone had obviously found Karin's record player and the strains of Don McLean's 'American Pie' echoed through the dark trees. Karin would have loved this.

The deck was strewn with plastic cups and there were empty beer bottles on every surface. Phoebe picked up an abandoned bottle of red wine and took a large swig, and then another. She was drunk. Drinking wine seemed to be the only solution to everything she'd been through in the past few hours. She moved towards the fire her dad had lit in an old tin drum on the grass and saw the Texan holding court. He was in his element. Wendy had obviously gotten sick of listening to the same old stories and gone home.

Phoebe spotted Tommy inside the house talking to her dad, an expression of worry on his face. She walked into the kitchen.

'Jenna's had to take Harry home to bed, but I really need to find it,' Tommy was saying.

'Are you sure you brought it? Maybe it's at your place,' her dad said.

Tommy made a face. 'Yeah, no, I definitely brought it. I always do.'

Her dad nodded solemnly. 'Could it have dropped out of your pocket? Maybe retrace your steps from the front gate.'

'I did that.'

'Have you lost your phone?' Phoebe asked.

Tommy looked tired. He nodded and blinked his eyes, as though trying to focus on her properly.

The landline phone on the table screamed to life, making Phoebe jump. She was right next to it, so she picked it up. It hardly ever rang.

'Hello?'

'Phoebe, is that you? Is Tommy still there?' Jenna was speaking quickly.

'Yes, he's right here.'

'Oh good, can you put him on please?'

'Is everything okay?'

'Just Harry stuff. Can't get him to sleep. He's screaming, beside himself. We stayed at the party too late.'

'Sorry to hear that. I hope he settles. Here's Tommy.'

Phoebe passed the phone over. The lines on Tommy's face looked deeper as he pressed the receiver to his ear. He nodded. 'Okay, yeah, no. I've looked everywhere. It must have dropped out and someone has taken it by mistake. I'll be right home.'

Phoebe followed Tommy out onto the deck. The music had turned to an upbeat Beatles track and several children were dancing. She said goodbye and watched Tommy walk into the dark.

'I've been looking for you everywhere.' Camilla was by her side, an empty wineglass in her hand.

Camilla took her elbow conspiratorially and steered her off the deck towards the river. She smelled of wine and barbecue smoke.

'Has he gone?' she asked. 'You owe me big time. I wasn't going to do it … I mean, I thought it was impossible … but then the opportunity just presented itself.' She made a twinkling gesture with her fingers.

'What are you … Are you drunk? I know I am.'

Camilla shoved something into Phoebe's hand. A phone. Jenna's and Harry's smiling faces beamed up at her. *'What?'*

Camilla was whispering now. 'Tommy was taking a photo of Harry and then he put the phone down on the table behind him. And someone started talking to him, and I …' She made a swiping action.

Phoebe's whole body froze. 'You took his phone? Are you joking? Please tell me you're joking. You're definitely drunk.'

'Well, I'm not. Joking. Obviously. I may be a little tipsy. I did this for you and for Karin. I don't entirely believe your theory but I want you to be free of it. So, we're going to crack into this phone and go through his stuff.'

Phoebe gripped Camilla's shoulders. 'Are you crazy? I'm pretty sure that's a crime. Especially since he's a Federal Police officer.'

'Yeah, well, so is killing someone,' Camilla dead-panned.

Phoebe took a deep breath. She needed to stay calm. 'I'm not at all sure about this …'

Camilla waggled a finger close to her face. 'Oh, no, no, no, you can't just about-face on all this. Being back here has reminded me of our childhood, all those hours we spent doing God knows what.' She looked out onto the dark water. 'I miss her, Phoebe. I can't believe …'

Camilla crumpled forward. Phoebe held her hand as she sobbed. She intuited that this was probably the first time Camilla had let herself cry, and she softened. Getting that phone was possibly the nicest, noblest thing Camilla had ever done. She put her arm around her sister and took the wineglass from her. Camilla sniffed loudly and wiped under her eyes with the heels of her hands. Her voice was still wobbly when she spoke. 'He called it from the landline, several times. There's no reception but I put it on silent, just in case.'

Phoebe shook her head and smiled. 'You're insane. Thank you, but we're not going to crack it.'

Camilla picked up a half-empty champagne bottle sitting nearby and fixed Phoebe with a determined expression. 'Maybe not, but we're goddamn going to try.'

# CHAPTER 23

All the emotions Phoebe had felt in the past twenty-four hours coalesced, pooling in the space behind her eyes. She pressed her knuckles into them and put the phone down. She looked over at Camilla, who had fallen asleep on the lounge, arm thrown behind her head and her knee up, as though she was sunbaking on a St Tropez beach. Phoebe drank the dregs of her cold tea and curled into a ball on the rug, pulling a cushion under her head.

Camilla knew a surprising amount about hacking iPhones, admitting she'd researched it after Rich's series of late nights in the office, when she suspected he might have been having an affair with a secretary. You only got six failed password attempts before it was disabled for one minute and then you only had one or two more tries before it shut down completely.

The passcode required six numbers. Phoebe tried the birthdays she knew: Jez's, Pauline's, who she'd never forgotten because she shared the same birthday as their own mum, Tommy's, Jenna's and Harry's birthdays, which to find out, Camilla had driven to the top of the hill and logged on to Facebook, and lastly a random combination of Tommy's,

Jenna's and Harry's birthdays. Nothing. It was an impossible task. The six attempts were up and the phone was disabled for one minute. Camilla was frustrated but Phoebe felt overwhelmed with relief.

Phoebe was so tired. The surrender to sleep came easily and she let it pull her under. Her dream greeted her. The woman with the black hair, drifting silently downriver, her white gown glowing phosphorescent in the rowboat. Her hair was a dark veil. Phoebe called out to her from the jetty, willing her to turn, wanting to see her face. But she didn't turn and then the woman was falling backwards, out of the boat, and she went under. Phoebe dived to catch her but it was too far. She was on Jez's jetty this time, not her own. She swam hard upstream, against the current, but the water felt thick and too black. She took a gulp of it and it was like tar filling up her lungs. Or blood. She woke up gasping.

She looked at the time glowing on Tommy's phone—3 am. She studied the screensaver of Jenna and Harry. Harry was quite a bit younger, and he wore a red hat with New York written in white, and a grey singlet with the number one on it. Tommy had obviously kept this because Harry's smiles were so rare. Phoebe felt a bubble of sadness rise inside her. Was she really trying to destroy another family, and one so fragile? She sat there in the dark, the feeling of dread growing in her gut.

There was one birthday she hadn't tried. Karin's. Her fingers trembled as she pressed in the date and she felt a roll of nausea in her belly. The phone buzzed its denial. She let out a ragged breath. She realised she'd been holding it.

She was about to settle back in to sleep when a word came into her mind. It was like a whisper, hazy with the aftermath of her dream. *Driftwood*. She lay down but couldn't get comfortable. She picked up Tommy's phone and stared at the key pad. The word Driftwood was too long but what about its number equivalent. What was the number of the house? 16. And the postcode? It came to her in a flash. All those times she had written it on the letters she had sent Jez. 2536. She punched in the number carefully. 162536.

A text message slid into view, a cursor blinking in a fresh message to someone called Tim. She was in. Phoebe's body spiked with adrenalin, a cocktail of anxiety, fear and excitement. She sat up and looked behind her to check no one was watching. She felt like a thief. An intruder. Behind the apps was a picture of the jetty at Driftwood, the sun sparkling brightly on the water.

She hesitated. No. It wasn't just about protecting Jenna, it was about protecting herself. She remembered Jez's hands on her body, she felt the warm promise of him deep inside her. If what she thought, what she now feared, was true, everything changed with Jez. The only person who she would risk Jez for was Karin. And she knew with a deep, unwavering certainty that the only person he would risk her for, was Tommy.

She looked at Camilla, now curled up facing the back of the couch, her top hiked up, lower back exposed. Their dad's snores rumbled softly from the back of the house. She wasn't alone in this anymore. She owed it to Karin, but also to her family, to find out the truth. An image of those dead flowers drifted into her mind. The deep sorrow of them. She imagined Karin choosing those blooms, lush and alive, carefully trimming their stalks, sorting them into the shape of words. Knowing the deeper meaning of them ran like an undercurrent beneath the surface. Perhaps never knowing they would be the last thing of beauty she would ever create.

Phoebe checked under 'K' in his contacts. Nothing. She found his Gmail account and scanned through it. Names she didn't recognise. She went into his text messages and checked everything that was a number without a name. She opened his WhatsApp and skimmed through the chats with mates, a picture of gigantic boobs they'd all shared. She went into his photos, skipping past the contents of his life—Harry on the beach, in the bath, on a bike. She felt the joy he felt for his little boy. There were pictures of Jenna too, mostly with Harry, behind oversized sunglasses, smiling. Cakes that had been baked, random objects—a dustbin, a mark on the road—probably related to work. A dog smoking a cigar. She felt her shoulders drop. He was a normal guy. Dogs and boobs and his kid.

She reached the same month, one year ago, and her heart tipped. There were ten photos. In miniature, she saw it. Red roses open, blooming yellow ones young and bright, the petals curled tight. The peonies were lush and full, the pink softly muted against the white lace of the tablecloth, and the snapdragons bent their lilac heads graciously to form the stems of the letters. It was beautiful. There was nothing sad about this note, it was bursting with colour. With love, with light, with hope. The flowers were formed into the words 'I'm sorry'. They had all seen pictures of dead flowers. These flowers were alive. If Karin had left a hidden message in the meanings of the flowers surely it was a beautiful one. Red roses for love, yellow for friendship, peonies for compassion and snapdragons for graciousness and strength.

Phoebe stared at the picture for a long time. The clock on the wall ticked out the seconds into the night. All she knew was that Karin had been happy the day she died, and that Tommy had seen the flowers alive. Her sister's last message was not for her family, it was for him. She wanted to shake Camilla awake, drag her exhausted body into the bedroom and wake their father, run next door and wake Ginny. But instead she sat there in communion with the seconds, filling up to minutes. What did it mean? What was Karin sorry for? Why was Karin dead? How was this picture on Tommy's phone? Why hadn't he told the police?

Nausea rolled through her and she pressed her hand against her belly. She was going to be sick. She pulled herself to standing, slid open the screen door, and the cold air buzzed against her cheeks. She was barefoot and shivering but she didn't care. She walked over the deck, sending a beer bottle rolling. It smashed on the ground below. She walked on towards the river, feeling sharp sticks, dry grass, dirt under her feet. She came to the river and stopped. It had broken the banks during the night and was now in retreat. Under the half-moon she could just make out the slats of the jetty in its shallows. There was a compulsion, childlike, to step onto this strange underwater jetty and so she did. It was numbingly cold and the tops of her feet glowed white beneath the water. She walked out into the river until she came to the jetty's end.

Phoebe almost expected the dream woman to be here but she was completely alone. She wanted to howl into the quiet night for the river to give back her sister. She wanted Jez to hold her and make everything better, take her back to that deserted beach where everything was possible and there was no one but the two of them. She'd lost Karin, she couldn't lose Jez again. She imagined showing him Tommy's phone. Even the betrayal of stealing it would cut Jez deep. She imagined his reaction to the photo of the flowers. He would never accept that Tommy could do something bad. He would make excuses, beg her not to take it further. But Karin ... Phoebe said her name out aloud. She hadn't been able to save Karin from this river so she wouldn't abandon her here, alone.

The first birdsong came from the trees across the water. It would be morning soon and Camilla would want to know if she'd cracked the phone. Phoebe wanted to stay here forever on her still, silver lake, suspended in time, floating, still free. She didn't want to have to choose between them. She looked down at the place where the jetty ended. The water was an oily black, like blood. She had one other option—to stop the pain thrumming through her, to make it all go away—but it was so awful, so sickening, and it filled her with anger. And she knew then what she had to do.

# CHAPTER 24

Phoebe went to find Jez as soon as dawn split open the dark shell of night. The early morning was muted, grey-blue with a dusting of fine rain. The river's greens were darker, gem-like in contrast to the bruised sky. She didn't bother to cover herself against the rain. She already felt sodden with emotion and cold, numb. She reached the gates of Driftwood, crossed the spongy grass and cut around the front of the house. No one was in the kitchen or lounge. Jez's window looked out onto a wooded area where trees obscured the river. Filmy white curtains were pulled across the low window. She could just make out the bed. He'd be alone. She knocked tentatively. Nothing. Then again a little harder. He appeared, his eyes slitted against the growing light, his hair tousled. Her heart expanded as he gave her a crinkle-eyed smile and opened the window. She climbed through, into the room. She could smell sleep, and him. The sheets were like the white caps of waves and she fell into them as they embraced.

'You're wet,' he said in her ear. He peeled the clothing from her body, scraped the damp strands of hair from her face with his thumbs. Phoebe said nothing. Maybe if she never spoke again they could exist forever in this perfect place of not-quite-day. There was no need for words. They knew each other's bodies. The way the sun had stamped his shoulders, the skin darker there, the flutter of his eyelashes as his eyes rolled back at her touch. She could feel the cool air from the open window against her bare breasts. His warm mouth covered them and the heat spread through her body. The translucent white of the curtains undulated softly in the breeze and she arched her back in response to him. His body was curled around her spine, fitted into hers like a perfect puzzle piece. She took all of the pleasure he gave her. The birdsong outside grew louder and the river began to teem with sound, as though still engorged. They rested in each other's arms and he fell asleep for a time, his breathing becoming light and even. She watched him and tried not to let her tears touch his skin.

Voices came from the main part of the house. They spoke in whispers and dressed quickly. The ground was still wet under the window but the rain had stopped. Sitting in the musky cabin of his ute she knew she couldn't put it off anymore.

'Let's get some takeaway coffees in the Bay,' she said, trying to keep her voice steady.

'Oh God,' he groaned. 'A bacon and egg roll. I'm starving after that little wake-up surprise.' His eyes flashed. He was happy. Happier than she'd ever seen him. 'Are you hungry?' he asked. His fingers found hers and wove through them. He kissed the back of her hand and she felt her heart squeeze with love, with dread. She allowed herself a second to feel angry. Angry that she couldn't just have the warm, easy love of him. Angry at herself for making Camilla steal Tommy's phone. But she couldn't, she just couldn't feel angry at Karin.

'Um, maybe.' She tried to remember the last time she'd eaten. It was some cheese and biscuits the night before at the party.

'Hey, are you okay?' He was onto her. She felt the tears again, threatening like the heavy clouds outside. She couldn't talk about it here with Tommy and Jenna inside the house.

'Just overwhelmed,' she said. 'Come on, let's get some food.'

They drove in silence for a short while and then he told her about his conversation with Asha last night at the hospital. She'd apologised for the things she'd said, and told him she was done. She couldn't keep going in their quest for a baby. They agreed that it had become the last chance to salvage their relationship. But Asha needed to be a mother. He'd told her that he'd been broken too and she deserved to have the thing she wanted so much: a child. It just wasn't to be with him.

'Did you tell her about us?' Phoebe asked, her heart aching with sorrow for Asha.

Jez shook his head his eyes on the road. 'I wanted to be completely honest. I wanted to ... to just come completely clean, but I couldn't.'

Asha had asked her brother to pick her up from the hospital today. Jez expected her back at the house around lunchtime.

They drove through the Bay and out on the coast road. The sun appeared like a gap-toothed smile through the clouds. They stopped opposite a strip of shops.

'The local tradies get their coffees and rolls here. It's pretty good,' said Jez.

Phoebe realised she had no bag, no wallet. 'I don't have any money,' she said, her hands fumbling in her lap. 'Sorry.'

He leaned over and kissed her gently on the cheek. 'Everything that's mine is yours.'

He opened the car door and crossed the road, leaving her fighting back tears. She got out of the ute to feel the sea breeze on her face. The ocean was choppy and the waves pounded the sand. The beach was almost deserted save for a few dog walkers. She sat on a park bench between two enormous pine trees. How was she going to talk to Jez about this?

He arrived juggling two takeaway coffees and brown paper bags already rimmed with bacon grease. He put the food down between them on the park bench and the smell of caffeine and fried bacon made her stomach growl. She felt sick with hunger but she couldn't eat. She took a sip of strong coffee and looked at him, his brow smooth and worry-free, all of his focus on his sandwich. There was no point delaying it. She waited until he had taken a bite to speak.

'Jez, do you remember when Ginny, my neighbour, told me Karin went away every few weekends and I didn't know about that? And it made me wonder if I even knew her?'

He nodded, wiping egg off his chin with the back of his hand.

Phoebe took a deep breath and let it out slowly. 'She also told me she rang Karin late one night when she was away from the cottage and she was with a man.' She paused. 'And you know how you told me Tommy had something … someone that Jenna never knew about?'

His jaw stopped mid-chew. She saw his face register these two pieces of information. He shook his head. He swallowed his food with some effort and then spoke. 'No, I don't think so.'

She was surprised at the surge of defiance she felt. 'No, you don't think so … what?'

'It wasn't Karin.' He put his sandwich down and wiped his fingers and mouth with a flimsy paper napkin.

'How do you know it wasn't?'

He was silent. He gripped the bench with both hands, his knuckles turning white. Phoebe could see his mind working behind his eyes.

'You don't know,' she said, her heart sinking.

He shook his head, brows creased together, and picked up his coffee but didn't drink it. 'He would have told me.'

She tried to stay calm, even though every inch of her wanted to shake him out of his delusion. 'Do you really think Tommy would have told you if it was Karin?'

He didn't answer, he just stared ahead of him at the crashing waves.

'Think about it, Jez, why do you think he might not have? Because Karin's dead.' She didn't want to be cruel but something dark and unexpected twisted in her chest.

His eyes flashed. 'Phoebe, where is this coming from? Do you realise what you're saying?'

A sound, incredulous, and not at all like her, came out of her mouth and she pressed her palms against her forehead. 'Of course. Of course I do. I'm not saying this lightly, Jez. Don't you think I want to be sitting here eating our breakfast in oblivion and contemplating an amazing new life together, instead of talking about Karin and Tommy?'

'Well then what? What the hell is going on?' he asked, swivelling his body to face her, a look of pleading in his eyes.

She had to steel herself to go on. 'I found something.' She took a deep breath. 'It links Tommy to Karin.'

'What?' His voice sounded hard.

'A photo on Tommy's phone.'

Jez's face screwed up in disgust. 'On his phone?'

There was no way to soften the blow. 'Camilla took it last night when he was over at our place for the party.'

Jez blinked in confusion, as though she'd slapped him. 'Camilla took Tommy's phone because she thought he was having an affair with Karin?'

Phoebe's body flooded with adrenalin. She pressed her hand against the pain in her chest. She didn't want to do this, didn't want to fight with him, but she made herself stay there, gripping the seat with her hands. She took a breath. *Tell him the truth. Just tell the truth.* 'No, Camilla didn't want to believe it. She didn't want to take the phone. It was my idea.'

'What the hell? What photo?' The wind snatched at his voice.

She swallowed hard, biting the inside of her lip until she could taste blood. 'When Karin died, the police found her suicide note, or they thought it was her suicide note. It was written in flowers on the kitchen table. It said, "I'm sorry". The flowers were dead by the time they found her body.'

'What does that have to do with Tommy?' There was a hint of defiance in his voice.

'He had a picture of the same flowers on his phone. The same words. "I'm sorry". But the flowers were alive.'

Jez stared at his hands, twisting in his lap.

'I'm so sorry, Jez, but don't you see? That means something. It means somehow he saw her, or was communicating with her right before she died. No one else has seen those flowers alive. Not the police, not even me.'

Jez looked up now, his gaze to the horizon.

She went on. 'I think her note was meant for Tommy. That's why the picture is on his phone. Karin wrote the words in flowers, took a photo of it and sent it to him. If that's true, it wasn't a suicide note. It was just a message to him saying she was sorry about something.'

Jez leaned forward, elbows on his knees, face in his hands. He glanced at her sidelong, as though he didn't know who she was anymore.

'Why wouldn't the police have found that photo on Karin's phone if she sent it to him?'

Phoebe shook her head. 'If she was having an affair with a married man ... I know what Karin was like. She would have deleted everything she sent and received from Tommy.' She looked at him straight in the eye. 'I know because it's what I would do.'

'You don't know any of this for sure. There's probably a really simple explanation.'

She laughed. The laugh wasn't bitter, it was pure. 'Jez, I want that to be true more than I've ever wanted anything— apart from my sister to be alive again. I don't want this to come between us. Not after everything we've been through.' Her voice broke. 'I love you.'

His lips curled into a quick smile but it didn't reach his eyes. 'Well, the only thing to do is to talk to Tommy, get him to explain the photo. Where's the phone now?'

'It's back at the house. Jez, I'll talk to Tommy, but I'm not giving him back the phone. Not yet.'

'What are you going to do with it?' His voice was flat, dreadful.

She shook her head. 'You know I can't give it to him.'

He moved closer to her on the bench. Her food fell onto the ground, its guts spilling out. 'You don't know what Tommy's been through. You can't do this to him.' His eyes were pleading with her. 'Jenna can't know about this. It will break her. What about Harry? We'll talk to Tommy, give him back his phone, sort it out. He'll explain the photo, I promise.'

She felt a hot surge of anger rise up through her body. 'It's not your promise to make, Jez. I don't trust Tommy.'

He took her hand and squeezed it. 'Trust me, then.'

Tears welled in her eyes. 'I can't. It's too big. It's bigger than you and me.'

He gripped her hand so hard it hurt. 'That's not true. It is you and me. Don't do this to my family. We've all been through enough.'

She snatched her hand back. 'What about my family and what we've been through?' She was crying now. 'My sister is dead. Tommy might have had his struggles but he's alive. He knows things about Karin's death that no one else knows. That's wrong, Jez. He's done a bad thing keeping it to himself.'

He hushed her, pulling her close, so that she could feel his heart through the thin fabric of his T-shirt. He stroked her hair. She pulled back and looked into his eyes. She couldn't stand seeing the uncertainty in them.

'Please, Phoebe,' he said.

She knew what he was asking. He was asking her to keep Tommy safe, just as she would ask the same thing for Karin.

She fought the instinct inside her to placate, to reassure and to smooth over. She shook her head and sat up, away from him. 'I'm sorry. I can't promise anything, Jez. This is Karin.'

His face was pale. 'This is Tommy. He's all I've got.'

It felt like her heart was being sliced into tiny pieces but she just nodded. 'I need to get back,' she said and stood.

# CHAPTER 25

Camilla was nursing her head at the kitchen table, a mug of black coffee in front of her, untouched. 'Where've you been? Argh. You could have warned me—these country folk sure know how to party. Dad's gone into the Bay to get bacon. He's dusty, too.'

Phoebe didn't respond. She sat down at the table and held out the phone.

Camilla straightened, her voice huskier than usual. 'No way. You got in?' She took it carefully and studied the image, working her lower lip with her teeth. 'Is that …?'

Phoebe's voice was a whisper. 'It's her note. Her flowers. But alive.'

Camilla's hand went to her mouth. She was silent for a long time. When she spoke her voice was thick with emotion. 'They're so beautiful. On his phone. Oh my God, how is this possible?' Her face was blanched with shock. 'You were right Phee.'

Phoebe shook her head and took a deep breath, the river drawing her gaze. 'I wish I wasn't, I really do. But it all fell into place when Jez mentioned Tommy's affair and I just knew.

I knew. Karin might have told me if it was some random guy but she never would have told me about Tommy.'

'Why? Because of Jez?' asked Camilla, her eyes softening.

Phoebe looked away. 'Yeah, because of Jez.'

Camilla blinked as though trying to focus. 'Well, this is evidence, Phee. We have to take this to the chief investigator.' She reached for her phone on the windowsill. 'Hang on, I've still got his email. He's based at the station in the Bay.' She was already back to her organised capable self.

Phoebe crossed her arms over her body, physically bracing for Camilla's reaction. 'Wait. I thought maybe we'd talk to Tommy first, get his side of the story.'

Camilla made a snorting noise through her nose. 'And give him a chance to make up an alibi? Change his story? No fucking way.' She took a long gulp of coffee.

Phoebe thought about Jez. Would he have already told Tommy about her suspicions? Their trip back in the car had been difficult. Neither of them had been able to be fake with each other, so they were silent. Jez's eyes were fixed on the road, the muscles working in his jaw, a vein in his forehead pulsing. He hit the steering wheel hard with the palm of his hand and swore loudly when someone pulled out in front of him in the main street of the Bay. His anger frightened her more than it should have. He dropped her at her house with a skid of tyres. She got out and turned back to him. His face softened as though he was going to tell her she was right and that he would be there for her no matter what. But he rubbed his chin and looked away.

'I'll see you later,' Phoebe said and closed the door on his awful silence.

She hadn't told Camilla about Jez; it just complicated things. Her sister would find out in the end. Phoebe knew Camilla was probably right about taking the phone straight to the police, but she was torn.

'Maybe we should give him a chance,' she said, watching as Camilla scrolled through the photos on the phone. 'I'm not saying give him the phone, just talk to him, you know? There could be a simple explanation. Or maybe he's been feeling guilty this whole time and wants to tell the truth. Maybe he's just covering up an affair.' She could hear the flimsiness in her own voice.

Camilla shook her head and drained the last of her coffee. She stood and placed the mug in the sink. 'This totally implicates Tommy in Karin's death. She either sent this to him in a phone message, in which case it could have a whole other meaning and it's not a suicide note like they thought. Or he was there at the scene and took a photo on his phone, which is totally creepy and I don't even want to think about what that might mean. Either way, he knows something about her death that we don't … and the police don't.'

'Why would he keep it on his phone if it implicates him?'

Camilla fixed her with a steely look. 'Why would he kill our sister?'

Phoebe's heart leaped at this, even though it was the thought that had been burning inside her. Her voice was wobbly, unsure. 'This isn't saying he killed her. Maybe they were just having an affair and he doesn't want that to get out.'

'We don't know what it's saying. But it's damn well saying something.' Camilla's eyes narrowed. 'You're the one who started this. Why are you backing out now?'

Phoebe shook her head, feeling her heart thump a little harder. 'I'm not backing out.'

'You totally are. We can't steal and hack into a Federal Police officer's phone and then go have a casual chat to him about it. I don't know, maybe he could have us arrested or something.'

'He wouldn't do that.'

Camilla cocked her head and raised one eyebrow.

'Okay, so you're probably right. I just feel—'

Camilla took a step forward and gripped her by the shoulders. 'You were right, Phoebe. I'm so sorry I doubted you. I thought you were a little crazy digging everything up … that it was all a bit pathetic, if I'm completely honest.'

Phoebe scoffed and hung her head but she didn't move from Camilla's grip.

'But something else is going on here and the police need to know about it. We're never going to get her back, but if someone hurt her …' Camilla's voice broke then and she took a sharp breath in.

Phoebe pulled her sister in close, smelling the sweet coconut scent of her hair and for the first time in her life, not resenting it. Camilla was right. Of course she was. She was seeing clearly, without the ulterior motive, the cloudiness of Jez. 'Okay. It's okay, we'll go to the police. We can go down there today.'

Camilla took a step back and pulled her hair off her face. 'I want to go now. Let's just go. Give me a minute. I'm such a mess.' She headed for the bathroom.

'Should we call first, do you think?'

'I think we just go,' she called from the bathroom.

Camilla emerged minutes later, smoothing down her jeans, lipstick freshly applied. She was different now, softer somehow.

The invisible barrier between them had come down. Phoebe picked up her handbag and was removing her phone from its charger when there was a knock on the front door.

She looked up to see Camilla's face crumple with alarm. 'Who could that be? Dad's due back from the Bay but he's got keys, hasn't he?'

The knock was louder this time. Phoebe's breathing quickened. A friendly neighbour didn't knock with such insistence. She shoved her phone and Tommy's into her bag. 'Take this,' she pressed her handbag into her sister's arms. 'Tommy's phone's in there. Go out the sliding door and climb over the fence to Ginny's house. Start walking up the road and I'll meet you at the top of the hill in a bit.'

Camilla's eyes flashed with realisation 'You think it's—'

'Yes.'

'Will you be okay?'

The knock was a loud thump now, as though someone was pounding with their fist.

'Just go,' Phoebe said, squeezing her sister's hands.

Camilla opened the sliding door and took a step out onto the deck and then Phoebe heard him. She could hear the relief in Camilla's voice and watched with a kind of cold dread running through her as Camilla came back inside with him. 'It's just Jez,' Camilla said, a smile on her face, the bag cradled in her arms like a baby.

Phoebe's eyes met Jez's and she saw that same heart-wrenching detachment was still there. She wanted to tell Camilla to run right now but no words would come.

Instead Jez spoke. 'We didn't think you were home.'

'It's Tommy at the front door,' Phoebe said, her voice strangely emotionless. The dread was thickening along her limbs. Her body was glued to the spot, like a bad dream where you try to move, to run, but nothing happens.

Camilla flashed her a questioning look and Phoebe swallowed, trying to work out what to do. She was too consumed by the emotion of seeing Jez, the knowledge that he must have told Tommy. And then suddenly Tommy was in the room with them. He was so tall. She'd never noticed how big he was. His face was flushed, from sun or emotion, she couldn't tell. His brown eyes were hidden behind sunglasses. He pushed them up onto his head and smiled.

'Ah, you guys are here. We thought we'd missed you. Jez said you found my phone.' He ran a hand casually through his hair. 'Thank God. Where was it?' His voice sounded normal, confident, only very slightly out of breath. But Phoebe could read Jez, and Jez was edgy. He was waiting.

Camilla's eyes darted from Tommy's to hers, unsure and wary. Phoebe felt protective of her sister suddenly, aware of how physically tiny she was for all her bluster. She'd always been the smallest person in the family and now standing next to Tommy, holding the bag containing the phone, Phoebe felt fear buzz along her skin. She tried to steady her voice, stay calm, play Tommy's game. The problem was, Jez knew her, too. He knew that her legs were trembling and her mind was reeling. *Tommy knows we've seen the picture.* It was that same ancient, subconscious part of her that had led her here and so she listened to it, she begged it to guide her.

'You nearly missed us. We were just going into the Bay, actually,' Phoebe said, trying to sound casual.

'We're just headed in. We can give you a lift if you want,' said Tommy, thumbing over his shoulder. Phoebe waited for him to mention the phone again but he didn't. She felt sick rather than relieved. Tommy was a Federal Police officer. He talked down hostage situations and strategised security for visiting heads of state. It wasn't the end of things, it was only the beginning.

'Thanks, but we're good,' Camilla said, her voice steady but her wringing hands betraying her. 'Got to get some petrol on the way in anyway.' She laughed, for no apparent reason.

*We have to get out of here, now*, Phoebe thought. She strode into the kitchen and located Camilla's keys on the kitchen table. It would be better to be in an Audi than her ageing Golf.

'Do you want to drive or shall I?' she asked without looking at any of them, bypassing the lounge and heading down the hall towards the front door, her strides unnaturally long. *Follow me*, she urged Camilla silently. Tommy would have to physically restrain them to stop them leaving the house. Was he capable of that? It really depended on what the picture on his phone meant. The front door was close. She heard the thud of footfalls behind her and she turned.

'Hey, hey, hey.' He loped towards her, his body loose as though he were kicking a ball on a Sunday afternoon instead of cornering someone in a narrow hall. Phoebe froze, her hand finding the cool metal of the doorknob. Tommy held his splayed palms up in a mock surrender. 'I just want to talk. No need to go running away. Can we talk?'

She saw Camilla standing behind Tommy, her face white and eyes wide. Phoebe hadn't been there for Karin and now she'd put Camilla in danger. It was up to her to finish this. She stood to her full height and looked Tommy in the eye. 'What do you want to talk about, Tommy?'

He laughed and rubbed his chin with his thumb. She noticed he hadn't shaved. 'Why don't we all just sit down and have a proper adult conversation about this?'

'About what? About your phone?'

'Look, Phoebe.' His voice was soft now. *I bet he's been trained to talk this way*, she thought. 'Let's just be upfront. I'm an upfront kind of person and I think you are, too.'

Phoebe laughed then, she couldn't help it. It sprang out of her, high and incredulous. 'You're an upfront kind of guy are you, Tommy? Is that why you're standing over me, not wanting me to leave my home because of a picture on your phone that you've kept hidden for a year?' Phoebe knew she probably wasn't playing her cards right but she couldn't stand his sanctimonious shit anymore. She could see him clearly now—the entitlement, the arrogance, the sense of control he exerted in all situations.

A memory flickered into her mind, the stray dog that time on the river. The treehouse. The way Tommy just shot the dog, even though they'd all begged to try to save him. How easy it had been for him. How much he'd wanted to do it. How much he was obsessed with that gun he'd found. But because he was the eldest, he'd been the one who had explained it all to their parents, and he had been hailed a hero for being grown-up and brave enough to put a dog out of its misery. For bringing them all back home safely. But Phoebe had seen his eyes when he'd held that gun to the dog's head. How could she have forgotten? Karin had never blamed Tommy. She had taken in so many stray dogs over the years, as though to absolve herself of what had happened to Bingo.

A hot rage flashed through her at the thought of what he might have done to Karin.

Tommy put his hands out in front of him as though sensing this change in her and trying to keep her calm. 'I know you feel angry and confused about the picture, but I want to explain it to you.'

'Okay. Great. I'm listening.' She looked into his eyes and could see desperation. It made her whole body go cold. 'Go ahead, Tommy, I'm listening. Camilla is, too.'

His expression darkened. 'You see, I think you have the wrong idea, the totally wrong idea, and I wouldn't want you doing anything stupid.'

She shrugged off the threat, emboldened by a mixture of anger, fear and adrenalin. 'So, you've resorted to threatening me now. What does it mean, Tommy? Please, tell us how you came to have Karin's flower note, a note that none of us has ever seen with the flowers alive, in your phone.'

Phoebe saw his eyes flash with pain, briefly, and then cloud with anger. He spoke through clenched teeth, his hands balled into fists beside his body. 'That's what I want to explain to you, if you'll just—'

'Just what? Give you back your phone?' She summoned all her pain, all her anger, all her strength and looked him right in the eyes. She saw his fear. 'It's not going to happen, Tommy.'

'You had no right to steal it.' He grabbed her then, his hand a suffocating grip on her upper arm, twisting it behind her back like she'd seen him do to Jez in play. She could feel his hot breath on her cheek. She yelped in pain as his fingers dug under her armpit. 'Where is it?' he asked.

She yelled out and lunged for the door, trying to shake his iron grip, kicking at his leg with her foot.

And then Jez was there. 'Get off her,' he said, arms on his brother's shoulders trying to pull him backwards.

She could see the large vein in Tommy's neck bulging. Her eyes met Jez's for a second. They were wild and sad and she understood that she had to run. She threw open the door and bolted for the car, her hands fumbling and clumsy with the keys. When she was in the cabin of the car she looked back, desperate to see her sister, but she was gone. *Please let her have run out the back.*

Tommy was thundering towards her now, Jez at his heels. Her pounding heart was all she could hear. Everything slowed as she started the engine. She struggled to put the car into first and skidded on the loose gravel until the tyres found traction. She didn't dare look back until she was out of the drive. There was no car. Tommy had been bluffing about the lift into the Bay; they must have walked up from Driftwood. They couldn't follow. Her whole body shook with relief as she caught sight of Camilla in Ginny's front yard, running, the bag in her arms. Phoebe skidded to a halt and leaned over to open the door.

Camilla jumped in and slammed the door shut, twisting to check they weren't behind. She slumped in her seat in relief. 'Oh my God oh my God oh my God,' she said, her hand against her chest, trying to catch her breath. 'Lock the doors.'

'They're locked,' said Phoebe, pulling away from the kerb and pressing her foot hard on the accelerator. Her body was still shaking. She kept her eyes on the road and gripped the steering wheel so hard her hands ached. 'He did something really, really bad, didn't he?'

Camilla reached out for her hand and squeezed it. When Phoebe glanced over there were tears in her sister's eyes.

# CHAPTER 26

When they reached the police station in the Bay, Phoebe half expected Tommy to be there, waiting for them, shaking his head in admonishment. That was the thing about Tommy—he wielded such natural authority that he always seemed one step ahead. Until now. Phoebe was on high alert as they walked up the concrete steps and pushed open the glass door, but no one stopped them as they moved into the fluorescent-lit foyer that smelled of sweet disinfectant and stale sweat.

'What if he knows someone here?' Camilla whispered as they waited at the front desk. 'What if we get in trouble for stealing his phone?'

'I've sent the picture to myself, to you, to Dad. He can try to stop this but it doesn't change the fact of that picture. The chief investigator of Karin's case is going to see that picture.'

'Graham Pickering, that's his name,' said Camilla. 'He's a nice man, we'll ask for him.'

'You can make a statement to Constable Lindy,' said the policeman behind the desk when he finally appeared and told them that Chief Inspector Pickering wasn't available. Constable

Lindy wrote everything down in a large, childish script, nodding as they spoke, and worrying a gold hoop earring in her right ear.

Phoebe imagined Tommy interrogating people in rooms that looked like this one. Everything was grey. The chairs, the tabletop, the walls. A life in monochrome. She had always pictured his job as powerful, perhaps because of the rarefied way he and everyone else referred to it. But she saw now that it involved a lot of plastic-backed chairs and cold coffee in paper cups. Phoebe wondered at the effect of being surrounded by crime every day. Had it made Tommy complacent? Is that why he'd kept the photo on his phone? Or was it that he felt immune to the law he upheld? Somehow above it, as that rookie cop had hinted at Tommy's party?

They explained to Constable Lindy what they'd found on Tommy's phone and how it related to Karin and her death. It took a while, and the policewoman didn't look as surprised as Phoebe would have liked. She said they would probably get a stern warning for stealing a Federal Police officer's phone. Camilla shot her a worried look but they handed over the phone.

Constable Lindy placed it carefully in a plastic evidence sleeve and zipped it shut. She assured them they'd go and talk to Tommy that afternoon. They were taking it very seriously, especially in the light of Tommy's physical assault. Phoebe had a mark on her upper arm—a deep red, darker at the edges like a blossoming mould spore. Constable Lindy photographed it and kept referring to it as 'the injury'.

Phoebe did most of the talking. Her voice didn't waver, except when she was describing Jez holding his brother back, remembering the pain in his face, the message in his eyes. When they left the station her hand found her phone instinctively. She wanted desperately to call him but she knew she couldn't. They were on opposite sides of a police investigation now. Just because he'd helped her escape his brother didn't mean he was on her side.

They recounted everything to their dad that afternoon. He scratched at the base of his neck, as he often did when he was thinking deeply, or troubled by something. Phoebe and Camilla had agreed to play down the extent of Tommy's violence, the desperation to get his phone back, in an effort not to alarm their father. He wasn't prone to alarm, but Phoebe saw pain skim the surface of his eyes when they explained the significance of the flowers being alive in Tommy's photo.

The next day Wendy and the Texan came around before lunch. They'd been at Driftwood when the police arrived on Sunday afternoon. They were shocked when the officers said they were looking for Tommy, and told them he and his family had just left for Canberra and that Jez had gone with them. They'd noticed Tommy was a bit distracted, but thought it was probably just work and that he wanted to get on the road. It was hard for Phoebe to explain why the police were there. She didn't talk in specifics, just that Tommy was somehow involved with Karin before her death.

Wendy kept shaking her head. Phoebe knew she was thinking of Jenna and Harry. The Texan said, 'We'll look after the house and garden.'

There were several days where they heard nothing. Phoebe made excuses to go into the Bay to get mobile reception, just in case Jez had contacted her, though deep down, she knew he wouldn't. She was tempted to keep driving and make the two-hour trip to Canberra just to know something, just to do something. Part of her wanted to find Jez and beg him to understand. Beg him to come back to her. Camilla called the station every day but the police weren't saying much, except that they were investigating. Wendy's only update was that Jez had called the house to say he'd be away for a bit and could they keep an eye on things. He was staying in the spare bedroom at Tommy's house in Manuka, and Wendy said it seemed like Tommy was still there.

Phoebe passed the days with a knot pulled tight inside her. She couldn't eat, couldn't sleep. She couldn't think about anything else. Part of her wanted everything to be a big misunderstanding, for Jez to come back to her with answers, for Tommy to have kept it all a secret to hide his affair with Karin. For Jenna to forgive him. For them all to move on. But another part of her was angry.

Their dad insisted on staying even though he had planned to return to Sydney, and Camilla made arrangements to remain until they knew what was happening. She spent an hour on the phone with their mother explaining the new developments.

'What did she say?' Phoebe asked.

'You know Mum. She went quiet, and then started talking to me about cushion covers for the master bedroom of one of our main clients at the moment.'

'Why does she do that?'

'You know she can't handle it. She just wants to get on with things so she doesn't have to feel anything. She cares, she just can't express it.'

Phoebe shook her head but she wasn't surprised. 'I used to think you were like that.'

'I am,' said Camilla, poking out her tongue.

It was deep autumn by now and the leaves were falling to the ground, crunching underfoot. Everything looked sparse, hungry, cold. Phoebe tried to keep tending her vegetable patch but it, too, was shutting down for the winter, the ground hardening beneath her fingers and cracking her skin raw.

Phoebe rang Woodend Hill about Karin's table and arranged to have it delivered to the cottage. It was so big they struggled to get it through the sliding doors and it didn't fit properly in the lounge or kitchen, so they had to leave it on the deck. Phoebe worried that the beautiful timber would swell and bloat with the weather, but what else could they do? She would have liked to take it to Driftwood but she felt cut off from that place now, as though the tether that had always held their two homes together had been severed.

She and Camilla took walks over to the village for coffee and went into the Bay for groceries. They visited Ginny to tell her what they suspected. They studied Karin's flower book again and decided it might be useful in evidence. Camilla dropped it off at the station that afternoon but no one was able to update her on anything.

Phoebe and Camilla were in the Bay having coffee when the police called. Phoebe passed the phone to Camilla when she saw the unknown number come up, her heart racing. She didn't have the strength to talk about it. Camilla used her professional power voice and put the phone on speaker so Phoebe could hear. Tommy had been called into the station and given a warning after Phoebe's assault. Camilla quizzed Constable Lindy about whether he'd be given special treatment as a Federal Police officer, but she said everyone was treated the same under the law. Camilla rolled her eyes. She said he'd been questioned over the photo on the phone. He'd demanded a lawyer and refused to speak. What did that mean in relation to Karin, Phoebe wanted to know? She told them the police were investigating further and putting together a case. But did they think that he'd been involved in Karin's death? Camilla pressed her, but all she could say was that they had reopened the case and were investigating.

Phoebe felt frustration buzz along her shoulders as Camilla hung up the phone. She dragged Camilla to the local pub where they sat in the beer garden drinking red wine until they had to call their dad to come and pick them up. Phoebe couldn't stand the not knowing. She couldn't stand the silence from Jez. She couldn't stand the waiting.

The next morning she woke early after another mostly sleepless night. The thought of doing nothing, of waiting one more day, was suffocating. She had to do something. She scrawled a note to her dad and Camilla then grabbed her car keys and her phone.

It was a Thursday, and the elegant, tree-lined streets of Manuka were peopled mostly by mothers pushing expensive prams. Phoebe didn't know Canberra well and used her phone to navigate to his house. Wendy had given her the address. When she pulled up opposite, Jenna and Harry were in the drive, getting out of their SUV. Jenna was unloading groceries from the boot in that deeply tired way she suspected was endemic to motherhood. Phoebe felt a stab of sadness seeing her engaged in such an innocent everyday activity. Jenna knew nothing, she was sure of it. Tommy was used to keeping secrets from her for his work. It wouldn't be much of a stretch to keep other, more personal secrets.

The house was completely different from what Phoebe had expected. She'd always seen Tommy and Jenna at Driftwood, in a natural setting. But this place was modern, and big, with little greenery. Shiny glass windows at the front reflected the sun, and there was an electronic metal gate and an intercom. There was a sterility about it that made Phoebe shiver. It was funny the assumptions she'd made. She'd imagined they lived in a place similar to Driftwood; she'd assumed Tommy was an essentially good person, a dedicated father and husband, and nothing more complicated than that. She felt pressure in her chest at the thought of Jenna. It was likely she still harboured the same innocent delusions about her husband. Was Phoebe really the one to shatter those? If not, then why had she driven all this way?

She sat perfectly still in her car, except for the rhythmic drum of her fingers on the steering wheel. She was torn. It was unlikely Tommy was home, but she couldn't know for sure. And Jez? Was he in the house? She made a split-second decision, killing the engine and slamming the door closed behind her before she could change her mind. She reached Jenna just as she was ushering Harry in through the front door. Phoebe felt shaky with nerves but she gave Jenna a wide smile as she called out from the bottom of the front steps.

Jenna's face morphed into its usual warmth and Phoebe felt relieved. 'Hi, Phoebe. What are you doing here?' She scooped Harry into her arms. 'Look, it's Aunty Phoebe, Haz.'

Harry gave his customary wave accompanied by his serious little look. Phoebe waved back, her heart sinking. What was she thinking? She had no place to tell Jenna anything.

'I needed to see if Jez was okay. I know it's been hard with him and Asha.'

Jenna smiled. 'You're a good friend. I don't think he's here, but come in for a cuppa,' she said, moving through the door into a cream-carpeted hallway with an ostentatious gold mirror.

'It's okay. I should be off. Just here to see old friends.' She hated herself for lying.

'Just come in for one cup. I could do with some adult company, Tommy's always home so late. And you can help me unload the groceries while the kettle's boiling.' Jenna laughed.

Phoebe followed her into the hall, relieved to hear that Tommy was at work. She picked up two bags of groceries as she passed.

'Oh, you're a sweetie,' said Jenna.

There was a carpeted staircase leading to a second level and they walked through a lounge with an enormous flat-screen TV, emerging into a spacious, cream tile and blonde timber kitchen. It opened onto a wide deck and grassy backyard, complete with miniature cubby house. It was the epitome of the Australian family dream home. Phoebe put the bags onto the granite kitchen island. Her hands were shaking.

Jenna settled Harry in front of the television in the adjoining family room and filled the kettle at the sink. 'It's so nice you've dropped in. I'm a bit pathetic today, really.' She shook her head. 'You just get a bit sick of ...' She shrugged and looked at the ceiling. 'You know.' Phoebe's heart lurched as Jenna put the kettle down with a thud and wiped under her eyes. 'Sorry, I'm feeling a bit sorry for myself.'

Phoebe rushed to her side. 'Don't say that. It's okay. Let me do this. You sit.'

Jenna slumped onto a stool, her head in her hands. 'Sorry, I'm just tired. Harry's been waking at night a lot lately and Tommy's been so jittery with work, doing late nights. He's got a massive case on.'

Phoebe felt her arms twitch involuntarily. *No, Tommy's been jittery because he's being investigated and he hasn't told you about it.* The anger she felt was as precise and sharp as a knife tip.

Jenna pressed her fingertips into the sides of her skull. Her eyes were unfocused as she spoke. 'And when he's got all this work stuff on he tosses and turns at night, and between that and Harry waking, I hardly sleep.'

'That must be hard,' said Phoebe, picturing Tommy writhing in the dead of night. Was he feeling guilty? How did he think this was going to pan out? That somehow he'd keep his involvement with Karin a secret from Jenna? His blind stupidity was astounding.

Phoebe searched in a cupboard for mugs. The routine of putting the tea bags in, pouring the water and milk and stirring, calmed her. She placed a cup in front of Jenna, who wrapped her hands around it gratefully. It was so tempting to sit down right now and free her from her misery. But it wasn't really freedom that the truth was offering—it was single parenthood with a disabled child. And it wasn't Phoebe's place to do this. She found herself lost for words as she sat down at the bench next to Jenna. She watched the other woman's shoulders slump as Harry started banging something repeatedly, making little distraught noises.

Jenna's voice was very calm, as though she was talking about a new product in the supermarket. 'Sometimes you just want to walk away, you know? From it all. I envy you so much, Phoebe. You're so free. When things didn't work out with your ex you could just run and go to the cottage. Start fresh. Once you've got kids, that's not possible.'

Phoebe looked into Jenna's eyes for a hint that she knew, that this was her way of telling Phoebe that she suspected something. But her eyes flickered and she laughed and shrugged in an exaggerated way. 'Sorry, I'm being self-indulgent. I'd better fix Harry something to eat or there'll be an epic meltdown.'

Phoebe wanted to reach out and grab Jenna's arm, shake it, and tell her that it was better to know the truth and endure its pain than to live in the shadows of lies. She thought back to her kind, warm-hearted sister and couldn't imagine her knowingly inflicting pain on a woman as lovely as Jenna. And yet Phoebe had started an affair with Jez knowing it would crush Asha. Did it make any difference that Jenna was nicer than Asha? She had justified it in the name of true love, used Asha's unkind nature to excuse her own selfishness. *He would be happier with me*, she'd told herself. Was this the same excuse Karin had used? Was it even an excuse?

'Jez, you have a visitor. We've just put the kettle on,' said Jenna, looking up from fixing a sandwich.

He was standing in the doorway behind her, wearing his work boots. Phoebe's heart throttled to life as their eyes met. His flashed with alarm and then he looked away. What was he afraid of? That she'd told Jenna there had been something between Tommy and Karin? What exactly did Jez know about the whole ordeal now?

'Just been helping a friend with his new bathroom,' he said. He shot her another wary look. Phoebe wondered if Jenna had picked up on the tension but she was busy buttering bread, Harry clasped neatly around her calves.

'Help yourself to a cuppa, Jez. I'm just fixing a sandwich for Harry. Can I make you one?'

He rubbed the back of his head. 'Thanks, Jenna, but I'm going out again. Just needed to grab something.' He hesitated and then turned to Phoebe, stiffly, as though his legs were made of stone. 'What are you doing in Canberra?'

She could tell he was trying to be casual but it still came out sounding like an accusation.

'Keeping me sane,' said Jenna, her mouth half full of bread. Harry started fussing, so she picked him up and jammed a sandwich into his hand.

Jez's eyes narrowed slightly and she could see a line of perspiration high on his brow.

'Just here visiting a friend. And I thought I'd drop in to see if you're okay.'

His eyes flickered with vulnerability but it was quickly replaced with something harder. 'I'm fine,' he said, his voice cool.

'Oh, and how's Asha going, Jez? Have you spoken to her?' Jenna asked, concern in her eyes.

'She's okay.' He paused. 'She's good. We spoke this morning. She's at her brother's. Flick's been amazing helping her out, and I've been checking in on her a lot. I might go and see her tomorrow.'

The words slit Phoebe deep, as though he had sharpened them specially. He was getting her back for being here, for muddying things even more.

She gathered up her coat and keys. 'Thanks for the cuppa. I'd better be getting back. I hope you get a better sleep tonight, Jenna.' She could feel Jez's eyes on her.

'Thanks, lovely. Have a good drive back and we'll probably see you on the weekend.'

*No you won't. There's no way Tommy's coming back to Driftwood.*

In the car, Phoebe leaned back against the head rest and squeezed her eyes shut. There was a knock at the window and her eyes flew open. Jez's face. She felt flustered and hot in the stuffy cabin of the car. She took a deep breath and lowered the window.

'What are you doing here?' His voice was strained and he looked behind, nervously.

'I could ask you the same thing.'

'What was I meant to do, Phoebe? Abandon my brother?'

'He hasn't told Jenna anything,' she said.

'Did you tell her?' His voice was high-pitched.

'Of course not, but he should.'

He shook his head and leaned closer. She could smell the musky heat of him and resented the effect it had on her. Up close he looked tired, the whites of his eyes pink-tinged. He lowered his voice. 'They had an affair, okay?' He shook his head again and ran his hands down his face. 'He came clean to me.'

'Oh my God.' She gripped the steering wheel. She had the urge to punch the horn, blast something. 'What about the—'

'The note, I know. There's a reason. He says he kept the note on his phone because it was sentimental. They had a fight. Karin wanted him to leave Jenna, and then she sent him the picture of the flowers, an apology, but ...' His voice trailed off. 'Well, we know how it ended.'

It felt like all the blood in her body had rushed to her feet. 'No, I don't think we do, Jez. Did he see her before she killed herself? Did he talk to her? Was he there?'

He flicked her a look full of warning.

'What happened?' Her voice was tight with frustration.

He looked away. He wouldn't meet her eyes. 'I don't know. He was pretty upset about it when he told me.'

'So, he just decided to completely ignore the police investigation into her death.'

'What was he supposed to do, Phoebe? Rock up and say, oh, hey, I was having an affair with her and she may have killed herself because I wouldn't leave my wife for her?'

Phoebe hit the steering wheel hard, her skin smarting. 'Yes, goddamn it. Yes! That's what he should have done.' She couldn't see Jez's face because her eyes were brimming with tears. She blinked them back so she could focus on him. His forehead was creased with worry.

'He's going to tell them,' said Jez.

'You're goddamn right he's going to tell them.' She revved the engine to life. She needed to think. She needed to get away from here.

'Are you sure you're okay to drive?'

She felt a surge of anger rush through her and for an instant wanted to slap him. 'What do you care?'

His brow contracted in hurt and she hated herself, but she went on. 'Why didn't you tell me when he told you they were together? And what the picture meant? You just left me waiting.'

'I was afraid you'd do this. Tell Jenna.'

Phoebe's voice was full of rage. 'I didn't tell her anything.'

'I know.'

There was a pause and she wanted him to move his elbow from her car so she could leave.

'He'll tell her. He'll tell the police,' said Jez. 'Please, just give him time.'

Her voice was cold now. 'I don't need to give Tommy anything. Can you move your arm, please?'

She drove away without looking back.

# CHAPTER 27

The dreams had stopped. Phoebe hadn't woken gasping, her skin damp, for two days. She found it hard to get to sleep but once she did it was a thick, dreamless slumber. There was some superstitious part of her that wondered, in the invisible spaces between logic, if the restless spirit that had woken her each night was more at peace now. Was it Karin's spirit? Now that the truth about Tommy had been uncovered, had the spirit been placated? She didn't believe such things, not really, not in the bright reality of day. But now it was deep night and she was awake. Not from a dream, though.

The noise, again. Tinny, like metal banging, from down near the river. She tiptoed past Camilla's room, knowing she should wake her.

As soon as Phoebe had told Camilla that Tommy had admitted to the affair, her sister had grabbed her phone to call the police.

'No.' Phoebe had snatched the phone from her hand.

Camilla's mouth opened in shock and then set into a grim line. 'What are you doing, Phoebe?'

'Jez promised me that Tommy would tell the police.'

'What? You believed him? Tommy's kept it a secret for a year and now you just believe he'll go and tell them? I'm sure as hell he didn't let that little fact of the affair slip when he was being questioned by the police.'

'There's Jenna to think about as well,' Phoebe said, pleading with her eyes.

Camilla made a scoffing noise. 'The sooner Jenna knows about this, the better. Her husband's a cheating scumbag.'

'I don't think it's that simple, Camilla.'

Her eyes narrowed and her voice dropped an octave. 'Okay, so I've suspected it for a while. Now I know. Something's going on, isn't it?'

'What do you mean?' Phoebe took a step backwards.

'Between you and Jez.'

Phoebe felt her face grow hot and Camilla sighed and shook her head. 'You're totally caught in the middle, aren't you? You're trying to protect Jez.'

Phoebe fought back the tears that were threatening. She was sick of crying. She shrugged and a strange and hopeless laugh came out of her. 'Yes. I'm in love with him. So what do we do?'

Camilla had stepped towards Phoebe and put her arms around her shoulders. She smoothed her hair and then drew back to look in her eyes. 'Okay, all right. We wait.'

Phoebe hesitated at Camilla's door now. The moonlight cast a silver glow along her skin. She felt a rush of love for her younger sister. She'd abandoned her life to be here. Her children rang on the landline at night, crying for her to come home. And she would, soon, she promised. Phoebe could see the change in her. The hard edges had softened, melting away like the summer heat. Phoebe sensed that despite the drama,

Camilla needed this time, this space. A novel lay next to her on the bedside table. It was, she said, the first time she'd read one in years. No, Phoebe wouldn't wake her.

The clanging noise sounded again from down near the water. Camilla didn't stir. It was probably nothing, probably coming from across the river. Phoebe would just get a glass of water and go back to bed. The moon drew long shadows across the kitchen floor and she drank thirstily, gazing out onto the river. It was a cold, still, autumn night. There was no wind in the trees, no ripples on the smooth mirror of water.

And then the sound again, louder, closer. It reverberated through her body. She stood very still, aware that her hands had become clammy. It sounded like the old metal fishing bucket being scraped along the jetty. Phoebe put the glass down and wrapped her dressing gown closer. A quiver of fear shimmied down her spine, but she opened the sliding door anyway.

The air was frigid on her hands and face and she blew into the cup of her palms. The humid smells of summer had muted now into something softer. A hint of eucalypt mixed with salt and woodfire smoke. She slipped on a pair of thongs, gasping as the freezing rubber met her skin. The dewy grass licked her ankles as she made her way down to the jetty. She shivered as she approached, her heart a noisy patter in her chest. There was a rustling in the bushes to her right and she jumped, her throat contracting in fright. She was being silly. It was probably just an animal moving the bucket around.

She looked back at the darkened house. She didn't believe in spirits but standing here alone, the night a dark blanket around her, she sensed her. Not Karin, but the completeness of her absence. She was gone. Forever.

The blackness was suffocating and Phoebe fought the urge to return to the house. And then she saw a shadow fall across the jetty. She walked forward, careful that her footfalls were silent. She heard a splash as something entered the water and she ran to the line of trees flanking the river bank. There was someone in the water. Fear froze her and she watched as a figure moved deeper into the water. It was a man. At first she thought it was Jez, but the body was taller. All she could hear was the sound of her own panicked breathing.

'Tommy?' Her voice echoed across the water.

He turned and she saw his face. It looked twisted and thin, not like him. The hollow sadness of his eyes made her breath catch.

'What do you want?' His teeth were chattering, betraying him, but even now, waist-deep in freezing water, the heavy metal bucket tied around his waist, he seemed the same, calm Tommy. Only the slowness of his words, the slight sway of his body, indicated that he was drunk.

'You should get out, Tommy, you're drunk and it's cold.' There was too much desperation in her voice. She told herself to remain calm. She knew he wouldn't respond to anything else.

'Not going to happen.' He kept walking deeper, the water now a silver ring around his waist, the bucket submerged.

'Please, Tommy, come out.' She stepped tentatively onto the jetty. 'We'll talk.'

'I can't. And you don't want me to. Not really.' He made a strangled sound, primal and awful. 'I killed her, Phoebe. I killed her. Not in the way you think. Not making her commit suicide. She didn't commit suicide.'

Phoebe's head began to spin. She tried to get her bearings but everything was moving—the water had become the night sky, the sky the water. Everything was black, wherever she looked. She was going to be sick. She lay down, bent over the side of the jetty and retched the acrid contents of her stomach into the water.

Tommy's voice had a hysterical note that frightened her. 'You knew all along. All she wanted was my love, and I … I couldn't.' He was crying now, his sobs rasping and pathetic. 'She made me choose and I got angry. So angry. I couldn't … I couldn't choose. I was too weak for her.'

Phoebe pulled herself up until she was on all fours. She could taste bile and blood and tears. Her whole body was shaking, her mind scrambling for traction. 'What did you do, Tommy? Tell me what you did.'

He shook his head, his arms wrapped around his trembling torso. She had to strain to hear his voice over the water. 'I haven't told anyone. Not even Jez. Sometimes I feel like it wasn't even me who did it. It was one of my cases. You detach. You don't feel anything anymore. So much death.'

Phoebe willed her body to still, her voice to issue from her mouth. 'Tommy, tell me what happened to Karin.'

She saw his eyes close. 'It was an accident. We were right here, on the jetty. I didn't mean for it to happen.' He let out a whimper and stopped, and she thought for a horrible second that he wasn't going to go on. His voice dropped to a whisper. 'The photo on my phone that you found … We'd had a fight. She was saying sorry for how she'd pushed me to choose who to spend my birthday with. I'd had to be with Jenna and Harry. Harry was sick. But as soon as she texted me the flower note I left work and came straight down. She had a picnic set up on the jetty. It was beautiful. Everything she did was always so beautiful.

'But then she said it was our last supper, that she couldn't do it anymore. That it wasn't fair to make me choose between her and my family all the time. She couldn't keep lying to everyone, hurting everyone. I wanted to leave Jenna for her, but how could I leave Jenna with Harry? I couldn't do it. I always said I would but I never could. I got angry with her. So angry for abandoning what we had. I wanted to keep her, Phoebe. I didn't want her to leave me, I couldn't bear it. She was the love of my life. But the look in her eyes … I could tell she'd already left me. It was over forever. I couldn't handle it. And she tried to get past me.' He paused and a groan came out of him.

A darkness rolled through Phoebe, the like of which she'd never felt. She could barely stand to look at his pathetic, shaking body.

'I tried to stop her, Phoebe. I wouldn't let her go and she slipped. I think she hit her head. And you know, she hadn't swum since that day she nearly drowned right here. You were there. We were all there. And she must have been unconscious because she didn't struggle. I saw her float down. Her eyes were closed. It's haunted me, her face. And I could have gone in and pulled her out, but I didn't. I didn't. I just stood there until it was too late.'

It felt like all the air had been sucked out of the world and Phoebe couldn't get enough into her lungs. She dry-retched into the water again. When she found it, her voice was low and violent. 'You let her die? How? How? How, Tommy?'

He shook his head and his hands went to cover his face. 'I don't know. I don't know. I was shocked. I couldn't lose her. I couldn't let her go.'

'But you lost her. You loved her and you let her die. I knew.' She hissed the word. 'I dreamt it over and over again. I knew.'

His voice was emotionless when he spoke again. 'So, you see, you need to go away now.'

A feeling, cold and thick like a hand, closed around her heart. Phoebe looked at him and felt disgust. She realised she wanted him to die. She wanted him gone from the earth. She wanted to have him feel the terror she saw in her sister's eyes that day she nearly drowned in the river. She wanted his final feeling to be the suffocating ache of his lungs filling up with water. She felt nothing as she watched his chest go under.

The water was at his chin. He was in profile, the moon illuminating his face. He had the same strong, straight nose as his brother and for a second, a millisecond, she saw it. How things might have played out. Asha having the baby, Jez being a great dad but still in his heart loving Phoebe. And maybe they would have succumbed. Maybe they would have started an affair again, even while his child grew. And maybe too, Asha and Jez would have found peace enough to stay together for the child they both adored. And would Jez have left his family for her? Maybe he couldn't have chosen, either. Maybe Jez loved her with such a need, such a violence, that he couldn't have let her go. Maybe he could have made a split-second mistake. Maybe all of us had this same horrible weakness when it came to the thing we loved the most.

'Tommy.' She said his name softly and he turned to her. She had never seen such sadness on a human face.

'I've lost everything,' he said, his voice strangely normal now. 'I'm not going to be able to be there for Harry or Jenna anyway now, so what's the point?'

She knew she had a choice. It was the same choice Tommy had had when Karin fell in right here. If Phoebe stayed silent he would leave this world now. And how much she wanted him to go. She wanted him to feel pain, to suffer for his cowardice.

Then she closed her eyes and saw her—the woman from her dreams, underwater, eyes wide with sadness. She was struggling to breathe. She was dying. But her lips were moving. Those cold blue, ghostly lips that had whispered into her dreams. Phoebe knew the words they mouthed without hearing them. 'I love him,' the woman said.

A memory came to her, fresh, alive, as though time had played a trick and it was yesterday. Karin, lying on the pontoon of the dam, a lazy arm under her head, book in hand. A daisy chain adorning her hair. And it was Tommy beside her, legs kicking at lily pads, his shoulders burnished by the sun.

Phoebe knew what she had to say. 'Your brother,' she said. And Tommy turned to her. 'You can't leave Jez. You can't put him through what I've been through.'

He was looking at her but he couldn't even see her. 'Please, Tommy. I don't want you dead.' Even though it was the truth, it hurt her to say it. 'It won't bring Karin back. It'll only hurt the person we both love.'

He went under then, and Phoebe knew what she had to do. She jumped and saw stars, it was so cold. The water was black. It felt like the beginning and the end of all things. It felt like death around her body, but there was a heat inside her and it made her arms and legs pump hard. She kicked down until she found his underarms and hauled him to the surface. His body was weightless despite the bucket around his waist and he didn't struggle. Her feet found traction on the slippery rocks close to shore and his body became newly heavy with gravity. She got him onto the sand and he coughed until he vomited.

'I'm so sorry, I'm so sorry, I'm so sorry,' he said, his face turned upwards in her lap, his body uncontrollable with cold. 'I loved her so much.'

He was a shell of a man, hollowed by the same pain Phoebe had known, tormented and whittled down by it. She smoothed the wet hair from his eyes. 'I know you did, Tommy. I know you did.'

# EPILOGUE

Phoebe saw the boat from a distance, a dinghy with a single figure, silhouetted against the setting sun. The craft seemed stationary, but when she looked closer she saw it was being carried slowly downriver by the tide. There was no fear now when she thought of her sister. At first she believed that avenging Karin had freed her from the fear and the darkness, but she understood now that it was saving Tommy, not jailing him, that had given her peace.

The evening softened around her, the rustle of leaves, the coo of doves, the tinkle of cutlery and laughter from up at the house.

Jenna's voice sounded from the balcony. 'Dinner, Phoebe.'

'Coming,' she said and wound in her line.

The smell of garlic and onions piqued the salty air. She liked to sit here each evening, alone. Or sometimes Jenna joined her. There was something about the closing down of the day that Phoebe needed to witness. She knew Jenna understood. Sometimes they talked, but mostly they sat and let the stillness fill them up. She understood why Jenna had moved to Driftwood, even though it was the source of her pain. When you lost things in life, the hole where they had been was folded into your body anyway, to be carried always. Jenna had lost the man she loved. She had lost her ability to trust. Phoebe had thought Jenna would hate her but the two of them were bound together. Their sadness and their loss came from the same source. And by being here, Jenna was no longer alone.

Phoebe thought about Tommy, the muted timbre of his voice in the courtroom. His downcast eyes, the nervous twitch of his shoulders. The quiver of his lips as he described the moment he let Karin drown because he was angry at her for leaving him. Jez told Wendy the defence team had wanted him to call it an accident, had wanted him jailed for the lesser sentence of involuntary manslaughter. They wanted to argue that he had Post-Traumatic Stress Disorder from his work. But Tommy told the court exactly what he'd told Phoebe. It hadn't just been an accident. He was sentenced to six years for voluntary manslaughter. It wasn't enough for Camilla, their mother or their dad. But for Phoebe, it was enough.

And Jez. He had stood stiff in shirt and tie at his brother's side the whole time. He had stayed at the Canberra house even when Jenna abandoned it for Driftwood and Tommy went to jail. It was strange now, that Tommy and Jez's childhood home harboured the rest of them, like secret stowaways. Phoebe had tried to speak to Jez. He knew about Tommy trying to take his own life, and that she had saved him, but he was shut tight to her.

She stood now and squinted upriver into the low, late-winter sun. She was waiting for him to come home.

Harry was in his flannelette pyjamas just inside the French doors when Phoebe reached the house. She banged the dirt from her shoes outside and lined them up with everyone else's. She could see Wendy pouring wine and the Texan thumping the table dramatically, laughing at something Flick was saying. Jenna spotted her and held up a bottle of white wine. Phoebe nodded. She opened the door and the warmth of the house, the smell of food, flooded her. She was about to step into it when something behind her, a sound, a feeling, made her turn.

Jez was standing there.

'Phoebe, you're letting the cold in,' said Flick, gesturing madly towards the door.

'Sorry. Hang on. You all start, I'll be in in a minute,' she said, and closed the door behind her. Her heart purred in her chest. She stood very still. 'Why do you have an oar?' she asked.

'You recognise it?' He ran his hands over the worn wood.

She walked towards him. He was leaner, as though the past few months had whittled him down. 'Should I?'

He started down towards the jetty and she followed him. How many times had the two of them walked this track? She had always followed him, without question. Even now, into the falling night, after everything, she followed him. There was a rowboat tethered to the ladder with a heavy rope. As she got closer she saw that it was filled with rose petals. Yellow, red, pink and white ones. She thought of her sister, and smiled, so she wouldn't cry.

'Flowers,' she said.

'It's your old boat. The one that got stolen.'

'It looks new. It's beautiful.'

'I painted it white and repaired the holes.'

All these months, he had been thinking of her. 'Will it float?' She stepped onto the jetty.

'Do you want to test it out?'

They walked to the end of the jetty and she climbed down the ladder after Jez. The petals felt soft underfoot. Their silky scent filled the air. She picked up a handful and held them to her nose. They reminded her of a time long ago, before she had known pain.

'They're for Karin,' Jez said gently, as he slipped the oar into place. He reached down and picked up a handful of petals and threw them over the bow, into the river.

Phoebe began to cry. The boat began to move, the sound of the oars in the water, their soft clunk against the hull, reminding her of being young. The five of them, piled in. Karin alone in the boat, while the rest of them jumped off the side, squealing their delight into the cool water.

'She felt safe in this boat,' Phoebe said. 'I'd forgotten.'

'I know,' said Jez. 'I remembered.'

It was dark now, the river black beneath them, but it didn't frighten her. The petals floated around them like luminous jewels on the surface of the water. And the trail of them led back to Driftwood.

# ACKNOWLEDGMENTS

There are so many people who go into the making of a book. Firstly, I'd like to thank my amazing readers: Karina Ware, Kirstin Bokor and Georgina Penney. Without your encouragement, this story wouldn't have come to be. Thank you to Danielle Townsend for reading from an editor's perspective, Abi Lewis for the long writing chats and Bec McSherry for emotional support over cups of tea.

Thanks to Jeanne Ryckmans and Jo Bulter from Cameron Creswell Agency for championing this novel.

I'm hugely grateful to the wonderful team at HarperCollins: Anna Valdinger, Catherine Milne, Barbara McClenahan, Kathy Hassett, Di Blacklock, Lucy Inglis, James Kellow and the sales and design teams.

Thank you to the booksellers too, who are so passionate about reading and supporting writers.

To Ben and Soph, thank you for being my home. And my lovely family: Mum and Dad, Anth and Beck, for your love and support.

This book is for my nanna, whose spirit lives on in our memories, on the jetty at Stray Leaves.

Vanessa studied English and Australian literature at Sydney University and dreamed of one day writing fiction. She then went on to immerse herself completely in writing about real people, working as a journalist for 18 years; Vanessa has been a news, medical and entertainment reporter for the *Daily Telegraph* and numerous other publications. She's happy to now finally be creating fictional characters. She lives in Sydney with her husband and daughter.